This book is dedicated to Jane

Author royalties from the sale of this book will be shared equally between East Cheshire Hospice, Macclesfield and St Ann's Hospice, Stockport.

I wish to thank Erlin Toong for typing the original manuscript, Darin Jewell of the Inspira Literary Agency for his encouragement and advice, Steve Linnell of Linnell Illustration for marketing material but, above all, the many patients that it has been my privilege to serve for giving me the inspiration to write this book.

Chapter 1

Whilst working in Casualty at the City General Hospital I had been completely unaware of the time, but it was already one in the morning and I was beginning to feel hungry. It was seven hours since I had last had anything solid to eat, having existed on occasional cups of sweet tea throughout my evening shift in the department. Although the night nurses had only come on duty at eight pm, their roster allowed them to return to the nurse's home at midnight, where they joined the nurses from the wards for a forty-minute break and a cooked meal. I had been working since nine in the morning but there was no such facility for me or, indeed, for the other doctors who worked through the night, although fortunately Bill, the night porter and Stan, the night security guard - an ex policeman - were happy to produce hot buttered toast on request.

"That's a lovely smell," said my next patient, in a soft Irish accent. His nose was held up in appreciation of the aroma, reminiscent of the boys in the gravy advert. His appearance suggested that he was a tramp. He looked dirty, unkempt and, as I discovered later, wore multiple layers of clothes underneath an old gabardine raincoat. He carried a woollen hat in his hand that I presumed to be responsible for the tidemark across his forehead. Below the line, the face was weather-beaten and brown, and strikingly pale above. He obviously spent much of his life out of doors and wore the hat most of the time. He was carrying a mug of tea, which struck me as unusual. Patients were advised not to partake of food or drink before they had seen the doctor, lest an anaesthetic be required subsequently. Notices to this effect were prominently displayed throughout the department. My initial 'foot of the bed' impression was that he didn't really look particularly ill; in fact he looked perfectly healthy, cheerful, rather pleased with himself, and had quite a sparkle in his eyes. I was somewhat surprised that he had smelled the buttered toast, because the aroma that reached my nostrils was one of methylated spirits.

"Top of the morning to you, Doctor," he said. "To be sure, 'tis a nice clear cold night, is it not?"

"You're Irish by the sound of it. Where exactly are you from?"

"I am indeed from Ireland," he said, "the Emerald Isle. God's own country. From a little village called Killybegs. It's right up in the north in County Donegal. Lovely spot it is too. Have you ever been there, Doctor?"

"Actually I have," I replied, recalling a holiday that I had enjoyed there with my parents many years previously, "and wild and beautiful it is too. But what brings you to this country?"

"Tis a long story to be sure, but I'm a priest."

I must have looked surprised as I tried to reconcile his present appearance with his stated calling, before he continued, now in a conspiratorial whisper.

"Well Doctor, to tell you the truth, I used to be a priest. I was a bit of a naughty boy. I became rather too fond of the taste of the communion wine and helped myself a little too freely. The Bishop of Donegal disapproved and sent me packing - not that he didn't partake of a little tipple himself, you understand."

Certainly an interesting character, I thought, a defrocked priest, down on his luck. It was tempting to delve a little deeper into his background but I was conscious of the time and, hoping to get a little sleep at some stage before morning, thought it best to move the consultation along. I asked him what the problem was.

"Tis me belly, Doctor, so it is," he said. "I've got a terrible pain in me belly." He went on to describe his troubles in more detail but it was a story that was difficult to untangle. The position of the pain that he described suggested that it might be coming from the stomach or duodenum but he insisted it troubled him when he moved his arms into certain positions and occasionally when he scratched his head, not a combination of symptoms with which I was familiar from my study of medical textbooks! He also described a pain behind his left eye - "Only my left eye, mind, Doctor" - when he passed water, again a complaint that I had not encountered in five years of study at medical school. It took nearly ten minutes to undress him because of his multiple layers of clothes. When he had taken off his jacket, three ragged sweaters and an old waistcoat, I thought that we should soon be rewarded by the sight of flesh but the further removal of two shirts and a couple of vests was required before we finally reached his skin.

Having achieved this, however, I discovered that the clinical signs in his abdomen were highly inconsistent. One minute the tenderness appeared to be on the left hand side, causing him to leap from the examination couch in an alarming fashion - later it seemed worse on the right. Yet at other times he would allow deep palpation without any apparent discomfort, whilst happily relating stories of his beloved homeland. After about half an hour, the only conclusion I had reached was that I really didn't have a clue what was the matter with him. It was at this moment that Sister walked through the door.

She beamed at him. "Oh, it's you, Charlie! So you've decided to pay us another visit?"

"Sure I did Sister, and can I say what a joy it is, to see your beautiful happy smiling face again."

"Have you had a cup of tea, Charlie?"

"Yes thank you Sister, a nice big mug. Hot and sweet and lovely it was too, brewed by one of your little angels."

"Would you like another drink before you go?"

"Would there be some nice buttered toast with that, Sister?"

Sister smiled. "Yes Charlie, there would, provided that you promise not to come back." Then, rather more severely, she added, "This is a hospital Charlie, a place for the sick and infirm. Not a port of call for ex-naval sea captains down on their luck."

By this time I had realised that Charlie had succeeded in getting two free mugs of tea, some hot buttered toast, and had spent a couple of hours in a nice warm environment, whilst successfully pulling the wool over my eyes - though his plan to spend the night between freshly laundered hospital sheets had been thwarted.

"He's actually not an ex-navy captain tonight Sister," I said. "He's a defrocked priest."

"Is that so?" she said, laughing. Then, turning to the patient whom she obviously knew well, "In that case, please say a couple of prayers for us, Charlie, whilst you are having that tea and toast, and then be on your way."

"I will, Sister. I will. And I'll say one for the nice young doctor too. May the Good Lord bless you and keep you both safe and warm in His arms," he said, "...'til I pop in and see you both again", he added, with a wink.

Later Sister apologised to me. "I'm sorry he got as far as the surgical cubicles, Dr Lambert, we usually manage to spot him and keep him in the waiting area. He pops in to see us every month or so, each time with a different story, but he's only after a bit of company...a little warmth and a cup of tea. He's quite a character though and he gets away with it because he's got the gift of the gab and that Irish charm."

Two months earlier, during the second week of July 1966, those of us who had been fortunate enough to graduate from the medical school attended the interview for our first medical posts. We all recognised the importance of this event and the mood was one of quiet apprehension. Our instructions had been to congregate in the corridor leading to the committee room in the administrative wing, which was situated in the oldest part of the hospital. Although during our medical training we had visited and were familiar with all the wards and clinical departments, this was an area to which we had not previously had access. I looked around with interest.

Despite the sun shining brightly outside, the corridor was dark and gloomy. The windows were small in size, few in number, and over-shadowed by the newer, taller, buildings that had sprung up as the hospital had developed haphazardly over the years. The bare brick wall of the outpatient block obscured the view on one side. Inside, dozens of anxious patients would be waiting their turn to meet the consultants; to tell of their medical complaints, to have investigations performed, or maybe to hear news - good or bad - about their medical conditions and prognosis. The level of anxiety there was probably just as great as that amongst the job applicants. Through the windows on the opposite side of the corridor there was a clear view of a shiny black hearse, which was discharging its load through the double doors of the hospital morgue. One of the funeral directors waved cheerily to the gathered throng, but received no response from the apprehensive graduates on our side of the glass.

The only furniture in the corridor was a line of old wooden benches placed along the walls, looking as if they might have served as pews in a church or chapel in a previous life. Above them, in battered gilt frames, hung the portraits of the learned doctors who had stalked the corridors and wards of the hospital over the last 150 years. These were the 'barber surgeons' who had undertaken amputations and cut for bladder stones in the days before anaesthetics, and the apothecaries who had used leeches and blood letting as a cure for a variety of different ailments. All wore formal robes representing the various colleges of which they had been members or fellows. Amongst them were two previous Presidents of the Royal College of Physicians, an obstetrician who had delivered royal babies and, of course, the hospital's most famous son: Lord Richard Rochfort, the pioneer of gastric surgery, proudly wearing the robes of the Royal College of Surgeons of England. The message from their stern faces, communicated through their eyes as they gazed down at this latest batch of young doctors, was clear. We were to uphold the dignity and gravity of our great profession and follow the guidance of the Hippocratic Oath throughout our working lives, as they had in theirs. The doctors in the portraits were, of course, all male.

The corridor was far too small for the number of people present. A few sat on the benches but the majority had to stand. There must have been sixty-five or seventy of us altogether. All the young doctors were well known to me as we had first met in the autumn of 1961 as 'freshers' at the medical school, and subsequently spent five years studying together. Medical students have quite a reputation for enjoying their student life to the full, and since for us this occurred in the era that was subsequently to be called the 'Swinging Sixties', it may be imagined that the last five years had been a period of non-stop partying, periodic intoxication and general debauchery. Perhaps it had been for one or two of my fellow students - but that would be to give a misleading impression of my own experience as an undergraduate. I had come to recognise that I am, by nature, an introspective individual; my preference being for the quiet company of a few good friends, rather than to be living it up as part of a large, boisterous crowd. Nor do I regard myself as being academically particularly bright. The success that I had in passing the various undergraduate examinations - and there were many of them - came as a result of prolonged periods of concentrated study, rather than as a result of any natural scholastic brilliance. I was extremely envious of those students who were able to party night after night and yet pass the exams without apparently having any need to study. Also, some seemed to be able to embark on deep and time-consuming personal relationships without it detracting from their studies, whereas I often felt ill at ease in the company of members of the opposite sex; possibly because I was one of three brothers and had attended an all-boys school.

The structure of the medical curriculum followed a logical pattern. The first five terms were spent studying anatomy - the structure of the human body - and physiology, the way in which the body functions. Anatomy was learned in part from formal lectures, but mainly from the dissection of the corpse of some kindly soul who had donated their earthly remains to medical science. Dissection of the human body was commenced within a week of starting the course, the Dean of the medical school obviously believing that an early test of a student's mettle and suitability for a medical career was appropriate.

The dissection room was a large, tiled, cool hall down in the basement of the medical school, containing ten or so porcelain tables upon which the bodies were laid, each preserved by the injection of formalin. The strong pungent smell from the preservative was overpowering.

This was my first experience of death and entering the hall for the first time was an unnerving experience. Each body lay under a white cotton sheet and even the initial step of removing the sheet from the body proved to be a considerable hurdle; not helped by the antics of the hardened senior students who amused themselves by turning the lights off from time to time, plunging the whole room into darkness. The bodies were cold, pale grey in colour, and the skin had a curiously waxy appearance. Fortunately their eyes were closed. Two or three of the students, fresh from school, could not overcome the revulsion that they felt at seeing, touching and making a first incision into the body and were unable to stay in the hall for more than a couple of minutes, thus forcing them to leave the course and abandon their potential career in medicine within a few days of starting. All were transferred to alternative paramedical university courses such as biology and pharmacy. At the time it seemed tough to subject young people to this challenge, particularly when they had worked so hard at school to obtain the exacting high A-level grades to win a place at the medical school but perhaps the dean was right; if they were squeamish, it was better for them to find out early in the course rather than at a later stage.

We spent five or six hours a week in the dissecting room, working away with scalpel and scissors, gradually revealing the three dimensional anatomy that is so difficult to visualise from the diagrams in a textbook. As we did so we slowly became accustomed to this unusual environment, and with time the atmosphere in the room lightened so that we chattered and exchanged light hearted banter as we worked. Sadly though, I must confess that much learned at this stage was of little relevance to those who did not subsequently pursue a career in surgery, and will have been long forgotten by most.

Armed with knowledge of the function and structure of the body, we moved on to the study of bacteriology, pathology and pharmacology. Bacteriology taught us the names and characteristics of numerous organisms and the wide variety of infectious diseases that they may cause; everything from septicaemia to syphilis, tetanus to tuberculosis. In pathology we learned about the changes induced by various disease processes such as infections, injury and cancer, the difference between benign and malignant tumours, and the manner in which infection and cancer spread through the tissues of the body. Pharmacology taught us about the drugs available to treat disease, though their range and effectiveness was considerably less than that of the modern and powerful drugs available today.

Finally, and many would say belatedly, we moved to the section of the syllabus that held the greatest fascination: the clinical part where we were taught how to take a patient's history and how to perform a thorough clinical examination. Obtaining a 'history' from a patient - persuading a patient to describe their symptoms and to inform you all about their previous health problems - is a considerable art and requires significant expertise. Initially, I felt that the patients who were obliging enough to allow us to practice on them must have regarded medical students as a nuisance; but they actually seemed to enjoy it, and no doubt it helped them to while away the hours as they lay in their hospital beds.

Much time was spent learning how to perform a physical examination. We practiced first on each other and then, once again, on our long-suffering patients. If you were referred by your general practitioner to be treated in a university teaching hospital you might very well get the best possible medical care, but you risked being pummelled, prodded and poked by some fairly heavy-handed medical students!

Equally fascinating were the attachments to the obstetrical and paediatric units. During our midwifery attachment each student was required to deliver twenty babies, and I was pleased to achieve this without any major mishap. It seemed to me that essentially most babies delivered themselves, that the main responsibility of the midwife was to catch the babe as it appeared, and that anyone reasonably adept at catching a cricket ball should perform quite well. Newborn babies, however, are a good deal more slippery than cricket balls and have a disconcerting habit of wriggling while you are holding them. The main concern of the senior midwife - who was always present to supervise with an eagle eye and sharp tongue - appeared to be that we did not drop the newborn infant onto the floor. As always, we asked permission to undertake the delivery but in practice the mothers in labour appeared not to mind in the least who was delivering their offspring, provided the end result was achieved as quickly as possible with the minimum of pain. The biggest hurdle of all - the final obstacle to be overcome before becoming a doctor, and the culmination of five years of hard graft - was the final examination for the degree of Bachelor of Medicine, Bachelor of Surgery (MBChB).

Every doctor has unforgettable memories of the cases presented to him in these clinical assessments and I am of no exception. My medical examination commenced with a requirement to analyse a sample of urine. There were four samples and we were informed that one sample contained sugar, one protein, one contained blood and that one was normal. Although the nurses on the ward could analyse urine for such abnormalities in twenty seconds using pre-prepared paper strips, we were required to conduct the analysis using old-fashioned laboratory chemical reagents. Since one of the four samples was red, the others being straw coloured, this was the sample that each student wished to be given and my silent prayers were answered when I was indeed passed the red sample to test. I quickly ran the test for blood, which was positive, and did not bother undertaking the tests for the other possible abnormalities, thereby giving myself ten minutes to prepare before meeting my clinical examiner. It seemed inevitable that the initial questions would revolve around the causes of blood in the urine and the treatment of these conditions, so I began to formulate in my head a list of all the possible sites in the urinary tract from which bleeding might occur - from the glomeruli and tubules of the kidney where urine is formed, to the tip of the urethra from which urine is voided. I also prepared mentally a list of the various disease processes that might be responsible for the loss of blood from each of these possible sites.

Our own Professor of Medicine - a kindly elderly man, whom I knew from my student training on his clinical unit - introduced me to the external examiner, a professor from London. The expression on his face did not encourage me. He looked bored and irritable, as if examining me was a chore that he would prefer to have avoided. His first two questions were extremely straightforward.

"Have you examined the urine sample?"

"Yes Sir."

"What did you find?"

"The presence of blood, Sir."

"That's quite right. Not too difficult I suppose, given that the urine was red." His voice was quiet and held just a hint of sarcasm.

It seemed to me that this was a reasonable start, but disaster was soon to follow. The examiner allowed a small, humourless, smile to cross his face and asked his next question...one that took me completely off-guard.

"Tell me, Lambert, about the causes of blood in the stool?"

I began my prepared answer. "There are many causes of blood in the urine, Sir," I said, "and if we take them one by one, starting in the kidney..."

"No," he interrupted, the sarcasm now more pronounced than before. "I said blood in the *stool*."

"In the stool, Sir?"

"Yes, Lambert, in the stool. That is the effluent that comes from the anus," he added unnecessarily. The voice was now mocking in tone. His bored expression had vanished. My examiner was warming to his task and beginning to enjoy himself at my expense.

My prepared answer disappeared into thin air. I noticed the smile on the examiner's face becoming a satisfied beam and wondered how often he had pulled this particular trick on other poor unsuspecting students.

My confidence, clearly misplaced, vanished in a flash as my brain suddenly seemed to stop functioning. The answer about the causes of blood in the urine that had been so well organised in my head was replaced by a complete void. It took several moments before I realised that the question could be addressed, as before, by taking all the possible sites from which bleeding might occur in the gut and then considering the possible causes from each; but it was only after a good deal of prompting by the examiner that I managed to stutter and stammer some sort of answer to the question. I saw the two examiners exchange a knowing look that clearly indicated that I was in trouble.

"Let's see if you can do a little better with your next case," said the visiting professor, and he asked me to listen to the heart of a breathless lady who was lying on a couch. My spirits rose slightly. In the previous three months I had listened to the heart sounds of hundreds of patients with many different cardiac problems and considered myself to be something of an expert, rarely having any difficulty in identifying the first and second heart sounds, the various murmurs that could be heard, and usually making the correct diagnosis. It was therefore with some confidence that I applied my stethoscope to the patient's chest, but once again I was to discover that my confidence was misplaced. The noise that I heard was unlike anything I had ever heard before - it sounded as if there was a concrete mixer churning continuously inside her. It was rasping and grinding and so loud that it completely obliterated the normal heart sounds. I wondered whether it might be coming not from the heart but from the lungs, and therefore asked the patient to stop breathing for a moment to try to discover if the sound was still present when there was no respiratory movement. This alarmed the examiner who commented, rather sarcastically, that he thought the patient was breathless enough already. He didn't think it would be wise to ask her to stop breathing in case she didn't manage to start again, a statement that in turn alarmed the patient! I became flustered. I had no idea what was causing this incredible noise and my examiner knew it. He had me on the ropes and, as before, was clearly enjoying my obvious discomfort, playing with me as a cat might play with a mouse. He asked me if I had reached a diagnosis, knowing full well that I hadn't. Whilst able to describe the sound that I had heard, with which the examiner agreed, I had to confess that I had no idea whatsoever of the cause of the noise.

The bell tolled to indicate that the time allotted for the examination was over. My torture was complete, and I was in no doubt that it also tolled to indicate that I was a doomed man. The examiner looked me straight in the eye and told me the diagnosis.

"This lady has pericarditis and therefore the noise is ..." He stopped and waited. Suddenly, the penny dropped. Why on earth had I not recognised it? It was an extremely rare abnormality but one, nonetheless, that was very characteristic that I ought to have recognised.

"A pericardial friction rub," I said.

"Caused by...?" the visiting professor wanted to know.

"Inflammation of the pericardium."

"Yes, Lambert. That will be all, thank you." The tone of the voice indicated, more clearly than the words, his opinion of my diagnostic skills. Despondently, I moved towards the door.

Our own Professor was more charitable. "Don't be too hard on yourself," he said. "You're not the first to be confused by the case this morning, and you won't be the last."

As I left the room, I mentally chastised myself. When told the cause of the 'machinery sounds' it was so obvious. The noise had not been coming from *within* the heart at all. This was a case of inflammation of the pericardium, the sack that *surrounds* the heart. As the heart moved there was friction between it and the sack within which it was contained, creating this rough sound. Since the heart was moving all the time, the noise was continuous. No wonder that the patient was so breathless. I felt certain at that moment that I had failed the medical examination and would have to spend the next six months swotting for the re-sits, whilst my friends and colleagues started work as doctors.

If my medical practical clinical examination had been a disaster, thanks to a major slice of luck my surgical examination proved to be a triumph. The examination took place on one of the surgical wards a couple of days later.

I was introduced to four patients in quick succession by the external examiner, this time a surgeon from Newcastle. Each patient had a swelling readily visible on the surface of their body: one was a hernia, others were a skin cyst, an abscess in a man's groin and a lady with an obvious varicose vein. Fortunately I was able to diagnose each correctly and to suggest an appropriate treatment.

My internal examiner was Sir William Warrender, the most senior surgeon at the City General Hospital, for whom I had a great deal of respect. I had undertaken part of my training on his 'firm' and found him to be a fatherly figure of the old school, patient with students, and a good teacher with the wisdom of long experience. He took me to the far end of the ward and introduced me to a generously proportioned West Indian lady of about fifty years of age.

"I would like you to have a look at the swelling on the front of this lady's left shoulder," he said. I said a polite "Good morning," to the patient and asked her permission to examine her shoulder, knowing that Sir William was the perfect English gentleman and this was certainly what he would expect.

There were a number of rolls of fat in front of the shoulder, but in addition there appeared to be a rather lobular, ill-defined swelling perhaps three inches in diameter. It was difficult to be sure whether this was a definite abnormality or merely a part of her general adiposity. When I felt the lump it did appear to be slightly firmer than the surrounding fat and had a vaguely nodular feel to it. It seemed probable that this was a simple lipoma, a common benign fatty swelling of little consequence. I was just about to say so, when my fingers detected a slight prominence of the skin overlying the apex of the swelling. I looked carefully at it and noticed that the skin in this area seemed perhaps to be even darker than that of the surrounding skin. In a fortuitous moment of true inspiration, a picture appeared in my mind of an artist's drawing that I had seen in an early edition of Bailey & Love's classic 'Textbook of Surgery'. This depicted a lady sitting in a chair feeding two infants simultaneously. One was suckling from her left breast whilst the other infant was feeding from a second breast situated on the same side. Just as a sow has a string of breasts on each side of the chest and abdomen, so too, albeit rarely, humans may have an additional nipple along a similar line and even more rarely may have some breast tissue underlying the extra nipple.

Wondering whether this might be such a case, I asked the patient whether she had a family and if so, had she noticed any change in the lump during pregnancy.

"Oh yes, Doctor," she said, not understanding that I was still a medical student.

"The lump got very much larger and became quite painful."

"In that case," I said to Sir William, "although this swelling has the appearance of a lipoma because it has this little nodule on the summit which is slightly darker than the surrounding skin, and since the entire swelling is situated on the 'milk line', I believe it may be an accessory breast with a rudimentary nipple."

Sir William initially looked doubtful but went to review the swelling for himself, then stood back whilst the external examiner did the same.

"My, my," he said, "and that would explain why the swelling got larger in pregnancy. I am always telling my students that common things occur commonly and that it is dangerous to diagnose rarities, but

I do believe that you are right. I must confess that we presented this lady today as a simple case of lipoma but with that accessory nipple over the top, I have to agree with you that this swelling probably is an accessory breast. Congratulations, Lambert!"

I left the ward with my head held high; delighted with the way the examination had gone, having successfully diagnosed a rare condition and having undoubtedly impressed my examiners.

When the exams were over, feeling utterly exhausted and with grave concerns that I had failed in medicine, I returned home for a couple of days to await the examination results. There was much partying for those who stayed in digs or halls of residency close to the hospital but I was content to relax with my parents, to revive friendships recently neglected, and to take some long solo country walks.

It was with much trepidation that I returned to the Medical School a few days later and joined the anxious group waiting for the results to be posted on the notice board. At exactly ten o'clock, as promised, the Hospital Secretary appeared and pinned up a single sheet of paper listing the names of the successful candidates. It was an enormous relief to discover that I had managed to pass in all subjects including, to my great surprise and delight, the medicine examination. It was to be many years before I came to understand that by the time medical students come to the end of their five years training, so much time, money and effort has been invested in them, that in practice they all qualify - although not necessarily at the first attempt. Eleven of my fellow students had to re-sit the exams, but they graduated six months later. I had become the first doctor in the Lambert family.

"Doctor Lambert!" I said the words to myself. "Doctor Lambert." How strange that sounded. Could I really be medically qualified? Was it really true that I was now a doctor, that I should start to practice medicine, that patients would entrust themselves to my care? Was I ready to carry that burden? My examiners had decided that I was; but it suddenly seemed to be a grave responsibility.

When told of my success my mother visibly swelled with pride, and spent many happy hours on the telephone telling all her friends and relations of my good fortune and basking in the reflected glory of my achievement. For myself, the feeling was mainly one of tremendous relief. For months the examinations had loomed in front of me as an enormous obstacle, but (not for the first time) I realised that, in life, an obstacle appears to diminish in size when it has been safely negotiated and when new challenges appear on the horizon. And there was now another hurdle in front of me: I had to find myself medical employment.

Chapter 2

As a graduate of a British medical school, a Bachelor of Medicine and Bachelor of Chirurgie (Surgery), I was entitled to put the letters MBChB after my name and allowed to call myself "Doctor". However, since I was not registered as a fully qualified doctor with the General Medical Council, I was only permitted to practice medicine under supervision. To become a fully registered doctor with the GMC and thereby licensed to practice unsupervised on the unsuspecting British public, it was necessary to undertake a twelve month apprenticeship as a provisionally, or 'preregistered', doctor.

It was for these 'house' officer jobs - so called because the doctor is required to be resident in the hospital - that interviews were now being held and for which I had applied. There is little doubt that the very first post that a doctor obtains is important and has a major influence on his future career prospects. An aspiring hospital consultant who fails to get a first post in a teaching hospital is disadvantaged from the start.

There was a delay in getting the interviews underway and the group of newly qualified doctors waiting in the dark and dusty corridor was, not surprisingly, becoming restless. To reach the committee room in which the interviews were to take place the consultants had to walk along the passage, through the group of newly qualified doctors. In contrast to the interviewees they all looked remarkably cheerful, as if this was a duty and responsibility that they relished. Perhaps they enjoyed having the power to decide the fate of the young graduates, perhaps it allowed them to reminisce about their own early careers, or perhaps it was merely an opportunity to have a break from their routine work and to have a chat with their colleagues.

As they passed, one or two of the consultants exchanged pleasantries with some of those waiting to be interviewed, and the significance of these short conversations was hotly debated. Was it an indication as to which candidate would be successful? Was it a case of simply trying to put the applicants at ease? Were they of any significance at all? Bill Jenkins, who had failed most of the examinations during his time at medical school - with the result that he had fallen back from the previous year and taken six years to qualify instead of the usual five - held the interview room door open respectfully for each consultant in turn; more in hope, I thought, than in any real expectation that it would be to his advantage. He was mocked by his friends for his troubles.

As I looked around I realised that all these young people - who had been my friends and fellow students for the last five years and who had all suffered the troubles and tribulations of the undergraduate years together - were now in competition with me for a job. The thought of friends turned rivals was unnerving.

It was amazing to see how well turned-out the applicants were. Gone were the casual slacks and sweaters that had been in evidence during lectures and tutorials. Suits, city shirts and smart ties were the order of the day and the girls, with one notable exception, were conservatively dressed and looked very demure. Most wore suits with straight or pleated skirts in navy, grey or black, pleasantly complemented by a white or cream blouse and high-heeled shoes. The ten days that had elapsed between the posting of the examination results and the interviews had allowed some rest and relaxation in the July sunshine and the graduates looked much healthier than they had at any time in the previous three months, the facial pallor that had resulted from the long hours of study having being replaced by much rosier complexions.

Because my performance in the final examination in surgery had been much better than my embarrassing medical experience, I had decided to apply for a house surgical position. As we waited for the interviews to get underway, I had no idea how many of us had applied for medical posts and how many for the surgical jobs. Clearly, it would be to my advantage if the majority had applied for medicine.

There were ten pre-registration house jobs available in each specialty. Of the surgical ones, two were on the orthopaedic unit, for which I had not applied. This was not a branch of surgery that was of interest to me, since the experience to be gained was too limited for anybody other than an aspiring orthopaedic surgeon. The remaining eight posts were allocated to the eight general surgeons who worked on four surgical units. The two posts on the professorial unit were always allocated to the two students who attained the highest marks in the surgical examination, and this year Richard Green and Helen Leach had both obtained distinctions. Richard was a studious bespectacled bookworm, who looked as if he would be more comfortable wearing an anorak and collecting railway engine numbers on Crewe station than working on a surgical ward. Helen, on the other hand, was irritatingly good at everything, regularly getting top marks in examinations without apparent effort, being captain of the university hockey team, and quite a beauty as well. These two were certainties for the two professorial jobs, though how Richard would fare as a surgical house officer I was not sure. Incredibly reserved, the sort that wouldn't say boo to a goose, he had the misfortune to be born with two left hands. It seemed unlikely that he would thrive in the dynamic world of the surgeons.

Another post was also effectively unavailable to me. The most recently appointed consultant surgeon, Sydney Potts, who had been in post for about five years, had already attained a reputation for appointing the prettiest female graduate as his house surgeon, irrespective of any academic or practical ability that they might possess - and standing next to me was Miss Elizabeth Chambers, whose choice of dress differed so markedly from that of the other girls. She looked stunningly attractive, with a black pencil skirt that ended two inches higher - and a sheer white blouse with a neckline plunging two inches lower - than one might expect for a formal interview. Further, the job of house surgeon to Sir William Warrender was almost certainly already allocated as well: Johnny Nolan was Sir William's nephew and was surely destined for that post. Frankly, not one of us would really begrudge such nepotism, since Johnny was a likable quick-witted rogue, whose pranks had provided several memorable moments during our student years. It was Johnny who had bricked up the entrance to the nurse's home one New Years Eve, and who had replaced the bust of the hospital's founder and benefactor with a skeleton dressed in a nurse's uniform on the "open day" when school sixth formers interested in applying for a place at Medical School were invited to look round. In many ways, it would be a waste of a good teaching hospital post if Johnny were to get Sir William's job, since it was known that his ambition was limited to joining his father's general practice in the leafier parts of Surrey, and a job in a peripheral hospital would serve him just as well. There were sixty or so of us waiting for the interviews to begin, but it seemed likely that only four posts were actually available to me.

The interviews were already half an hour late and, as the delay dragged on, conversation inevitably turned to an individual's prospect of success. It transpired that one or two of our group had already been to speak with particular consultants, to express an interest in being appointed to their posts. This was a course of action that I had decided against; believing that with so many potential applicants for so few jobs the busy consultants would find this a nuisance. It was, however, no surprise to learn that Liz Chambers had actually been along to see Mr Potts, who had expressed delight that "*she wished to be considered for his post*". From her attitude it was obvious that she had interpreted this as confirmation that this job was hers.

The mood amongst the group, initially one of some restlessness, had progressed to irritation by the time that the solid oak door leading to the committee room finally opened and Frederick Swindles, the secretary to the Medical Board, appeared, holding a clipboard and calling for attention. Frederick was an insignificant greying man of about fifty years of age. He tried to insist on being called Frederick but inevitably he was known as Fred. He was wearing a crumpled brown jacket over a home-knitted woollen cardigan, a shirt and tie of discordant colours, and scuffed shoes. His working life was spent at the beck and call of the consultants; not that he altogether resented this. He recognised that they despised and bullied him but his association with them gave him a certain kudos in the hospital that he reinforced by name-dropping at every available opportunity. Having started as an office junior, he had been promoted over the years to his present post but had never left the secluded security of the administrative department. Twice a year, however, he emerged to organise the house officer interviews, a role that he relished and anticipated with great enthusiasm. Being small in stature, he had to stand on one of the benches to call for attention. Gradually the room quietened as conversation ceased.

"Good morning ladies and gentlemen," Fred began, "or should I say, *doctors!*" This was an opening line that he used regularly and of which he was somewhat proud. He allowed himself a slight smile.

"May I take this opportunity of welcoming you today to the City General Hospital for the formal interviews for the pre-registration house officer posts in medicine and surgery. I am sure that you all recognise and appreciate the great honour that it would be for you to work in this prestigious establishment, which has been a seat of medical learning and research for many years and which has been graced by the presence of so many famous physicians and surgeons, some of whom are immortalised in the portraits on the walls surrounding you. I am proud to have known some of them, albeit only those who worked here in recent years."

Again he allowed himself a slight smile at another of his prepared comments. "I am sure that those of you fortunate enough to be appointed today will wish to continue with the high standard of medical care that they..."

"Get on with it," a voice shouted from the back of the crowd. Fred looked irritated by the interruption that he clearly regarded as impertinence. He paused for a moment but continued unabashed, "...will continue to uphold the high standards of medical care that were set by your predecessors. Now, coming to the business of the day, as you will know we are holding interviews for pre-registration house physician and pre-registration..."

Again there was an interruption from the back. "We know all that. Get on with it!"

Again Fred ignored the interruption and carried on regardless. He was not going to have his big moment spoiled by these disrespectful hopefuls.

"The successful applicants will be compulsorily resident and monies will be taken from their annual stipend for accommodation and food. In addition..."

Medical students, who have been together as a group for five years, know how to deal effectively with such situations. Without any prompting, a gradual stamping of the feet started at the back and spread to the front of the group; quietly at first but building gradually in a crescendo to a level where Fred's voice could no longer be heard. When he was forced to stop speaking, a ragged cheer went up. He held up both arms, one holding the clipboard, and slowly silence returned. Fred Swindles' big day was being spoiled but he continued bravely, if more briskly. Eventually he addressed the arrangements for the interviews. We were all eager to learn why so many of us had been called for interview at precisely the same time and we were soon to find out.

"There are sixty-six applicants for interview today. I trust that you are all here. I will now call out all your names. Anyone who isn't here should inform me at once." *Brilliant*, I thought. *No wonder the administrative staff are held in such low esteem.*

All the names were duly called and it transpired that all applicants were present. Fred continued: "You will be called into the interview room to meet the consultants in two groups. The groups will enter in alphabetical order. The first group will be doctors with surnames from A to M - that is Dr Abbot to Dr McDonald - and the second group will be doctors whose surnames range from N to Z - that is to say, Dr Nelson to Dr Whiteside. You will therefore need to organise yourselves into two columns, with Dr Abbott at the front of the first column and Dr Nelson at the head of the second." There was a gradual movement as the candidates began to organise themselves according to these instructions, with Mike Abbott going to the front by the committee room door, and the others sorting themselves out behind him.

"Wait, wait, wait," shouted Fred, "I haven't finished yet. In turn, I will lead each column into the committee room. Inside, you will find the consultants sitting behind a row of tables on the right hand side. The column will line up opposite the consultants with Dr Abbott at the far end and Dr McDonald, as the last one to enter the room, by the door. When you are all in place, I shall call out your names one by one, and you will each answer to your name in turn. At the completion of this exercise there will probably be a pause and there may be some conversation between the consultants - but in due course, when you get a signal from me, you will exit the room - with Dr McDonald, as the last doctor in, being the first out. You should not speak unless spoken to by one of the interviewing panel, other than to answer to your names. Subsequently, the second group of thirty-three doctors will enter, with Dr Nelson leading the way in and Dr Whiteside leading the way out. Is that clear?"

These arrangements sounded ludicrous and for a moment there was a stunned silence. Then the inevitable flurry of questions began.

"Are we subsequently to be interviewed separately?"

"No."

"How can the consultants possibly interview thirty-three applicants at once?"

"The consultants make the arrangements for these interviews," replied Fred defensively, "not me!"

There was a query from the back of the room. "Will there be any opportunity to ask questions?"

"There will be no opportunity to ask any questions. As I said, you will answer to your names and you should not speak unless spoken to."

"When shall we know which of us has been successful?"

"I expect the results to be available within five minutes of the end of the interviews. After the second group comes out, I will go back into the committee room and will be given the names of the successful candidates, which I shall then read out to you."

This sounded to be a most bizarre and unsuitable way for a *'prestigious establishment'* - as Fred had described it - to appoint its medical staff, and there was a general muttering of discontent. However, it appeared that there was nothing that we could do about it, and no time for further grumbling.

Fred held up his hand again and called for silence. "Now please form up into the two columns, with Dr Abbott's column on the left side of the corridor, and Dr Nelson's on the right."

It took a moment or two to organise this and then Fred, having checked that the consultants were ready, led the first column, of which I was a member, into the committee room. We were now in the oldest part of the hospital, another area that was new to me. It was a large room, oak-panelled, with an arched stained glass window at the far end. It looked as if it might have been the chapel of the original hospital, retained when the more modern wards were added. Again there were portraits on the wall, each with a brass plate giving the name and vital dates of the distinguished doctors of a bygone era that had worked here. Also, standing on pedestals, were bronze busts of two of the hospital's most famous sons.

Just as Fred had described, the consultants were seated behind leather topped committee tables on the right hand side of the room. No doubt all the applicants were able to identify them, at least by sight. During our training we had visited many of the units in the hospital, being taught by the consultants who worked there, and most had delivered lectures to us at some time or another. Looking down the line I was surprised to see only four consultant surgeons present. There was only one orthopaedic surgeon, nobody was there to represent the professorial unit, and there was just a single surgeon from each of the other three units. Sir William Warrender representing Surgical Five was the most senior. There were more physicians present than surgeons but again, by no means were they all present. Dr Digby, a consultant radiologist who was the current chairman of the consultants committee, sat in the centre. There were no house officer posts in radiology, so I presumed he was there simply to act as chairman and to organise the proceedings.

It was difficult to know where to look and how to stand. It seemed impolite to look at Fred and to ignore the interviewing panel, yet equally inappropriate to try to catch the eye of one of the consultants. I decided that the best option was to focus on a point on the wall just above Dr Digby's head. Standing with hands in pockets was clearly too casual but standing rigidly to attention did not seem appropriate either; so I settled for the hands behind the back 'Duke of Edinburgh' pose. Suddenly I realised that Fred had started to read out our names, and had already reached Dr Green. In response, some of the candidates were replying "Sir"; some said "Good morning," some simply "Present." The whole exercise seemed utterly ridiculous and reminded me of the attendance register read out every morning at primary school. It struck me that there was a danger that I might reply "Here, Miss," when my name was called, but I managed a polite "Good morning," when the time came.

At the end of the roll-call there was a pause, whilst some muttered conversation between the consultants occurred, interspersed with surreptitious glances at the line of interviewees. One of the physicians got up and went to speak with the orthopaedic surgeon whilst looking in the general direction of the "A to D" doctors, before returning to his place. In due course, each consultant nodded to the chairman, who in turn nodded to Fred, and we were led out of the room. In less than five minutes the whole charade was over and we were back in the corridor.

Without any delay, the second column was marched in for their 'interviews'. There was a general disbelief amongst our group at what had happened.

"That was a fiasco," said one.

"What a waste of time."

"I felt like a model at a seaside beauty competition."

"Or like a suspect in a police identification parade," was another view.

There was a general consensus that the consultants must already have decided in advance of the interviews whom they were going to appoint, presumably from knowledge of the student's performance during the clinical attachments on their units or from the marks gained in the final examination. It appeared that the purpose of the exercise was simply to check they had put the right name to the right face and to ensure that two consultants did not both wish to appoint the same candidate.

All too soon, the second column of doctors was back from their 'interviews'. Fred returned to the committee room, and those in the corridor were left to wait for the results. Johnny Nolan said that he thought he got the faintest nod from his 'Uncle Bill', but no one else seemed to have been given any sort of visual encouragement. If we thought that the results of the interview had been predetermined, this impression was reinforced when Fred re-appeared within two minutes with a list attached to his clipboard that looked suspiciously like one that had been present before the performance began.

Once again, with great aplomb, he stood on one of the benches and called for attention. His preliminary remarks had been a big moment for him, but this was to be his finest hour. He held the future of all these young doctors in the palm of his hand, their fates listed on the paper he was holding. He had their attention, he was totally in control - or so he thought.

"I am pleased to say that Dr Digby, as Chair of the Consultant's committee, has passed to me a list of the successful candidates for the pre-registration house posts at the City General Hospital due to commence on the first of August, 1966. Those of you whose names are called out as the successful applicants should stay behind afterwards and I will take you back into the committee room so that we can undertake certain necessary formalities."

Again the rumble of stamped feet began from the applicants, eager to know the result of the interviews and irritated by this procrastination. However, these few precious moments of power only occurred for Fred twice a year, and he was not going to be denied. He continued, and indeed caused further frustration by repeating his last sentence. "Those of you who are successful will be required to stay behind and I will take you back into the committee room to undertake various formalities. You will be required to sign a contract of employment, to make arrangements..."

There were mutterings of "Oh for God's sake," and "Get on with it!" from the back of the hall, but Fred continued undeterred. "You will also be required to attend tomorrow morning at nine am to meet the resident housekeeper, where you will be allocated rooms in the medical residency, and you will given bleeps by the switchboard supervisor - for which, a small deposit will be required."

He continued in this vein for two or three minutes, despite frequent interruptions. Finally, he turned to the paper attached to his clipboard, and after an unnecessary, but nonetheless dramatic pause, came to the information that we were all desperate to hear.

"The successful applicants for the pre-registration jobs at this hospital are..."

Immediately he had the total undivided attention of us all. Slowly, and with prolonged pauses after each name called (he would have been superb at announcing the elimination results of one of the present day television talent shows), he gave the names of the successful doctors, starting with the medical posts. Although I had not applied for any of these, it was nonetheless of interest to know who had been successful. At the completion of the list of names, each linked to the post to be held, a wide range of emotions were on display; relief for some, disappointment for others. There was a general exodus of those who had applied for the medical posts but who had been unsuccessful. It would have been perfectly feasible for Fred to continue to read out the names of the successful applicants for the surgical jobs but he decided to wait until those who wished to leave had done so, and until he again had silence.

Finally, he said "I will now read out the names of the successful applicants for the pre-registration house surgical jobs. Surgical One: Dr Bennett and Dr Holme."

These were the two orthopaedic posts for which I had not applied.

"Surgical Two: Dr Green and Dr Leach." As expected, these were the two distinction candidates.

Names were read out for the two successful applicants for Surgical Three and Surgical Four. This just left the Warrender/Potts Surgical Five jobs, and I was certain that one of those was destined for Miss 'Miniskirt' Chambers and that Johnny Nolan would work for Sir

William. It seemed that I was not destined to start my medical career at the teaching hospital. Disappointed but not surprised, I turned to leave.

"The house surgeon for Sir William Warrender will be Dr Nolan." Johnny would work for his Uncle Bill as expected. There was another long pause. "Finally, the house surgeon for Mr Potts will be Dr Lambert."

For a moment I was absolutely stunned. There must be some mistake. Had I heard correctly? It had been indicated to Liz Chambers that the job was hers. How had I got a job at the teaching hospital - and with Mr Potts of all people? He always selected the prettiest female graduate.

Johnny Nolan came bounding over to my side, a huge smile on his face. It would have been hard to find anybody more pleasant to work alongside.

"Well, that's a turn-up for the books!" he said. "I thought Liz had Mr Potts' job sewn up, all cut and dried."

"I just can't believe it," I replied."I didn't even go and see him to express an interest in the job. Liz did, and was virtually promised it."

"I know. Potts always goes for the classy young birds and your figure and legs don't match hers at all! Maybe Sydney is having a midlife crisis, or perhaps changing his sexual orientation."

"I'm not sure about that but I'm delighted to get the job, though I can't understand how it could have happened. I simply can't believe it."

As we continued to chat, waiting to do the paperwork that we had been told about, the disappointed unsuccessful candidates trooped past. They included Liz Chambers, who looked hard in my direction. She remained tight-lipped and looked extremely angry but held her head high as she stomped out in her high heel shoes.

"She'd better wear something a bit less revealing for the interviews at the Middleton Hospital tomorrow," said Johnny, "or she'll miss out on a job there as well. Look, after we've filled in all those forms that Fred was talking about, let's go and find somewhere to have a drink and celebrate."

The formalities took half an hour or so and soon enough we were in a local pub happily toasting our success. It had been a most bizarre interview but somehow or other it had turned out well, and I was absolutely delighted. Good fortune, I realised, tastes all the sweeter when it comes unexpectedly.

Chapter 3

There was an opportunity for some rest and relaxation in the ten days before I took up my post, so I joined my two younger brothers who were enjoying their school summer holiday youth hostelling in the Lake District. Tramping over the hills in glorious sunshine was a wonderful way to recharge my batteries, both physical and mental, after the months of revision and the stress of the final examinations and interview. I found a sense of freedom and space in the high mountains and on some days wandered off on my own to seek out the quieter ridges and summits. Sitting on a mountain top, looking down at the panorama of fields and lakes far below, I contemplated the life as a doctor that now lay before me, and wondered whether I was sufficiently prepared for the challenge ahead. It was known that doctors had a rate of mental illness three times the national average, a suicide rate three times the norm and, for those that were married, a rate of divorce three times what would be expected. I also realised that not all house officers successfully completed their twelve months as a resident hospital doctor. I wondered how I would cope; would I last the course?

I could happily have stayed in the Lakes for a month or more but - realising that it would be beneficial to pick the brains of the outgoing house officer, to get some advice and inside information about the job that I was about to do - I left my brothers to enjoy their holiday and travelled back to the city.

It was well recognised - indeed, expected - that most new house officers would make several blunders or embarrassing *faux-pas* in the first few weeks of their job. Staff at the City General Hospital still told with amusement a story about Eleanor Briggs, the house officer that I was about to meet.

The first cardiac arrest to which she was called occurred at three am one morning and, knowing how important it was to get to the patient and commence resuscitation as soon as humanly possible, it had taken her less than sixty seconds to rush from her bed in the residency to the scene of the patient's collapse on the ward. Kneeling on the floor beside the collapsed male patient, she had commenced resuscitation with gusto in textbook fashion, implementing external cardiac massage and mouth-to-mouth respiration. Unfortunately, engrossed in this life-saving work, she had forgotten that when rushing from her bed she had simply thrown a white coat over an extremely skimpy diaphanous silk nightie and dashed barefoot to the ward. She was completely unaware of just how revealing the view was from the front, or indeed the rear. Inevitably the male medical staff also involved in the resuscitation were significantly distracted and had difficulty concentrating on the job in hand - but despite this the resuscitation was successful, at least initially. What the patient thought on being returned to the land of the living by this nubile young woman is not known, since unfortunately he collapsed a second time shortly afterwards, some say from overexcitement. It is reported that later a rather stern night sister took Eleanor to one side and explained that even in an emergency, it was permissible - indeed advisable - to pull on a pair of slacks and a sweater!

Eleanor and I met in one of the side rooms of the male ward on the Sunday afternoon, the day before I commenced my job on the first of August. I did not know her well. She had only been a somewhat distant figure, albeit a striking one, from the year above me at medical school. Tall and slim, with good looks, an attractive figure and blonde hair, she was a typical Sydney Potts selection for house surgeon.

As I looked at her now I thought that although the figure was still there, she looked a little slimmer - having perhaps lost some weight - but more noticeable were the subtle changes about the face and hair. She had a slightly jaded expression, a hint of weariness had crept into her demeanour, and a few frown lines had appeared on her forehead. Her eyes had lost their sparkle and the blonde hair, which had been her crowning glory, looked slightly unkempt and in need of a good brush. Whether this indicated a lack of time or a slight loss of self-esteem was difficult to say, but the six months that she had worked on the unit certainly seemed to have taken their toll.

I quizzed her about the two consultants, particularly about their likes and dislikes and the 'do's and don'ts' which would smooth my transition from student to doctor. She described Sir William as being immaculately dressed with manners to match, saying that he was invariably courteous and unfailingly polite, whether to nurses, doctors or patients, and never deviated from his calm, unhurried manner. He had apparently been in post since the inception of the National Health Service in 1948 and was well respected, both inside the hospital and in the wider medical fraternity. Although Eleanor clearly liked him and enjoyed working for him, she also described him as being a 'bit of an old woman', prone to repetition and to reminiscences about his own younger surgical days. She didn't know his exact age but thought he must be close to retirement.

"His ward rounds go on interminably," she said, "but if you can keep your concentration, which isn't always easy after a disturbed nights sleep, you will learn a lot of surgical common sense. He is a vastly experienced surgeon and always eager to share his knowledge with his team. By the way, it also helps if you have an interest in horticulture. He is a bachelor who lives in the lodge at the back of the hospital, and has a large garden. When he's not on the ward he can be found tending his prize vegetables, and he's always pleased if his junior staff show an interest."

"And why was he knighted?" I asked.

"I really don't know," replied Eleanor, "but I believe Johnny Nolan, the other new houseman, is his nephew, so presumably he will be able to tell you."

"And what about Sydney Potts?" I asked.

"Well," said Eleanor, a frown crossing her face, "I suppose he's completely the opposite. He's younger, has only been in the post for four or five years, and is probably still striving to get himself established. Obviously he is bang up to date with all the latest medical theories and research, so you will have the opportunity to learn modern surgical ideas and treatments. Indeed, he is a bit of a showman, and keen to demonstrate his clinical knowledge and surgical abilities. He puts on a real five star acting performance in theatre, especially if there are some young nurses to impress. Basically, he's a good technical surgeon too, probably better than Sir William - at least he would be, if he didn't tend to get a little bit impatient and rush things. You need to be on your toes when you assist him in theatre or you will feel the sharp end of his tongue. He hasn't got Sir William's bedside manner either; he can be very short with patients at times. Everyone says that he prefers his patients to be asleep, anaesthetised in theatre, rather than awake and able to talk to him and ask questions. Oh, and as I think everyone knows, he does fancy himself a little bit with the ladies; we were all rather surprised to hear that you had got his job. In fact, I had much the same conversation that I am having with you now with Liz Chambers about a fortnight ago; she seemed to think that the job was hers."

"Yes, I know that. She told me the same thing and I was amazed to hear that I had been appointed."

Eleanor continued. "Mr Potts' main interest outside his work is sailing. He's got a yacht that he sails offshore. He asked me to crew for him whilst he sailed his boat up to Scotland earlier in the summer."

"What, just the two of you?"

"No, no, it's got four or five berths and he needs to have at least three or four people on board to sail her any distance. 'My thirty-six footer' he calls her, and each spring he sails up to Scotland, leaves her there for the season, and in late summer he sails back again. I believe she's moored somewhere in Anglesey during the winter. He likes to make suggestive remarks about 'rubbing her bottom down' and 'spending the night with her'. In the summer, when he's not on duty, he spends his weekends in Scotland - presumably with his family - but he needs assistance to get the boat there and back at the beginning and end of the season. It wasn't my cup of tea at all. I get terribly seasick when I'm on the water and in any case, if I get any time off duty, I use it to catch up on my sleep. On the last trip this spring, he took the senior registrar, Simon Gresty, and I was very surprised that Simon agreed to go. He's not the outdoor type at all and I heard afterwards that he spent a lot of the time with his head over a bucket. Mind you, he probably didn't feel able to say 'no'...he's applying for consultant posts now and needs a good reference. Mr Potts will be looking for a crew very soon to sail the boat home. You are sure to be invited."

It suddenly occurred to me that this might be the reason for my appointment to the house officer post. In the past I had done quite a lot of dinghy sailing, both inland and on coastal waters, and if Mr Potts had somehow heard about this - after discovering that his female house officers opted out and his senior registrar was a land-lubber - perhaps he regarded me as a better bet as potential crew.

I was also keen to hear Eleanor's views and get some background on the two ward sisters with whom I should soon be working. We had been told repeatedly by our tutors and by previous house officers of the importance of establishing a good relationship with the nursing sisters, who could make or break a newly qualified doctor. If they chose to they could offer helpful advice and assistance to the new houseman, especially in the first few weeks of the job when they were unfamiliar with the routine on the ward. On the other hand, there were endless tales of arrogant young house officers who foolishly believed that nurses were subservient to doctors, that it was the doctor's role to give instructions to the nurses and who, as a result, had been made to suffer for such disrespect.

"Well, the two nursing sisters are as different as chalk and cheese," Eleanor said. "Sister Rutherford on the female ward, or Gladys to her friends, is absolutely wonderful. A real brick. She is well-respected by all her nurses and also by the medical staff, including the two consultants, and is loved by all her patients. She mothers us all in a firm but friendly fashion. She has been in the job a long time, has no ambitions to be promoted to a teaching or administrative nursing post, and she is certainly someone you can turn to for advice. Her third grandchild has just arrived, and I'm sure she makes a wonderful granny. But beware of Jean Ashbrook on the male ward; she tends to blow 'hot and cold'. Sometimes she can be just about tolerable, but other times she can be the devil in disguise. One of her patients once asked me if it was a 'monthly' thing, but there is more to it than that. Initially I used to think that it was personal - that she just hated me because I was a female doctor - but I have come to the conclusion that she dislikes all doctors. She seems to believe that she could do our job better than we can. Some say that she actually wanted to do medicine - that she applied to medical school but failed to get the necessary grades at A-level - and she certainly seems to have been taking her frustration out on doctors ever since. Others say that she needs a man to sort her out and that she is a frustrated spinster, but unless she changes her attitude, I can't think that any man would be prepared to take her on. But," Eleanor added, "she does know her stuff, and she does run the ward efficiently."

"So what advice can you give to someone who will be working with her for the next six months?" I asked.

"Well," she said, "my advice would be that you don't take her attitude too personally or too seriously. Remember that she treats all the junior doctors the same. Don't imagine that it is only you that will feel the sharp edge of her tongue. Keep a sense of humour. My belief is that she is constantly looking for an opportunity to get the better of the house officer. Just accept that from time to time she will win one of her little battles with you and that on other occasions you will win. Regard it as being a game of tennis with the advantage swinging to and fro. But don't let her get on top of you." I presumed that she was speaking metaphorically and not physically!

"And any other advice?"

"Yes," she said. "Don't try to buck the system." I did not understand what she meant and asked her to explain.

"You may think that you have been employed here as a doctor. You have, but you are also expected to be a clerk, a porter, a cleaner, a nurse and a general dogsbody. You may imagine that having been appointed as a doctor at the City General Hospital that you have some kudos, some prestige, that you hold a position worthy of respect. Outside the hospital that is true, people will look up to you, but inside - forget it. You are the lowest of the low. The hospital system has been in place for the last 40 years, and it's still going to be there in 40 years time. You are not going to change it. If you are going to survive, accept it and learn to live with it."

Still reflecting on this advice, I went home and enjoyed a good night's sleep, better than I was destined to have for some time to come. Keen to create a good first impression and to be as well prepared as possible for Mr Potts' Monday morning ward round, I arrived early at the hospital the next day. By seven forty-five am I was walking along the corridor to the Surgical Five unit, wearing my new white coat and sporting the badge which proudly displayed my name and medical position.

'Dr Paul Lambert, House Surgeon to Mr Potts.' I still found it hard to believe. One pocket held a copy of the British National Formulary which listed the details, doses and side effects of all the pharmaceutical agents licensed for use in the UK, a second pocket held my stethoscope and tendon hammer - symbolic instruments of my trade - and the third pocket held pens and pencils and the hospital bleep, which I had been so pleased and proud to receive from the hospital switchboard. How naïve I had been not to recognise that this was, in reality, not a modern aid to good communication but an instrument of torture, an unforgiving taskmaster, a destroyer of sleep...something which, in less than a month, I would gladly have thrown from the highest cliff into the deepest sea!

Approaching the ward on that first morning I felt a sense of pride in what I had achieved, and in my new found status. But I was also acutely aware of the many challenges ahead; and conscious that this pride, and the confidence that it engendered, might be shattered in an instant by a question from a patient or nurse to which I did not know the answer, or worse, by being faced with a situation - perhaps an emergency - with which I could not cope.

On reaching the ward office, I could see the nurse's handover in progress through the glazed portion of the door. This is a ritual, repeated morning and night, on every ward in every hospital in England on a daily basis. The staff nurse, who with her two student nurses had cared for the patients through the night, was relaying to sister and the oncoming day staff information concerning the progress of each individual patient. I knocked quietly on the office door and entered the room.

"Good morning, Sister," I said. "If you don't mind, I would like to take two or three sets of patient records from the notes trolley, and get to know some of the patients before Mr Potts' starts his ward round."

Sister Ashbrook looked up for a second but then, without acknowledging my presence, instructed staff nurse to resume the handover. The staff nurse did as she had been told.

As I stood by the door, I heard her say "In bed one, we have Dennis Needham, the hernia repair from five days ago. He is due to go home today. A district nurse has been arranged to remove his stitches. Dennis is single but a neighbour is coming to collect him, although she is not able to get here until about two pm because of her other commitments. The bed therefore won't be available until this afternoon." There was a pause for questions, but none were forthcoming.

"In bed two, we have Stuart Taylor, yesterday's varicose veins operation. There was a bit of oozing of blood from the groin wound in the night, but nothing serious. His pulse and blood pressure were not affected and the oozing stopped with a bit of pressure. He is already up and about this morning." I saw a couple of the nurses look in my direction, but Sister continued to ignore me.

"In bed three, we have the young lad, Peter Thompson. Aged sixteen, he had an acutely inflammed appendix removed two days ago. He has not been so well during the night. He has been feeling faint, has sweated a lot, and he spiked a temperature of 102 degrees. He has been started on antibiotics and we have increased his observations to two-hourly. His temperature came down with aspirin and cold sponging but the medical staff wish to be informed if it spikes again, as they want to take blood for culture."

Again, there was the odd glance in my direction. The notes I needed were on the far side of the group of nurses and I could not reach them without disturbing the group by moving at least one of their chairs. I coughed softly and tried again.

"Excuse me, Sister."

Sister looked up angrily. "Shh, don't interrupt. Can't you see we're busy?"

By this time one of the nurses looked quite apprehensive; aware, no doubt, that there was the potential for tension to develop if Sister continued to ignore me. But ignore me she did.

After a glance in my direction, staff nurse continued yet again. "In bed four, we have Max Quigley, admitted yesterday with haematemesis and melaena. He's only forty-two years old and apparently something of a big noise in the city. He has a long history of indigestion and the bleeding is thought to be coming from a duodenal ulcer. He has got blood running through an intravenous drip at the moment but it seems there is a possibility that he will have to go to theatre if the bleeding doesn't stop."

"How many units has he had?" asked Sister.

"Three so far."

"And how much blood is available for him in the blood bank?"

"Three further units, but the transfusion is running a little behind schedule at the moment. He is certainly unstable and needs careful monitoring."

I decided that I had been ignored long enough, that Sister Ashbrook was being deliberately awkward and provocative, and my patience was being tested to the limit. There was little point in trying to familiarise myself with the patients without their case-notes and they were out of reach beyond the group of nurses on the far side of the room.

"Sister," I said, making a move in the direction of the trolley, "if you don't mind, I'll just get a few notes and then be out of your way."

Sister Ashbrook was sitting at the desk facing the door with the nurses from both night shift and day shift in a semicircle around her, their backs to me. A mother hen with her brood. As I spoke, heads turned in my direction and I was faced with a sea of at least eight faces. Sister's was red and angry.

"Stay exactly where you are," she said, her voice crisp and cold. "Surely you know that medical *students* are not allowed in my office until nine am?"

There was just the slightest emphasis on the word 'students'. It was clearly an instruction to leave forthwith. Had she not seen the white doctor's badge that I was wearing proudly on my lapel in place of the dark blue student badge? Or was this a deliberate snub and her first opportunity to gain an advantage over a hesitant new house officer?

"I do apologise, Sister," I said in a deferential voice. "I should have introduced myself. I have been appointed as the new surgical house officer. My name is *Doctor* Lambert." I gave a slight but definite emphasis to the word Doctor.

"Then, *Doctor*," – again, the slight emphasis on the word Doctor - "if you are new and inexperienced, you need to learn that it is quite inappropriate to burst into my office and interrupt a nursing handover meeting in this manner. I should be grateful if you would leave us and return when the meeting is over; we shouldn't be more than twenty minutes or so."

I looked at the group of nurses. All their faces were now turned in my direction. Sister's expression was stern and uncompromising. She had clearly decided that she would have her way in this little battle. A couple of the staff nurses adjacent to her clearly found the situation amusing and were only just managing to conceal their smiles, with difficulty. The more junior nurses looked anxious, and I thought that there might even have been a touch of sympathy for me in their expressions.

This was clearly a watershed moment in my relationship with Sister Ashbrook. I knew beyond any doubt that this was not her office, but the clinical office shared by nursing, medical and paramedical staff. The office, after all, contained the medical notes and various items of medical equipment that were used by the medical staff. It held the laboratory and radiological investigation cards for the doctors to use, and the small library of books that were shared between the doctors and the nurses. Similarly, there was no doubt that I was entitled to take medical notes if I needed them; indeed it would be impossible for me to do my job without them. The notes were an essential part of medical care and had to be available to the medical staff twenty-four hours a day.

I remembered the warning that Eleanor had given me the day before and particularly her advice not to take Sister Ashbrook's behaviour too seriously or personally. But why was she like this? Had she made an innocent mistake, not noticing my doctor's badge and forgetting that it was the first of August, when the new house officers arrived? Had she really believed initially that I was a medical student and then been too proud to admit her error? Or was she simply trying to impress her brood of nurses? On balance, I felt it more likely that she was simply trying to establish her supremacy, to show me who was the boss from the very start. Whatever the real reason, she was putting me in a difficult position. Rightly or wrongly, and many will think me a wimp, I decided to withdraw. I left the room and closed the door quietly behind me. If this was a game of tennis, as Eleanor had suggested, it was definitely fifteen-love to Sister Ashbrook.

I wondered what I should do until the nursing handover was finished. I still wanted to review some patients with their notes before Mr Potts arrived - but I was damned if I was going to stand outside Sister's office and wait twenty minutes like a naughty schoolboy outside the headmaster's office - and so I decided to return to the residency.

Had I taken the right decision? I remained in no doubt that everything I had done and said had been entirely appropriate, that I had every right to enter the office to collect the notes that I required, and that Sister's actions had been obstructive and rude. Accordingly, I would have been well within my rights to have stood my ground - perhaps I should have done. Equally, to have done so would have raised the stakes considerably, and had I proceeded to push through the group of nurses to access the trolley and take the notes that I required, in defiance of her instructions, the situation would have been exacerbated. She would have felt that her authority had been undermined in front of her nurses and would have been even more likely to make life difficult for me in the future. As it was, I had undoubtedly lost face in front of the nurses; but on balance, I felt that my decision to withdraw gracefully (and, I hoped, with some dignity) had not been unreasonable. I certainly intended to sort the matter out, one to one with Sister Ashbrook, at a later stage.

Returning to the residency, tail somewhat between my legs, I met Mr Khan, the registrar on the unit, coming in the opposite direction.

"Hello Paul," he said, "or should it be Dr Lambert now? I was delighted to hear that you have been appointed to join us. I hope you will enjoy your six months working on the unit." It was a much warmer welcome than I had received in the clinical office!

"But you are going in the wrong direction," he continued. "It's useful to review the patients on the ward before Mr Potts does his ward round, to catch up with any events that have occurred during the night. The boss expects us to be up to date with our patient's clinical problems at all times. The houseman usually joins me on my early morning round."

"That is exactly what I was trying to do," I said, and went on to explain what had happened.

"Ah," said Mr Khan, "so you have already had your first spat with Sister Ashbrook, have you? That didn't take you long. Well, you come with me." Then, with a twinkle in his eye, he added, "Let's go and stir things up a bit."

Together we walked back to the ward office and he knocked on the door, which remained firmly closed as the nurses continued with their morning handover. Without waiting for a reply he entered and, slightly hesitantly, I followed in his wake.

"Good morning Sister, good morning nurses," he said, in the cheeriest conceivable voice. "I believe you have already met our new house officer, Dr Lambert." Without waiting for a reply, he continued, "If you don't mind, Sister, Dr Lambert and I will just collect a few medical notes and then leave you all in peace to have your little chinwag."

He went straight up to the medical records trolley, displacing a couple of the nurses as he did so, and plucked out a selection of notes.

To my amazement, he then burst into song. It was a tune with which I was very familiar; 'Territory Folks' from the musical *Oklahoma*. I knew the words well enough too. They came from the Hospital Revue that the doctors and nurses had performed and in which he had played a leading role the previous Christmas, in the Great Hall in the Nurses Home. In a rich clear tenor voice he sang the verse:

"Oh, the Surgeons and the Sisters must be friends,
Oh, the Surgeons and the Sisters must be friends.
Surgeons need to stitch and sew,
Sisters need to show them how,
The Surgeons and the Sisters should be friends."

Without a break, he went straight into the chorus:
"Doctors and Nurses should be friendly,
Doctors and Nurses should be pals,
Doctors yearn to be Nurses' sweethearts,
Nurses yearn to be Doctors' gals."

When I had re-entered the office, I had been determined to keep my head down and avoid catching Sister's eye, but at this performance I simply could not resist turning to look at her to witness her reaction and that of her group of nurses. All the faces bar one were wreathed in smiles. One or two of the nurses laughed openly. For a moment I thought that the nurses were going to break into spontaneous applause, heightening Sister's humiliation - but clearly, if they considered this, they thought better of it. The laughter subsided and Mr Khan handed me a pile of notes to carry as he turned towards the door. I was, after all, the house officer, and he was the registrar.

"Thank you, Sister," he said as we left the office. Without looking back, I closed the door quietly behind us.

"That was very brave," I said, "or possibly very foolish."

"Not at all," Mr Khan replied. "Sister and I have an understanding."

"And what is that?"

"Well," he said, "Sister and I agree to dislike each other, but I have a respect for the way in which she runs the ward, and I think that she has a respect for me as a surgical registrar. It is not an ideal arrangement and it is not the way I would like it to be; but as a relationship, it seems to work."

I wondered if I would ever have the confidence to pull off a trick such as the one that I had just witnessed. I thought probably not, but it had been a memorable start to my first day on the ward and, thanks to

Mr Khan's intervention and support, we had scored a point over Sister Ashbrook.

It's now "Fifteen All", I thought, but recognised that my relationship with Sister had got off to a very sticky start. She had been humiliated in front of her nurses and I knew that she would be looking for a chance to get her own back as soon as an opportunity arose. Unfortunately, that opportunity arose all too soon.

Chapter 4

In the office Mr Khan had been in ebullient mood, putting on a performance that would have graced a music hall stage, but on entering the ward he became serious and businesslike.

"This morning," he said, "we need to have a quick look at all Mr Potts' patients, both on the male and the female wards, before he arrives. He usually starts his consultant round at around nine-thirty and he will expect us to be up to speed with each and every patient, to know who is making satisfactory progress and to have identified those with problems. The main role of a consultant is to care for his patients but he is also watching to see that his junior staff are performing well, so we need to give a good account of ourselves. It doesn't look good if the boss identifies a problem that we have overlooked. That gives us approximately an hour to make sure that everything is tidy." Then, helpfully, he added, "Since this is your first morning on the ward, I will present the patients to Mr Potts today – but, of course, thereafter it will be your responsibility. "

The ward was of a 'Nightingale' design; a large, open-plan rectangular room, with a line of a dozen beds down each side. With its large windows and high ceiling it was light and airy, with just a slight scent of antiseptic in the air. For convenience, each consultant was allocated beds on one side of the ward: Mr Potts' patients on the left and Sir William's patients on the right. Starting with the first bed on the left, Mr Khan picked up the observation chart from the rail on the foot of the bed, glanced at it briefly, and then addressed the patient.

"Good morning Mr Needham, how are you feeling this morning?"

"Fine, Doctor, thank you."

"Your rupture operation appears to have gone very well, and, as you know, we are planning to let you go home today. Do you have your post-operative instruction sheet?"

"Yes I do, thanks."

"And you understand that the district nurse will call next week to take out your stitches?" The patient nodded. "And you have a date for your review in the follow up clinic?"

"Yes, I do."

"Do you have any questions you want to ask before you leave?"

"None at all, thank you. Doctor, by the way - thank you for all your help these last few days."

"You're welcome."

We moved on to the next bed. Again, Mr Khan addressed the patient by name and asked how he was feeling and whether he had enjoyed a comfortable night.

"I feel well enough, thank you, but in the night the nurses seemed a bit anxious about this wound in my groin."

"Paul, perhaps you could screen the patient, so that we can have a look?"

The screens had four cotton panels printed with a floral design, each panel held within folding rectangular metal frames mounted on casters. Three such screens were required to provide adequate privacy for the patient. A great deal of time was spent both by nurses and junior doctors moving these screens during the course of every working day. When I had arranged the screens around the bed, Mr Khan looked at the dressing covering the varicose vein wound in the groin. Although the nurses had put an extra pad over the wound, the amount of blood visible on the dressing was minimal. Mr Khan reassured the patient.

"There is no cause for any concern, Mr Taylor," he said. "There really has been no significant blood loss. It is quite common for there to be a bit of oozing after a varicose vein operation, and the amount here is little more than we normally see. The nurses will put a nice fresh dressing on the wound for you and I anticipate that you will be able to go home tomorrow as planned." The patient clearly looked relieved.

"Do you have any questions?" asked Mr Khan. "No thanks, Doc," was the reply, and again we moved on. In the third bed was the young boy whose appendix had been removed a few days before.

"Now how are you today, Peter? You look a bit flushed."

"Funnily enough Doctor, I don't feel as well as I did yesterday. I feel a bit sickly and I couldn't face anything to eat for breakfast this morning. I didn't get much sleep last night and felt very sweaty, feverish and cold. The cut in my tummy feels more painful today too."

"I see that your temperature was quite high in the night," said Mr Khan, "and you've still got a temperature this morning, which suggests you've got an infection somewhere. Let me have a look at you."

He listened to the patient's chest but found no sign of infection, and then looked at the wound. This was quite red and inflamed and there was a small amount of purulent fluid oozing from it. Again, Mr Khan addressed the patient.

"I'm afraid it does look as if you've got a slight infection in this wound. We will get a sample taken from it to make sure that you are on the right antibiotic, and the nurses will be along later to redress it. I shall also ask them to take a couple of your stitches out so that the infection can escape to the surface. Perhaps some stronger painkillers would help to make things more comfortable. Don't worry though. This is just a bit of a nuisance rather than a major problem, but it may delay your going home for a day or two." He prescribed a larger dose of pethidine on Peter's chart, then turned to me.

"I see you've got a pen and paper - can you please arrange for a full blood count and a wound swab for bacteriology? If he spikes another temperature he will need blood cultures as well."

Mr Khan's conduct on the ward round was exemplary. He was open and personable with the patients, speaking to them in language that they understood, and we were progressing around the ward speedily, without giving any impression of being rushed. Clearly, with his long experience as a surgical registrar, he was completely comfortable with clinical situations that were, for him, quite routine.

It was obvious when we saw Mr Quigley in the fourth bed that he was far from well. He looked pale and anxious. His charts revealed a fast pulse and low blood pressure despite the blood that was being administered through a drip in his right arm. Mr Khan took a careful history of the patient's longstanding dyspepsia. He said that he had experienced indigestion for many years and that this had been particularly severe in the last few weeks, during which time he had taken little by mouth except milk and antacids. He blamed his problems on stress at work, but admitted to smoking thirty cigarettes a day. Mr Khan inquired about any drugs that Mr Quigley might have taken, knowing that a number of tablets, even common ones such as aspirin, can cause ulcers on the lining of the stomach. He also asked searching questions about alcohol intake, aware that should surgery be needed to arrest gastric haemorrhage the most difficult situation to deal with is when juicy varicose veins develop in the gullet and stomach after the liver has been damaged by alcohol. As it happened, Mr Quigley drank very little alcohol - usually only a small glass of sherry, and then just once or twice a year on special occasions. After completing his history and examination, Mr Khan spoke to the patient.

"As you know, there is some bleeding going on, probably from the stomach or the duodenum. We are going to replace the blood that you have lost with these blood transfusions," he indicated the drip in the patient's right arm, "but should the bleeding not stop then I'm afraid we would have to recommend an operation for you."

"Does that mean that it's serious?" asked the patient.

"Clearly, any bleeding has to be taken seriously," came the reply. "If you were bleeding from the surface of the skin, we could easily stop it, simply by stitching it up or by applying some pressure - but because your bleeding is internal we would need to give you an anaesthetic, and perform an operation to reach the bleeding point. Mr Potts, your consultant, will be here to see you in about an hour and we will be asking him for advice."

He turned to me. "Paul, please find out how many pints of blood we still have available and, whatever the number, make it up to six. In addition, can you make sure they've got plenty of serum in the lab so that if we need to cross-match any more blood in a hurry, there will be no delay whilst we take a further blood sample. Also, if the blood pressure drops below ninety or the pulse goes above 110, I want you to call me at once."

We had spent quite some time with Mr Quigley but fortunately the remaining male patients were straightforward, and when all had been reviewed we walked across to the female ward, passing Johnny Nolan and Simon Gresty, the senior registrar, coming in the opposite direction. They had been reviewing Sir William's patients, having started with the ladies. Mr Khan's review of the patients on the female ward was equally efficient and in less than an hour we had returned to the clinical office on the male ward to await the arrival of Mr Potts. By this time, I had accumulated half a dozen jobs on my notepad and wondered when I should find the time to get them done.

While we were waiting, Mr Khan took the opportunity to give me some general advice about the role of the house officer and the responsibilities that I would have for the next six months. Essentially, it was my job to know everything that was clinically relevant about every one of Mr Potts' patients at all times. That included the patient's history, details of abnormal physical findings, and, particularly, their investigations.

"There will be times," he said, "when you will also have to be the spokesman for the patient. Sometimes patients are a little timid, particularly when faced with some of our more formidable colleagues. Occasionally, if a patient fails to tell a consultant something that you know to be important and relevant, you will have to speak up for them."

Mr Khan continued, "There is one point that I need to emphasise. Should you feel uncertain about anything, at any time - if, for example, you feel that you may be out of your depth - then do call someone more senior for support. It is better to call unnecessarily than not to seek advice when it is truly needed." As we were talking Johnny and Simon Gresty joined us, having completed their review of Sir William's patients, and a few minutes later Mr Potts arrived.

Perhaps slightly less than average height and stockily built, I judged him to be forty or forty-five years old. His dark hair was well-oiled and swept back, but showed a hint of grey around the edges. His face was tanned, or possibly weather-beaten, from a weekend spent sailing in Scotland. He wore an immaculate suit and with his suntanned face he looked an impressive figure, despite his lack of inches. Awaiting his arrival we had been reclining in our chairs, but now jumped promptly and smartly to our feet.

"Good morning," said Mr Khan. "I trust you've had a good weekend?"

"Yes, thanks," boomed Mr Potts, with a voice that seemed unnecessarily loud in the confines of the office. "Good weather, calm seas, and a fresh breeze, perhaps blowing four or five from the west. Tried out the new spinnaker on the run from East Loch Tarbert to the Isle of Arran and it worked a treat - a great improvement on the old jenny. So, yes, we've had an excellent weekend, thank you." He paused and looked around. "Now I see that we have some new faces with us this morning. Who have we here?"

"Yes," responded Mr Khan, "we have two new house officers. Can I introduce you to Dr John Nolan and Dr Paul Lambert?"

There is a convention that surgeons are referred to as 'Mister', whereas physicians and all other doctors are called 'Doctor'. This distinction is historical and goes back to the days of the barber-surgeons who were intensely despised by the medical establishment of the time. Referring to them as 'Mister' was a deliberate slight and implied that they were not proper doctors. Over the years the status of surgery and surgeons has changed; so that when a doctor passes the examination to become a Fellow of the Royal College of Surgeons of England, he is entitled, indeed pleased and proud, to be called 'Mister'. Johnny and I would therefore be called 'Doctor', but everyone else on the unit would be called 'Mister'.

"Welcome to you both," said Mr Potts. "And which of you is working for Sir William?"

"I am, Sir," said Johnny.

The boss turned towards me, "And you are working for...?"

"For you, Sir," I said.

Mr Potts frowned and looked puzzled, and there was a slight pause. "Then where is the delightful Miss Chambers?" he asked, turning to Mr Khan.

Again there was a pause, longer this time, but I sensed that it was for me to reply. "Well, Sir," I said with some hesitation, "I'm not absolutely sure, but I think she will be at the Middleton Hospital."

"And what is she doing there?" demanded Mr Potts.

"Well, to the best of my knowledge, she got a house physician job there, Sir." For a moment, there was silence as Mr Potts digested this information.

"Damn the old rogue," he said finally, "she is supposed to be working here. The instructions I gave were quite specific. They could not have been clearer. I tell him I am unable to attend the interviews because I'm operating elsewhere and he..." He left the sentence unfinished.

Suddenly, it became crystal clear to me what had happened. Mr Potts had obviously arranged to do some surgery at one of the private hospitals, had asked Sir William to attend the house officer interviews on his behalf, and told him to appoint Liz Chambers. Sir William, however - the elderly bachelor - had presumably taken a look at Liz, noted her appearance, hadn't liked what he had seen and had overruled his junior consultant colleague. He had then appointed me in her stead, possibly on the basis of the West Indian lady with the extra breast we had seen together in the final examination. I had been appointed by a happy mischance. Surgical serendipity, in fact!

Mr Potts turned to me again. "I take it that you now have a contract of employment here?" he asked.

"Yes, Sir," I replied quietly, clearly aware of the way in which his mind was working.

"And you think that Miss Chambers is a house physician at the Middleton Hospital where, presumably, she too has a six month contract?"

"To the best of my knowledge yes, Sir," I said.

He turned to the general assembly and said, icily, "If you all will please excuse me, I have some telephone calls to make. May I suggest that we re-assemble here in thirty minutes?" With that, he promptly left the room.

For a while there was silence in the room. It was clear to everyone present, including Sister Ashbrook, that I had been appointed against his wishes and should not have a job at the hospital at all. Further, Mr Potts had gone to see if he could correct matters.

"Well, I'm pleased to have you onboard," said Mr Khan.

"And so am I," added Johnny.

Sister Ashbrook remained silent, still irritated, no doubt, by her earlier humiliation during nurses' handover. She would probably be delighted if Mr Potts was successful in transferring me to the Middleton.

Mr Khan, ever practical, turned to Johnny and me. "I am sure that you have both got some investigations to arrange following the walk round the wards this morning, and probably some bloods to take as well. There is no point in wasting time. I suggest you get on with those and we will meet again here in half an hour."

For the next thirty minutes I was extremely apprehensive as to what would happen when Mr Potts returned, and I found it difficult to concentrate on the tasks in hand. I genuinely doubted that he had the power to cancel my contract but if he hadn't, how was he going to treat me for the next six months? It was unlikely that he would be kindly disposed to a houseman who had been appointed to work for him in defiance of his express wishes. And if my contract was cancelled it would be six months before any more house officer jobs became available, unless I was shunted to the house officer post that Liz Chambers was doing at the Middleton.

As it turned out I need not have worried, for when Mr Potts returned he had lost his tense angry expression and had a wicked smile on his face. Ignoring the others, he spoke directly to me.

"Lambert," he said, "as you will have guessed, you were not my first choice as house surgeon - but I welcome you nonetheless, and hope that you have a rewarding time whilst you are with us. It would not be right for you to suffer simply because you have become a victim of my senior colleague's wily ways." A wave of relief swept over me; I wasn't about to be kicked out after all.

"You were quite right - Miss Chambers has indeed been appointed to a house physicians post at the Middleton Hospital – but, of course, she will be looking for a house surgeon's post in February, when I will make sure that I make both the house officer appointments for this unit. I think Sir William will be surprised when he finds out who his next house surgeon is going to be! I have just spoken to him and the old rascal said he wasn't sure how he or some of our elderly male patients would cope with Miss Chamber's miniskirts, or indeed whether the plunging necklines might upset the nurses, and that is the reason he did not appoint her. In due course - in six months time, in fact - he is going to find out. I only hope that his blood pressure can stand the shock!"

Now smiling broadly, he added, "We are running behind schedule. Let's get on with the ward round."

Led by Mr Potts, Mr Khan, Johnny and I, together with Sister Ashbrook, staff nurse and one of the student nurses, took the trolley containing the medical notes and we went, in procession, onto the ward.

It was noticeable how different his approach was to that of Mr Khan. Gone were the open questions that invited a frank and honest reply from the patient. Mr Potts' approach was much more abrupt.

"You're feeling better," he might say. Although the slight inflection in the voice suggested that this was a question, the words were actually a statement, and, should the patient not be feeling better, they actually had to contradict the consultant to make this known. Mr Khan's approach would have been quite different. "How have you felt since I saw you last?" would have been his approach. There was, in fact, very little communication with the patients at all. Whereas Mr Khan stood face to face, Mr Potts stood at the foot of the bed with his entourage, at some distance from the patient. The conversations that took place involved the gaggle of doctors and nurses at the foot of the bed, the subject of the discussion scarcely being involved at all. Management decisions were debated in hushed voices, almost suggesting that it was inappropriate for the patient to hear what was being said.

It was also noticeable that Mr Potts encouraged brevity, and also had great trust in the competence of his long serving registrar. Mr Khan might say, "Yesterday's hernia Sir, no problems at all, probably home on Wednesday."

Mr Potts would wave at the patient from the foot of the bed and say "Good, good," and we would move onto to the next patient. It was easy to see that the patient would feel excluded from such consultations that in some cases barely lasted fifteen seconds. Even Mr Potts's review of Mr Quigley only lasted a couple of minutes. Mr Khan expressed his concern that the situation was unstable, and Mr Potts agreed that surgery would be indicated in the event of further bleeding, but his only words to the patient were "Don't worry, we'll sort you out one way or another." In particular, he did not ask to be informed in the event that surgery was required. I realised that, as Mr Khan had indicated, an important part of my role as house officer was to speak up for the patients and keep them informed of decisions taken about them on the consultant's ward round.

When the ward round was over, Mr Potts lingered for ten or fifteen minutes, drinking a cup of coffee in the office and chatting about the excellent sailing that was available in the sheltered waters off the west coast of Scotland. This was frustrating as I knew there were a lot of jobs waiting for me to do, although nothing had been added to my list during the consultant round, everything having been identified by Mr Khan on his preliminary visit.

Three patients had been admitted from the waiting list during the course of the morning, and after a quick lunch I set off to clerk them. Armed with the first patient's notes, I pulled the screens around the bed of a pleasant thirty-three-year-old lady, who had come into hospital to have her varicose veins treated. She told her story in a brisk and concise fashion; it appeared that the troublesome veins had developed after a recent pregnancy. As well as examining the veins on her legs it was also necessary to examine her heart and lungs to ensure that she was fit for a general anaesthetic, and I offered to get a chaperone.

"No need to bother, young man," she said. "When you've had two babies, you cease to worry about such things."

She proved to be physically fit and I made the necessary notes in the patient records and marked the site of the veins on her leg with a black marker pen. The varicose veins were very prominent when she stood but would be collapsed and much less conspicuous when she was lying horizontally on the operating table. The marks helped to ensure that the operating surgeon removed all the veins that were troubling the patient.

Pleased with my progress, I moved onto the second admission, an obese lady in her seventies whose investigations in the outpatient clinic had revealed gallstones. This time, taking the history proved to be very frustrating. I needed to know the site of the pain, its character, and how long it had been present.

"The pain's in my belly Doctor," she said, "all over, really."

"In every part of your belly?"

"Well, no," she replied, "mainly here." With her left hand she lifted up a pendulous right breast and pointed with her free hand to an area beneath her ribs.

"And how long does it last?"

"Well, it's there all the time," came the reply.

"All the time - you mean throughout the entire day and night?"

"Well, no - not all the time, Doctor - but a lot of the time."

"Have you got it right now?"

"No," she replied.

"Have you had it at all today?"

"No, not today, Doctor."

"So when did you last have it?"

"Oh, some time ago now. I really can't remember."

"And when you do get it, how long does it last?"

"Well, it's like a lightning flash, Doctor. It's gone in a second."

It seemed she would have me believe that this was a pain that was present all the time; but she could not remember when she last had it, and when it did occur it only lasted a few seconds!

"And how severe is it when it comes?" I asked.

"Oh, Doctor," she said and her eyes rolled to the ceiling. "I can't tell you how bad it is."

"How does it compare with labour pains?" I asked.

"Oh, far worse than that."

"So what do you do when it comes?"

"Well doctor, as you know, a woman's work is never done. I just get on with my jobs 'til it passes. You have to, don't you?"

I quietly wondered how many women managed to do their housework in the throes of labour. The real trouble came when I tried to discover how long she had been experiencing the pain.

"Oh, years and years, Doctor," she said. I tried to pin her down.

"Would you say weeks, months, or perhaps years?"

"Oh, a real long time Doctor," she said. "Years and years."

Pushing her, I asked, "Could you say how long?"

"Well, I had an attack at our Billy's wedding, and another when we had that holiday in Wales."

"And how long ago was Billy married?"

"Oh, that's difficult to say Doctor. Quite some time, because they've got the twins now."

"And how old are the twins?"

"Oh, probably coming up two or three," she said, "but it took a long time for the babes to arrive. Our Billy's wife had to have some tests, you know. She went for some fancy new treatment in London. Then it took a long time for her to catch. Not that there's anything wrong with our Billy, you understand."

I reverted to my original question. "So how long do you think you've had the pain altogether?"

Unfortunately, she reverted to her original answer. "Oh, years and years, Doctor!"

It was clear that I was going round in circles and making little progress but I had to decide how to record these symptoms in the notes. In the end, I settled for *"Patient finds difficulty in giving details of the pain, states that it is present constantly yet intermittently, is severe in intensity but doesn't interfere with housework, and has been present for a long time – probably many years."* I was just completing this entry when my bleep rang with its urgent tone.

"Excuse me," I said and dashed to the phone. "Patient collapsed, Surgical Five Male ward," the switchboard operator said.

I set off down the corridor at a run, anxious to know the nature of the emergency and concerned about my ability to cope. As I entered the male ward one of the student nurses passed me, carrying some bloodstained sheets. "It's Mr Quigley, Dr Lambert, in bed four. Sister's already in there."

Passing through the screens that surrounded the patient's bed, it was immediately apparent that Mr Quigley had suffered a further significant bleed. His was face was as pale as the sheet upon which he was lying. There was evidence of bloodstained vomit on the floor and the characteristic odour of melaena in the air, the result of altered blood in the stool. Sister Asbrook was at the bedside and it was obvious that she was accustomed to dealing with such situations.

"Hello Dr Lambert," she said briskly. "A further major bleed about five minutes ago. Blood pressure is down to seventy-five over thirty-five. I think we will need a second drip in the other arm. I've got the drip and cannula available if you would be kind enough to slip it in."

Fortunately I was able to pass the cannula successfully into the vein at the first attempt and very soon we had blood running into both arms. The patient's blood pressure improved a fraction.

"Has Mr Khan been informed?" I asked.

"Yes," said Sister. "He's just with a patient in the out-patient department but says he will be here within ten minutes. I've spoken with the patient's wife as well, and asked her to come in."

This was clearly a different sister to the one with whom I had fenced earlier that day. Although I was the doctor and she the nurse, with her years of experience she had effectively assumed the lead without trying to be overly superior. For myself - attending my first emergency - I was pleased that she was there and welcomed the fact that she had taken control.

When Mr Khan arrived, he was brisk and businesslike.

"We need to take Mr Quigley to theatre as soon as he is stabilised. I will have to go back to the outpatient clinic shortly as there are still some patients waiting to be seen, but these are the things I want you to arrange. Book the emergency theatre: it's Monday, so it's Surgical Three's day. Tell them that, all being well, we should be ready in about an hour. If they have already got some cases booked they will have to postpone them unless their patients are as urgent as ours, which is unlikely. Contact the emergency anaesthetist and make sure he sees the patient before the patient is taken to theatre. Did you take some extra blood to the lab for cross matching earlier today?"

"I did," I replied.

"Fine, then ring the lab and make sure they have those six units available as soon as possible. Get the patient's consent for *"whatever necessary to stop gastrointestinal bleeding and to treat the underlying cause*". Finally, speak with the patient's wife and make sure she understands the gravity of the situation. People believe that nobody should die from haemorrhage on a surgical ward but, regrettably, it does happen from time to time. Be sure to warn her of that possibility. I must go back to the clinic now but don't hesitate to give me a ring if there is any further deterioration - otherwise, I will meet you in theatre in about an hour."

With that he was off and I set about the tasks that I had been given. It was impossible not to be impressed by the way in which both Sister Ashbrook and Mr Khan had reacted to this life-threatening emergency. There had been no sense of panic under pressure; both had been calm, clearheaded and decisive.

I rang the Surgical Three theatre first to check the availability of the theatre suite. Unfortunately there were already a couple of surgical urgencies booked by the on-call team of the day - a patient for an appendicectomy, and another for drainage of an abscess. These cases were urgent, but not life-threatening. The theatre day staff were due off duty at eight-thirty pm, regardless of what cases were undertaken, and accepted our emergency without hesitation. Similarly, the on-duty anaesthetist accepted the case readily enough, but asked that the patient's clotting studies be undertaken; which meant a further sample of blood needed to be taken.

Unfortunately the Surgical Three surgeon, a senior registrar, was far from pleased when I spoke to him on the telephone. It was already 4.30pm and he clearly had plans for the evening.

"Damn it," he said, "surely your case can wait? It won't take me more than ninety minutes to knock off an appendix and an abscess. Bring your case to theatre after that."

A senior surgical registrar versus a house officer undertaking his first day's duty is scarcely a fair contest, but I knew I had to stick to my guns. I explained the gravity of our patient's condition, stressing that he was actively bleeding, and in an unstable condition.

"Tell me," said the senior registrar, "how long is this case going to take? How long am I going to be kept waiting?"

"I really don't know," I replied. "I guess that depends upon what we find when the abdomen is opened." He knew in this heart that this was true.

"Is your case really so urgent?" he insisted.

"I'm afraid the patient's blood pressure is down to seventy-five over thirty-five," I said, "despite receiving four units of blood in the last three hours. You could discuss the matter with Mr Khan if you wish," I added defensively, thinking that I might need some extra moral support. However, the force of this clinical argument defeated him.

"All right," he snapped, "but get a move on, don't waste any time." He slammed down the telephone.

Back on the ward I took the blood sample requested by the anaesthetist and went, slightly apprehensively, to meet Mrs Quigley. I had no previous experience of speaking to relatives, let alone giving them bad news; such matters had not been part of the medical curriculum. Her attitude surprised me.

"He really is a very stubborn man," she said. "He's had this ulcer for years and years and I have told him so many times that he ought to go to the doctor to seek advice. Finally, when he did go, the doctor recommended that he go along to see a specialist - but would he go? No. The stubborn man simply said he was far too busy at work to take time off."

Remembering Mr Khan's words, I emphasised to her that her husband really was a very sick man, that he had lost a lot of blood and that the surgery was not without its risks.

"Is this ulcer due to his smoking? Will he have to stop his smoking now? If I've told him once I've told him a hundred times that he'll smoke himself into an early grave."

"Ulcers can have lots of causes," I replied. "Smoking, stress, and irregular meals can all play their part, but some people just seem to be prone to them. I'm sure that it would be wise to give up smoking, provided he pulls through the operation. It will be a major operation and he is quite ill at the moment."

Quite suddenly, she reached out and held my hand.

"You mustn't think I'm a hard woman, Doctor. I do care for him; it's just that he's been so stubborn for so long about this ulcer. Will you tell him that I wish him well?"

"Look, why don't you go and tell him that yourself? There will be a few minutes before he goes into surgery."

I had often scrubbed for theatre cases as a medical student but always as a second or third assistant, holding a retractor at arm's length with aching arms, unable to see what was happening in the depth of the wound. On this occasion, being the sole assistant to Mr Khan, I stood immediately opposite him as he worked and was able to see every step of the procedure.

When the patient had been anaesthetised and draped, Mr Khan opened the abdomen through a long incision in the midline above the umbilicus. He quickly displayed the stomach and duodenum - both of which, at least from the front, looked entirely normal.

"Ulcers may occur on any aspect of the stomach or duodenum," he explained, "but, due to the position of the blood vessels, it is ulcers on the back wall that cause bleeding. You may not see any abnormality looking from the front but if you feel carefully you can usually detect the firmness of the ulcer on the back wall, which will indicate where the problem is. Feel the area in the first part of the duodenum, and you will see what I mean."

As I felt, it was quite clear that the tissue in the area where the stomach joined the duodenum was no longer soft and pliable but was harder and more rigid. Mr Khan incised the wall immediately in front of this area so that the inner lining of the bowel became visible, put tissue-holding forceps on each edge of the cut, and as I held these open, he displayed the ulcer on the back wall of the duodenum. It was about a centimetre in diameter and was covered with a blood clot.

Theatre sister handed him some strong catgut mounted on a needle and he under-ran the ulcer, taking large bites of the surrounding tissue. As he did so the blood clot was disturbed, and a fountain of bright red arterial blood sprayed six inches upwards into the wound.

"Impressive, hey?" he said as he looked at me across the theatre table. "It's no wonder that his blood pressure dropped so fast."

Just as quickly as the fountain had started it stopped, as he tied the sutures over the ulcer. With a minimum of fuss, he closed the incision in the front of the duodenum and then divided the vagus nerve that stimulates the stomach to produce acid. Without this stimulus there was every prospect that the ulcer would heal and not recur. He closed the abdomen, put a dressing on the wound, and we removed our theatre gowns.

We then retired to the surgeon's room where he wrote an operation note detailing the operative findings and procedures that had been undertaken. I prescribed the patient's post-operative pain relief and, after consulting Mr Khan, a post-operative fluid regime.

"The anaesthetist has put down a nasogastric tube which will enable the nurses to draw off gastric juices and keep the stomach empty whilst it heals," Mr Khan said, "but the patient will be 'nil by mouth' for at least thirty-six hours. He will need three litres of clear fluid every twenty-four hours via his drip, but he may need some blood as well. Get his blood count done again now, let me know what the result is, and then we'll decide how much more blood he needs to top him up."

As we walked back together to the ward I was surprised to notice that it had gone dark, and the lights were shining brightly from the windows of the wards as we passed. During the operation, I had been totally unaware of time. I had been so engrossed in the surgery that it seemed to me that the operation had taken no more than a couple of minutes, but in practice it must have taken a couple of hours. No doubt time would have passed more slowly for the Surgical Three senior registrar who was waiting to perform the two operations that had been deferred.

It had been suggested that Mrs Quigley should wait on the male ward whilst her husband was in theatre, and we had promised to speak with her after the operation. The evening visitors to the other patients on the ward had long since left and we found her sitting alone in the visitors' room, with a cup of tea that the staff had provided for her. She jumped to her feet as we entered the room, and immediately came across and addressed me. She looked strained and anxious.

"I've been waiting to see you, Dr Lambert. Do tell me how he is - do tell me that he is better!"

I introduced her to Mr Khan, explaining that he was the surgeon that had done the operation and was better placed than I to tell her the situation. To my surprise, he gave a significantly gloomier prognosis than seemed justified. Surely, I thought, the bleeding had been stopped; the patient was only middle aged, had previously been healthy and would, as a matter of course, make a full recovery. However, Mr Khan explained to Mrs Quigley that this had been a very major operation, that the situation remained quite volatile, that there were still significant hurdles ahead and that we would not know for several days if all would be well.

Subsequently, I asked him if he was not being unnecessarily pessimistic about the patient's outlook. "Perhaps a little," he admitted, "but let's be realistic. There is a significant chance that he might re-bleed, not least because we have effectively replaced all his own blood with anticoagulated blood from the blood bank. He's had a long anaesthetic with all its attendant risks, and there is always the danger of a pulmonary embolism." This was the complication that all surgeons dreaded. All too often after an otherwise successful operation, a blood clot develops in the veins of the legs and floats up to the lungs, causing instantaneous death.

Mr Khan continued, "Rather than being overconfident about the prognosis and then getting egg on your face if the patient has a major complication or even dies, it is much wiser to make relatives and indeed patients fully aware of the risks, even if this causes a little extra anxiety in the short term."

He explained that the same philosophy applies on the medical wards when patients have heart attacks. The majority of patients, perhaps eighty percent, will recover without complication - but the remainder may die without any warning. It was an important lesson to put to one side for future use.

Nine hours had passed since lunch, and I was famished. The evening meal was served in the residency at seven pm, to coincide with the visiting time on the wards. Unaware of what arrangements, if any, existed for doctors who missed the evening meal, I went to the dining room in the residency to investigate. Fortunately, food had been left for latecomers in a heated cabinet. The slices of beef had dried and turned to leather at the edge, the mashed potato had formed a thick skin and the peas had hardened, but a generous portion of gravy helped to make it digestible. I was half way through the meal when I was bleeped by the staff on the ward, to be informed that one of the day's admissions was grumbling that a doctor had not seen him since he arrived in the hospital at ten am that day. The night staff had noted that he had not been clerked in and the tablets he took regularly at home for his angina had not been prescribed for him. Would I please go down to the ward to sort things out?

With all the excitement and my involvement with Mr Quigley, I had completely forgotten that one of the routine admissions remained outstanding and had not been clerked. It also struck me that I had not written a word in any of Mr Potts' patients' notes all day. I returned to the ward to attend to these duties, and it was after midnight before I was able to return to my room and get to bed.

Sleep did not come easily; my mind was too alert and too full of the day's events. What an introduction to life on a surgical ward it had been! I had been on my feet and working virtually non-stop for some sixteen or seventeen hours. It had been a rollercoaster of different experiences and emotions, but the management of the bleeding ulcer had demonstrated to me the attraction - almost seduction - of surgery. Mr Quigley was a man in his mid-forties who without surgery would have bled to death, but the operative intervention and the technical skill of the surgeon had completely reversed the situation. All being well, a man's life had been saved today. It was no wonder that surgery was the most glamorous of hospital specialities, or that the general public held surgeons in high regard.

Only the day was not yet over. At one am the telephone rang. One of Mr Potts' patients couldn't sleep - could I please go to the ward to write up some night sedation? And at four am I was roused from sleep to replace one of Mr Quigley's drips that had stopped working!

Chapter 5

The next few days were a living nightmare for me as I became progressively more exhausted, dispirited and disillusioned. Starting work before eight-thirty each morning, I did not stop until eleven or twelve at night, yet still got dragged from my bed later to attend to some problem on the ward. Try as I might to be organised and in control I found myself buffeted from pillar to post by requests to do jobs, all apparently urgent, that required my attention. I was taking a history from Mr Taylor when informed that the ambulance was waiting to take Mrs Jones home, and that she needed a prescription writing for the drugs that she required. I was busy taking blood samples for analysis when bleeped to be told that Mr Salisbury was waiting to go to theatre but that his 'consent for operation' form had not been completed, and I was examining a patient with a postoperative chest infection when asked to attend to Mrs Myers' intravenous drip that had stopped working and needed to be replaced. With so many interruptions, the simplest task took hours to complete, and often, returning to my original patient, it was not possible to complete the job smoothly. Mr Taylor, from whom I had been taking a clinical history, was now eating his lunch, and the patient whose chest I had been examining had been whisked off for an X-ray.

It was obvious that an efficient house surgeon was critical to the smooth running of the unit and that his input was required to a greater or lesser extent at every stage of the patient's journey - from admission, to theatre, to discharge - yet it was glaringly obvious that I was not that well-organised, efficient person. It was not simply that there were so many jobs to do; it was that I had been thrown unprepared into this complex clinical environment and did not know precisely what was expected of me. I did not know the ward routine, the personnel, or where to find the equipment needed to perform practical procedures, and ended up running around in circles achieving very little. I had studied for five years at medical school in preparation for my career as a doctor, I knew the symptoms and signs of diseases both common and rare, knew how they were diagnosed and understood the role of surgery in their treatment. Yet I was failing to cope within a week of starting my job on the very first rung of the medical career ladder. It was disturbing and depressing. Observing the calm way in which all the other staff went about their duties only served to heighten my feeling of inadequacy. The nurses, cleaners, and porters were all completely at home in this environment and worked in a relaxed, unhurried, yet efficient manner.

Thursday arrived; my fourth day in the job, and a day I was dreading. In addition to my responsibilities on the ward there would be even more pressure, since this was to be my first exposure to Casualty duties. First though, I was required to attend Sir William Warrender's ward round, just as Johnny Nolan had attended Mr Potts' ward round previously. Being present at each of the consultant's ward rounds enabled us both to become familiar with all the patients on the Surgical Five unit, so that each would be able to offer medical cover when his opposite number was off duty; not that this was a very frequent occurrence. From a training point of view, a further advantage was that it allowed the house officers to compare the different approaches of the two consultants to clinical problems, and indeed the contrasting styles of Sir William and Mr Potts was striking. Perhaps the only similarity was that both consultants were always immaculately dressed in formal suits with city shirts and ties - though Sir William, as a final flourish in the summer months, would add a rose or a carnation (grown in his own garden) to the buttonhole of his jacket.

I judged that Sir William was in his early sixties, probably within a few years of retirement; tall and distinguished with almost-white hair, his face usually holding a kindly expression indicative of his gentle manner. Whereas Mr Potts was distant and brusque with his patients, Sir William was adored for his excellent communication and interpersonal skills. He always found time to reassure patients, to explain to them the nature of their surgery, potential complications and details of their expected convalescence. Whilst much appreciated by patients hearing them for the first time, these explanations proved a test of patience for the doctors and nurses when the same patter was repeated four or five times during his twice-weekly ward rounds. Whereas Mr Potts would complete a ward round in between sixty and ninety minutes, Sir William's rounds usually took four to four and a half hours, by which time legs were beginning to ache and patience was wearing thin.

Regrettably, from time to time, the discussions on the ward round were not confined to medical matters, and did not always remain focussed on the clinical problem relevant to the patient beside whose bed we happened to be standing. Whilst it was interesting to hear Sir William's view on a wide variety of subjects - he was happy to speak on any matter from politics to potting sheds - it was frustrating to be aware that time was passing and that a full day's duties awaited when the ward round was over. If the patient's occupation was, say, hairdressing, Sir William was likely to entertain the assembled junior doctors and nurses with comments about a pop singer's outrageous haircut; or if it transpired that a patient had been on holiday on a particular Mediterranean island, Sir William would happily discourse at length on the flora and fauna of the island. Since his hobby, indeed his principle passion after surgery, was gardening - particularly the vegetables that he grew in his own garden - most ward rounds were interspersed with advice on how to grow the finest turnips, the sweetest tomatoes or the largest cucumbers. It was his house officer's and his registrar's responsibility in these circumstances to guide the conversation back to clinical matters as surreptitiously as possible.

House officers received no formal teaching during their employment, ours was a traditional apprenticeship, but invariably on these ward rounds some sound nuggets of good old-fashioned surgical common sense emerged. The danger, though, was that as the ward round dragged on, and the house officer became restless and allowed his attention to slip, these pearls of wisdom could be missed. It was a question of separating the wheat from the chaff - a horticultural analogy that Sir William would have liked.

Johnny led Sir William round his patients, aided by Simon Gresty, the senior registrar. I had no official role to play and was simply an observer, but soon witnessed both the great man's sound surgical advice, as well as some of his idiosyncrasies.

The third patient that we saw was a man called Barry Webb, who was recovering from a recent operation to remove his gall bladder. On his bedside locker in a glass specimen jar, looking like a collection of small black pebbles, were the gallstones that had been the cause of his troubles. After a few minutes of polite conversation with the patient, during which the recent warm wet weather was discussed in some detail ("Good growing weather for the peas and beans," Sir William observed), the patient was politely asked how he felt, and in due course Sir William inquired about the wound. With some pride, Barry opened his pyjamas and revealed his surgical wound, six inches in length, situated under the ribs in the upper part of the right side of the abdomen. Neatly stitched, with no hint of any infection, it was healing beautifully.

"Haven't I got good healing flesh?" said Barry, clearly pleased with himself. Sir William turned to the doctors and nurses encircling the foot of the bed.

"There, you see how it is," he said. "If the wound heals beautifully and the patient makes a smooth post-operative recovery, credit goes to his 'good healing flesh'. However, if there is a problem with the wound, perhaps an infection - or worse, a wound that fails to heal - it's a case of 'what's gone wrong with your stitches, Doctor?' It's a bit tough on the surgeon, isn't it? We can't win either way." His audience smiled politely.

Simon commented, "The wound really is healing well and Mr Webb is recovering nicely. He is a credit to you, Sir."

I looked up rather sharply at the senior registrar. It appeared to me to be a rather fawning remark but Sir William seemed not to notice. He simply said "Thank you, Simon." Then, turning back to the patient, he asked "Have you moved your bowels since the operation, Mr Webb?"

"No, not yet. I had some rumblings in my belly earlier, as if there was some wind rolling round, but no action yet."

"Aha," said Sir William and held up his right hand, his long bony index finger pointing at the ceiling. This prompted a little flurry of activity. Sister Ashbrook snapped her fingers; a junior nurse ran off to get the rectal tray, and a second nurse disappeared to fetch a clean towel from the linen cupboard. A fingerstall was produced from the rectal tray and passed to Sir William. The consultant slowly and carefully rolled the rubber sheath onto his erect right index finger, an action that induced an alternative parallel image to enter my head. I glanced at Johnny, who seemed to have the faintest smile on his face, and I presumed that the same thought had occurred to him. I looked around the rest of the group but no similar thoughts appeared to have entered the heads of the nurses - or if they had, they were sufficiently self-controlled that their faces did not show any reaction.

With the fingerstall in place, Sir William was handed a three-inch square of lint, in the centre of which a slit had been cut. Designed to protect the knuckles from any soiling during the forthcoming examination, this was placed over the index finger, which still remained pointing aloft. Sir William turned to Johnny, his new house officer.

"Now, young man, you must learn from my experience. No one should be too superior or too proud to perform a humble rectal examination. If you don't put your finger in it, sooner or later you will put your foot in it! Always remember that the examination of the abdomen begins in the groin and ends in the rectum."

"And we all need to learn from your experience Sir," said Simon smoothly. Again, the remark seemed awkward and out of place but, as before, Sir William appeared not to notice.

The patient was turned onto his left side and his knees were drawn up. His pyjama trousers were lowered and his buttocks were adjusted so that they were overhanging the edge of the bed. The screens had been pulled round the bed, offering privacy from the other patients on the ward, but not from the doctors and nurses accompanying Sir William on his round. It seemed an unnecessary indignity to perform the examination with such a large audience, but this did not seem to upset either Sir William or the patient.

Again, the surgeon's right index finger was held in the air, and another nurse appeared holding a small glass jar containing the glycerine that was to act as lubricant. Sir William plunged his finger into the jar and then, with considerable relish, into the anus of the patient who gave an involuntary start, taken slightly by surprise by this sudden rear end attack. Sir William pushed his finger to the very hilt, beaming broadly as he did so.

"Sister," he announced, "the patient's bunged up. Two suppositories, please." These appeared as if by magic, were lubricated, and were passed to the senior consultant, who deftly thrust them into the patient's rectum. By this time yet another nurse was standing at Sir William's side, with a paper bag held open, into which Sir William placed the (now offensive) rubber sheath and lint. He then marched off to the washbasin situated half way down the ward, followed by the nurse with the freshly laundered towel over her arm, looking for all the world like a waitress at an expensive restaurant.

The whole episode had been quite a performance. The teamwork shown by the nurses was impressive, and suggested hours of practice. An impish thought occurred to me - perhaps this was an exercise organised by the ward sister in advance, with the various nurses being designated different tasks. Nurse One collects the rectal tray, Nurse Two passes the finger stall, Nurse Three passes the lint, Nurse Four produces the lubricant, Nurse Five has the suppositories ready, Nurse Six holds the paper bag open and Nurse Seven accompanies Sir William to the sink with the freshly laundered towel - whilst Sister ensures that the whole performance proceeds with the precision and discipline that would be demanded by a regimental sergeant major at an army camp.

It was not altogether a surprise to find that the whole pantomime was repeated further down the male ward, and indeed later on the female ward. I wondered whether perhaps the teams of nurses from the two wards had competitions to see who could perform the exercise most efficiently, just as a team from the Royal Artillery competes with a team from the Royal Engineers to assemble a field gun in the Royal Albert Hall during the Remembrance service each November.

The very last patient whom we saw on the female ward was an eighty-two-year-old lady, Elsie Bewley, who was being prepared for a major bowel operation. She had been passing blood in the stool and her investigations had revealed that she had a tumour in the lower part of the bowel. The next day a length of colon was to be excised, and there was a possibility that she might be left with a colostomy and be required to wear a bag to collect her stool on the abdominal wall. Sir William started to explain to her the various operations that might be required and the effect that these would have on her. It would only become apparent during the procedure exactly what type of operation was required, so the patient would go under the anaesthetic not knowing whether or not she would wake up with a permanent colostomy. Her life would be very different and there would be many new challenges to face, if it proved necessary to remove the anus and rectum and create an artificial stoma.

"Don't bother me with all those details, Doctor. You just do what you've got to do. I'm sure that you know what's best for me," she said.

Sir William persisted though. "I really think you ought to know what the possibilities are. It is quite important."

But again, Elsie interrupted. "You're the Doctor, you know best. You just do what you've got to do."

Although Sir William tried again to inform the patient of the various surgical procedures that might be performed, it became clear that she simply did not want to know. She was much more comfortable leaving all the decisions and the responsibility with her consultant.

As we all sat down for a cup of coffee in the clinical room when the ward round was over, Elsie's attitude to her proposed surgery became a topic of conversation. Sir William took up the theme.

"It is always right to offer patients as much information about their conditions and their operations as they wish to receive, but have you noticed how some patients want to know everything there is to know, whilst others wish to know nothing at all? Their attitude is, simply, 'You know best, Doc.' That philosophy is all very well, but it does put a great responsibility onto the surgeon. By and large, you will find that younger patients require more information than older ones. Also, in general, the elderly are far more grateful for our efforts and more accepting of minor complications than the younger ones."

"Why do you think that is?" he was asked.

"It's probably due a number of different factors. Most elderly folk have known significant hardship at some stage in their lives; they have lived through the war, of course, and many will remember what life was like before the National Health Service existed when, unless you were wealthy, there was little or no treatment available. Also most have learnt to accept the various aches and pains that come with advancing years. I find that that there are some cultural differences as well. Folk from London seem to want more information than folk up here in the North of England, and those from the city generally want more information than those from country areas. Remember though that it is wise, indeed your responsibility, to give everyone as much information as possible. Better too much than too little."

With that, Sir William finished his coffee, politely thanked the doctors and nurses for their help on the ward round and announced that it was time for him to go for lunch.

The morning had passed pleasantly enough and confirmed everything I had heard about Sir William's gentlemanly and fatherly manner. In practice I had merely been a spectator on the ward round and had not been required to make any input, but I had been aware that time was passing and that my own duties were being neglected. I had not managed to complete all the venepunctures before the ward round began, there were three elective patients to be admitted and, since it was Surgical Five's intake day, it was probable that there would be some emergency admissions coming to the wards during the course of the day. All these things needed my attention before I attended casualty for the night shift at nine pm, and with that in mind, I walked with Johnny across to the residency for a very quick lunch where we reflected on the morning's events.

"That was quite a performance," I said, "particularly the rigmarole with the suppositories. How many do you think Sir William put in during the course of the morning?"

"I wasn't counting."

"But it must have been eight or ten."

"At least."

"And what do you think of Simon?"

Johnny thought for a moment. "I've only been around for a couple of days but he seems to be a bit of a slime-ball. Sucks up to the consultants all the time. He is in his final year as a senior registrar now; his next stop is a consultant post, private practice, and a nice house in the suburbs with an acre or two for the pony. But he's yet to make that vital step, so perhaps it is simply a matter of him needing a good reference."

"Well, he just seems like a bit of a creep to me," I said. "I wouldn't be impressed by it."

"I don't think my Uncle Bill is too impressed either, but he is too much of a gentleman to say so."

I asked Johnny how his Uncle Bill had come to be knighted.

"The truth is, I'm not absolutely sure. Officially it was for 'services to surgery' and he certainly has made a number of notable contributions over the years, particularly at the time of the introduction of the National Health Service way back in 1945. As you know, Aneurin Bevan developed the concept of an NHS, which had originally been proposed by Lord Beveridge who suggested nationalising all the existing hospitals and organising them on a regional basis. At the time, most doctors were against the plan - mainly because they thought it would result in their losing income, but also because they felt that in a nationalised service their professional freedom would be eroded. Between 1945 and 1948 it became a political hot potato and at that stage Uncle Bill was quite vociferous in support of the proposals, speaking to groups of doctors and trying to persuade them of the potential benefits. Now, of course, most doctors are strong advocates of the NHS, feel a great loyalty to it and defend it at every opportunity. Uncle Bill has always been one for supporting the underdog and saw the advantage of such a service to the man in the street, to those who were unable to afford any medical care at all and had to depend on charity. I suspect that is the main reason he was honoured, but it probably didn't harm his reputation when one of the minor Royals got appendicitis as the Royal Train was passing through the city on its way to Balmoral. Uncle Bill whipped his appendix out, the patient made an excellent recovery, and Uncle Bill got a letter of thanks on Palace headed notepaper that he still keeps. It is framed and hangs on the wall of his study. All in all, I think his honour is well deserved."

After lunch I returned to the wards, and was making good progress with the routine admissions when I was 'bleeped' by the male ward. When I rang, I was informed by one of the nurses that there was a problem with Mr Quigley. The nurse did not know the nature of the problem but said that Sister Ashbrook was already in attendance trying to sort things out. My heart sank. The most likely explanation was that he had started bleeding again. I knew that there was no longer any blood cross matched for him and was not sure whether the laboratory was still holding a sample of serum in readiness.

Hurrying onto the ward, I saw that the screens around Mr Quigley's bed were indeed closed and there was considerable activity going on within. Fortunately it was quickly apparent that the patient had not suffered any major haemorrhage for he was sitting upright in the bed looking reasonably alert, and even had a bit of colour in his cheeks. The observation chart at the foot of the bed showed that the blood pressure and the pulse rate were entirely stable, which was very reassuring. Sister Ashbrook was at the bedside with one of the staff nurses, and one look at her face told me that she was displeased.

"Why you doctors can't anchor these drips in more securely I will never know," she said. "Does no one ever teach you that the cannula should be secured with adhesive tape, the forearm should be splinted, and the splint should be held in place with at least two rolls of three-inch crepe bandage? When the nurses do the job the drips never come adrift."

It was clear at whom the remark was aimed. I was about to point out that it was the anaesthetist in theatre who had inserted this particular drip, not me - but the expression on Sister's face told me that this would be unwise, and I thought better of it.

"The nasogastric tube seems to have come adrift as well," I said, knowing that passing these tubes was usually a nursing duty and hinting that perhaps the nurses were not always as perfect as she would wish to believe. Too late, I realised that this played straight into her hands, for Sister remembered when the tube had been inserted.

"Yes," she replied pointedly, "but the nurses didn't put this particular tube in place, did they? The anaesthetist did that in theatre."

"Probably at the same time that he inserted the cannula in the arm, Sister," I said innocently. My remark was greeted by a long cold stare, but there was no verbal response. At least it was comforting to know that senior anaesthetists, as well as humble house officers, could be held responsible for mishaps. Sister barked out her instructions.

"Well *Doctor*," – again, the slightest emphasis on that word - "please set up a new drip, pass a clean nasogastric tube, and rewrite the intravenous infusion regime so that Mr Quigley can catch up with the fluid that he should have had in the last couple of hours."

She turned on her heels and marched off, closing the screens behind her.

It was clear that, as Eleanor had warned me, Sister Ashbrook blew hot and cold. We were back with the 'I am the senior sister and you are a junior doctor' routine that I had encountered when I first arrived on the ward. Gone was the helpful team leader she had been when Mr Quigley had his major bleed and collapse three days previously. Mr Quigley looked at me, sympathy written large on his face.

"She can be quite a Tartar when she wants to be, can't she, doctor?"

"She certainly can!"

I noted that on this occasion, nothing was prepared in readiness for me; no drip set, no drip stand, and no intravenous needle, as had been the case previously. Sister Ashbrook had left me to get these items, and the nasogastric tube.

When it comes to the process of accessing a vein - whether by inserting a cannula through which to give fluids, or performing a venepuncture to obtain blood samples for analysis - a number of factors are relevant. Some patients have many veins on their arms, readily visible immediately below the skin; whilst others, particularly women, children, and patients with a generous fatty covering have fewer, deeper veins that are more difficult to locate. In either case, each patient only has a finite number of available veins. When a patient has been in hospital for some time, it becomes increasingly difficult to identify a vein that is still patent and usable. In effect, a law of diminishing returns exists, and it was a relief therefore to find that on this occasion the cannula slipped into one of Mr Quigley's veins easily. Very soon I had the drip running satisfactorily, secured with adhesive tape, the forearm well splinted and secured with the statutory two rolls of three-inch crepe bandage. All that remained now was to pass the nasogastric tube, after which I would be free to complete my clerking of the patients that had been admitted for surgery the next day.

I had never previously passed a nasogastric tube - this being a task that the nurses normally undertook - but I didn't anticipate any difficulties. At any one time on a surgical ward, there would be half a dozen patients being treated with these tubes, and I had never been aware that the nurses had encountered any problem in putting them into place. The tube is passed through the nose into the back of the mouth, over the back of the tongue then down the gullet, so that its tip comes to rest in the stomach. It is made of transparent plastic, roughly two feet long, with a diameter about that of a drinking straw. It has a small metal bead at the gastric end so that, should there be any doubt as to its position, an X-ray can be taken to confirm that the tip is indeed resting in the stomach. Its function is to allow the acidic digestive juices that the stomach produces to be aspirated, thus keeping the stomach empty, which was particularly important in Mr Quigley's case...it would have been unwise to allow these corrosive juices to come into contact either with the sutures so recently placed to stop the bleeding, or with the ulcer itself, since that would prevent it from it from healing. Although Mr Quigley understood the purpose of the nasogastric tube, for one had been in place for the last forty-eight hours, as I had reminded Sister, this had been inserted when he was anaesthetised in theatre. Accordingly, he did not know how it had been inserted. I explained that the tube would be slipped up his nose, he would feel it pass over the back of his tongue, and then it would slide smoothly down into his stomach. He didn't seem in the least alarmed at this prospect and I was similarly relaxed about the procedure, with which I did not anticipate any problems.

Taking the tube out of its plastic bag, I gently fed it up the left nostril. It went in about half an inch and then hit a blockage. I withdrew it and tried again, this time pushing a little more firmly but again it came to a full stop, suggesting that it had reached a fairly solid obstruction. Once more, I was forced to take it out and wondered whether at some time he had broken his nose, and whether the channel up the nostril had been narrowed or deformed as a result.

"Let's try the other side," I said. As on the left, the tube seemed to meet some resistance inside the nose but this time by pushing a little harder the tube advanced, and I seemed to be making some progress. Suddenly Mr Quigley winced, apparently in some discomfort, and his free hand went to his nose.

"Don't worry," I said, using my most soothing voice and gently guiding his hand back to his side. "We are getting somewhere now."

The tube had graduated marks on it to indicate how much tube had been passed and when twenty inches had disappeared into the nose, the end, with its metal tip, should have reached the stomach. Ten, fifteen, and then twenty inches of tube passed easily into the nose without any resistance being met. Unfortunately, Mr Quigley was now getting a bit alarmed. For some reason he seemed unable to speak, and pointed anxiously to his cheeks, both of which were now swollen like a hamster's pouches. Quite suddenly, in front of my eyes, the metal tip of the plastic tube emerged like a viper's tongue from between his lips. He opened his mouth, and easily visible inside was twenty inches of plastic tube, all coiled, twisted and buckled. Clearly the tube had not been going down the gullet to the stomach at all - it had taken a wrong turn at the back of the mouth! I wondered what on earth I should do.

I was tempted to ask him to spit it out through the mouth, hoping that the whole tube, including the last few inches that were still dangling from his nose, would follow. The tube, however, was wider at the top, and having taken a quick look at it, I doubted that it would in fact pass down through the nose. The alternative was to pull the tube backwards through the nose and hope and pray that it wouldn't tie itself in a knot somewhere at the back of the throat as invariably happens whenever I handled plastic coated electrical cabling or a plastic hosepipe! If that were to occur, it might be impossible to remove the tube either upwards or downwards and the patient might have to go back to the operating theatre to have it retrieved. I felt a cold sweat on the back of my neck.

I decided that withdrawing it through the nose was probably the better option and slowly and carefully started to pull the tube upwards. To my great relief the hamster pouches gradually decreased in size, the snake's tongue disappeared and the tube came out without undue difficulty. A wave of relief swept through me as I realised that, although I had caused some temporary distress to the patient, no serious harm had resulted.

I apologised profusely to Mr Quigley, gave him a couple of minutes to recover and then tried again, using the right nostril. Once again there was the early resistance, which caused the patient a little discomfort, but as before this was overcome with a little extra pressure. Gently, I eased the tube onwards, going more slowly this time. I judged it would probably take five or six inches to reach the back of the mouth and when we reached that point I stopped, asked the patient to open his mouth and found, thankfully, that the tube was nowhere to be seen. I advanced another inch, re-inspected the mouth, and again was delighted to see no sign of the tube. Certain that the tip of the tube was now beyond the mouth and safely descending the gullet, I pushed another two inches up the nose with renewed confidence. Suddenly, and without any warning, Mr Quigley's hands grasped at this throat and he started gasping for breath. He started a paroxysm of coughing and his cheeks, previously pink, started to take on an ominous purple look. Hands still to his throat, he tried to speak, but without breath was unable to do so. There was a wild fear in his eyes. It was obvious that the tip of the tube had not come down the gullet but had gone down the wrong way and was in the trachea, the passage leading to his lungs, completely blocking his airway. At once I pulled the entire tube out. For a couple of minutes Mr Quigley was greatly distressed, coughing repeatedly, making a high pitched wheezing sound and gasping for breath, but slowly the colour returned to his cheeks and in time he regained his composure. When he had recovered a little, I put my hand around his shoulders and apologised yet again for causing him so much anxiety and discomfort.

"Don't worry, Doctor," he said. "I'm sorry I'm being such a nuisance, you've got your job to do. We'll try again, but just give me a moment or two to catch my breath."

I wondered whether this was an appropriate time to call for assistance. Mr Khan had already told me that if house officers met any difficulties or were uncertain how to proceed in any clinical situation they should not be afraid to call for help, and that failing to call for help when it was required was a greater sin than calling unnecessarily. I recognised that I was having difficulty but also aware that I would undoubtedly lose face with the nursing staff if I asked for assistance. Surely, I thought, passing a nasogastric tube shouldn't be such a difficult job. It was something that the nurses did, day in and day out. Whilst I was contemplating these matters, I received some encouragement from Mr Quigley: "Come on Doctor, let's get it over with."

With the benefit of hindsight, I know that I should have called for assistance. But I didn't, not least because the person that I would have had to ask was Sister Ashbrook. Having decided to make one final attempt, and with some trepidation, I threaded the tube once again into the right nostril. Approximately six inches of tube disappeared up the nose before the disaster happened. Mr Quigley was sitting up in his bed and I was standing about twelve inches away immediately in front of him. Without warning, and accompanied by a loud retching noise, he vomited. A pint and a half of stale blood mixed with yellowy green bile hit me in the middle of the chest. Involuntarily, I took a step back. Within a few seconds a second vomit occurred, this time landing on my shoes, on the ward floor, and also splashing beyond the confines of the screens that surrounded the bed. In a flash, Sister Ashbrook appeared. She assessed the situation instantly - the patient still retching, a pool of old blood and bile on the floor, and me - still holding the nasogastric tube in my right hand, with the patient's vomitus down the front of my white coat, dripping onto my shoes. She turned to the student nurse that accompanied her.

"Nurse Meredith," she said, "please show *Doctor* Lambert the *correct* way to pass a nasogastric tube, and then clear up this unholy mess."

Was it my imagination or was there again the slightest emphasis on the word 'Doctor' and the word 'correct'? With eyes to the ceiling, she turned on her heels and left. Undoubtedly, this was a notable victory for Sister Ashbrook. Thirty-fifteen, if not forty-fifteen to her! I could imagine her gloating over the episode for many weeks to come.

Nurse Meredith's first concern was the patient. She took his hand.

"I'm sorry you've been sick, Mr Quigley," she said, her voice quiet and sympathetic. "Let's start by rinsing out your mouth." She handed him a glass of water and invited him to gargle with it, and to spit into the vomit bowel that had been on the bedside locker.

"I'm just going to get a face cloth to wipe around your mouth," she said, and she slipped out between the screens. In a couple of minutes she was back, tidying up around the patient's mouth and mopping his brow. She spoke again in her gentle reassuring voice.

"I'm afraid that we really do need to have this tube in place. It is an important part of your treatment. Is it alright if I try and pass it for you?" The patient looked apprehensive but, after a pause, nodded faintly.

She produced a clean new nasogastric tube, a pad of lint, and a small glass bottle containing glycerine. Pouring the glycerine onto the lint, she then folded the lint over it and drew the nasogastric tube through the folds so that its entire length was thoroughly lubricated.

"Now," she said, "I'm going to pass this tube slowly into your nose and I want you to nod for me when you feel it touch the back of your tongue. I have a glass of water here and when the tube touches the back of your throat, I want you to take a couple of sips of water and then swallow. Is that clear?" The patient again nodded weakly. She passed the glass of water to him.

Ever so gently, she threaded the tube into the patient's left nostril and advanced it slowly. With the lubrication easing its passage, there was absolutely no resistance at all in the nose. When about five inches had disappeared, the patient nodded.

"Now," she said, "any time you like, just take a little water from the glass and swallow down a couple of sips." The patient did as he was told and when Nurse Meredith saw the patient swallow, she advanced the tube effortlessly.

"All we need is a couple of swallows. That's it, you can stop drinking now." As she advanced the tube to its full length, the act of swallowing automatically guided the tube into the gullet and away from the lungs.

The whole episode had taken about twenty seconds, had been perfectly painless for the patient, and quite effortless. Nurse Meredith busied herself anchoring the tube to the patient's nose and then looked across at me.

"It's Dr Lambert, isn't it?" she said. "I was in the office on Monday morning when you first came on duty. I'm sorry that you didn't get a more pleasant welcome from our nursing Sister."

"Thank you," I said, "and thank you as well for showing me how to pass the tube. I'm very grateful. I'm afraid we weren't shown how to do that at Medical School."

She looked me up and down - her eyes passing up from the vomit on my shoes to my soiled white coat, and on to the embarrassed expression on my face. She smiled.

"Now, what are we going to do with you?"

This was a question that I had already begun to ponder. I certainly didn't relish the prospect of walking through the ward in my present state, passing Sister Ashbrook on the way and then walking along the hospital corridors to tidy myself up in my room, though I was sure that Sister would have enjoyed the sight.

"You stay here for a minute while I slip out and get another white coat for you from the linen cupboard. I need to bring back some sheets and freshen up this bed as well."

When she returned I noticed that the white coat was actually hidden amongst the sheets and pillowcases that she had brought. Behind the patient's screen, I changed my white coat and used the old coat to wipe down my shoes. Nurse Meredith was smiling broadly now.

"You really look quite respectable again Dr Lambert," she said, "but you really don't smell too good. You slip away and change your shirt while I tidy up here. I'll get one of the other nurses to help me."

"Thank you," I said. "You've been extremely kind to a doctor in distress!"

Severely chastened, I left, and managed to escape from the ward and to reach the residency without attracting too much attention. I realised that I had been foolish and in my heart knew that it served me right that I had been publicly humiliated. There was a lesson for me to learn here. When you don't know what to do, don't be too proud to ask for some advice - which is exactly what Mr Khan had said to me a few days before!

Chapter 6

If the British public were better informed, they would know that it is not wise to fall ill or have an accident during the first week of August. At that time of the year, throughout the United Kingdom, thousands of totally inexperienced newly qualified doctors are released onto the wards to practice medicine for the first time. The situation is exacerbated since all the outgoing house officers, who have by this stage gained some experience in medicine and surgery, move to posts in other specialties such as paediatrics, obstetrics or psychiatry - in which, once again, they have absolutely no practical experience. Common sense suggests that this has a detrimental effect on the quality of patient care and indeed recent research has clearly demonstrated that the morbidity and mortality rates of hospitals are increased at this time of the year.

This major annual upheaval occurs on the morning of the first day of August and inevitably leads to some impossible logistical problems. Eleanor, whom I had replaced as house officer on Surgical Five, held a contract that required her to be resident until nine am on the first of August at the City General Hospital; and a new contract that required her to be at work in her next post - in obstetrics, forty miles away at Stockbridge - at exactly the same time. One might have expected that consultants and managers would reduce the workload on the wards in consideration of these problems, but this was not the case. These arrangements not only put patients at risk but also placed medical staff in an unenviable position, as my introduction to emergency duties on August the fourth illustrated. With three whole days experience behind me, I was to be involved in the management of all the surgical emergencies that might arise due to accident or illness, as I faced the challenge of working as the casualty officer for a major city centre hospital with a catchment population of half a million people. Furthermore, for twelve hours during the night, I would be 'first on call'; the frontline doctor...the first to attend the new patients presenting in casualty.

The clinical workload arising from accident and emergency surgical problems was shared equally between the four general surgical units, each being responsible for managing such patients on one day of the week. Surgical Five were responsible for Thursdays. Similarly, weekends were shared on a one in four basis, the weekend running from nine am Friday to nine am on Monday. As a result, every fourth week our team was 'on take' from Thursday morning until the following Monday morning – a total of ninety-six hours. Both house officers were required to be on duty throughout this period. Although the hospital employed casualty officers, they only worked on weekdays and then only from nine am to five pm, the housemen being responsible for manning the casualty department during the evenings, nights and weekends. Fortunately, the department was also staffed by some long-standing and extremely experienced nursing staff, including a couple of excellent senior nursing sisters.

It was custom and practice on Surgical Five's emergency day for one of the house officers to work in casualty from five pm to nine pm, and the other to undertake the twelve hour nightshift from nine pm through until nine am the next day. Johnny and I agreed that the evening and night shift should alternate between us on successive urgency days, and we tossed a coin to decide who should do the first long night shift. I lost!

During my first few days in post, I had become acutely aware of my lack of experience in all manner of different problems on the ward, and inevitably this was having an effect on my morale and self-esteem. It was not that I lacked knowledge of theoretical matters such as diagnosis and clinical management, but rather, an ignorance of the way that situations were handled in actual practice. I knew when blood should be cross-matched for a patient but was unaware of the actual steps required to achieve this; whose job was it to take the specimen to the laboratory, who brought the cross-matched blood back to the ward and, more importantly, what checks had to be carried out before the blood could be given to the patient? I knew that a patient with an infectious disease had to be reported to the Public Health Department but, although this was apparently one of my duties, I had no idea how or when this was done. Facing my first experience as a casualty officer, I was aware of the deficiencies in my training and felt significantly ill-prepared and apprehensive. Inevitably, I wondered how I would cope, indeed whether I *should* cope. It was a daunting prospect.

The actual casualty department was a drab affair. Designed to be functional rather than attractive, the décor had suffered at the hands of rowdy youths and drunks over the years. There was a large and rather dirty waiting area, whose only furniture was a number of wooden hard backed chairs and a table bearing some old comics and magazines. The lino on the floor was stained and cracked at the edges and the walls were covered with tired, dog-eared health promotion posters advising patients how to avoid conditions from which some of those attending were already suffering! Beyond this there was a clinical area comprising eight cubicles: three allocated for medical cases and five for surgical cases. Two of the medical cubicles were equipped with heavy, blue and white oxygen cylinders and mobile suction machines; they shared a mobile ECG machine, but there was none of the modern hi-tech diagnostic and resuscitation equipment found in a modern accident and emergency department, which is expected to have one or two cubicles equipped to the standard of an intensive care unit. The surgical cubicles held only a leather topped examination coach and a single wooden chair.

I derived some comfort from knowing just how helpful and supportive Mr Khan was, and from being aware that I could call on him if I got into difficulties. Equally, I was conscious that there would be times when I was on duty in the accident department when he would be unavailable, perhaps because he was operating in theatre or busy attending to a patient on the ward. Mr Gresty and Mr Potts, of course, were also on duty - but during the evenings, at night and throughout the weekend they would be at home and not immediately available. Also, there would be occasions when a number of patients with multiple injuries would arrive simultaneously, perhaps from a major road traffic or industrial accident; circumstances in which prompt action taken the minute the patient arrived at the hospital could be life saving. With my three days of experience as a doctor, was I ready for the challenge? Ignorance, they say, is bliss; so perhaps it was just as well that the general public were unaware of the lack of experience of the casualty officer waiting to treat them should they need emergency treatment!

Nine o'clock came and I took over from Johnny. He looked relieved to have survived his four-hour shift without any major problems. Fortunately, my first couple of hours on duty were also reasonably uneventful, since the first few cases were all fairly routine; cuts and grazes, one or two needing stitches, mainly just requiring dressings. There was a lady with an abscess - tense, red, and angry in her armpit - that, although painful, was very close to the surface and looked as if it might burst within a day or so. I was able to freeze it with an ethyl chloride spray and, knowing that there were no important anatomical structures in the vicinity, boldly plunged a scalpel blade into it, releasing the pus and greatly relieving her pain. She was very grateful and it was rewarding to be able to perform a small technical procedure with immediate benefits for the patient.

I learned a useful 'trick of the trade' when a young man arrived who had inadvertently hit his thumbnail with a hammer. There was no question of the underlying bone being broken, but he had an extremely painful blood blister underneath his nail. One of the staff nurses became quite animated.

"Have you dealt with one of these before?" she asked. I shook my head.

"Good," she said, "I'll show you what we do. It's a little job that I enjoy." She went to the office and returned with a paper clip, a candle and a match. I wondered quite what voodoo witchcraft I was about to witness.

She took the paper clip and straightened it out until she had a short piece of wire, and heated one end in the candle flame, much to the horror of the patient who was watching and wondering what torture lay in store.

"Don't be alarmed," she said, "finger nails have no nerves in them. I promise that this isn't going to hurt at all."

She took the red-hot wire, and with its end burned a neat round hole in the nail, directly over the blood blister. Three or four drops of blood erupted from the cavity beneath, gently sizzling like fat in a frying pan as they met the hot wire, and immediately, with the release of pressure from beneath the nail, all the patient's pain vanished. Once again, we had an extremely grateful patient.

The next case took considerably longer to sort out. Mrs Dearden was a plump fifty-year-old lady who was already known to have gallstones. She had previously seen a consultant from one of the other surgical units in his outpatient clinic, had already had some X-rays that showed the stones, and was on the waiting list to have her gallbladder removed. Without doubt, the pain in her back and right side which had caused this casualty attendance was again coming from the gallbladder. The diagnosis was not difficult but it was obvious she needed to be admitted for pain relief, and it took half an hour or so to take her history, examine her and to record all the information in her notes. Then there were blood samples to be taken and telephone calls to be made. First to the laboratory, then to Mr Khan - who agreed that she should be admitted - and finally to the ward to check that a bed was available.

Having been keen to deal with this patient carefully, I had not rushed, but now I was behind schedule and Sister gently mentioned to me that a considerable backlog of cases had built up in the waiting room. "Nothing particularly urgent or serious," she emphasised, "but they are getting restless. The first three are in the cubicles. Oh, and by the way, I have put a cup of tea for you in the office, but you might like to take it with you as you work." Later I was to realise that patients, when kept waiting, usually complain bitterly to the nurses and give them a hard time...but when they are finally seen by the doctor, immediately become charming and polite!

As a student, there had been no time pressure; it had not mattered how long it had taken me to assess a patient and I had often spent a couple of hours with a single patient, talking to them, examining them and then carefully writing up detailed notes. But this was a completely different environment. As well as being required to do a thorough job, making judgements that affected people's lives, which took time, I was working against the clock.

Finally, I saw a couple of drunks who had sustained minor abrasions in a disturbance outside a night club, and at about three am a lady, also the worse for wear, who happened to be passing on her way home from a party and thought that she could get some advice on a long-standing problem with her ingrown toenail.

"I thought that if I popped in to see you now," she said, "it would save me waiting at my general practitioner's surgery. You can wait for over an hour to be seen there."

I explained that this was a department for accident and emergency cases, not a clinic for long-standing minor problems, and tried to send her on her way. I quickly regretted using the word 'minor' for she started to tell me how painful and disabling it was. Sister had already warned me that the Department could not afford to get a reputation as a substitute for general practice, otherwise it would be snowed under with inappropriate cases, so I did not relent.

"I don't see why you can't see me now," she grumbled as she left. "There's no one else here!"

In that respect, the patient was right. All the surgical cubicles were indeed empty, and when I popped my head into the waiting room that was empty too.

At the back of the department, off the main corridor leading to the rest of the hospital, there was a small drab room that used to be a storeroom but which was now designated as the duty doctor's bedroom, provided so that the house officer could snatch an hour or two of sleep - provided that the patient flow allowed. It was barely large enough to hold a bed, a chair and a bedside locker. Having worked continuously from eight-thirty in the morning, I was mentally and physically exhausted and longed to get some rest. The room was unattractive but that did not matter. It had a bed. That was all I needed...I simply wanted to put my head on a pillow and get some sleep. I went in search of Sister and found her in the office writing out the duty rosters for the nurses for the following week.

"If it's alright with you," I said, "I think I'll try to get some sleep now."

"Fine," she replied, "we'll let you know if you are needed. By the way, I may not see you in the morning as I have to leave early, but thanks for your help tonight." It was nice to be thanked and I recalled that Sir William had thanked his staff earlier in the day at the end of his ward round. It struck me that it was not strictly necessary to thank a fellow member of a team - we were both required to do the work - but it cost nothing, and made me feel valued and appreciated.

The heat in the room was oppressive. Although there was no radiator, a metal central heating pipe, three inches in diameter, passed along its length. There was no window, and since the room was accessed directly from the casualty department's main corridor, leaving the door open to lower the temperature was not an option. I had brought pyjamas with me but it was clearly too hot for them. I stripped down to my underpants, threw my clothes on to the chair and, taking off all the covers except for a single sheet, got into bed. Tired as I was, sleep did not come easily. I tossed and turned, reviewing in my mind the events of the day, particularly the patients that I had seen and the decisions I had made in casualty. Also it was difficult to relax knowing that, any second, I might be awakened and expected to deal with some major emergency. It took some time but eventually I slipped into a fitful sleep.

I had probably slept for about an hour when the telephone rang.

"Sorry to trouble you, Doctor Lambert," - it was Sister's cheerful voice - "but I've got a little job for you."

"I'll be right there Sister." I replied, immediately fearful that the case might be beyond my experience and expertise.

I slipped into trousers and shirt, pulled my white coat over the top, and within a minute was back in the department - only to be surprised to discover all the surgical cubicles empty. An ambulance man, however, was hovering in the corridor, looking relaxed with a cup of tea in his hand. The kettle in the casualty department was clearly one of the most frequently used items of equipment.

"Oh, there you are Doc," he said. "I've got a B.I.D. for you." Doctors use many abbreviations and synonyms, but this was not one I had heard before.

"You've got a what?" I said.

“A B.I.D. in the back of the van, if you’ve got a minute, Doc.”

“What is a B.I.D.?” I asked.

“A Brought in Dead.”

I had no idea what I was supposed to do with a ’Brought in Dead’. In fact, I had never heard the expression before. I decided that I had better seek enlightenment from Sister.

She explained that it meant that the ambulance men had somebody in the back of the ambulance whom they believed to be dead, possibly somebody who had just collapsed and died in the street, or possibly someone who had been the subject of a 999 call but had died before the ambulance managed to reach them.

“And my role?”

“Well,” she explained, “they need a doctor to certify that the patient is indeed dead. If they are ‘brought in dead’ we don’t admit them and they don’t come through our front door since there is obviously nothing we can do for them. Instead they are taken directly to the city morgue and dealt with by the Coroner, who arranges a post-mortem examination to ascertain the cause of death and to make sure that there are no suspicious circumstances. The ambulance crew need a doctor to sign the death certificate for them.”

It struck me that I had spent years learning how to make hundreds of different diagnoses but always on the assumption that the patient was alive. No one had told me how to be absolutely certain that someone was dead. Diagnosing death was certainly something I could not afford to get wrong; I didn’t want to feature in a ‘Patient wakes up in City Morgue’ newspaper story.

I went with the ambulance man into the back of his ‘van’, as he called it, but I needn’t have worried about getting this particular diagnosis wrong. The body was in an early state of decomposition, having been found by a caretaker in the back yard of an office block known to be frequented by the homeless. The smell was overpowering. I felt for a pulse, listened for heart sounds, and checked the reflexes in his eyes. This rather amused the ambulance men who clearly regarded such tests as unnecessary, but they didn’t say anything. I duly pronounced the patient dead. Inevitably there was a form to sign, but fortunately there was no requirement to make any supposition about the cause of death. All that was necessary was to certify that this decomposing corpse had indeed died and I had no hesitation about this. I washed my hands thoroughly and returned to my room.

It felt as if I had not had more than two or three minutes sleep when the phone rang again, although the clock insisted that an hour had passed.

This time it was to see a lad of about nineteen years old, who was clearly drunk. He had fallen down some steps on his way home from one of the nightclubs in the city centre and the gross deformity of his ankle indicated that, without any doubt, his ankle was broken. It seemed equally obvious that an X-ray was required to judge the nature and extent of his injury. I rang the duty radiographer and apologetically told her the nature of the problem.

The response was immediate and aggressive. "What on earth do you expect me to do about it at this time of the night?"

"Well I thought it would be appropriate to get it X-rayed," I said, perhaps with just a trace of sarcasm in my voice.

"And what would be the point of that?" she snapped back. "Are you going to be able to anaesthetise him whilst he is drunk? Do you suppose that the orthopaedic surgeons are going to reduce the fracture in the middle of the night? Immobilise it, give him pain relief, and X-ray him in the morning." With a bang, the telephone receiver went down.

Whilst I was shocked at the rude and abrupt manner I had to admit, on reflection, that she was quite right. Nothing would be gained from X-raying him at five in the morning and, once again, I realised that whilst I had a great deal of medical knowledge, my training had left me inadequately prepared for the practicalities of medical life.

Once again, I returned to the cubbyhole that was my bedroom for the night and, hot and stuffy though it was, I drifted into a heavy sleep. I was wakened by a knock on the door and one of the nurses walked in.

"Wakey wakey," she said in a bright and cheerful voice, sounding like Billy Cotton at the beginning of his 'Big Band Show'. "It's seven thirty in the morning, time to rise and shine."

She had sparkling eyes and a smiling generous mouth, set in a full round face framed with curly dark hair. It was, however, her figure that was most striking, acting as a magnet to my gaze. Moll Flanders in a nurse's uniform. With the top three buttons of the dress undone and with the collar folded back, she revealed far more of her generous cleavage than Matron's regulations on nurse's uniforms allowed. I felt my face flush and my senses quicken.

"I've brought a cup of tea for you, Paul," she said, using my Christian name in a further breach of Matron's rules, although we had never met before. The bedside locker was on the far side of the bed from the door and the obvious thing for her to do was to walk around the foot of the bed to leave the tea on the locker. This, however, was not her way of doing things. Instead she leant across the bed, her cleavage coming within a few inches of my face. The view of her breasts and the smell of her perfume were intoxicating, indeed stimulating, despite the weariness I felt from the lack of sleep. Having deposited the drink on the locker she feigned to slip and steadied herself with a hand on my bare shoulder, her face directly in front of me, her lips only a couple of inches from mine. For one dreadful moment, I thought she was planning to throw her arms round me and kiss me.

"We like to look after the doctors here," she said, "especially the good looking ones." The voice was husky and suggestive. Others, I am sure, would have relished such a situation, perhaps would have turned it to their advantage, but I felt decidedly ill at ease. Many would have responded with some clever remark or witticism but I was embarrassed, tongue-tied and, conscious that I was dressed only in my underpants, quickly drew the sheet up under my chin.

"Don't be shy, Paul. I'm a nurse; I've seen it all before." She sat down on the bed, just the sheet separating her shapely knee from my thigh. I could feel its warmth through the thin material.

"The night staff are going off duty now, but I've got a quickie for you." Again, the suggestive voice and smile. I must have looked alarmed for she added, "Don't worry, I'm not going to eat you. Mind you, you do look rather tasty." She put a finger on my nose and then very slowly traced a path downwards across my lips, caressing each in turn, lingering on my chin and then seductively stroking my neck and upper chest, until its descent was arrested by the sheet that I held tightly with both hands across my body. Her eyes had been following the course of her finger but now they found mine. The smile on her face was teasing and provocative.

"Never mind," she said wickedly, "there's always next time." She retreated a foot or so and I began to feel slightly less vulnerable. Fortunately, she then became a little bit more businesslike and reported on the patients that had attended the department whilst I had been asleep.

"There is one patient with a small cut in cubicle one. We've sewn it up and he's agreed to stay to let you see him. There are also three sets of notes for you to sign."

"What are they?" I asked, puzzled.

"Patients we've seen while you've been resting. We didn't want to wake you so we've sorted them out. We just need you to sign the cards before you leave."

"But how do I sign the records if I haven't seen the patients?"

"Oh, you are the innocent one aren't you?" she said. "We will have to do something about that. Well, most doctors just sign the notes as if they have seen the patients. The alternative is for you to say that we treated them but that they didn't wait to be seen by you."

"But that's not quite true either, is it?"

The playful voice returned. "You do take things seriously, don't you, Paul? I can see that I shall have to give you some personal tuition...show you how to relax and have a good time. Strictly speaking, it isn't *entirely* true, but doing it this way saves you getting up every twenty minutes to see the patients who dribble in through the night. At least we've given you a couple of hours sleep. Anyway, I'll leave the cards out and you can decide what you want to do with them. I must dash."

Suddenly, the voice became suggestive again. "It's been nice to meet you, Paul." She fingered the top of the sheet that separated us. "I hope to see much more of you soon." She bent forward and gave me a kiss on the forehead. Again, there was a sensuous mix of cleavage and perfume. She moved to leave but by the door she turned, a twinkle in her eye and a smile on her face. "By the way, I'm moving to Surgical Five theatre next week. I'll see you there."

I drank the cup of tea in bed and then slowly dressed, wondering what I should do about the patients whom the nurses had seen and discharged. I saw the patient that they had stitched, wrote in his medical record, and discharged him. I signed the other three cards having recorded that the patients hadn't waited to be seen...not that I was completely happy about doing this, but at least there was an element of truth in this statement. I sincerely hoped there would be no comeback.

Whilst writing up the case notes I had heard the sound of activity, and, leaving the office, found two of the surgical cubicles occupied. The receptionist had taken up her position for the new day and a new team of nurses, all bright and fresh, had come on duty and were being allocated their various duties by the Day Sister. I put a hand to my armpit and then to my nose. There was an unmistakable smell of body odour and I felt the stubble on my chin. Sister took me to one side and her words were most welcome.

"Although you are on duty until nine am," she said, "I suggest you go to the residency and freshen up. If anything urgent turns up we will bleep you, any other cases we will save for the casualty officers when they arrive at nine am."

I walked slowly back to the residency feeling hungry, tired and also somewhat light-headed. The nursing staff who had shared the night work with me in casualty had been off-duty the day before, were off-duty again now, and had enjoyed a meal break during the night -

whereas I had worked all day yesterday, through the night, and now, with my head still throbbing gently from the heat in the bedroom, knew that I faced another full day's work - commencing within the hour with a ward round with Mr Potts. Somehow, it didn't seem quite fair!

Back in the residency I refreshed myself with a long hot shower and then went for breakfast. The other house officers, particularly those who had not as yet done a stint in the casualty department through the night, were keen to know how I had got on. I related the experience of my early morning cup of tea.

"That will be Sue Weston," someone suggested. "She's got quite a reputation. If she's coming to Surgical Five you'd better watch your step, Paul."

I felt considerably better when breakfast was over. Somehow, eating bacon, eggs, toast and marmalade and having a large mug of coffee at eight-thirty in the morning established a baseline for the day, and the slight disorientation that I had felt leaving casualty disappeared. I also felt a sense of satisfaction from knowing that I had come through my first night as a casualty officer. It had been tough - I had needed assistance from Mr Khan and the nursing staff, and there was still a full day's work in front of me, during which I should have to stay alert and avoid errors - but I had survived.

Chapter 7

Thanks to my overnight duties in the casualty department and the need to have a shower and a shave, it was after nine am when I arrived on the ward. Mr Khan had already completed his review of the male patients and was half way round the female ward when I joined him. He brushed aside my apologies for my late arrival.

"I know that you have been undertaking the overnight accident room duties," he said, "so there is no need to apologise. It was inevitable that you would be late. I didn't hear from you in the night. Was it fairly quiet?"

I said that I wasn't sure what constituted a quiet night since I hadn't done enough of them yet to know what was normal, but added that I did manage to get two or three hours sleep.

"That must be about average," he said then added generously, "To give you a flying start today and to save you some time, I will finish the round whilst you start preparing the investigation cards and, if you like, I will introduce the patients to the boss on the ward round. I am sure you will be looking for an early finish today. We will meet on the male ward at nine-thirty for Mr Potts' ward round."

I thanked him but suggested that I would like to present the patients, provided that he would come to my assistance should I forget anything of importance. Mr Khan agreed, albeit with a knowing smile that left me wondering if my enthusiasm was leading me into trouble.

An early finish would indeed be most welcome. Over breakfast I had considered the day's workload and had come to the conclusion that a finish by three-thirty or four pm was quite feasible, provided that there weren't too many interruptions. I knew that it would not be possible to complete the venepunctures before Mr Potts' ward round, but he had the reputation of conducting his rounds in a businesslike fashion and if he started at nine-thirty, it seemed likely that he would be away by eleven am. All that would then remain would be the necessary blood samples and three admissions. That should allow me to finish by mid-afternoon. I had made no special arrangements for the evening and planned nothing more than an evening meal, maybe an hour or two in front of the television or a chat and a beer in the residency, followed by an early night.

Mr Potts duly arrived in the office and wasted no time in commencing his ward round. In accordance with his usual practice he led us to the first bed on the ward and I as his house officer followed in his wake, pushing the notes trolley in time-honoured fashion. With the patient's records in my hand as an aide-memoir, I started to present the first case to my boss in the manner that I had been taught as a student.

"This is Mr Harry Peters, Sir. He's forty-two years old and has worked as a postman for many years. He is married with three teenage children. He was admitted about eight days ago from the waiting list with a long-standing history of upper abdominal pain, mainly on the right side, radiating to the back. It tended to come on after food, particularly fatty food. He has also been troubled with a good deal of flatulence, again associated with the ingestion of fatty foods. His weight recently has..."

Mr Potts interrupted. "This is last week's cholecystectomy, isn't it?"

"Yes Sir. At operation he was found to have stones in his gall bladder, but there were no stones in the common bile duct. His recovery to date has been unremarkable. He is now taking fat-free fluids and it is planned to start him on a light diet tomorrow. The chest is clinically clear, and the wound is..."

Again Mr Potts interrupted.

"Yes, yes, yes - are there any problems?"

"No, Sir."

"Good, then let's move on and not waste any more time."

And move on we did, leaving a slightly bewildered Mr Peters in our wake. I made a mental note to return to him after the round to explain that Mr Potts was well pleased with his progress, that there were no problems with his postoperative recovery and that it was anticipated he would get home on schedule.

Having spent years learning how to take and present a good case history and examination, and having been required to pass the exacting final MB ChB examination to prove myself capable of doing this, it was galling to discover that this was not what my consultant boss wanted at all. What he wanted to hear was: *"This is Mr Peters. Eight days post cholecystectomy. He's got no problems"* - which was, of course, exactly the manner in which Mr Khan had been presenting cases to Mr Potts a few days earlier. Was this brevity common to all consultant surgeons as part of their 'dynamic surgical personality', or was it a peculiarity of Mr Potts? Or was it, in reality, a necessity due to the constraints of time? It was difficult to know.

Thereafter I abridged my presentations and, to my surprise, if I stated that the patient was making a good recovery, Mr Potts took my word for it. Just occasionally he would look to Mr Khan for confirmation and he would simply nod to concur. These were the abridged presentations, much derided by the physicians, about which we had been warned. In due course, when I took up a house physician's post I would have to revert to complete presentations. I knew that there existed a good deal of (mainly) friendly rivalry between physicians and surgeons, not dissimilar to that which exists between the residents of Glasgow and those of Edinburgh or between Liverpool and Manchester, each being pleased if they can score a point over the other. If in six months time whilst presenting a patient to a consultant physician I omitted some important clinical detail, the likelihood was that the physician would smile sadly and pass a comment to those accompanying him on his ward round on the bad habits that the surgeons had allowed me to develop.

I knew also that physicians often spoke of the 'womb-like' existence of the surgeon, referring to his life in an air-conditioned operating theatre, supported by maternal nurses supplying him with the instruments and needles he needs whilst operating, nurturing him with coffee and hot buttered toast between cases and generally attending to his every need in this sheltered environment. Whilst the actual practice of technical skills in theatre is the highlight of the job for most surgeons, in practice the surgeon's time is spread more or less equally between three areas of activity; the operating theatres, the wards, and the outpatient clinics where the majority of his patients are seen for the first time. Although I had not yet seen Mr Potts operating, it did seem that the technical side of the job in theatre was the most attractive for him and that he regarded the pre-operative and post-operative care of the patients on the ward as a necessary chore that came with the job. His rounds were conducted in a brisk, indeed sometimes brusque manner, and his communication with the patients was minimal.

We saw all the patients on both the male and female wards in just over an hour. The boss then stayed with us for about ten minutes having a cup of coffee and chatting in the office, and thereafter I was left to get on with the schedule that I had planned for myself. The round had produced only a small number of extra jobs; one patient who had developed a chest infection needed to have a chest X-ray and a bacterial analysis of a sample of his sputum, so that he could be prescribed the most appropriate antibiotic. The only other task was to ask Dr Darby, the Consultant Cardiologist, to come to our ward to advise on one of our patients who appeared to have some form of cardiac problem. She was breathless, had some chest pain, and her electrocardiogram showed some changes which none of our team felt confident about interpreting.

No doubt the cardiologist would be pleased to play 'one-upmanship' on a surgical ward.

Having filled in all the laboratory request cards and taken all the necessary bloods, I had just started to clerk the first of the day's admissions when my bleep sounded. Although I had been pleased to be allocated a 'bleep' less than a week before, indicative of my new status in the hospital, the pride that I had initially felt was fast disappearing as I realised how easy it was for others to contact me, to add to my workload and to disrupt my daily schedule. The switchboard informed me that Sir William was in the surgeon's room in theatre and wished to speak with me. Apologising to my patient, I walked to the theatre and found Sir William and his nephew Johnny, looking relaxed and sharing a cup of coffee and a biscuit.

"Ah, Lambert," he said. "I am pleased that you were free to come and join us." It was custom and practice for consultants to address their house officers by their surname. By assuming that I was 'free', rather than working with a patient, he made it sound as if it was a casual request which I could have declined had I so wished, rather than an instruction from the boss which had to be obeyed!

"I'm afraid that there has been a little problem with the marking of patients," Sir William continued. "Two patients arrived in theatre for today's list on whom the operation site had not been marked. I also understand from the theatre staff that one of Mr Potts' varicose veins patients arrived in theatre yesterday and the marks on the legs were almost invisible."

At first I failed to understand how this affected me. The patients on that morning's list had been clerked by Johnny, and I knew with absolute certainty that all the patients that I had clerked had been marked appropriately. I had marked them myself.

"But I marked them myself," I said, "very boldly, with a black marker pen."

"Yes, I do realise that," said Sir William gently, "but it appears that you used a washable marker pen instead of an indelible one. You need to remember that all patients are bathed and shaved after you have clerked them, before they go to theatre. Remember that to avoid unnecessary mistakes, every patient must be appropriately marked. I want you both to go down to the stores department today and pick up an indelible marker for future use."

He went on to explain that every year somewhere in the country, a surgeon either operates on the wrong patient or performs the wrong operation, and there were even examples of the wrong limb being amputated. Such mistakes, he said, were all indefensible and completely preventable.

"I know we all pay for medical negligence insurance, but when these things happen it's not good for the reputation of the profession, or indeed for the career of the individual surgeon concerned – and, of course, it's an absolute disaster for the patient."

He went on to explain that of equal importance in preventing such calamities was to write the patient's Christian name and surname, their hospital number, and the type of operation to be performed in full, both on the patient's consent form and on the operating list. No shorthand or abbreviations should be used. The side on which surgery is to be performed should be written in capitals, so a patient for a hernia operation is listed as 'RIGHT inguinal hernia repair', not as 'RIH'. Similarly an amputation is recorded as 'LEFT mid thigh amputation', not as 'LMTA'. He turned to me.

"Which is your first finger?" he asked. I held up my index finger.

"Most people in this country would agree, but did you know that there are parts of the world where the thumb is regarded as the first? The lesson is that their descriptive names - thumb, index, middle, ring and little - should be used."

He went on to describe other safeguards. "All the documentation should be checked as the patient leaves the ward, again as they arrive in theatre, and a third time by both anaesthetist and surgeon before any procedure begins. Accidents happen," he said, "when these basic procedures are not followed."

The lesson was an important one but Sir William, who at times could be a bit pedantic, did rather labour the point, and illustrated it by telling how a surgeon friend of his who was due to give a lecture had ended up in Newcastle-under-Lyme when his true destination was Newcastle-Upon-Tyne. It seemed a rather weak example to illustrate the point when only the week before the national newspapers had carried a story about an unfortunate man who was listed as the third patient on a theatre list but had actually been operated on second - because the man scheduled to be number two had decided at the last minute not to proceed with his vasectomy!

I was unhappy at being reprimanded (albeit gently and constructively) so soon after my arrival on the unit. In my eyes, Sir William Warrender was an eminent senior surgeon and one of my bosses. He was to be respected, his advice heeded and his instructions followed for the benefit of the patients, but not least because he was able to have a significant influence on my career. My next post would be a house physician's job and if I had his support and a good reference, my prospects would be good. With a bad reference, I might end up as a GP on a far-flung Scottish island or on a £10 assisted passage to one of the colonies. The situation for Johnny was quite different; Sir William was his uncle, and his future in his father's practice in Surrey was assured. I had noticed that the exchanges between them in front of patients or the nursing staff were always appropriately formal and correct. No one would have suspected that there was a family connection, particularly as they had different surnames. Away from patients though, the relationship was much more relaxed. Johnny dropped the "Sir" that he used in public and Sir William referred to his nephew by his Christian name. Johnny evidently regarded Sir William as a benevolent uncle.

When we left the surgeons' room, we walked together back to the ward. A smile crept over Johnny's face. It seemed that he had some mischief in mind.

"If we really took him at his word, we could have some fun with this," he said, with a twinkle in his eye. "I've got a man coming in next week for a circumcision. I shall draw a bold black arrow all the way down from his umbilicus to the tip of his manhood."

"You scarcely need to mark a circumcision," I said. "He's only got one appendage to choose from, there really can't be any confusion."

"Nonetheless," said Johnny, still smiling, "we've been told to mark it and mark it I shall, as prominently as I can! We've also got a lady being admitted with piles. I shall draw concentric circles around the area, possibly in different colours, to make it look like an archery target, or a dartboard."

He paused. "Did my Uncle Bill say anything about the proper name for the different toes? I have a patient coming in for an operation on a toenail. I think it's the middle one, but he didn't tell us the correct anatomical name for that. Is it called the middle toe or the third toe?"

"Call it the roast beef one," I said.

"What on earth do you mean?"

I started to recite the traditional nursery rhyme, so well known to children. "This little piggy went to market, this little piggy stayed at home, this little piggy had roast beef, this little piggy..."

"That's it," said Johnny. "I shall write *'Ingrown toe nail on the right roast beef toenail'* on the list that goes to theatre and on the consent form. It will keep the nurses amused and it does accurately describe the nail for surgery. Have you got any suitable cases for marking?" he said, looking at me.

"With respect, I think you and I are in slightly different situations Johnny," I said. "I rather doubt that Mr Potts would find such behaviour amusing!"

Our conversation was interrupted by a call from the laboratory. It was an anxious sounding technician from the haematology department.

"Dr Lambert, you've sent down a request for estimation of haemoglobin level this morning on a man called Walter Franklin on your male ward. The card says he had a hernia repaired yesterday. I thought I ought to ring you; his haemoglobin is only twenty percent of normal. I've checked with the blood bank and they have no blood cross matched for him - I think you'd better get a sample down to us straight away."

For a moment I was stunned, I had seen Mr Franklin not a couple of hours previously on Mr Potts' round and he looked as right as rain. There was no suggestion that he had lost much blood. I dashed back to the ward, collected the blood letting kit and ran to his bedside. However, when I got there he was sitting up in bed, reading the newspaper and looking pink and healthy. His observation charts showed a rock steady pulse and blood pressure. He wanted to know why I was in such a rush. Surely his haemoglobin couldn't be so low. I wondered if the samples could have got mixed up in some way. Had I labelled some bottles incorrectly? Was there another of my patients who was bleeding and had a low haemoglobin? This seemed unlikely as any patient with a blood count of twenty percent would be extremely ill and none of my patients were particularly sick at all - we had seen them all less than two hours ago, and none of them was giving the slightest cause for concern. Perhaps the laboratory had mixed up the samples at their end.

I took a sample for repeat haemoglobin estimation as well as one for cross match and sent them urgently to the lab for further analysis. I rang the technician to tell him that the samples were on their way and asked him to phone me as soon as the result was known. Within 50 minutes he was on the phone again, sounding much more cheerful this time.

"The haemoglobin's 95% this time," he said. "That's odd isn't it? So strange, in fact, that I've spoken with the boys next door in the biochemistry laboratory to see whether they had received any specimens from Mr Franklin this morning."

"They will have done," I said, "I sent down electrolytes as well."

"Yes, I know - and according to the biochemistry laboratory, the patient has virtually no potassium in his blood at all and more salt than you would find in the Dead Sea. According to these results, the patient ought to be dead! Can I ask you Doctor, does the patient have a drip up?"

"Yes," I said.

"Is the drip running a sodium chloride solution?"

The penny dropped and suddenly I realised exactly what he was trying to say and precisely what I had done wrong. The patient had a drip into his forearm and I had taken the first blood sample from the crook of the elbow, about three inches higher. The initial sample had been a mixture of a little blood and a lot of the salt solution that was being administered.

"Oh my God," I said. "I've taken blood from the drip arm, haven't I?"

"It looks like it," he said, "but not to worry - it does happen from time to time, and usually at this time of the year. Can I suggest that you take a sample from the other arm, just for the record?"

It was another lesson learned the hard way. There was one consolation though; fortunately Sister Ashbrook was off-duty and with reasonable luck she wouldn't get to hear about it, otherwise the tennis score would have tipped even more strongly in her favour.

I returned to the patient that I had started to admit before being called to see Sir William in theatre. The admissions on Fridays for the short Saturday morning list were usually relatively fit young patients having minor surgery who could be expected to have a straightforward recovery over the weekend, when the staffing levels in the hospital were a little thinner on the ground than they tended to be during the working week. They should not take too long to admit, I thought, and it still seemed as if my work could be completed by late afternoon and allow me to catch up with the sleep that I had lost whilst working in casualty – but, unfortunately, there were further interruptions.

Firstly, the anaesthetist who was scheduled to do the Saturday morning theatre session rang and wished to know what operations were planned on the next day's list. I had imagined that he would come and see the patients himself pre-operatively - to introduce himself, to check that they were not taking any medication that would interfere with the anaesthetic, and to see that they were fit for surgery - but it seemed that this was not the case, and he was happy to take my assessment of their fitness. I explained that I had not as yet had an opportunity to see them myself, so he asked that I give him a ring at home after I had seen them. It was a surprise to me that he was prepared to accept an assessment by a doctor with less than a week's experience, indeed even more surprising that he instructed me to prescribe their premedication drugs for them.

The next interruption bought more bad news and a great deal of extra work. It came in the form of a telephone call from Mrs Atkins, one of the secretaries in the surgical office.

"I'm sorry to trouble you, Dr Lambert," she said, "but we're off home now. May we leave you to write out the operating lists for tomorrow's surgery?"

I looked at my watch; it was a quarter to five. Mrs Atkins explained that it was the responsibility of the house officer to bring the proposed operating list to the office during the course of the afternoon so that the secretaries could type it out and circulate it. The job, however, became one for the house officer if the list was not presented by the time that the secretarial staff went home.

"You'd better explain to me how many copies are required and where they have to go to," I said.

"You'll need to write out eight copies," was the response. "Four for the theatre, one to each ward, one to the anaesthetic office and one is left in this office for filing. Oh, and by the way, there is quite a large pile of notes building up for patients who have been discharged."

I was struck by a premonition that worse news was to follow. "Tell me more," I said.

"Well, it is the house officer's job to dictate a letter to the general practitioner on every patient who has been discharged, and we've got a pile of twenty or more waiting in the office. The general practitioners need to know what has happened to their patients whilst they have been in hospital, and what medication they are taking when they leave. A patient may well need to see his GP within a few days of going home and the GP will be lost without information from us, so the discharge letters need to go out promptly. If you come in on Monday morning, I can show you the pile of case notes and let you know where the dictating machine and tapes are kept."

She rang off and I considered the outstanding jobs that needed to be completed before my day's duty was complete and I could get some rest. This single telephone call had given me a significant extra workload. The discharge letters would obviously have to wait until Monday, but I decided that the duplication and circulation of the operation lists would have to be done virtually at once if the theatre staff were going to be able to prepare the surgical instruments for the next day's cases. As I anticipated, writing out the lists longhand proved to be a boring and time consuming clerical job and I vowed to ensure that the list went to the secretaries in good time in future.

By the time that I got round to admitting the last patient of the day, I was surprised to find visitors standing outside the ward. It was seven o'clock and they were waiting for the bell to announce the commencement of visiting time. With just this one job to perform before my day was over, I decided to proceed with the clerking behind screens during the visiting period, reasoning to myself that this patient had only left his nearest and dearest relatives a few hours before, that they would still have half an hour together after I had completed the admission procedure, and that in the circumstances it was justifiable to put myself first and let the visitors wait. Finally, tired and hungry, all duties complete - having been on continuous duty for almost thirty-six hours and actually working for all but two or three hours - I returned to the residency.

After the evening meal, I sat down with Johnny and one or two of the other newly appointed house officers in the common room. It had been a bad day at the end of a difficult week and I was acutely aware that since starting the job I had made a number of errors. It had been incompetent to take blood from the arm into which saline was being infused, and with hindsight I realised that when I encountered difficulties with Mr Quigley's nasogastric tube, I ought to have swallowed my pride and sought advice. Perhaps some of it was due to inexperience, and maybe the mistake with the saline drip had been due to tiredness; after all, thanks to the casualty duties, I had only had a couple of hours sleep the night before. Inexperience and tiredness were, however, not the only explanation. The other house officers shared their experiences. They had all encountered similar problems and we came to the conclusion that we had been inadequately prepared for the duties that we were required to perform. Our medical school training had been very detailed but it had been theoretical. Important practical lessons had been omitted. We also recognised that more information ought to have been given to us about the content and nature of the job. I had taken it upon myself to speak to Eleanor, the outgoing house surgeon, to try to learn more about the role that I was about to play - yet didn't know that I was supposed to ring the anaesthetist about the operating list, or that the details of the operating list had to be given to the secretaries by four-thirty pm, or that it was my responsibility to write discharge summaries for the GPs. Surely the tasks expected of us ought to have been listed and explained? Surely some form of induction programme should have been arranged? Wearily, I wondered how many more house officer jobs there were of which I still remained ignorant.

Johnny wasn't as tired as I was - he had not yet done his first overnight stint in the accident department - but despite his natural cheery disposition, he too felt that the first week had been difficult. As he said, you start the day with six jobs to complete and by lunchtime you have ten jobs on your 'to do' list. We were forever playing catch-up. Further, it was all too evident that a houseman was not merely a doctor; he also needed to be a porter, a nurse and clerk. I remembered the battle that I had fought to get priority for Mr Quigley's emergency operation. In addition to his medical skills, the houseman needed diplomatic, mediation and communication skills as well. It was clear that if I were to survive for six months in this post I would need to find some inner strength and resilience. Johnny and I thought the weekend would probably bring some respite but, knowing that the following week was likely to follow the course of the first, we decided to take our troubles to Sir William and seek his advice on how to manage our jobs and our time more effectively.

Chapter 8

During the weekend the clinical workload did indeed slacken significantly. Each morning I went to the two wards and reviewed Mr Potts' patients on my own; spending time with them, getting to know them better, and becoming more familiar, not only with their clinical problems, but with each of them as individuals. It was very satisfying to be able to do this in a leisurely fashion without any time constraint. Fortunately they were all making good progress, I identified no new clinical problems and there was no occasion on which it proved necessary to call for more senior advice.

In the afternoons, having discovered that the keys for the clinical office were kept on the ward, I searched through various drawers and cupboards until I found a dictating machine and some audiotapes. Yet again, I realised that my training for the job had been deficient - at no stage had I been given any advice on how to write a medical letter. I sat for a long time considering what information a GP would require should a patient consult him within a few days of leaving hospital. It seemed to me that he would not want a full account of the clinical history and examination at the time of admission to hospital, since he should already be familiar with that. Rather, he would need to know the diagnosis that had been reached in hospital and the treatment given, an account of the patient's condition at the time of discharge, together with the arrangements made for the patients' further management, and particularly the care that was expected from the GP. Since the patient's medication was frequently changed during the hospital stay, it seemed important to include details of that as well. I decided that each letter should have standard paragraphs covering these areas. By and large this worked well, although it was later pointed out to me that GPs also need to know precisely what information patients themselves had been given about their condition, especially when they had a malignant process and a poor prognosis. If a GP were informed in a letter that his patient had incurable cancer and a life expectancy of only a few months, it would place him in an invidious position if he were unaware whether the patient shared this knowledge. Dictating these letters proved especially time-consuming for those patients who had been admitted and discharged before the first of August. These were patients I had never met and I had to familiarise myself with the details of their hospital stay by reading the notes, frequently finding that the information required had not been recorded and was not available. I consoled myself with the thought that dictating these discharge letters would become an easier task when it came to compiling reports on patients whom I had helped to manage on the wards.

Most importantly of all, over the weekend I managed to get two reasonable nights sleep, which recharged the batteries. It was a much refreshed house officer who came on duty the following week. Knowing that Sir William had seen fifty or more house officers come and go whilst he had been a consultant, I was sure that he would be able to offer useful advice on the role of the house officer and was looking forward to hearing what he had to say on the matter. It had been arranged that we would have the opportunity to have a chat with him after his next ward round and it was in a mood of cheerful anticipation that I joined Johnny and Simon Gresty in the office on the female ward to await Sir William's arrival.

Sister Gladys Rutherford was there too and although I had only been in post for a week, it was apparent that she was a kindly nursing sister of the 'traditional school'. Whilst being quite strict and professional, certainly not one to stand any nonsense either from the medical or nursing staff, she ran her ward efficiently, managing to achieve this without fuss or bother. She appeared to be both well-liked and respected by the two consultants, and the result was a well-organised ward where the atmosphere was calm and relaxed, in contrast to the slight tension that always seemed to exist on the male ward where Sister Ashbrook was in charge.

Simon Gresty looked at his watch and frowned. Sir William was late and there had been no message to explain why.

"I hope that this ward round doesn't take too long," he said. "A consultant job has been advertised at the Medchurch District Hospital in the Midlands for which I wish to apply - they are looking for a general surgeon with particular expertise in abdominal surgery. I have arranged to speak with the retiring consultant at three pm this afternoon to find out more about the post, and I don't want to upset him by arriving late. He's offered to show me round and to give me more details about the hospital and the sort of replacement that they are looking for. If you show your face, you know, and let them see that you are really interested, you are much more likely to be short-listed and called for interview."

Sister Rutherford chipped in. "I suggest that you mention to Sir William that you want to leave a little early. I am sure that if you explained the reason, he would understand and not mind in the least."

"No, no, Sister. I couldn't possibly do that. Sir William would expect me to be on his round throughout, to tell him how his patients are progressing. There are a couple of cases on which I particularly need his advice. If I were not here, he would have only the new houseman to show him round and that would never do. I wouldn't like to take the risk of offending him."

This was the first time that I had been with Simon other than on the consultant ward rounds, where his manner had been formal and when his performance had been impressive. He always had the facts and figures about all the patients at his fingertips, never needing to refer to the notes or to retrieve details from a laboratory report. It was, however, his attitude to his consultant that I had noticed and disliked. It wasn't just respectful or deferential. Somehow it was more than that - almost fawning, even obsequious, at times. This contrasted with his demeanour towards the house officers and nursing staff, to whom he appeared somewhat distant and haughty. He was a tall man, perhaps thirty-seven or thirty-eight years of age, with angular features - a sharp nose and chin, clear blue eyes, with his hair well greased and swept back. His face often carried a superior expression - especially, it seemed, when addressing a house officer. I could not deny, however, that his knowledge of surgical matters appeared comprehensive and, although I had yet to see him operate, by reputation he was a fine technician.

I find it curious that within a few minutes of meeting somebody for the first time, it is possible to get an intuitive feeling as to whether this is someone whom you could come to like, someone who might perhaps become a friend - or, alternatively, whether this is a person whom, even at this first encounter, you decide you would prefer to keep at arm's length. In my mind, Sister Rutherford emphatically belonged in the first category and Simon quite definitely in the latter. Curious also that these early impressions rarely change, indeed often become consolidated, with time.

Simon looked at his watch again.

"Perhaps if we could persuade Sir William to do fewer rectal examinations we would get round faster," suggested Johnny, noticing Simon's anxiety.

"Or insert fewer suppositories," I added, remembering the ritual that was enacted each time. "That would save time as well."

These remarks earned us a slight reproach from Sister.

"Sir William has a traditional bedside manner," she said. "Some people may regard it as a bit old fashioned, but he takes a personal interest in all his patients. They all have great respect for him, and they benefit from the personal attention that he gives them."

Simon continued to look anxious. "Look, it's ten-thirty already," he said. "I bet it's half past one or two o'clock before we're through. I'm afraid that I'm going to be late for my appointment at Medchurch."

"If we had a sweepstake to guess the time that the round finished," Johnny suggested, "at least the time would seem to go faster. Or perhaps a sweepstake to estimate how many suppositories he inserted during the course of the round might be even more fun."

Sister gave him another disapproving look, but said nothing. Perhaps she felt that Johnny, as Sir William's nephew, was allowed to say such things. By this time Mr Khan had joined us and seemed enthusiastic about the idea of a sweepstake.

"I would have said that, on average, about eight suppositories were inserted per round - so my money is going on eight." I suggested four. Johnny suggested ten.

Initially Simon was reluctant to participate. "I'm not sure that this is a good idea," he said. "What would happen if Sir William found out? I am sure that he would disapprove. I don't want to blot my copybook."

"Don't be such a spoilsport," said Johnny in a tone that one would not normally expect a houseman to use to a senior registrar. "I can assure you that the old boy is not without a sense of humour. It's not likely that he will find out but even if he did, I am sure that he would only regard it as a bit of fun. And it would do no harm to the patients; they are going to have the suppositories inserted whether we count the number or not!"

Reluctantly Simon agreed to join in, and decided on twelve. We all suggested that this was excessive but Simon just touched the side of his nose. "Don't forget that I have worked for Sir William longer than you."

Sister, however, could not be persuaded to participate. She looked rather prim and said she would rather not be involved. Without her actually saying so, it was clear that she did not approve.

"If you are not joining in, perhaps you would be prepared to keep the score?" Mr Khan asked.

"Certainly not," she responded crossly.

"I'll keep the score then," said Johnny. "I'll start with some investigation cards in my right hand white coat pocket, and I'll transfer one to my left hand pocket each time a suppository is inserted. It will be like the umpire counting the six balls of an over in a game of cricket."

Mr Khan reminded us that there was one aspect of the sweepstake that we had forgotten. "How much is the stake going to be?"

"Not more than sixpence," I said quickly. "We don't get paid until the end of the month and I don't have a lot to spare."

And so the great suppository game began that was to provide hours of harmless entertainment and amusement during Sir William's seemingly endless ward rounds in the weeks to come.

In due course, Sir William arrived and Simon gave a sigh of relief.

"Good morning," he said, addressing the assembly in general. "I do apologise for being late. One of my patients in the private wing has developed a severe chest infection and I have been sorting out a chest X-ray and some physiotherapy for her."

Then, turning to Johnny and me, he added, "Mrs Atkins in the secretarial office tells me that you two would like to see me after the ward round for a bit of a chat. That's fine. I wanted to catch a word with both of you anyway because I have got a little favour that I want to ask of you."

I groaned inwardly. The reason we wanted to see him was to discover if some of the jobs we were doing were unnecessary, and to find out if there was a more efficient way of organising our work. The last thing we wanted was additional work. Was this yet another task delegated to house officers of which we were still unaware?

We set out on the ward round; Sir William followed by the two registrars, the two house officers, Sister Rutherford and a gaggle of nurses. The patient in the first bed was Mrs Farrington who was due to be discharged later that day, having had a hernia repaired. Having checked her chest and wound for any evidence of infection, duplicating the examination that Simon had undertaken earlier that morning, Sir William asked about her bowels. I saw Johnny's hand move expectantly to his white coat pocket, but when the patient assured Sir William that her bowels were in good working order he assumed his normal posture, looking a trifle disappointed. I did wonder whether the patients, when chatting amongst themselves, discussed the experience of being at the receiving end of Sir William's digital examinations - and if they did, whether the word went round that it was wiser to deny any slight constipation, even if their bowels were a little on the stubborn side.

It was the third patient that we saw on the round who actually volunteered to the boss that in the six days since her stomach operation she had not managed to get her bowels working. Perhaps, I thought, she had not heard of the fate that befalls anyone brave enough to make such a confession to Sir William, or perhaps she felt that her bowel problem was sufficiently severe as to need his radical therapy, rather than the rather more gentle laxative therapy that she would have received had she had a quiet word with Sister Rutherford. Immediately Sir William's index finger pointed rigidly towards the ceiling, summoning the rectal tray, and he reiterated the stock phrases that we were to hear so often.

"No one should be too superior or too proud to perform the humble rectal examination. Mark my words, sooner or later if you don't put your finger in, you'll put your foot in it. Remember that the examination of the abdomen starts in the groin and ends in the rectum."

The seven nurses set about their duties with exemplary efficiency; a finger stall was placed on the upheld finger, gauze applied to protect the knuckles, lubrication applied, and at the completion of the military operation two suppositories had been inserted, and Johnny had transferred two cards from his right hand coat pocket to the left, a smug, self satisfied look on his face. The suppository sweepstake had begun.

In no way did the little game detract from the seriousness with which each consultation was undertaken. The ward round was conducted at a leisurely pace, each patient was thoroughly assessed and examined, and due consideration was given to an appropriate course of management. As always, Sir William's explanations to the patients were thorough and much appreciated, though tedious to the staff that had heard them all so many times previously. The suppository sideshow simply provided a little extra interest.

Six cards had been placed in Johnny's left hand pocket by the time we had reviewed all the female patients, and - with the men still to see - having suggested just four suppositories, I had already said goodbye to my sixpence!

On the male ward, we were joined by Sister Ashbrook. The ward round by the senior consultant was one of the highlights of the week and the patients were sitting neatly in their beds, maintaining a respectful silence. All the chairs and lockers had been tidied and sheets and pillowcases straightened. Since it was not possible for the cheerful hubbub of routine nursing duties to proceed in these circumstances, most of the nurses on the ward joined the round. In no time at all, the rectal tray was in action again. It continued to surprise me that Sir William seemed not to appreciate that to have the spectacle of rectal examination and suppository insertion witnessed by all the accompanying doctors and nurses might be embarrassing for the patient. Perhaps he did, but felt that to demonstrate that he, a senior consultant, considered it sufficiently important to perform a task that others might find demeaning, overcame any concern that he might have had about the patient's feelings. Standing across the bed from the boss, I tried to avoid eye contact with the patient. Instead I looked across the top of the patient's bare buttocks as Sir William started to perform his examination and noticed Kate Meredith, my saviour from Mr Quigley's nasogastric tube disaster, standing behind him. I watched her as Sir William started his patter. "No one should be too superior or too proud to perform the humble rectal examination," he reiterated. "If you don't put your finger in..."

Kate was looking at me. She smiled and started to mime the phrase that she had heard so often, in time with Sir William's words. I smiled back but unfortunately Sir William noted my amusement. He had completed his digital assessment of the rectal contents and was about to insert some suppositories. He withdrew his finger and looked across at me.

"No, Lambert," he said, wagging a soiled finger at me. I saw a small fleck of faeces flick off and land on the white bed sheet. "This is no joking matter. I'm absolutely serious about the need to examine all patients thoroughly, and that includes a rectal examination. If you omit it, sooner or later you will miss something important. Many a general practitioner has treated a patient with rectal bleeding as a simple case of piles, but if they had examined the rectum properly, they would have recognised immediately that the patient had a carcinoma of the rectum. Many a surgeon has treated an appendicectomy patient for a wound infection, but had they put their finger into the rectum they would have recognised that the patient's fever was due to an abscess deep in the pelvis. For surgeons, thoroughness should be routine. It is the key to good clinical practice and safe patient care."

It was galling to be reprimanded so publicly but I was not in a position to say that I had not been laughing at Sir William at all. I noticed that Sister Ashbrook seemed to be enjoying my discomfiture and mentally added another fifteen points onto her tennis score, thinking bitterly that she must already have scored more than enough points to have won the first game. Simon Gresty then irritated me more by deciding to add his two pennies worth.

"You are quite right to remind us, Sir - we all need to benefit from your experience."

Wretched creep, I thought, noting that my earlier impression of him had been not been misplaced.

When the ward round was over - Simon having irked me further by winning two shillings on the sweepstake - Johnny and I went with Sir William to his private office, which was situated adjacent to the secretarial office. By comparison with the utilitarian furniture on the ward, it was really luxuriously furnished - presumably at his own expense, as the NHS would never have funded such extravagance. There was a leather-topped desk, intricately carved antique oak armchairs with leather seats, and what looked suspiciously like a drinks cabinet in the corner. On the walls hung some rather fine watercolours, his University and College degrees behind glass in matching frames, together with photographs of him wearing the fur lined gown of the President of the Royal College of Surgeons of England. There was even one of him standing in a group of College dignitaries with the young Queen.

On the ward Johnny's relationship with his uncle had been formal and professional, just as one would expect between a house officer and his consultant. In this private environment though, he was completely relaxed, whereas I felt slightly ill at ease; partly because of my recent fall from grace, and also because of a concern that Sir William was about to allocate some extra duties to us. The boss, however, appeared either to have forgotten the recent incident on the ward, or decided that nothing more needed to be said on the matter. He spent some time showing us round the room, speaking of the various occasions when the photographs were taken and telling us the names and backgrounds of some of the other surgeons depicted. Finally he turned to us.

"Well, I think you boys wanted to talk to me."

Johnny and I looked at each other, wondering which of us should voice our concerns. I had imagined that Johnny would speak up but to my surprise, he left it to me. I wondered how I should begin.

"We are grateful to you, Sir, for sparing us some of your time. The reason that we wished to see you was that we feel that we need some advice, and since we know that you must had dozens of housemen working for you over the years, we feel that you will be able to give us the benefit of your experience."

Somehow the words seemed rather formal and inappropriate. I wondered if I was sounding as much of a creep as Simon, but battled on regardless.

"The truth is that we both feel that we have struggled during this first week of our job. The change from student to pre-registration house officer has not come as easily as we thought it would, and neither of us feel that we are performing very well."

"In what way?" Sir William asked.

"Speaking for myself," I said, "I feel that I just can't keep up with the number of duties that are allocated to me, at least if I am to do them justice and perform them properly. I feel as if I'm drowning in all the jobs that there are to do. When I go on to the ward in the morning, there may be six or seven tasks waiting for me to complete. By lunchtime though, having completed only half of them, there will have been so many interruptions - each bringing in more work - that I find myself way behind schedule, now with ten or twelve jobs outstanding. Frankly, I don't feel able to cope. We wondered if you would be able to advise us or guide us as to how to perform more effectively."

Sir William smiled. "Well, I'm glad that you feel able to come and discuss it with me, but I can't say that I've noticed any problems; whenever I have been on the ward, everything has appeared to be well organised. It is true that the transition from student to doctor can be a difficult one - and, certainly, being a house officer can be very stressful and tiring, particularly at the beginning - but I can assure you that it does get easier with time. When you've been in the job a little longer I'm sure you'll cope." He smiled and started to reminisce. "I remember when I was a house officer at the London Hospital, down the Mile End Road in the East End of the city, how hard we worked, both on the wards and in the theatres. Two consultants had to share one registrar and a single house officer in those days, you know, which meant that the house officers got a lot of responsibility; much more than house officers today. We received no pay at all; indeed we had to pay for our lodgings, so we actually ended up out of pocket for the honour of working for the hospital! But it was a marvellous experience and the patients there were the salt of the earth, mainly dockers working on the London waterfront. They had to be tough and able to tolerate some rough treatment too, as anaesthetics were nothing like as good as they are today."

He became wistful. "We had some good times as well though, and some wonderful colleagues too, people that became friends for life. Harry James was one; he's now a professor in Newcastle." He pointed to a young dark haired man on the second row of one of his group photographs. "He married a sister on Flanagan ward. What was she called...? Yes, I remember now, she was called Harriet, a pretty little thing she was. She was Harriet Dawkins before she was married. Then there was James Doherty. He became a surgeon as well. We used to compete for the same jobs when we were training and I still see him from time to time when I'm examining for the final examination at the Royal College in London. Then there was Neil Hancock - he was quite wild when he was young and got up to all sorts of tricks. Once he captured a lamb and put it in the medical superintendent's garden...there was a great fuss about that, as you can imagine! It kept the medical superintendent and his wife awake, bleating away all night, crying for its mother. Would you believe he is now the most boring man you could possibly imagine? He's a physician, specialising in caring for geriatric patients in Brighton."

He was lost in his memories and we were making no progress. I tried to bring the conversation back to our own problems of how to perform more effectively and how to avoid embarrassing episodes. I hadn't wished to tell him about the mistakes I had made during the previous week but I did admit to the error in taking blood from the drip arm, in an attempt to focus him on giving us some constructive advice. He laughed heartily when he heard that the technician had rung me with the very low haemoglobin and a potassium level that was incompatible with life.

"You won't get it right all the time - indeed, it is unrealistic to expect never to make any errors," he said. "If you set your sights on being perfect, you will make your life unbearable. You have to be humble. You have to have humility...that's what I was trying to indicate to you during the ward round just now, Lambert. An arrogant surgeon is a danger to his patients. The surgeon who doesn't know his limits is a liability. Everyone is bound to make a few mistakes; it's inevitable. The secret is to make sure you learn from them, to avoid making the same mistake twice. That's why I'm delighted that you've come to see me about this, as it shows me that you're willing to learn. Now, before you go, I've got a favour to ask."

Inwardly, I groaned. Yet more jobs to be heaped on our shoulders, I thought; but I need not have been concerned.

"As you will know, I am very keen on my garden and like to grow vegetables in my spare time for the local shows. The hospital late summer fête is to be held in about a fortnight, and I would be grateful if you two would keep an eye on my marrows for me. I'm afraid I shall be away for the next two weekends and don't want them to be neglected. I've got some college business in London to which I must attend and I wonder if you would be kind enough to nurture them for me? The attention given to them in the last couple of weeks before the show is critical. I've won prizes in two of the last three years and would very much like to make it a hat trick of wins. Unfortunately, this year my best marrow is not quite up to scratch; we have had a long cool summer and the marrow really needs a bit of intensive care, ideally a settled spell of warm weather. I would be very grateful if you could help me with it when I'm away at the weekends."

The task did not sound too onerous and would be a welcome diversion from work on the wards so we readily agreed; not that it would have been politic to do anything else! As far as a houseman is concerned, what your consultant boss wants, your consultant boss gets! He went on to describe the attention that the marrows required and to give us extremely detailed written instructions on their feeding, watering and general care. The time and care given to the marrows seemed to be every bit as important to him as the time and care that he lavished on his patients. We assured him that we would be extremely attentive and that he had no reason to be concerned.

It seemed the interview was over, and Sir William got up and escorted us to the door.

"Anyway, I hope that this little chat has helped you both. I am pleased that you came to see me. Remember that you should never be afraid to ask for help. My door is always open."

Johnny and I walked slowly back to the office on the female ward. We sat down, looking and feeling rather glum.

"Well," I said, "that was a complete waste of time. We must have been in there thirty minutes or more, we've heard some amusing anecdotes, but got no useful advice whatsoever."

"I honestly felt that Uncle Bill would have been a bit more help than that," said Johnny, slightly apologetically. "I suppose he comes from a different generation and that life in hospital was different when he was on the house." We sat in silence for a moment or two, feeling that there was nothing that we could do except to soldier on as best we could, hoping that we would cope better with the demands of the job with the passage of time and as we gained experience.

Sister Rutherford entered the office and was quick to notice that we both looked somewhat dejected. "Why so glum?" she questioned cheerfully. "You both look as if you've lost a month's wages."

It would have been easy to say "Nothing's the matter at all, Sister," but I remembered what had been said about the help that experienced ward sisters could give to house officers. Whilst there was no way I would have shared my troubles with Sister Ashbrook, it was different with Sister Rutherford. She listened sympathetically to what we had to say and expressed regret that we hadn't had a more constructive meeting with Sir William.

"I'm not sure that I'm the right person to help," she said, "but I have no doubt at all that a chat with Mr Khan would be beneficial. It is not his personality to volunteer to help - he would be afraid that you might feel that he was interfering -but if you were to approach him, I am certain he would be able to give you some constructive suggestions."

Since the alternative was to struggle on, drowning in our workload, we decided that nothing would be lost if we took her advice.

Chapter 9

The second week in the job proved to be just as difficult as the first. From morn 'til night I went round in circles, seemingly chasing shadows: dashing from one job to the next, constantly being interrupted, and reacting as best as I could to the various challenges and obstructions placed in my path. Although I made an early start each morning it was usually ten or eleven pm before my duties were complete, yet I was still woken once or twice in the night to attend to some problem on the ward, often something that I had overlooked during the day. I became increasingly tired, disillusioned, and seriously concerned that I would be unable to see the job through to its conclusion in six months time. Following the frustrating and disappointing meeting with Sir William, the need to seek advice from Mr Khan became an imperative. Fortunately, the opportunity to discuss matters with him arose a few days later.

The second weekend arrived and thankfully the pace of the clinical work again slackened. We had been told that Mr Potts could be relied upon to stay away from the hospital on Saturdays and Sundays unless one of his patients was particularly unwell, but that Sir William often came in on a Saturday morning. This was generally regarded, by both the nursing staff and the junior medical staff, as a hindrance, since - unless there was a difficult clinical problem that required the advice of a consultant - it simply interrupted the morning's routine and delayed the time by which the work was completed. Nominally, he came in to check if there were any seriously ill patients that required his advice, but in practice it was mainly for a coffee and a chat. He was a bachelor, he lived onsite, and, had he been asked, he would probably have agreed that he regarded it largely as a social visit.

Unless it was an urgency weekend, one of the house officers on each unit was permitted to go off duty on Saturday lunchtime and was not required to be back until Monday morning; although in practice, most stayed in the hospital for the weekend, simply because they did not have accommodation of their own and lived at a distance from their parent's homes. The responsibility of the Surgical Five house officer who remained on duty was to care for the patients of both consultants over the weekend, and also to admit three or four patients for Sir William's Monday morning list.

On the Saturday morning, Johnny and I had separate duties to perform. He went with Simon to the theatre and assisted the senior registrar with an operating list. Meanwhile, Mr Khan and I undertook a ward round, reviewing the patients of both consultants. By noon however, Johnny and I were able to sit down in the office with Mr Khan, eager to seek his advice about the problems that we had encountered. We apologised for detaining him, but it was typical of him that he seemed pleased to help. I explained, as I had explained previously to Sir William, that we had experienced many difficulties settling in, felt that we had not been adequately prepared as students for the job expected of us and knew that we weren't coping with the workload. It was difficult to describe to him exactly how I felt. The tiredness was not entirely physical. I was young, healthy and reasonably fit, and being on my feet for sixteen or eighteen hours a day was not a problem. Partly it was mental - living on my nerves, constantly fretting that I had overlooked an important part of a patient's management, lacking confidence in my own ability and anxious that a decision that I had taken was inappropriate or that a practical procedure I had performed would in some way put a patient at risk. But mainly it was due to sleep deprivation. I never got a decent nights rest. Sleep was elusive due to the concerns and anxieties constantly in my mind. And when I did fall asleep, I was woken either by the phone or by my bleep demanding my presence on the ward. The result was that my brain felt dulled, my mental reactions slow and I had difficulty concentrating on the job in hand; all of which increased the probability that I would make mistakes. I mentioned that Johnny and I had already tried to discuss the matter with Sir William, but unfortunately had learned nothing of value from him. We had merely stimulated him to reminisce about his own time as a house officer.

Mr Khan laughed. "You must forgive him," he said. "Those were very different days. In Sir William's time as a house officer, the number of drugs in use was very limited and those that were available were not very effective. Those were the days before penicillin - indeed, at that time there were no antibiotics at all, and no diuretics. In fact, there was morphine for pain, chloral hydrate for patients who couldn't sleep, digitalis was the only drug available for heart conditions - and that was about it. Doctors didn't carry bleeps and patients didn't have cardiac arrests. If the heart stopped beating, they died. Also, believe it or not, if a patient had a hernia repair, they stayed in hospital for fourteen days, seven of them on bed rest, so the turnover of patients on the ward was a fraction of what it is today. If I am going to help you, you must tell me more precisely what aspect of the job you are worried about. I actually feel you have coped with your first fortnight as well as could be expected. Many new house officers when they first arrive cause considerably more chaos than you two have in your first two weeks, and in all honesty, I can't say I've noticed any particular problem. You must appreciate that the transition from student to doctor represents a fairly formidable challenge. No one finds it easy, particularly if you start on a busy surgical unit."

We explained to Mr Khan in some detail our problems, emphasising that the greatest difficulty was fitting all the tasks into the time available and our inability to complete any job without constant interruptions.

"Let me see if I can help you," he commenced. "You are absolutely right, of course. Time management is of the essence, and it is all down to good organisation. Let me try to give you a few examples. Inevitably, a great deal of your time is spent in filling in forms; forms to request X-rays, forms for blood tests, forms for bacteriology tests, routine forms when patients are admitted and discharged. Whenever possible, try to do them in advance. You are given the names and hospital numbers of all the patients who will be admitted from the waiting list before they actually arrive on the ward. Today is Saturday, but you already know now who is coming in each day next week as an elective admission. You can anticipate the investigations that they will require and write out the X-ray and laboratory request cards over the weekend whilst it is quiet. Similarly with the operating lists. You already know which patients are coming in on Tuesday for the Wednesday list and on Thursday for the Friday list, so make out the lists in advance. Occasionally you will have to make a late adjustment if a patient cancels or if an additional patient is added - but, with advanced planning, you should always get the list to the secretaries in time and never be left in the position of having to write out half a dozen operating lists that you have to circulate to the wards yourself.

One of the problems for hospital doctors, and not just for housemen," he added, "is getting enough sleep. You will not work effectively if you are exhausted and you will be more likely to make mistakes. Inevitably you are going to get called from time to time, from your nice warm beds to the ward in the middle of the night. That cannot be completely prevented, but it is possible to reduce the number of times that this happens. Every night before turning in, visit each of the wards and quickly review every patient with the night sister or staff nurse. It may take a quarter of an hour or twenty minutes but it will dramatically reduce the chance of being called back to the ward after you have gone to bed. When going round, make sure that all the patients are written up for night sedation. There is nothing more irritating than to be woken yourself at two or three in the morning to be told that someone else can't sleep, and then having to drag yourself to the ward to spend twenty seconds writing up a prescription that could have been written before you turned in! By the time you get back to bed you will be wide-awake. It is probably best to prescribe night sedation for every patient. If you ask if a patient wants a sleeping tablet, many of them they will say that they don't need one; but it can be noisy on a hospital ward at night and patients who sleep well at home will not necessarily do so in hospital. Apart from any noise the nurses make, there are bound to be a few snorers, even on the female ward. Whilst doing your evening round, also check that the intravenous drips are running satisfactorily and that the night staff know which drips need to be replaced if they fail, and which don't. Some patients are having infusions because they are short of blood or fluid. Obviously these need to be maintained through the night. However many other patients are receiving infusions because they are only taking limited fluids by mouth, perhaps after an operation or in preparation for surgery the next day. Such a drip doesn't need to be replaced during the night. You don't take a drink during the night and neither need they.

While we are talking about sleep, remember what your mothers used to tell you about going to bed at night. Mine used to say, 'one hour at night is worth two in the morning'. Sometimes, when the day's work is done, it is too easy to collapse into an easy chair in the residency and sit chatting - perhaps grumbling - about the workload and how tired you are, when in fact you could be in bed and catching up on your sleep."

Mr Khan then went on to discuss teamwork. "Paul, you have been appointed as house officer to Mr Potts - Johnny, you as house officer to Sir William - but its far better if you regard yourselves as two house officers jointly caring for all the patients on the Surgical Five unit. Work together as a team. When you are both on a consultant ward round, one of you will be busy presenting the patient's details to the boss, but the other should not be twiddling his thumbs. He can be recording the consultation and the management decisions in the notes, and if any investigations are requested, he can be writing up the appropriate investigation cards. Then when the ward round is over all the jobs generated on the round will have been done, instead of still waiting for one of you to do them. There are other ways you will benefit by working as a team. Generally, the occasion when you will lose most sleep will be when you work overnight in Casualty. I would particularly recommend that after one of you has done that duty, you arrange for him to have the next night undisturbed. Tell the wards and the switchboard that the other house officer is on call, switch off the bleep, take the bedside telephone off the hook and ensure that you catch up on your sleep."

Every one of Mr Khan's suggestions made complete sense, and as he continued I was already beginning to feel more optimistic. It was easy to see how we could be better organised - indeed, I wondered why we had not thought of some of these solutions ourselves. Perhaps we would have done had we not both been so tired! Some of the advice that he gave related to the bleeps.

"Don't let the bleep rule your life. If you're with a patient, perhaps during a consultation, and the bleep goes, it is disrupting to you and the patient if you immediately dash off to answer the phone. Often there will be a student nurse or a medical student around who can answer the bleep for you; ask them to do so and take a message for you. They will normally be quite happy to do it, and it's good experience for them. Also, when you are bleeped, try, if possible, to complete the job you are doing before you move on to the next. The call will often be about a matter which is not urgent and which you can fit into the schedule that you've already got planned for yourself. Anyway, as I said at the beginning, you both appear to have performed perfectly well in the last couple of weeks; better perhaps than many others I have known. Keep it up - but if you feel you have problems, please do not hesitate to come and tell me about them. I want you both to work hard but also to be happy on the unit. Remember," he added with a smile, "it is in my best interests for you to work effectively. If the house officers perform well, it makes my life as a registrar so much easier."

Johnny and I thanked Mr Khan for taking the time with us. We both realised the advice which we had received was based on considerable experience and could already appreciate that it would be of tremendous benefit to us in the weeks ahead. We went to lunch in a much more optimistic frame of mind.

In the afternoon, we decided that it was time to fulfil our promise to Sir William and to attend to his vegetable marrows. Sir William's house had originally been the lodge to an old hall, which had long since had been demolished to make room for the hospital. It adjoined one of the city's municipal parks but was separated from it by a high fence, presumably to protect it from the local youths. It had a garden, amounting roughly to half an acre, which was immaculately maintained and was clearly Sir William's pride and joy. We walked round the side of the house and found ourselves on a small covered veranda boasting an old bamboo easy-chair surrounded by tubs and troughs, overflowing with late summer colour; where no doubt Sir William sat and rested, admiring his handiwork, when the day's work was done. A gravel path led down the garden with a neatly clipped lawn to one side, beyond which were mature apple and pear trees, laden with fruit. Within the lawn was a circular bed of magnificent roses in full bloom, no doubt the source of Sir William's buttonholes. On the other side of the path was a well-maintained herbaceous border, again ablaze with colour. Dianthus, oxalis and lavender occupied the front of the border and behind them achillea, verbascum, dahlias and chrysanthemums jostled for space with the delphiniums. Further back, shrubs such as fuchsias, maples and spirea added different textures and extra colour. Obviously Sir William lavished just as much attention on his garden as he did on his patients.

Beyond the flower bed, furthest from the house, was the vegetable plot, and it was clear that this was where the consultant devoted his greatest efforts. Parts were free of plants, having been harvested of the early summer vegetables - presumably broad beans and lettuces - but even these areas had already been covered in compost to prepare the ground for the following season. Other areas held the mid season and autumn crops such as the peas, carrots, dwarf and runner beans, and these were still being harvested. All looked extremely healthy and there was not a weed to be seen between the various rows. I took the liberty of plucking a pod of peas to taste, and then helped myself to a few more, as they tasted so good.

"You had better take those empty pods back to the residency or hide them in the compost heap," said Johnny, "and remove all evidence of your crime."

At the far end of the plot the turnips, sprouts and swedes were waiting to be cropped in the wintertime. In pride of place, in the sunniest part of the vegetable garden, were the marrows. There were three of them and it was difficult to decide which was the best. They were about four feet long and so wide that it would have been impossible to encircle them with both arms. Light green in colour, with broader stripes of a rich darker green along their length, they rested on purpose-built net hammocks that held them off the ground, protecting them from slugs and preventing any soiling or discolouration of their skins from pressure from the ground. The elasticated net material from which the hammocks had been made bore a remarkable similarity to the elastic hosiery used on our patients after operations on their varicose veins. The marrows were growing in the most beautifully fertile, fibrous, soil.

Sir William had given us written instructions, typed no doubt by the hospital secretaries, detailing exactly how to water the marrows and precisely how much feed to give them. There were two different feeds; a granular general fertiliser, and a liquid one to be diluted and applied with a watering can. This apparently contained the trace elements necessary to remedy any deficiencies in the soil. It was akin to dispensing vitamins and tonics to frail or malnourished patients on the ward, except these were by no means frail specimens. They were giants, bursting with health. Rather, it was like giving performance-enhancing drugs to weightlifters!

We had also been asked to look carefully for any evidence of slug activity and to lay slug pellets if necessary, and aditionally we had been instructed to check that the hammocks were giving adequate support to the marrows, keeping them off the ground and preventing any stretching of the stalk. We dutifully fulfilled these tasks. It was impossible not to admire and be impressed by the size, colour and texture of such magnificent specimens. They certainly impressed Johnny.

"They're fantastic," he said. "I've absolutely no doubt they will win First Prize at the hospital's summer fête."

"I'm not so sure," I replied. "I've been to one or two of these fruit and vegetable shows and some of the exhibits are quite amazing. I've seen carrots two feet long and beautifully symmetrical. Some gardeners grow them in especially designed plastic drainpipes in a mixture of sand, compost and nutrients. I've seen leeks as thick as a man's arm, cauliflowers as big as footballs, and on occasion I've seen marrows larger than these." At first, Johnny was disinclined to believe me, but I assured him it was true.

"Then in that case, I think perhaps we should give Uncle Bill's marrows a bit of a helping hand," said Johnny.

"Meaning?" I asked.

"Well we could select one - perhaps this one in the centre is the pick of the bunch - and drip feed it for twenty-four hours or so, get it to swell up a bit. If we infuse the marrow with two or three litres of saline, we could really plump it up. We're not overlooked here, so no one would know. The potting shed protects it from being seen by anyone in the park and it can't be seen from the hospital because of the house."

"I'm not sure that's wise." I said. "Your Uncle has old fashioned values. I doubt that he would approve."

"I'm sure that he wouldn't. He's not the sort of person who would dream of doing anything underhand. But you know how badly he wants to win, and he's not going to find out, is he?"

I was not at all sure and had a premonition that something would go wrong. Perhaps the infused fluid would drip back out of the puncture wound, making the interference obvious, or worse, we might even kill the marrow. But Johnny's mind was decided.

"Come on," he said, "we need to get a few bits of equipment."

We slipped back to the ward and returned with a drip stand, infusion tubing, four large bags each containing two pints of saline, and a long needle. Johnny carefully inserted the needle into the marrow just at the point where the stalk was attached so that it would be invisible thereafter, and I rigged up the drip stand, delivery set and first saline bag. The drip worked beautifully and the bag was empty within a few minutes, although there was no visible change in the outward appearance of the marrow. The infusion slowed when we infused the second bag, although there was still no obvious change in the marrow's size. Johnny suggested that it might take a little time for the skin to stretch and said he would return later to infuse the third and fourth bags.

That evening we joined the other house officers, both medical and surgical, in the residency, and chatted about our early experiences as house officers. The residency was situated in a detached block some fifty yards from the main hospital buildings, connected by a covered walkway. It had been so hectic during the first two weeks that I had spent very little time there, but it proved to be a pleasant place with a warm and friendly atmosphere where the residents could relax when time allowed. Each doctor had his own small room, simply furnished with a single bed, chest of drawers, wardrobe and desk. Each had a washbasin. The bathrooms were communal, but adequate in number. The heart of the residency was the main lounge, a large room with old but comfortable armchairs and settees haphazardly scattered throughout. At the far end was a bar where beer was available on a 'serve yourself' basis. An honesty book was provided for individuals to record their alcoholic intake, bar bills being settled at the end of each month, and to my surprise the amount of beer drunk never failed to tally with the entries in the book. As the weeks rolled by, I discovered that mine was one of the smaller accounts that resulted. The beer was provided at a discount price by a local brewery. Alcohol was available to patients as well. We regularly prescribed a bottle of brown ale to be taken during the evening, mainly for the male patients though also occasionally for females, as an alternative to night sedation - a custom that has been lost over the years.

In addition to the main lounge there was a small television lounge, a snooker room, and two dining rooms, one designated for male doctors and one for female doctors. This arrangement that had been perpetuated by our predecessors seemed antiquated in the extreme and by common consent was immediately abandoned, which suited everyone, especially the catering staff.

A particular pleasure afforded to us in our own dining room was the service given by Bridget Connelly. Bridget, or "Bridie", as she was known to one and all, was in her fifties, came from County Kerry on the west coast of Ireland - as indeed did a number of our best nurses - and was the member of the staff who was in charge of our catering. She loved her job and, in turn, we appreciated the attention that she gave to us. She mothered us, fussed over our diets and chided us for rushing our meals. She regarded us as her family. Nothing was too much trouble for her. Each morning she provided a full English breakfast from a hot trolley. Lunch and dinner were wholesome meals, were nicely presented, and she was always careful to leave hot food for doctors who were late for meals, which was essential given the unpredictable nature of our work. Bridie regarded feeding young doctors as being just as important as attending to the needs of the patients and would try to prevent us returning to the ward mid-meal should we be bleeped to attend to a medical problem. "You finish your meal," she would say, "I'm sure the patient can wait. Who is going to look after them when you fall ill from missing your meals?" And anyone who used strong language at the dinner table was sharply reprimanded. "That's not good enough, young Sir. People look up to you. Don't you go letting yourself down."

The residency became my home for six months and during that time - like Sir William before me - my working colleagues were to become my life-long friends, whose careers I would follow with interest and about whom, no doubt, I would reminisce in due course, to the irritation of the next generation of junior doctors.

That evening, there was an informal meeting of those resident doctors who had decided to stay in the hospital for the weekend. In practice this was the vast majority, as few had decided to go home so soon after starting the job. It was the custom that a President, Social Secretary and Treasurer should be elected. The role of the President was to call and chair any meetings that might be necessary, and also to represent the views of the resident doctors to the hospital administration or to the consultant body, should this ever prove necessary. The responsibility of the Social Secretary was to organise occasional social events. In practice, this amounted to making sure that the supply of beer to the mess did not fail, and arranging a residency party every two or three months. The role of the Treasurer was to ensure that bar bills were paid, that the brewery was reimbursed for barrels of beer provided, and that social events were self-funding. None of the jobs was regarded as particularly onerous.

In due course Johnny was unanimously appointed as the Mess President, as it was felt that his personality was appropriate for the job and that his family connections would facilitate any dialogue with the consultant body that might be required. Helen Leach - who as a medical student had combined a full social life with excellent academic achievements and who was currently working as a house officer for the Professor of Surgery - was appointed as Social Secretary, and the Treasurer's post went to John Probert, one of the house physicians. I was pleased, though not surprised, that no one nominated me for any of the jobs. If nominated it might have been difficult to say no, but I felt it would have been folly to take on an additional voluntary job, given the difficulty that I was experiencing coping with my workload.

There was then a general exchange of views on the experiences that we had shared during our first two weeks as doctors. By and large, it was felt that the house physicians had fared somewhat better than the house surgeons, probably due to the slower pace of life on the medical wards. Others had already received advice, usually from their consultants, on how to perform their house officer's duties efficiently, which largely concurred with the advice that we had received from Mr Khan. It seemed inexplicable that we had not been better prepared for the house officer role. There was no justification for 'throwing us in at the deep end' when the lessons we were now learning the hard way could have been taught to us in advance. There was an obvious, urgent and overwhelming need for some form of induction programme. It was a mystery to us why nothing of that sort had been arranged and it was agreed that Johnny, as the new Mess President, should propose to the consultants the development of an induction programme for incoming house officers.

The next day I wasn't able to accompany Johnny to Sir William's garden as I was busy clerking Mr Potts' new admissions but he reported that all was well, that the marrow we had infused looked plumper and healthier than before, and he suggested that we review the situation next weekend, to see whether a further infusion was necessary.

The following Saturday, therefore, (Johnny having confirmed that Sir William was indeed going to London to attend a meeting of Royal College of Surgeons), he and I went to review the situation in the vegetable garden. It was satisfying to observe that, thanks to our administrations, the centre marrow had grown considerably both in length and breadth over the previous seven days. My concern that the saline might have killed the marrow was clearly unfounded. With its extra weight it now nearly touched the ground despite the support from the hammock and we saw that, since our last visit, Sir William had placed straw underneath it for added protection. The marrow's skin appeared to have ripened and the slight wrinkles that there had existed previously had filled and disappeared. We felt that the marrow's colour had improved too, with a greater distinction between the darker and the lighter green stripes that passed along its length.

We fed and watered all three marrows as before and, as Sir William had instructed, placed some slug pellets around their stems and adjusted the hammocks to take the strain off the stalks. Johnny walked round the marrow in the centre and looked at it critically from all sides. Thanks to the treatment we had given it now significantly outshone its neighbours, and was clearly going to be the one that Sir William would select as his entry in the show.

"I think," he said after some deliberation and with the confidence that comes from complete ignorance of growing vegetables, "that it would benefit from one further top-up infusion."

I was less sure. I pointed out that we didn't want the marrow to win by such a margin that people became suspicious. However Johnny, as before, was adamant, and quickly overcame my objections. We returned to the ward and gathered together the equipment just as we had done the previous weekend. There was, however, a problem. On this occasion, perhaps not surprisingly, the stocks of saline in the ward storeroom were low and there was a danger that if we depleted them further there might be none left, should one of our patients need it.

"The nurses are a bit slow in replenishing their supplies!" said Johnny with pretence at innocence. "I think you had better have a word with Sister Ashbrook, Paul."

To avoid reducing the stocks further but also to avoid raising any suspicions on the ward, we took four big bags of dextrose sugar solution as an alternative. The last thing I wanted was a further confrontation with Sister.

"This will be even better than saline. Dextrose is pure carbohydrate," said Johnny. "Marrows are full of sugar so this should work a treat. These extra bags should guarantee first prize."

We set up the drip as before and ensured that it was running freely. Johnny said he would come back later that day to change the bags and review the situation on the Sunday before his Uncle returned. He needed to take the equipment back to the ward and remove any evidence that the marrow had been given a helping hand.

The day of the garden fête duly arrived and was blessed with glorious weather. It was a blazing hot day without a cloud in the sky, and the temperature rose by mid-afternoon to eighty degrees. Unfortunately, throughout the afternoon I was occupied with various problems on the ward and wasn't free to accompany Johnny to the show - but heard about the great day in considerable detail later.

Shortly after lunch, Sir William rang him to request his assistance to take the marrow from the garden to the marquee in the park where all the entries for the different categories of vegetable were to be displayed and judged. Working very slowly and gently, they cut the stalk, took the marrow out of its hammock, and placed it carefully on soft cushions in a large wheelbarrow. Apparently it was so heavy that the two of them needed all their strength to lift it. Taking great care to avoid any bumps in the path, the marrow was wheeled to the competition tent in the show ground, labelled, and placed on the trestle table that had been allocated for the marrows, cucumbers and pumpkins. Johnny was then obliged to walk round the rest of the show with Sir William, waiting for the judging to take place. Sir William was known to almost everyone there and stopped frequently to have a chat with colleagues, friends and acquaintances. Almost everyone asked about his marrows and offered him good wishes for another successful day. After a while Johnny excused himself, and walked around the various stalls and amusements. He threw cloth balls at plastic ducks, fished for prizes in the Lucky Wishing Well and took a turn on the Bottle Tombola. Having met a couple of nurses who, like him, were in need of a drink on such a warm day, he escorted them to the beer tent for some liquid refreshment. He stayed there for an hour or so until, late in the afternoon, he heard the public address system announce that the judges had completed their work and that the prize giving ceremony was about to commence. He finished his beer and then - conscious that he ought to be supporting his uncle rather than socialising with the nurses, and eager to see if the assistance that we had rendered the marrow would reap its unjust reward - he drifted back to the competition tent.

The heat in the marquee was stifling but Johnny was pleased to see that his uncle's marrow was larger than the others by some margin; indeed, it dwarfed the efforts of the other competitors. Furthermore, whereas the others had deep wrinkles in the skin, Sir William's marrow had a shining glossy skin and looked to be in the very best of health. It was certainly the most magnificent specimen on show and there was no doubt that there could only be one winner.

Judging of the root vegetables had been completed and the results of the peas and beans were being announced, as Johnny joined his uncle amongst the considerable crowd that had waited to see if the father figure of the hospital was once again destined to win the 'Best in Show' prize for his marrow. The judging of the marrows was to be the grand finale of the fête and there was a feeling of expectancy as the chief judge eventually moved to stand, microphone in hand, behind the tables upon which the cucumbers, courgettes, pumpkins and marrows lay. He announced the first, second and third prizes for the cucumbers first and then the three prizes for the courgettes. Each announcement was greeted with polite applause. He then moved to stand behind the pumpkins and was announcing the first prize when a short but loud rasping sound interrupted him - as if somebody had inadvertently passed wind. The judge stopped mid-sentence, but since all now seemed quiet, he continued. The winner of the pumpkin prize stepped forward to receive a rosette from the judge, who went on to announce the second and third place winners for the pumpkin prizes - but whilst doing so he was again interrupted two or three times by much louder, longer and this time somewhat moister sounds, which seemed to be coming from the marrow table. He looked anxiously at the marrows but spotted nothing amiss.

Finally, as the chief judge moved to the marrow table, the noise returned - louder, wetter, and now continuous. All the eyes in the crowd turned to search for its source, a source that unfortunately was now all too apparent. A mixture of foul yellow liquid and gas was belching from the base of Sir William's marrow; a patient with dysentery could not have performed better. Further, as the discharge continued, the marrow was visibly shrinking, its skin crinkling and collapsing. The judge and audience watched the spectacle with a mixture of amazement and horror, and handkerchiefs were taken to hold over noses as the marrow continued to shrivel and shrink until it was nothing more than an empty green sack in a sea of offensive yellow fluid. A foul stench filled the air.

There was a mixed reaction from the audience. Initially there was a gasp of surprise from the assembled throng but unfortunately someone started to laugh, and soon the entire crowd was roaring with laughter. Johnny was so horrified that he dared not look in Sir William's direction, but knew that his uncle must have been appalled, indeed humiliated, since everyone knew to whom this particular marrow belonged. The judge proved to be quick-thinking and cool-headed and, unfazed by the spectacle unfolding before him, rapidly regained his composure. Whilst waiting for the crowd to quieten - he had to call for silence at least twice - he calmly slipped the card that had been on the top of the pack in his hand to the bottom. He laid his hand on the marrow that had been the second largest and announced that this had won the first prize and subsequently gave the second prize to the marrow that would have been third.

"There will be no third prize for marrows this year," he announced.

After Johnny had completed his tale, I felt shocked and extremely guilty about my involvement in the escapade. Why had I allowed myself to get involved in such tomfoolery? Sir William had done nothing to deserve such a public humiliation; I knew that he would be mortified. Johnny, however, appeared to be quite relaxed about the whole affair and seemed to find the whole episode highly amusing.

He simply commented, "It must have been the combination of the sugar solution and the recent warm weather. We obviously introduced some bacteria with the fluid, and it fermented inside the marrow. Next time we'll stick to normal saline and improve our aseptic technique!"

Chapter 10

It was inevitable that the drama of the Late Summer Fête would dominate conversations and gossip in the hospital during the following week. Many of the staff had witnessed the demise of Sir William's marrow and had supposed, at least initially, that the disaster had been an Act of God. Unfortunately, all the members of the residency knew that the marrow had been doctored, as Johnny and I had made no secret of our visits to the vegetable plot during the previous two weekends. Inevitably, therefore, it was only a couple of days before it was widely known that there had been foul play and, thanks to the efficiency of the hospital grapevine, by Monday lunchtime everyone was talking about it. Two contrasting views emerged from the staff. Some regarded the event as a tremendous joke and I received a number of compliments on my part in the escapade. On the other hand, many felt that it was unkind, indeed inexcusable, to play such a trick on a kindly senior and well-respected figure. In many ways, these opposing views reflected the respective sentiments of Johnny and myself. Whilst Johnny had no regrets about the matter, I felt that Sir William must have been embarrassed and hurt, particularly as the events had unfolded so publicly. There had been no intention to cause distress, of course, but that did little to assuage my feelings of guilt. A further concern was that it seemed likely that it was only a matter of time before Sir William learned the truth about the cause of his exploding marrow, and my worst fears were confirmed during a ward round a few days later. By this time, even Johnny had begun to share my concerns that eventually his uncle would learn the truth and discover the names of the culprits. Whilst waiting in the office for him to arrive we both felt slightly ill at ease; but when he appeared for the round we relaxed when we saw that he was his usual charming self, and in his characteristic benevolent mood. As always, he wore a rose in his lapel, only quite small but beautifully formed, that no doubt had come from the rose garden we had admired on our way to his vegetable patch. Pending his arrival, we had, as usual, placed our bets on the number of suppositories that would be inserted during the course of the morning. There were two medical students with us on this occasion who also put money into the kitty, and one of them asked for clarification of the rules.

"Is it winner takes all?"

"Yes," said Johnny. "There isn't enough money in the pot to have a first and second prize."

"And what happens if nobody guesses correctly?"

"In that case, there is no winner and we have a rollover, with double the money in the kitty next time."

Once again Sister Rutherford's face displayed her disapproval, but she said nothing. Had she not been there a couple of the nurses might well have joined in the sweepstake, but with their nursing Sister present they were restrained from doing so.

On the ward round, Sir William was introduced to a slim and anxious looking forty-year-old factory worker, Ernest Singleton, who had been admitted from the waiting list to have surgery on his duodenal ulcer. During the discussion that ensued at the bedside, I learned another valuable lesson from Sir William; the concept of '*earning your operation*'. Johnny presented the patient's history to Sir William in the usual way. Mr Singleton had been experiencing a burning indigestion in the solar plexus area that troubled him for an hour or so after his evening meal. He needed to take alkaline mixtures such as bicarbonate of soda to relieve the symptoms. Very occasionally he would wake at one or two in the morning with the same indigestion, and would go downstairs to the kitchen to relieve it with a drink of milk. As always, Sir William questioned the patient in his thorough fashion, and during this interrogation it transpired that Mr Singleton had only suffered these symptoms for three or four months – and, while there was no doubt that the barium meal X-ray confirmed the presence of a duodenal ulcer, the patient had done very little to help to cure himself. He was still smoking thirty cigarettes a day, he continued to take irregular meals, and drank spirits every evening. He had not experienced any of the serious complications of ulcers, such as vomiting, perforation, or the type of bleeding that had threatened the life of Mr Quigley.

"You must make the patient earn their operation," Sir William said to us. "Mr Singleton has done little or nothing to try to cure the ulcer himself. He has not tried a gastric diet nor has he moderated his drinking or smoking habits, which may well have been responsible for the ulcer in the first place. Should you decide to operate on him, perhaps removing a portion of the stomach, you may well rid him of his ulcer, but afterwards it is highly unlikely that he will digest his food normally. Almost certainly he will be left with some fresh discomfort after meals. With his stomach reduced in size, he may only be able to take small meals, perhaps feeling bloated after just a single course - and these new symptoms may be quite severe and irreversible. A patient who has only had ulcer symptoms for three months will not thank you if your operation leaves him with some discomfort for the rest of his life. Having removed a portion of the stomach, you're never going to be able to replace it. In addition, you have subjected the patient to the risk of an operation that, whilst generally safe, still has a small associated mortality. Make the patient earn his operation," Sir William reiterated. "Often if a patient moderates his habits and takes an appropriate diet, he will be able to cure the ulcer himself and avoid an unpleasant operation. If not, and he continues to suffer unpleasant ulcer symptoms for three or four years, he will be quite understanding and tolerant if you leave him with some symptoms after the operation."

Mr Singleton, sitting in the bed at Sir William's side, heard all this advice, as was indeed intended. He clearly understood the point of the argument and was taking note of what was said.

"You mean to say, Doctor, that the operation itself may cause me to have some discomfort and some difficulty digesting food, and that it is possible that I might be able to cure the ulcer myself without an operation?"

"That's right," said Sir William. "If we do an operation for you, we will permanently alter the plumbing of your stomach. It will no longer be as the good Lord designed and I am afraid that it is highly unlikely that your digestion will go completely back to normal." We moved away from the patient's bed, but Sir William continued to expand on this theme.

"As surgeons get older they should get wiser, and mature like a good wine. You should not do an operation just because you can do an operation. Remember the old surgical adage: *A good surgeon knows how to perform a good operation, a better surgeon knows when not to operate at all.* Particularly, this is true for malignant disease. With your surgical skill and a good general anaesthetic you may well perform some brilliant and heroic operation - but if the cancer is so advanced that you cannot cure it, so that it continues to spread and kills the patient within three months, have you really helped by bringing your patient into hospital, giving them an anaesthetic and a painful operation from which it would take even a healthy patient six weeks to recover? Would he not have been happier having two months at home with his family? Remember it's the quality of life, not merely the quantity, which is important."

Sir William started to reminisce. "I remember when I was first appointed as a consultant here, more years ago than I care to remember. Having trained in London under a Professor who was an expert in gastric surgery, I had learned how to remove the whole of the stomach, and how to bridge the gap by joining the lower end of the gullet to the duodenum. As you know, cancer of the stomach is a very unpleasant disease from which most patients die - but the Professor had half a dozen patients who were cured by this operation, which was quite new at the time. I arrived here keen and eager to show what I could do and we admitted a man called George Newcombe. I shall never forget him. I opened his abdomen and found that he had a cancer of the stomach that I thought might be curable by removing the whole of his stomach. I did suspect that there might be some spread of the cancer to the liver but, as a young surgeon with a big ego, I decided to proceed with the new operation. It was a terrible decision and, although I felt guilty about it afterwards and had some sleepless nights, the one who really suffered was the patient. Everything that could go wrong went wrong. The gullet did not heal to the duodenum and he got a severe infection inside his belly. Because the gullet was leaking we were not able to feed him and he had a miserable death over the next five or six weeks. It taught me a lesson I shall never forget."

He turned to Sister Ashbrook. "I bet you remember George Newcombe, don't you Sister, or was it before your time?"

Sister, overlooking the fact that she was probably still in kindergarten when Sir William was appointed at the City General, answered politely "I think that must have been before my time, Sir, when Sister Bostock was here."

"Oh yes, Sister Bostock, I remember her so well. You are quite right; she was in charge of the male ward when I first arrived. She ran the ward with a rod of iron. I remember how she used to line up the nurses to inspect them each day when they came on duty...it was like watching a sergeant major inspect his troops on an army parade ground. Skirts to show no more than three inches of ankle, caps and aprons to be stiffly starched, not a hair to be visible beneath the nurse's cap and black shoes to be polished so that you could see your face mirrored in them. Those were happy days. She used to run the ward in military fashion too. Every bed had to be made with 'hospital corners', bedside cabinets had to be in exactly the right position and were not to display more than one vase of flowers, all of which had to be removed from the ward at night. Most of the patients were so afraid of her that they would only speak when spoken to and they all sat to attention whenever she passed. How things have changed over the years."

Much as I enjoyed Sir William's ward rounds, it was frustrating that he would drift away from important clinical matters and would happily digress for long periods. Whilst some of his reminisces were quite interesting, others were less so, particularly if you had heard them a couple of times before. When this happened I felt that it was Simon's, or possibly Johnny's responsibility, to guide him gently and surreptitiously back to clinical matters. I looked across to Simon and tried to pass a non-verbal message to him but he was clearly not prepared to take the initiative, despite the fact that, having worked for Sir William for two years, he must inevitably have heard these old stories on numerous occasions. My attention began to wander and I decided to concentrate again when Sir William returned to clinical matters. I inched closer to Johnny, wondering how many investigation cards he had transferred across to his left hand coat pocket, hoping that exactly ten would be there by the end of the round. There appeared to be half a dozen or more there already, but exactly how many I could not be sure.

Looking around the group of doctors and nurses who were accompanying Sir William on the ward round, I noticed Nurse Meredith standing next to Sister Ashbrook. Since we both worked on the same ward I had obviously seen her regularly, and had spoken to her several times about our patients, but each time this had occurred a subtle change came over me. There was something about her that attracted me. Whenever I spoke with her I felt slightly anxious, slightly hesitant, and a little ill at ease. I got butterflies in my stomach and was conscious of my heart thumping in my chest. Somehow, I felt more alive. What was it about her? I looked across at her again. In many ways she was quite unremarkable, the sort of girl you could pass in the street and not really notice. She was of average height, slim, with a neat figure and mousy brown hair that was held neatly under her nurse's cap. Was it just that she had been kind to me and come to my rescue when I was struggling with Mr Quigley's nasogastric tube during my first week on the ward? No, there was more to it than that. I admired the way that she handled herself on the ward. She moved easily through the sick patients with a smile here and a kind word there. In many ways she appeared to be a younger version of Sister Rutherford, who was so lovely to the patients on the female ward. It struck me that she seemed at ease with herself, content with her lot, enjoying her work, undertaking her job without any fuss or bother and certainly not drawing attention to herself in any way. I looked at her face. She had a fresh complexion and blue eyes but she could not be described as a classic beauty. It was not a face that you would see on the front page of a fashion magazine - but it was one, nevertheless, that I found highly attractive.

Quite suddenly she caught my eye and smiled. I realised that I must have been staring at her. How long I had been looking at her I did not know, but I was certainly oblivious to what Sir William was saying. I managed half a smile in return but later reflected that this may well have had the appearance of a grimace. I turned and looked away, feeling embarrassed. Again, I was aware of the butterflies and the heartbeat in my chest, and knew that my face had become flushed. I tried to concentrate again on what Sir William was saying but he was still reminiscing on surgical times gone by, when he was a trainee surgeon. I decided to risk another glance at Nurse Meredith. She must have been waiting for me to do so, because she immediately caught my eye. She seemed to be amused at my embarrassment but her face was soft and calm, in no way angry, and again I benefited from one of her gentle smiles. It was a beautiful smile, full of warmth and friendship. It struck me again that she was at ease with herself and quite comfortable with the silent communication occurring between us, whereas my heart was thumping so hard that I feared everyone on the ward round must hear it.

I recalled that Sir William had chided me previously for lack of attention on his ward round and thought it wise to stop my daydreaming, so I forced myself to concentrate on what he was saying. He was now reflecting on how surgical practice had changed over the years, and the need for surgeons to change with the times.

"Michael Stanbury was a medical student with me who went on to become a chest surgeon in Edinburgh. When he was first appointed a consultant, almost all the operations he performed were for tuberculosis, rib resections for drainage of empyemas[1] and the like. Then, of course, along came all the anti-tuberculosis drugs, and that sort of surgical practice simply melted away. It just wasn't needed any more. Like all thoracic surgeons he then started to perform resections for lung cancer, sometimes just removing one lobe of the lung, sometimes the whole lung. There is a growing weight of evidence, you know, that suggests that cigarette smoking is the principle cause of the increase in lung cancer that we have seen recently." He looked hard at Johnny and I. "I hope neither of you two smoke."

Without waiting for a reply, he turned to the nurses and added, "It saddens me to see how many young nurses have started to smoke too. It is easy to start a habit such as smoking, but nothing like so easy to stop." I noticed that he was too much of a gentleman to ask specifically if any of them did smoke, which was as well, since I knew that at least two of them did.

---

1 A collection of pus in the chest

I looked up and noticed that whilst Sir William had been speaking, Sister Ashbrook had dispatched Nurse Meredith to the office. Was there a genuine job for her to do there, or had Sister spotted the exchange between the two of us and decided to intervene?

We had been standing on one spot for half an hour or more and eventually the ward round did get moving again, but thanks to Sir William's tales of surgical days of old, we were significantly behind schedule when we finally arrived at the last bed on the ward. It was occupied by a man in his early thirties who had been admitted the previous day with a large abscess in his left armpit. There was a swelling at least the size of a hen's egg that was bright red, warm to the touch and extremely tender. Because of the pain, he was quite unable to let his arm hang by his side.

Sir William turned to Johnny. "Now young man," he said, "this clearly is a nasty abscess, but tell me - what precisely is an abscess? What's it made of?"

I looked up in surprise. This was an unusual development. There is a tradition in British hospitals - unwritten, but a tradition nonetheless - that junior doctors are not asked searching questions by consultants in the presence of medical students. Custom and practice is that medical students are asked first, and only if they are unable to answer is the question then addressed to one of the medical staff. This saves any embarrassment should the answer be known by the student but not by the qualified doctor.

In this case the answer to the question was easy enough, and Johnny had no hesitation in replying "It's a collection of pus, Sir."

Sir William turned to me. "That's right. Now, Lambert, what exactly is pus - of what does it comprise?" Again this was a simple enough question, and I had no difficulty in responding.

"It's the product of the digestion of the blood and tissues Sir, due to infection."

"Correct." Then, turning to Johnny he asked his next question. "And what causes the infection?"

"Bacteria, Sir - in this case, probably staphylococci."

For some reason that I did not understand, the questions were being asked alternately to Johnny and myself, and Sister and the nurses were beginning to pay particular attention; persistent probing and interrogation like this was not Sir William's usual style at all. Sir William continued, now addressing me.

"And how do these bacteria get into the tissues?"

"Presumably via a breach in the skin, Sir."

"Yes, but the skin is a very strong thick layer, isn't it? It should be impermeable to bacteria."

Suddenly I saw, with total clarity, exactly where this questioning was going. With horror I realised that I could predict exactly the question that I was going to be asked next.

"And if the abscess remains untreated, Lambert, what happens next?"

"The pressure within it increases and the patient feels an increasing amount of pain, Sir."

"And if the pressure goes untreated, Dr Nolan, what will happen as a result?"

"The abscess will burst, Sir," replied Johnny in a flat voice, for he too had appreciated the purpose of this interrogation.

"Yes," said Sir William sternly. "The abscess will burst and a large volume of creamy yellow pus and foul-smelling gas will escape, and the skin over the abscess will collapse."

It was now painfully obvious to everyone present that Sir William realised why his prize marrow had exploded during the prize giving ceremony at the hospital fête. Further, since the grilling had been directed at both Johnny and myself he also knew that we were both involved, otherwise his questions would have been addressed solely to Johnny. Whilst I had not initiated the interference with the marrow I had been a willing and active participant in the escapade, and now deeply regretted my involvement.

As was usual at the end of his ward round, Sir William stopped in the office for a cup of coffee with Sister and his medical colleagues, during which Johnny and I were notably subdued. Simon however was ebullient, had a very self-satisfied expression on his face, and was clearly enjoying our discomfort. The more I saw of our senior registrar, the more he irritated me and the more I disliked him. When Sir William had finished his drink, he rose to leave the office. I stopped him at the office door.

"May I please have a quiet word with you, Sir, in private?"

"I think that would be a good idea. Would that nephew of mine like to come as well, do you think?"

Johnny had already joined us at the door. "Yes Sir, I would."

We walked in silence to his office, where Sir William made himself comfortable in the armchair behind the leather-bound desk. He invited us to sit opposite him.

"Now," he said quietly, "I think you said you had something to say to me."

"Sir," I began, "I should like to apologise for interfering with the marrow. At the time it seemed no more than a silly prank and we really didn't mean to do any harm. I was horrified when I heard what had happened during the prize-giving ceremony and realise how embarrassing it must have been for you. I do recognise that it was a childish thing to do, and I am truly very sorry."

Johnny was quick to intervene in an attempt to take the bulk of the blame. "I must confess that it was my idea and that I was the prime mover. I actually had to persuade Dr Lambert to join in, so you should not be blaming him." There was a moment's pause. Sir William's face normally held a gentle, relaxed expression, but he now looked stern and serious.

"I want you to know that at the time I was extremely upset, but I now understand that everybody in the hospital knows exactly what happened and why. My greatest concern was that people might think that I had tried to cheat by inflating the size of the marrow but it appears that since the fête, I have been the only person in the hospital not to know the truth; that it was in fact you two. So, fortunately, no real harm has been done." There was a long pause; then he seemed to relax and smile.

"You have obviously caused a lot of amusement in the hospital, albeit at my expense, and some good did come out of the day. Despite the sensation with the exploding marrow, I did manage to win some prizes at the fête. I had first prize for the longest carrot and, for the first time ever, won a prize for a truss of tomatoes. You two are full of tricks, aren't you? Your marking of operation sites on patients was very entertaining for the theatre staff recently, particularly the patient with piles, and I confess that the theatre sister had to explain to me what was meant by a 'roast beef toe'. Perhaps if I had ever married and had children, I would have known! However, I thought that marking my boots 'L' and 'R' was a step too far. I'm not quite so old that I need that sort of assistance." I looked sharply at Johnny because this was news to me, and it did seem a little unkind.

Sir William continued. "I suppose medical students and junior doctors have always got up to silly japes. I confess that as a young man I played my fair share of foolish tricks..." He embarked on a long and convoluted story that involved him putting earwigs under the door of Matron's bedroom when he was a resident doctor.

I relaxed. Sir William wasn't a bad sort at all; a bit old fashioned, maybe, but kindly and benevolent and obviously quick to forgive. He was much liked by all his patients too, no doubt because his bedside manner was superb. It was no wonder that he was so well respected in the hospital.

He finished his story. "Well," he said, "you two had better get back to your duties now. By the way, the last time you were in this office you told me that you were finding it a little difficult to settle into your new duties. Is it easier now, following our little chat?"

Johnny and I responded in unison, "Yes Sir, it is. Thank you, Sir." It is true that we were finding it easier - although in truth this was due to Mr Khan's advice, not Sir William's.

Chapter 11

As the weeks passed, Johnny and I gradually began to feel more settled and comfortable in the jobs that we were doing. Certainly the hours that we worked were long, we were on our feet most of the time, the nature of the work was exacting, meals were often rushed and sleep became a precious commodity - but thanks to Mr Khan's advice, particularly in relation to using our time more effectively, the 'inability to cope' feeling of early weeks was overcome.

I did not mind working the long hours; they were no better or worse than those of any of the other house surgeons and I recognised that, as a result of being better organised, I was developing into a useful member of the team. Indeed, the sense of belonging to a team was strong, as was our team spirit. We were proud of the work that we did on Surgical Five and proud of the results we achieved for our patients. The wards became 'our' wards and the patients there became 'our' patients. All the staff on the unit - be they doctors, nurses or ancillary workers - wanted to do the very best that they could for them. In fact, we wanted to be better than any of the other surgical units. There was a sense of belonging and I felt appreciated by my peers. I even developed a reasonable working relationship with Sister Ashbrook - though she was not a person that I would ever come to like - and felt confident that I was performing my house officer duties to a satisfactory level.

With time and experience, I had become familiar and at ease with the weekly cycle of ward rounds, theatre lists and those long nights in the accident department. A great many of the duties were routine, and whereas in the early days I needed to stop frequently and ask for advice and guidance, I was now able to undertake such work with the minimum of fuss or bother. I had now witnessed most of the clinical situations that arose on a surgical unit, knew what was expected of me, and what I should do in different circumstances. With experience, I had become adept at the various practical procedures that fell to the house officer and was able to tackle them without fear of failure. Any concern that Mr Potts didn't want me as his house officer and yearned for the feminine charms of Miss Chambers had completely vanished! No longer did I feel an interloper, unwelcome in a strange environment, as I had felt at the start of the job. I knew that I had become an important member of the surgical unit, essential to the smooth running of the ward.

It was great to have Johnny as a partner. He was always cheerful and hardworking and we forged a good partnership. We shared the heavy workload, stood side by side on ward rounds, balanced the duties on urgency day and generally covered each other's backs. The advice that Mr Khan had given to us on teamwork in those early days had proved invaluable and I had already decided to impart this information to Liz Chalmers when she took over from me as Mr Potts' house officer in February.

In much the same way that morale was good amongst the members of the Surgical Five team, an excellent sense of camaraderie developed amongst the doctors in the residency, which did much to lift spirits and encourage teamwork amongst the junior doctors. None of us had found the transition from student to doctor easy - but as a result of being thrown together, facing common challenges and sharing the same difficulties, a bond was created between us - much as would develop amongst a group of young squaddies thrown together on the parade ground, facing a tyrannical sergeant major.

Although the residents came together for breakfast and lunch these meals tended to be rushed, as ward duties took priority. The evening meal however, taken whilst the visitors were on the ward, was generally more leisurely. Later, when each of us had finished our day's work, we would congregate in the lounge and, over a drink of coffee or beer, would cheer ourselves up by having a communal grumble; usually about the inequity of the staffing structure in British hospitals.

When we had been appointed, there had been no formal job description or personal specification. There had not even been a formal application form. A notice had been posted, simply announcing that any graduate interested in working as a house officer should give their name to Frederick Swindles, Secretary to the Medical Committee. We amused ourselves by envisaging what an honest description of our current house officer jobs might look like.

It was suggested that the 'Job Purpose' should read:

'To work as a ward based medical or surgical slave, to enable the City General Hospital to exploit the requirement that all newly qualified doctors should undertake a compulsory year as a resident, prior to full registration with the General Medical Council.'

We felt that the 'Key Tasks' should be listed as: -

1. To be on duty for 120 hours per week, never actually working for less than eighty hours per week.

2. To be at the beck and call of consultants both surgical and medical at all times of the day and night, and to undertake whatever duties that they demand, regardless of whether these demands are necessary or reasonable.

3. To be in several different places in the hospital at the same time and to undertake multiple tasks simultaneously.

4. To act as a Casualty officer every fourth day whilst concurrently having responsibilities on the ward.

5. To complete all tasks successfully without breaching hospital policies or falling asleep whilst on duty.'

We agreed that the official document should also state that: *Remuneration will be £750 p.a. from which £250 p.a. will be deducted for board and lodgings.*

Whilst many of the these grumbles might be regarded as slightly 'tongue in cheek', in reality the aspect of our employment about which we were genuinely deeply unhappy was our rate of pay, which amounted to ten pounds a week; one pound ten shillings per day, equating to an hourly rate of approximately two shilling and six pence (or in modern decimal coinage about twelve pence). This hourly rate of pay was significantly less than any other employee at the hospital at the time - including the cooks, porters, and cleaners.

Finally, we agreed that the 'Person Specification' should read: -

'This post requires a hardworking, long suffering, thick-skinned young doctor who will require dogged determination and an excellent sense of humour to survive.'

In truth, dark humour was one of the things that kept us going.

Only in later years, when the hours that we worked were reduced because they were seen to be unacceptable, did I realise that, as well as the disadvantages of which we were so aware - particularly the chronic tiredness from which we all suffered and to which we never truly became accustomed - there were advantages for both the medical staff, and particularly for the patients, with the staffing arrangements as they existed at that time. Certainly the hours were long, but of critical importance was the fact that the key members of the surgical unit - consultant, registrar and house officer - were all 'on call' at the same time. Whenever the consultant was 'on take', his registrar was always resident and 'on duty' with the house officer in the hospital. This meant that registrars got well trained both in operative technique and in the assessment of surgical problems, for it was in the consultant's interest to train his registrar. The better a registrar was trained, the fewer times a consultant had to leave his bed at night to travel to the hospital to attend to an emergency. The same was true with the relationship between the house officer and the registrar, since the quicker the house officer gained competence, the sooner the workload of the registrar decreased. Furthermore, both house officer and registrar quickly learned how their consultant wanted particular clinical situations to be managed, so there was consistency in application of policy. Additionally, there were important advantages for the patient. They had a single point of contact with the medical team; the house officer, who was available to them morning noon and night, and with whom they could develop a personal relationship, someone who had seen them previously on a ward round with their consultant and knew everything about their medical problem and their management plan.

Over the years, changes have been introduced both by the British and European Parliaments, and as a result the situation is now very different. All junior hospital doctors, including house officers, undertake shift patterns; shifts lasting between eight and twelve hours, with a maximum permissible time on duty of forty-eight hours per week. When on duty the house officer may be responsible for one hundred or more patients on four or more wards, most of whom he will have never met previously. Because the number of house officers, registrars, and consultants is no longer equal, and all are on slightly different rosters, a consultant may be on duty at different times with any one of half a dozen registrars. He may therefore be phoned at night and asked for advice by a registrar who is a stranger to him, and of whose surgical knowledge and technical expertise he is ignorant.

The problems these changes have caused for patients are obvious. He or she will be admitted when they first arrive at the hospital by a house officer whom they may never see again during their hospital stay, and will then be managed by a succession of new doctors, each having to familiarise themselves with the patient's clinical problem from scratch. The system that existed in the sixties was not perfect but it did offer tremendous experience for young doctors, continuity of care for patients, and superb training for the aspiring surgeon.

These changes in medical staffing have also resulted in a major change in the social environment within the hospital. Since the doctors covering the hospital at night now follow a shift pattern, it is expected that they will be on their feet and actually working when on duty, and therefore they are no longer provided with accommodation. As a result, the concept of a 'resident's mess', similar as it was to an officers' mess in the armed forces, has disappeared, as has the social life that accompanied it. In the sixties, parties were held in the residency that had become our home whilst we were employed 'on the house'. We also hosted a formal dinner for the consultants twice a year, and occasionally even managed to stage a Christmas Revue.

To date, our group of residents had not held a party - a fact that had not gone unnoticed by the more social animals amongst us - and one evening Johnny, as Mess President, suggested to Helen Leach (who had been appointed Social Secretary) that the time was ripe. We were pleasantly surprised to hear that Helen had already given consideration to the matter, and indeed had started to make preliminary arrangements.

"There is a problem, however," she said. "Some of you will know that the last party held by the outgoing house officers - the so called 'end of year' party - got completely out of control, and that the Hospital Secretary and Dr Digby, the Chair of the Medical Committee, decreed that there should be no future parties." There was a groan from the doctors who had been listening.

"However," she continued, "I've been along to see them both and pointed out that it would be grossly unfair to penalise our Mess for the misdemeanours of our predecessors, and I have managed to persuade them that we should be allowed to have a party. They have set a number of conditions, though, that they insist must be followed. Further, they have said that if we do hold a party and there are problems, then that will be the end of residency parties for good."

There was silence as we waited for her to tell us exactly how severe these restrictions would be and whether they would be so severe as to make an enjoyable party impossible.

"They insist on four things. Firstly, that the number of people present should be limited to eighty and that admission should be by ticket only. Secondly, that two porters should act as doormen, paid at our expense, to ensure that nobody enters without a ticket - bouncers, if you like. Thirdly, that the party should end strictly at one am, and finally, that either a consultant or Matron should be present."

There was general dismay when these conditions, particularly the last, were heard. A number of angry voices were raised in protest.

"How can we possibly let our hair down and enjoy ourselves if one of the consultants is present, or worse still, if Matron decides to come along? Who is going to be able to get friendly with one of the nurses or to steal a kiss with Matron watching? The party will be a complete flop, a damp squib. We might as well not bother."

It quickly became apparent that Helen and Johnny had already considered these matters in advance of them being raised by their colleagues. Helen spoke first.

"I do understand why the management have concerns...I was at the last party and it did get out of control. It was a "bring your own" affair and there was far too much alcohol around. This lounge was a total wreck afterwards, with vomit and broken glass everywhere. The hospital cleaners declined to clear up the mess and industrial cleaners had to be employed, at the residents' expense. A number of outsiders gate-crashed the party; nobody knew exactly who they were or where they came from. They certainly seemed to have no connection with the hospital at all. There was a suggestion that it became known at a local pub that there was a party going on here, and the drinkers from the pub simply wandered in after closing time. A fight broke out between some of the doctors and some of these intruders, furniture was broken, and at least one person had to be treated in Casualty. Worst still, when the party finally broke up, someone looking for the exit onto the street whilst completely drunk wandered onto one of the wards and caused a disturbance there. It did the reputation of the hospital no good at all, particularly as the incident was reported in the local press. If you look at the conditions one by one, I honestly believe that we can still host an enjoyable party. I don't think it unreasonable that we should limit the number of people attending. We want this to be *our* party for *our* friends, not one for the entire world and his wife. Equally, it would be no great hardship to have porters acting as doormen. It will save one of us having to guard the door throughout the evening, and there will be more than enough money in the kitty from the bar profits to pay for them."

"But what about this condition about a consultant or Matron being present - that really would put a dampener on it!" This time it was Johnny who replied.

"Again, I don't see that as too much of a problem. It might mean bending the rules a little bit, as I think the intention is to have one of them present throughout the evening, but I thought I could invite my Uncle Bill along to 'declare the party open'. If he did that, at perhaps eight or eight-thirty, there would scarcely be anybody here. I'm sure I could persuade him not to stay for more than an hour or so; and in any case, if we turned the music up loud enough I have no doubt that we could drive him away, even if he didn't retire gracefully."

Everyone was considerably cheered by these suggestions, as the residents came to realise that it would be perfectly possible to have an enjoyable evening despite the restrictions, and soon the discussion began to focus on the practical arrangements that would have to be made. When a date had been agreed, a discussion followed on the types and quantity of drinks that would be required, and volunteers were sought to decorate the lounge on the day of the party. Some were delegated to make suitable posters to place around the hospital to advertise the event, and others to prepare the tickets. It was agreed that each resident should be allocated five tickets - one for themselves and four to be distributed at their discretion. In the event that they didn't need all of their tickets, they were not to be left unused but were to be passed back to Helen to be available to other residents on request. Immediately there was a hubbub as a debate developed as to who should be invited.

"Who's going to give Nurse Susan Weston a ticket?" shouted Johnny at the top of his voice. The memory of my early morning cup of tea in the accident room returned to haunt me. Most of the residents thought that it would be a great idea to have her there, and it became quite clear that she had a significant reputation. It appeared that I was not the only one that had experienced her 'special treatment' in the Casualty Department bedroom!

"It certainly won't be me who will invite her," I said to Johnny. "You could very well get more than you bargained for from that one."

"Well, I wonder whom you will be taking? Perhaps a certain young lady from the Surgical Five male ward?"

"Did you have anyone particular in mind?"

"I would imagine a certain young nurse at whom you have been making eyes across a crowded ward round," he said, "not to mention across the top of a patient's pink buttocks." Then, teasing, he added, "I know that you're a bit shy and reticent, Paul...would you like me to ask her for you?"

"That's very kind," I said primly, "but I am quite capable of asking her myself." He laughed.

"In that case, I'll make you a promise. I'll make sure the lights are turned down low and that there are some nice slow numbers for you to smooch to during the evening."

I was certain that none of the other residents would have the slightest difficulty in asking a girl to a dance, but Johnny was right...the truth was that asking her for a date would not come easily to me.

For a couple of days, I wandered around with a dance poster and some tickets in my pocket, wondering how to approach the task, and cursing myself for my lack of confidence where matters of the opposite sex were concerned. I knew, of course, that I was being stupidly shy and inhibited and that it should be the easiest thing in the world for a young man to go up to a pretty young woman and say "We're holding a party on Saturday, would you care to come?" It seemed that no one else found this the slightest problem except me, to whom it appeared a formidable hurdle. Fortunately, a golden opportunity arose when I walked into the ward office one morning when Kate and one of the other first year nurses happened to be there, but even then I managed to make a hash of it. I took the poster out of my pocket and started to pin it on the notice board, when Kate walked over.

"Oh, that's great. I heard there was a dance coming up. When is it to be?"

"Saturday the nineteenth," I replied, "in the Doctors' residency. I have some tickets in my pocket, if you two girls are interested."

I immediately kicked myself. Why on earth had I said "two girls"? The obvious thing to have said was "I would be very pleased if you would come as my guest, Kate."

Kate looked at me with mock seriousness, yet with a twinkle in her eye. She answered, in a grave voice that might well have been Lizzie Bennett's in Jane Austen's 'Pride and Prejudice', "As far as I am aware, I have no prior engagement on that particular evening, Dr Lambert. Speaking personally, I would be delighted to attend, but I have been led to believe that the Doctor's residency after dark on a Saturday night is not a suitable venue for a young lady of high repute. Indeed, I believe that many a young lady's reputation has been severely tarnished at such gatherings."

With equal gravity, I replied in a voice that I hoped sounded both serious and sincere, with words that might have come from the lips of Mr Darcy. "I also have heard such rumours, dear lady - but can give you my personal assurance, as a gentleman, that such rumours are much exaggerated."

"I am much encouraged to hear that, kind Sir - but even so, I am certain that Mama would never allow me to attend such an event unaccompanied."

"My dear, I understand that no lesser a personage than Sir William Warrender himself will be in attendance. I am sure that your Mama would agree that such a noble and esteemed gentleman would not grace an engagement that was in any way lacking in propriety. In any event, I shall be pleased to make it my personal responsibility to see that you come to no harm and are safely returned to your Mama at the end of the evening."

"You are most kind and considerate young Sir...in that case, I shall be pleased to attend."

She did a mock curtsey and held out her hand to be kissed. Gravely, I took her hand and put her fingers to my lips, and for a second looked deep into her eyes.

We had both been acting out parts from a romantic novel, but I was elated. I had done it - I had asked her to the dance and she had accepted. I had known for some time that I was extremely fond of her – no, not merely fond of her, much more than that - and from the look on her face, I felt certain that she had some feelings for me. With luck, the party might be the beginning of something special.

Chapter 12

It was early one evening in the middle of October when David Entwistle came into casualty. Although I was not aware of it at the time, he was a patient who was to change the entire course of my life. He was a tall, extremely slim sociology student from the local university. Nineteen years of age, he had been at the university for less than a month, and was accompanied by his tutor from the hall of residence where he was living. As a medical student, I had envied undergraduates studying for degrees such as sociology, politics or English Literature, who appeared to have no more than eight hours of formal tuition a week; a contrast to the much longer hours endured by those of us at the medical school. Such students had ample time to lead a full university life, to participate in the various societies and clubs that were available on the university campus, and were also able to supplement their university grants by taking part-time jobs, which supplied the funds to support the hectic social life that appeared to be their main preoccupation. His history was absolutely classical. He had previously been entirely fit and well but, approximately twenty-four hours before, had noticed a rather vague, griping discomfort in the central part of his abdomen. He had thought little about it, assuming that he merely had a slight stomach upset, but during the day it had got progressively more severe and had settled in the lower right corner of the abdomen. Having lost his appetite, he had eaten next to nothing since morning and had felt nauseous, but hadn't actually vomited. The nurses had already taken his temperature and found it to be mildly elevated. On examination, he was healthy apart from his abdominal problem, albeit built like a beanpole. The tenderness in the bottom right corner of his abdomen was extreme, and his muscles resisted and tightened when I put a hand on this area because of the acute pain that this caused. This was undoubtedly a case of acute appendicitis. It was equally clear that he needed to be admitted, so I spoke with Mr Khan on the phone to ask him to confirm the diagnosis and to seek his permission to admit the patient into the hospital, with a view to surgery. Mr Khan, busy on the ward, accepted my diagnosis and left me to make the necessary arrangements.

By this stage, I had learned how to streamline procedures for the benefit of the patient and to minimise delays for the medical staff. Accordingly, I checked that he did not have any allergies or hypersensitivities, that he was not on any medication, and that there were no other factors that might cause difficulties for the anaesthetist. He had not eaten anything for the last four or five hours and I reminded him not to eat or drink anything before his anaesthetic. I took the necessary samples of blood before he left the accident room so these could be processed whilst he was being moved to the ward. I booked the theatre and spoke with the anaesthetist whilst he was still in the casualty department, and obtained his written consent for an appendicectomy operation. Three months earlier I would not have undertaken any of these jobs until Mr Khan had seen him, which would have resulted in a delay in getting him to theatre that ultimately would have cost me two hours of sleep. With the experience and confidence now acquired, I was in no doubt that Mr Khan would agree with my diagnosis and that later in the evening, when Johnny had relieved me in the accident room, I would assist in theatre whilst Mr Khan removed the appendix. Because the illness was of short duration and the patient was young and slim, it promised to be a quick and straightforward appendicectomy operation. Little did I realise just how wrong this assumption was to be.

Just as I had anticipated, at eleven pm David was being anaesthetised. Mr Khan and I changed into our green theatre pants and vests, scrubbed up in the now familiar manner, and donned gowns and gloves. The patient, endotracheal tube in his throat and intravenous drip in his arm, was brought through from the anaesthetic room and lifted gently onto the operating theatre table. The abdomen was widely exposed and Mr Khan painted the skin with an iodine antiseptic solution, placing surgical drapes around the proposed operation site in the usual fashion. Everything was prepared for the operation to begin.

Mr Khan spoke to the night theatre Sister who was also scrubbed and standing opposite him at the table, her tray of surgical instruments, needles and swabs at the ready. "It seems very quiet tonight Sister - have you got any other cases booked?"

Sister did not recognise the trap that was being set for her, nor indeed did I appreciate the significance of this innocent sounding question. "No," she replied. "It's somewhat unusual, but I am pleased to say that this is the only case."

Mr Khan turned to me. "Paul," he said, "come and change places with me."

I looked across the table at him, not understanding the reason for his request, then suddenly realised what was being suggested.

"Are you sure?" I said. "I haven't done one before, you know."

"I know," he replied, "but you must have assisted at a dozen or more."

I saw the theatre sister and the anaesthetist exchange a meaningful glance. Both had seen that the patient was young and slim and knew Mr Khan to be a skilled and experienced operator who could be expected to complete the procedure in thirty to forty minutes. They both realised that this was not going to be such a quick operation after all. For the theatre sister, this only meant a longer operation and the possibility of being late for the one am meal provided for night staff, but for the anaesthetist this meant getting to bed late and missing sleep. He made no comment, but a frown crossed his face. Mr Khan, who had seen the exchange, clearly understood what was going through their minds.

"We've all got to learn," he said. "There's a first time for everything, whether it's our first appendix, our first solo anaesthetic, or our first case as a scrub nurse."

With some trepidation, I changed places with him and picked up the scalpel. My heart was beating fast. It was true that I had assisted at quite a number of appendix operations, but seeing one and doing one are quite different things. There had been no time to prepare myself mentally for the test that was imminent, though I suspect that was Mr Khan's intention; I should probably have been much more nervous had there been a long time to think about it. I was grateful also that it was to be Mr Khan who would guide me through the procedure, and not one of the consultants. Looking at the area of virgin skin in front of me, I felt the sweat forming on my brow.

I knew exactly where to make the incision. It would be two inches long and centred on McBurney's point in the right iliac fossa. Holding the scalpel in my right hand, I made the initial incision, drawing the knife carefully along the skin. Lifting the blade away, I saw that I had created the faintest scratch - no more than a red line on the skin, without causing any bleeding at all. Mr Khan started a running commentary that he was to continue with throughout the procedure.

"Use your left thumb and forefinger to tense the skin," he said, "and then the skin won't move away from the blade. You are bound to be tentative at first but you just need to apply a little more pressure."

I made a second cut, and again lifted the scalpel away. At one end of the wound the incision was not quite superimposed on the first scratch, thus resulting in two parallel lines. Also, whilst the skin was cut completely through in the centre of the wound, it had not completely parted at either end. The pressure that I had exerted had not been uniform along the length of the cut.

"You will need the full length of this incision," said Mr Khan, "so make sure you're through the skin at both ends. That's better. Right - now deepen the wound through the fatty layer, remembering that this patient is quite thin and you will soon be down to muscle. Some patients have a fatty layer two or more inches thick, but in this young man it won't be more than a quarter of an inch."

Slowly, nervously and hesitantly, but with intense concentration, I followed his instructions. "Fine. Now, you will see that there is quite a lot of bleeding from those small vessels in the fatty layer deep to the skin. Place a swab over your side of the wound to compress the bleeding points, and I will do the same over mine. There. That temporarily stops the bleeding for us. Now, as I take my swab away little by little, it exposes the bleeding points one by one, and you can cauterise them using the diathermy machine."

This was the first time that I had used the diathermy machine. It involved identifying and grasping the bleeding vessel in the points of the electric forceps, and pressing the pedal on the floor with one foot. Knowing what length of the vessel to grasp with the forceps was a matter of judgement. Too large a bite and an excessive amount of tissue would be coagulated, leaving a lot of dead tissue with a risk of infection afterwards. Too little and the bleeding was not stopped. One or two of the bleeding vessels were too large to be coagulated with the diathermy machine, so these were clipped with artery forceps. They now needed to be tied in a reef knot with thread, and I had to do this two-handed. Left over right and under, then right over left and under, pulling the two half hitches up in opposite directions, just like tying up a Christmas parcel with string. I had seen the consultants and Mr Khan tie knots effortlessly - one-handed, taking only a second or two - and I was conscious that my efforts were slow and clumsy in the extreme.

"If we're going to make a surgeon of you," said Mr Khan, "you're going to have to learn how to tie knots left-handed."

This was true. A right-handed surgeon ties all his knots left-handed, never letting go of the end of the thread at any time, and some specialist surgeons have particularly difficult knot skills to acquire. The Ear, Nose and Throat surgeon, when performing a tonsillectomy operation, has to tie a knot to control the major tonsillar artery in the confined space at the back of the throat. A modern surgeon performing keyhole surgery has to tie knots inside the abdomen using long handled instruments, whilst only able to see what he is doing by watching the television monitor. And when knots are tied to control large bleeding arteries, it is vitally important that they do not come undone!

Beneath the fatty layer the abdomen has three layers of muscle, but in this patient, who was extremely thin, these layers were not well developed; which is no doubt why Mr Khan had decided that this patient was suitable for me to perform my first operation. By this time, I had ceased to feel nervous. My entire concentration was devoted to following Mr Khan's guidance to the very best of my ability. Nor was I conscious of the other personnel in the theatre; not even aware of the theatre sister, even though she was standing opposite me and handing me the surgical instruments as and when they were needed.

Slowly, I dissected my way through the muscles, and arrived at the glistening peritoneal layer that forms the inner lining of the abdomen. Mr Khan pointed out that, whilst my skin incision was two inches long in the deepest part of the wound, I had only exposed about a half an inch of peritoneum.

"Your incision has got shelving edges," he said. "They need to be vertical, otherwise you won't have enough room in which to operate when we actually get within the abdominal cavity."

He supervised whilst I increased the length of the incision at the level of the fat and muscle layers, until it met with his approval. "Don't be fooled into thinking that the best surgeon is the one who works through the smallest hole and leaves the shortest scar," he said. "The best surgeon is the one who operates safely, and it isn't safe to struggle to complete an operation through the shortest possible incision. Now, I want you to open the peritoneum and then, if you don't mind, I will put a finger into the abdomen proper and we'll find out exactly where this young man's appendix is situated."

Having seen many appendix operations, I knew that the position of the appendix was very variable. Sometimes it would be immediately accessible, sitting exactly where the incision had been made, but often it was tucked behind that part of the large bowel called the caecum. Typically, when the appendix gets inflamed, a fatty apron called the omentum, known to surgeons as the 'abdominal policeman' because it guards against the spread of infection, moves to the inflamed area and attempts to wrap itself around the inflamed appendix, confining the sepsis to a limited area. Indeed, when I looked into my incision, all I could see was the pale omentum obliterating everything else. Mr Khan, from his side of the operating table, probed within the abdomen with his index finger. Using only his sense of touch and his previous experience he was locating the appendix and identifying the structures to which it was adherent. He withdrew his finger.

"Pop a couple of fingers into the abdomen and you'll find that the omentum is stuck to the inner aspect of the muscles, about an inch from the lower end of the wound. I want you gently to slide a finger between the muscle wall and the omentum. I've started it off, so you should be able to feel the plane that I want you to separate."

The incision was only large enough to allow the insertion of two fingers, and the area to be dissected was out of view, tucked underneath the lower portion of the wound - but I thought that I could feel the plane that he had described, the one he wanted me to separate. I was, however, apprehensive that I might not be in the correct plane, and concerned that if I worked in the wrong area I might damage some adjacent structure.

Mr Khan continued, "It's like separating two segments of an orange with your eyes closed. Just slide your finger gently up and down the cleft and you'll feel the omentum peeling away from the muscle layer."

Tentatively, and once again conscious of moisture on my brow, I separated the two a little, then asked Mr Khan to check that I was progressing satisfactorily.

"Yes, absolutely," he said, "you are in exactly the right place. Just continue along that line." Reassured, I continued to work between omentum and muscle, and soon the two sides were apart.

"That would be classed as a fairly light adhesion between the two structures," Mr Khan said. "In due course, you will find many cases where the appendix has been inflamed for a longer period, and where the two sides are much more firmly stuck together - just as sometimes orange segments will fall apart easily, and at other times they can be difficult to separate without breaking into the fruit. Now, if you put your finger in again, you will feel the appendix. It's about the size and shape of a chocolate finger biscuit. We are in luck today because nothing else is adherent to it. Identify it and then gently rotate your finger all the way round it to increase its mobility, then hook your index finger around it and flick it up into the wound."

As before, it was nerve-racking to be working unable to see exactly where my finger was, not sure how much pressure to apply and unable to be certain that I was not damaging any neighbouring structures. I felt a cold trickle of sweat run down the small of my back. I was afraid to continue with the manoeuvre, and again asked Mr Khan to check that things were progressing satisfactorily. Having checked, he once more reassured me that all was well and very slowly I progressed with the dissection, until eventually the turgid, inflamed, appendix was visible in the wound.

Mr Khan applied a pair of tissue-holding forceps to the end of the appendix and for the first time it was now possible to see its whole length - from the red, angry, inflamed tip, right down to the point at which it entered the colon - and also to see the blood vessels feeding it. The next task was to divide these blood vessels and apply ties to them. Applying forceps to the blood vessels and cutting them with scissors proved to be straightforward but I was concerned about applying ties to them, as they were clearly enlarged and carrying much more blood than was usual because the appendix was so inflamed. It was vitally important that these ligatures were absolutely secure.

"It's probably worth putting a third half hitch on them for extra security," said Mr Khan. "Those vessels would bleed very freely if the ties were to come adrift."

Laboriously, I applied my Christmas parcel knots to the vessels, putting a third and then a fourth half hitch on for good measure. Mr Khan then showed me how to detach the appendix from the large bowel by cutting across its base with a knife. He asked me to take a specimen swab from the inflamed portion to send for bacteriological analysis, so that we would know which antibiotic to use if the patient subsequently got an infection, and finally demonstrated how to bury the stump of the appendix in the large bowel. We were now ready to close the abdomen, and Sister passed me the suture used to close the peritoneum. Mr Khan, however, asked me to stop.

"Now," he said, "what have you forgotten?"

I was flummoxed and could think of nothing that I had overlooked, although the truth was that, during the operation, I had not been thinking for myself at all. My entire concentration had been given to listening to Mr Khan and following his instructions to the very best of my ability.

"What are you going to ask Sister to do?"

It was a request from surgeon to scrub nurse that I had heard a great many times, indeed one that I had heard during every operation that I had ever witnessed. Suddenly, I realised.

"Sister, please may we count the swabs and instruments to make sure that they are present and correct?"

"That's right," said Mr Khan. "Too often it is left to the nursing staff to do the check, but it is the surgeon's responsibility to assure himself that all swabs and instruments are accounted for. That means an examination of the operation area by the surgeon, concentrating particularly on the space within the abdomen; and two counts, conducted jointly by the surgeon and the scrub nurse, of instruments and swabs. It is sad but true that every year some surgeon in the UK will manage to leave either a swab or an instrument inside a patient."

I checked the wound and abdomen, then counted aloud whilst Sister identified all the swabs that had been used, most of which were now hanging on the swab rack against the theatre wall. Then Mr Khan guided me, step by step, as the abdomen was closed. The edges of the three muscle layers were sutured back together one by one, and we checked that there was no further bleeding in any part of the wound. I closed the subcutaneous fatty layer and then, finally, sutured the skin. Again, I was conscious of my clumsy knot-tying technique, but the wound - the only part of my handiwork that the patient would see - did look reasonably respectable when it was finally closed. Sister handed me a dressing, which I applied to the wound. My first appendicectomy operation was complete.

I stripped off my hat, mask, gloves and gown, feeling completely drained. Looking at the clock, I found that it was after one am. The operation had taken over two hours, but during the procedure I had not been conscious of the time at all.

"Thank you, Sister," I said, "for being so patient." I then turned to the anaesthetist, adding "And you too; I know Mr Khan could have done the operation in half the time."

"Probably less," Sister said, "but as he said, we all have to learn. That really wasn't too bad for a first attempt."

The words were not spoken unkindly, indeed might have been taken as a compliment. Suddenly, with the completion of the operation and the lifting of the tension, I felt exhilarated. I could have laughed aloud. I had been working non-stop since eight-thirty in the morning, but I didn't feel in the least bit tired. I had done my first proper operation, had removed an inflamed appendix, and Sister had implied that I had done all right; that it had been a reasonable effort. I felt good and was proud of myself. We went back into the surgeon's room for a cup of coffee and a biscuit.

"If we are going to make a surgeon of you," Mr Khan reiterated, "you're going to have to learn how to tie left handed knots. In most situations in surgery, there simply isn't enough space in the wound for you to be tying knots with two hands. You must learn how to throw a half hitch with your left hand and then slide it down into position using your index finger. Let me show you how."

He went out of the room, returning with a length of suture material, and gave an impressive demonstration of how it was done. He was able to tie a secure reef knot, one-handed, in five seconds. He passed the thread to me, and laughed at my early ungainly attempts.

"It takes practice," he said. "Take some suture material away with you and practice in your own time."

"I will, and thank you for your patience this evening. My first proper operation - I can't believe that I've actually removed an appendix. If you will excuse me now, I'd like to take a quick walk around the wards and check that things are tidy there before I go to bed."

"Paul," he said with his quiet smile, "I'm afraid you've not finished here yet. There are one or two jobs for you to do. You need to write a detailed description of the operation in the patient's hospital notes and record the procedure in the theatre logbook. Then there are the post-operative instructions for the nurses to be written, not to mention the patient's post-operative medication for pain relief and the fluid balance chart."

In my buoyant mood, the adrenalin still pumping through my veins, I was forgetting that I was still the houseman, the most junior member of the team. Paperwork was the house officer's responsibility, and this was Mr Khan's way of bringing me down to earth.

Clerical duties completed, I walked quickly around the wards to ensure that everything was tidy, thereby reducing the chances of being disturbed during the rest of the night. I then returned to the residency, pleased and proud of myself, rather hoping that someone would be there whom I could tell of my achievement. The lounge, though, was deserted; the other housemen were either still working on the wards or had gone to bed. Later in my bedroom, as perhaps I should have expected, it took a long time to get to sleep, thanks to the many thoughts that were buzzing in my head.

As I lay in bed, Mr Khan's remark '*making a surgeon of you*' came to mind. I had never really thought of surgery as a career - merely as a necessary stepping-stone to completing the pre-registration house year to enable me to become fully registered with the GMC. I had been too busy actually doing the job to have had time to think further ahead. Nonetheless, something had been awakened within me, as it had during my first week in the job when assisting at Mr Quigley's operation for a bleeding duodenal ulcer. The operation that I had just performed, though not as dramatic as the arrest of haemorrhage from Mr Quigley's ulcer, nevertheless had been the turning point that had changed the course of the patient's illness. Both illnesses, had they been left untreated, were potentially fatal; and surgical intervention had been the event which had eliminated the disease and returned the patient to health. Performing an appendicectomy operation certainly made me think about a career in surgery, but also demonstrated to me just how much knowledge there would be to assimilate, and how much technical skill I needed to acquire.

Sometime later I woke in a cold sweat, gripped with sudden fear. The euphoria I had felt on completing the surgery had been replaced with an acute attack of self-doubt. Had I tied the arteries taking blood to the appendix properly? Could the ligatures have slipped and the patient be quietly bleeding to death on the ward? Perhaps the ligature on the base of the appendix had come adrift, so that faeces in the large bowel were spilling into the abdomen and the deeper part of the wound. If that were the case, David would be toxic and extremely ill by morning. Suppose he died, a bright young man in his first term at university? I tried to be rational. Surely Mr Khan would have intervened had he not been happy with any of the steps in the operation - but then again could he tell, simply by watching, just how tight those ligatures were? I tried to get back to sleep, but couldn't. There was a devil in my head that simply wouldn't be quietened, stoking my self-doubt.

Again, I tried to be logical and reasonable. The instructions that I had written for the nurses were that observations of pulse, blood pressure and temperature should be taken through the night. Surely the nurses would ring me if the patient showed signs of bleeding or sepsis. But then I remembered that the observations had only been requested every two hours (that was the routine after an appendix operation), and I became concerned that this might not be frequent enough. If a ligature on the blood vessel had come adrift immediately after they had taken a set of observations, it might be another two hours before the nurses noticed that the patient had deteriorated and was quietly bleeding to death. Finally, unable to sleep and agonising over the situation - visualising all manner of calamities that might have occurred to my patient - I could bear it no longer and rang the ward to speak with the staff nurse.

"Hello," I said. "Paul Lambert here...can you tell me how David Entwistle is? The lad who had his appendix removed earlier?" I tried to sound unconcerned.

Staff nurse sounded surprised at the question. "Yes, he's fine," she said. "He's come out of his anaesthetic. He asked for a drink a little while ago but the instructions were that he should have nothing by mouth, so we've just given him a mouth wash."

"Are his observations alright?" I asked anxiously.

"Yes, absolutely fine," she said.

Reassured, I settled back into the bed. *Now,* I thought, *I shall be able to get to sleep*. But sleep wouldn't come. I tossed and turned and fretted. Common sense told me that there was nothing to worry about, but a lingering doubt at the back of my mind would not allow me to relax. An hour passed, and then another, and finally, unable to stand it any more, I decided to go to the ward to check on the patient personally.

"Hello," said Staff Nurse, surprised at my sudden appearance. "We weren't expecting you. Is there a problem?"

"I've just come to check on David Entwistle," I said.

"He's fine, no problems at all."

Nonetheless, we went together to see how he was. He was fast asleep, appeared to be in no discomfort, and his observations were, indeed, absolutely normal. Staff Nurse was clearly puzzled that I should have left my bed and come of my own accord to the ward at five in the morning, to see a patient who was causing no concern whatsoever.

"Was it a difficult operation? Are you expecting some troubles? Do you want us to do some extra observations?"

"No," I said. "It wasn't difficult, but it was my first appendicectomy."

"Ah, now I understand. Well, as you can see, he is absolutely fine. You go back to bed and I promise we will ring you if there are any problems – but, as you can see, he looks entirely comfortable."

I did return to bed and finally got some sleep, but I had learned very soon after performing my first operation that there would be no point in attempting a career in surgery unless I was able to carry the responsibility and pressure that went with it.

Chapter 13

I was awaiting the arrival of the weekend with eager anticipation, for Saturday was the day of the party. The date had been specially selected as a day when neither the Surgical Five unit nor Surgical Two unit were on call - these being the respective units of Johnny Nolan, the Mess President and Helen Leach, our Social Secretary. Both Johnny and I had our clinical duties to attend to on the Saturday morning, but after lunch Helen and one or two volunteers joined us and we set about organising the residency lounge in preparation for the party. Helen explained that, in her experience, the key requirements for a successful party were low lights, loud music, and an adequate supply of alcohol.

We pulled the settees and armchairs to the sides of the room, which was then decorated with fairy lights, balloons, and posters of exotic places that Helen had obtained from a local travel agent. The bar was decked with tinsel and streamers, and the extra barrels of beer and the cheap white wine that had been bought were carried across from Johnny's bedroom, where they had been stored. We realised that nobody had thought about providing any soft drinks, so one of the volunteers was despatched to the local shops to obtain an adequate supply. Glasses and mugs were brought from the hospital kitchen - but only after the catering manager, who remembered the damage caused at the last doctors' party, had been promised that we would pay for all breakages.

"That sorts out the drinks," I said, "but what about the low lights?"

"And why are you particularly interested in low lights, Paul?" said Johnny provocatively.

"No particular reason," I responded innocently. "It's just that Helen said it was essential for a good party."

"No particular reason, my foot!" retorted Johnny, "You want to snuggle up to Kate Meredith, and everyone on Surgical Five unit knows it and wants you to as well. The two of you have been making eyes at each other long enough. I've been trying to organise another sweepstake to predict when you would give her the first kiss, but there have been no takers. Everyone agrees that tonight is the night! It's time you two got together and I'm going to make damn sure that it happens at the party."

"And what do you mean by that?"

"Never you mind, old son. You just do what comes naturally this evening and put the whole of the Surgical Five unit out of its misery."

"And what about these low lights, then?" I repeated. It was Helen who replied.

"Take a look at the light switches. I've persuaded the electricians to put dimmer switches on them all...we can have the lights as bright or as dim as we wish. We can turn them off completely, if you want, Paul," she added, eyes sparkling.

"That just leaves the music?"

"All sorted," said Helen. "One of the porters, a chap called Barry, is an amateur disc jockey. He does gigs most Saturday nights, and he will be along later this afternoon with all the gear that he needs to set up in advance. However we need the help of a few strong men to roll the carpet back, so that there is an area for dancing."

"You seem to have thought of everything," I said, impressed with all the details that Helen had organised.

"I've added one final touch to make sure that nothing spoils the party mood - I've disconnected all the telephones in the room. The last thing we want is the phone ringing every five minutes."

Between them, Helen and Johnny did indeed appear to have thought of everything, and by four pm the lounge was fully prepared for the party. The room looked festive and welcoming. At that moment, my bleep sounded. I went to my room to answer it and was surprised to be told by the switchboard that Mr Potts was calling on an outside line.

"Lambert, there you are. I'm afraid I've got a little job for you. A patient of mine in the private patient's hospital has got some problems and I'm arranging for her to be transferred to the female ward. In fact, she has already left, so she should be with you at any time. She's bleeding from the back passage and the situation is potentially unstable. We really don't have the facilities here to deal with her. Clerk her in, will you, sort out the bloods, and put up a drip? She's not particularly well at the moment so you had better get Khan in to help you."

I thought quickly. "Sir, it isn't our urgency weekend. Surgical Three unit is on call today. Mr Khan may not be around."

"Well, give him a ring anyway. If he's not available, you will have to get the duty registrar to help you. But it would be better if it were Khan. And perhaps you could give me a ring when you have got things sorted." With that he rang off, and no sooner had he done so than my bleep sounded again. This time it was Sister Rutherford.

"Paul, a lady called Mrs Deakin has just arrived on the ward. She has been transferred from the private hospital by ambulance. We weren't expecting her. Do you know anything about her?"

I told her the little that I knew. Having known Sister for a number of months now I had yet to see her irritated or upset, but now she was both angry with Mr Potts and concerned for the patient.

"Mr Potts shouldn't admit patients to the private hospital if they don't have the facilities there to deal with emergencies," she said severely. "This patient is very sick, Paul. She has clearly lost a lot of blood. Can you come at once, please?"

Mrs Deakin was a lady in her forties and it was immediately apparent that Sister's concern was not misplaced. She was pale, felt faint, was sweating and looked frightened. "The blood is pouring from me, Doctor," she said. "Can you do anything to stop it?"

The first thing to do was to administer oxygen, get a drip up, and arrange for an urgent blood transfusion. Then I was able to ask her a few questions. She told me that for the last three or four days she had passed a small volume of blood with her stool, but during the morning had passed large quantities of blood and blood clots. When I attempted to examine the rectum a vast amount of fresh blood poured out. Mr Potts had suggested that I might need some help from Mr Khan so I rang his home, hoping that he was available.

A female voice answered, "Hello, this is Mr Khan's house."

Mr Khan himself had no discernable accent but this lady had a distinctive Indian voice. It made me realise how little I knew about Mr Khan; I knew nothing of his home circumstances at all, nor where he lived, and had never inquired whether he was married or perhaps had a family.

"Good afternoon," I said, "this is Dr Lambert from the hospital. Is it possible to speak to Mr Khan, please?"

"Oh hello," the voice replied. "You must be Paul, Mr Potts' house officer. Mohammed has often spoken about you. If you will hold the line please, just for a minute, I'll see where he is." Again, it struck me that I didn't even know Mr Khan's Christian name. Mentally, I corrected myself - first name.

Mr Khan arrived on the ward ten minutes later and assessed Mrs Deakin carefully. Together we stayed with her for the next hour, infusing plasma, and then as soon as the transfusion was available, two pints of blood. With the patient now more stable with an improved colour and blood pressure, Mr Khan discussed the situation with Mr Potts on the phone and he decided he would identify the bleeding point and arrest the haemorrhage using an operating telescope. Accordingly, I proceeded to obtain her written consent for the anaesthetic and procedure.

Although I had been involved in the management of a number of patients who had vomited blood, this was the first case of rectal bleeding that I had seen. Mr Khan explained that this was a difficult situation with which to deal. The bleeding might be coming from any part of the colon or rectum and locating the actual bleeding point was difficult. Then he surprised me.

"It's the hospital party tonight, isn't it? I'll stay here and make sure Mrs Deakin doesn't come to any harm. You go off and enjoy yourself. I'm sure Mr Potts and I can cope."

"Are you absolutely sure?" I said, scarcely able to believe my luck. It was highly unusual for a registrar to volunteer to be on duty whilst the house officer went off.

"Absolutely certain. I hear you've got a prior engagement, give my regards to Nurse Meredith."

I looked up, surprised, to see Mr Khan laughing at me. Was Johnny right? Had everybody on the ward been talking about us? Had they really been considering a sweepstake behind our backs? Mr Khan smiled..

"Go on, be off, before I change my mind."

I felt that I really ought to stay with him - not that I could add anything to the combined brains of a consultant and registrar, but because it was the 'right thing to do'. But it was too good an offer to refuse. Kate had accepted an invitation to the party. Nothing was going to make me miss it, and I was hoping and praying that the evening would be a success.

"That's most kind of you," I said. "Thank you very much."

It had been decided that drinks would be available from the bar from eight-thirty pm, that 'last orders' would be at midnight, and that two of the resident doctors should act as bar men at any one time, each pair being on duty for one hour. To ensure that other social gatherings would be permitted in the future, it was agreed that no drinks should be served after twelve-fifteen am and that the party should finish strictly at one am, as the management had decreed. I felt obliged to volunteer to do a period of bar duty but had asked to be allocated the eight-thirty to nine-thirty slot, as it seemed unlikely that the party would really get going before nine-thirty or ten pm.

The evening did indeed start quietly. At eight-thirty the only people present were the resident doctors awaiting the arrival of their guests, and the two porters standing guard at the door, ready to act as bouncers should the need arise. By nine pm a steady trickle of people drifted in, each coming straight to the bar for a drink. One of the first to arrive was Sir William, looking conspicuous but immaculate in dinner jacket and bow tie, inevitably with a buttonhole taken from his garden. If he was conscious that he looked out of place amongst a younger generation who were smartly but casually dressed, he did not show it. Johnny escorted him to the bar and I offered him a drink.

"So, you're a barman tonight Lambert, are you? Another one of your many talents?"

"I thought I'd give it a try Sir, just in case I don't make a career in medicine or surgery." I wasn't fishing for a compliment, but I got one.

"There's no danger of that Lambert - you're doing fine." He was beaming, and clearly in a congenial mood.

"Now, what are you serving at this bar? Can you manage a whisky and soda?"

"I'm afraid not, Sir. I can only offer you a pint of slightly warm beer or some rather cheap white wine."

"In that case, I'll have a small glass of the white wine please."

Sir William started to chat about the changes that had taken place in hospital life over the years, drawing comparisons between the social life in the residency when he was a junior doctor in the early nineteen-twenties and the present day - but Johnny had decided to get Sir William in and out of the party as quickly as was compatible with common decency and he interrupted the conversation shortly afterwards, inviting Sir William to formally declare the party open.

"It only needs to be very short and succinct," he hinted hopefully, if not with great subtlety. Like me, he was obviously conscious that there was a danger that Sir William would start reminiscing at length about hospital parties in the nineteen-twenties and speak for half an hour or more - or worse, deliver a lecture on the dangers of alcohol.

Fortunately, Sir William took the hint and, with uncharacteristic brevity, simply made the point that young people who worked hard were entitled to enjoy periods of relaxation. With that, he formally declared the party open, and expressed the wish that we would all have an enjoyable evening. He said nothing about steps that might be taken if the party became too rowdy, although clearly he knew that the previous residents' party had gotten completely out of hand.

As soon as his little speech was over, the disc jockey put on a slow waltz and Helen, our delightful social secretary, asked Sir William for a dance. Sir William accepted with obvious pleasure and, holding Helen formally at arm's length, acquitted himself well on the dance floor, deserving the appreciative round of applause that he received from the residents and guests. As soon as the waltz was over the lights were dimmed, the volume of the music raised, and Johnny thanked his uncle for his attendance. Once again Sir William took the hint, politely thanked us for the invitation, and departed.

All the while I had been waiting for Kate to arrive and soon after Sir William's departure I saw her come through the door, accompanied by a girl I had not seen before. Previously I had only seen Kate in her nurse's uniform (in which she looked very attractive), but now her appearance was absolutely delightful. She wore a simple black dress, more modestly cut than others in the room. Her hair, previously covered by her nurse's cap, now tumbled in soft curls to her shoulders. Delighted to see her, my spirits high, I left the bar and went to greet her. She responded with a warm smile that set my pulse racing. Remembering our 'Pride and Prejudice' conversation when I had invited Kate to the party and given her the tickets, I affected my grave and serious Mr Darcy voice.

"Dear Ladies, I must declare that I am delighted to welcome you to our little soirée, and do trust that you had a comfortable journey."

I gestured at the rather old and worn furniture in the room. "You will see that we live in rather straightened times, and I do appreciate that the accommodation here is somewhat more humble that you would normally expect. Nonetheless, I hope that the entertainment that we have arranged for your amusement will be acceptable to you. I must apologise that, having recently fallen on hard times, I can no longer afford to employ a manservant - but should you wish to quench your thirst, I would be pleased to serve you with a drink myself."

Kate replied in kind. "You are most considerate, Sir. The journey in the carriage was indeed most tiresome, and I am sure that if we were to partake of a small glass of wine that would be most refreshing. If I may, Sir, I would like to introduce my companion, Sally. I did beg Mama to allow me to travel unaccompanied, but she insisted that Sally should come with me as my chaperone. Mama still has reservations about a young lady visiting an establishment such as this."

As she said these words, she curtsied prettily and held out her hand. As before, I touched her fingers to my lips, but thought the play-acting had gone on long enough and reverted to normal conversation.

"Hello Sally - can I get you a drink as well?"

I led the girls to the bar and served each a drink. They both opted for wine mixed fifty-fifty with lemonade. I explained I was required to serve drinks at the bar for a further fifteen minutes but thereafter would be free to enjoy the evening.

We sat and chatted, although newly arrived partygoers needing refreshments periodically interrupted our conversation. I learned that Sally was also a student nurse and had joined the hospital's nursing school at the same time as Kate. She was now on a medical ward. The two had become firm friends and spent much of their off-duty time together. Kate explained, however, that this arrangement was soon to change.

"As part of our training, we are moved around the hospital every three months or so, to give us experience of different types of nursing. Also, from time to time we are taken off the wards completely and have two months of academic training in the School of Nursing. Sally has been allocated to the accident department and I'm about to start on nights. Indeed, I've already completed my last day on the Surgical Five male ward."

"Does that mean that you're leaving Surgical Five altogether?" I asked, hoping that the anxiety didn't sound in my voice. She looked across at me.

"No," she said, smiling that gentle smile that sent shivers down my spine. "I've simply been switched from days to nights, and from Surgical Five male to Surgical Five female."

"That's excellent. You'll still be there to rescue me the next time a patient vomits all down my shirt and trousers."

It was indeed wonderful news. I visited both wards each night before turning in and often had a drink and a chat with the night staff. It was a good omen - perhaps our friendship would flourish.

John Probert, one of the medical house officers, came up and joined us in conversation. Apparently completely at ease, he asked to be introduced to Kate and Sally in a way that I would have found difficult, if not impossible. Why did I find it so awkward to go up to a girl and simply say "Hello" and have a chat, when I had no difficulty whatsoever in commencing a conversation with a patient? On the ward, I could go straight up to someone that I had never seen before, introduce myself, and then engage with them for half an hour covering topics that at times were very personal - yet when in the company of a pretty girl I became hopelessly self-conscious and tongue-tied.

Conversation was easier with John present and we gossiped freely about life in the hospital, sharing stories about hospital staff and events. The girls related tales about Matron and the various ward sisters, whilst we shared reminiscences with them about the consultants.

At nine-thirty pm Richard Green came to relieve me of my bar duties, most of the guests had arrived, and the party was in full swing. John invited Sally onto the dance floor. I turned to Kate.

"Would you care to dance?"

"I thought you'd never ask."

Thanks to the sofas and armchairs around the edge of the room, the area for dancing (where the carpet had been removed) was very limited. This was the era of rock and roll but space restricted the dancing to jigging on the spot, and the volume of the music limited conversation. After about half an hour, Johnny took the microphone from the DJ.

"By special request of all the staff on the Surgical Five Unit," he said, "I have selected the next number especially for a good friend of mine. He has been working far too hard recently and not spending sufficient time relaxing in the company of the opposite sex - so, Paul, this next dance is especially for you and Kate!"

Now I knew what Johnny had been referring to earlier, when we had been preparing the room, but I was slightly irritated that he should embarrass me in public. I wondered if Kate knew that we had been a topic of conversation on the unit.

"Have people really been talking about us?" I asked.

"Yes, they have, for quite some time now. Did you not know?"

"Honestly, I didn't. Maybe I go around with my eyes and ears closed."

"Or maybe you just work too hard."

The strains of the pop song 'True Love Ways' sung by Buddy Holly came out of the loudspeakers, a song more suited to smooching has probably never been written. The lights were low, I held Kate in my arms, and we rocked gently to and fro to the rhythm of the music. Although the room was crowded, with people all around us, I was conscious of nothing else but Kate so close to me; the faint smell of her perfume, and the soft touch of her hair against my cheek.

"This is nice."

"Lovely," she murmured.

Totally relaxed, I felt that this was heaven. We had our arms around each other and I could feel the closeness of her body against mine. Any fears that she might not welcome this vanished as she snuggled ever closer to me, gently swaying in time to the music. For a second, she pulled away and looked up at me, her eyes meeting and holding mine. No words were spoken. She simply smiled, then put her head back on my shoulder and we danced on, moving as one to the music. Had I the power to stop the world from spinning and have it stand still in its orbit - this is the moment I would have chosen. A moment that I would cherish, savour, and nurture forever in my heart.

A tap on my shoulder interrupted these blissful sensations. It was Richard.

"Sorry to interrupt Paul," he said apologetically, "but you're wanted on the telephone out in the corridor. Sounds urgent."

"Who on earth wants me?"

"One of the nurses in Surgical Three theatre. Sounds as if they want you there fast."

Silently, I cursed. This was a moment I had dreamed about for months, an occasion that I scarcely dared imagine would actually come about, a sensation that I wanted to go on forever - yet in an instant the magic spell had been broken and the moment had been snatched from me. I apologised to Kate, led her by the hand off the dance floor, and suggested that she sat on one of the chairs at the side whilst I answered the phone, promising to be back in a matter of seconds. Out in the corridor, the telephone was hanging off the hook. It was indeed a member of the nursing staff from Surgical Three theatre.

"Dr Lambert, I have been asked to get you to come to the theatre as soon as possible."

"What, immediately?"

"Yes, immediately. Mr Potts is waiting to start the operation."

"You say Mr Potts is there?"

"Yes, and he wants you here now."

I couldn't make sense of it at all. To operate within the bowel through a telescope required the patient to be put into the lithotomy position, the position in which it is customary for women to give birth. Damn it, there was only just space between the legs for the surgeon - there simply wasn't room for an assistant as well. Anyway, why did Mr Potts need an assistant? It was a one-man operation. In any case, where was Mr Khan? Had he gone home? Surely he would not have left the boss on his own. Perhaps Mr Potts felt that if the consultant had to work on a Saturday evening the houseman should be there as well, I thought bitterly. I hurried back to find Kate and apologised profusely, explaining the situation.

"I shouldn't be more than thirty or forty minutes. Do you mind waiting?"

"No, I don't mind," she said, a little doubtfully. "I've got Sally for company, but please do get back as soon as you can."

Assuring her that I would, I ran to the Surgical Three unit.

Arriving in the theatre, I found Mr Potts and Mr Khan already scrubbed in readiness for the surgery. I was surprised to find that the patient, Mrs Deakin, although in the lithotomy position, was draped in readiness for an abdominal operation. Mr Khan explained quickly that they had identified the bleeding point within the rectum and that it was bleeding profusely but, despite their best endeavours, they had been unable to arrest the haemorrhage using the operating telescope working through the back passage. The plan now was to remove the entire rectum and anus, in an operation that involved one surgeon dissecting the bowel from above through an abdominal incision, whilst the second surgeon dissected the bowel upwards from below, starting at the anus. As the two surgeons each worked to separate the bowel from the surrounding structures eventually they would meet in the heart of the pelvis, and the length of bowel, in this case the rectum and anus, including the bleeding ulcer, would be removed. As soon as I heard this news, I was horrified. My concern ought to have been that a woman, only in her forties, would end up with a permanent colostomy and have to wear a bag to collect her stools on her abdominal wall for the rest of her life. I ought to have been concerned that she had not been warned about this possibility, nor had she given her consent for it, although it was probably covered by the '*whatever necessary*' phrase in the small print on the standard consent form. I ought to have been concerned that this operation carried a significant mortality risk - but my sole concern was that I knew this operation would last at least three hours, and I had told Kate to expect me back in approximately thirty minutes.

Mr Potts had already started his incision in the abdomen, as had Mr Khan in the perineum.

"Come on, Lambert, hurry up." The consultant looked across at me and growled, "Don't just stand there dithering. I need some assistance here. I can't do this operation all on my own." As I started to scrub my hands and arms, I beckoned one of the nurses to me.

"Do me a favour," I said urgently. "Ring the lounge in the doctors' residency; there's a party going on there. See if you can get a message to Nurse Meredith for me to tell her what's happening. Tell her that I'm going to be stuck here for hours. And do apologise for me, please?"

In two minutes she was back. "I think the telephone there must be broken...I'm afraid that I can't get a ringing tone at all."

I suddenly remembered that all the telephones in the lounge had been disconnected. I begged her to try and contact Kate using the telephone in the corridor, and she disappeared again obediently. By the time she returned, I was at the table assisting Mr Potts. He had already opened the abdomen and started to dissect the large bowel. Mr Khan was well into the dissection at the lower end.

"Do you mind if I give a message to Dr Lambert, Mr Potts?"

"No, carry on."

She turned to me. "I'm afraid there's no reply, the telephone just rings and rings."

"Then could you please bleep Dr Nolan and pass my message that way, if you don't mind?"

When she returned she didn't dare to interrupt Mr Potts a second time, but caught my eye and shook her head.

I was devastated. The evening had started so promisingly, but this was a disaster. I would now be stuck in the operating theatre for at least three hours whilst Kate would be on her own at the party, not knowing what had become of me. She had said that Sally would be with her, but Sally and John had been getting on well and would probably feel that Kate was not their responsibility and, in any case, decide that she was quite old enough to look after herself.

I pictured her sitting on her own, looking at her watch from time to time, and getting angrier with me for letting her down as every minute passed. Then a worse thought struck me. Perhaps she was no longer on her own. Perhaps I was no longer in her thoughts. Perhaps she was in the arms of another, continuing to enjoy the party. It was inevitable that a pretty young girl sitting on her own at a party would be invited to dance. I was aware I could do nothing about it and, feeling bitter and angry, cursed fate that had played such a trick on us. Mr Potts' voice brought me back to reality.

"For God's sake, Lambert, you're not helping me in the least. You're supposed to be using that retractor to help me, not to hinder me. Hold those tissues out of the way so that I can see what I am dissecting and for God's sake, use your swab to mop away the blood."

Feeling utterly miserable, I tried to concentrate on being a good assistant but my mind was elsewhere, tortured by the thought of Kate in another's arms. My eyes regularly drifted to the clock on the theatre wall as its fingers showed eleven pm, slowly moved to eleven–thirty pm, and then dragged on towards midnight. It was after one am when the last suture was inserted and dressings applied to the various wounds, and a plastic bag was placed over the stoma on the abdominal wall, through which Mrs Deakin would move her bowels for the rest of her life.

Taking off his bloodstained theatre gown and throwing it into the skip in the corner of the surgeon's room, Mr Potts looked at me critically.

"You've been very subdued tonight Lambert - is everything alright?"

"Yes, Sir, fine thank you. Perhaps a little tired, that's all."

The last thing I was going to do was to share my problems with my boss. Mr Potts accepted this explanation, but Mr Khan was more perceptive.

"Paul, I can write up the operation notes, drug charts and post-operative instructions for you if you would like to disappear. I am sure that there are other matters that you need to attend to."

I smiled at him gratefully, said "Goodnight," to Mr Potts, and made my exit.

Head down, I walked slowly and sadly back to the residency and dragged myself to the lounge. The party was over and a number of the residents were tidying up the room, emptying the ashtrays, collecting up the glasses, and boxing the empty wine bottles. The DJ was busy packing away his records, microphone and loudspeakers. It was hard to believe that less than four hours before, here in this room, I had enjoyed those magical moments when I had held Kate in my arms. Johnny came across, looking angry.

"So there you are. I get everything set up for you - low lights, soft music - and you go and disappear! Where the hell did you get to?" Quickly, I explained, and he was immediately sympathetic. I asked after Kate.

"Was she alright? Did you see what happened to her? Was she with her friend Sally?"

"Sally and John Probert stayed to the very end. They seemed to be getting on well together. I saw Kate dancing with Simon early on but what happened to them later, I don't know. They certainly weren't here at the end."

"Simon. You mean Simon Gresty?"

"Yes."

"And did they leave together or did Kate leave on her own?"

"Look Paul, I'm sorry. I really don't know. I know they were together early in the evening, but what happened after that I couldn't say. I'm sorry."

I wondered if he really did not know or whether in fact he did, but was protecting my feelings. Johnny could clearly see the anger and frustration mirrored in my face.

"I'm sure that she'll understand, Paul, when you explain to her what happened. It was just one of those things. There was nothing you could do about it. Ask her out again as soon as you can."

I should have stayed and helped to clear up the lounge but I was tired and felt utterly dejected. I excused myself and went back to my room. How could an evening which started so well end so miserably? And what must Kate be thinking of me? Would she understand that the

matter was truly out of my hands, beyond my control? Would she give me a second chance or was our friendship at an end? I was determined to contact her first thing in the morning.
Although not disturbed by any medical calls, I got very little sleep that night. I lay in bed, bitter, aggrieved, and full of self-pity, thinking how unfair it all was. For months now, I had devoted myself exclusively to my clinical duties and to the patients on the ward who were my responsibility. I had always put them first - and yet, the first and only time when I really wanted a few hours just for myself, they had been denied. There had been no other occasion since I had started the job when one of our patients had needed to go to theatre at a weekend, other than when we had been 'on take'. Then, exactly at the wrong moment - just as the party was getting going and I held Kate in my arms - not only did a patient have to go to theatre, but it turned into a three hour operation, and I was not even able to get a message through to her to explain my absence.

I was also extremely anxious to know what had happened to Kate. If her friend Sally was enjoying John Probert's company as Johnny had suggested, it seemed unlikely that she would worry about Kate. I hoped that Kate might have slipped quietly back to the nurses home when she realised that I wasn't coming back, but it seemed, from what I had heard from Johnny, that she had got together with Simon. Simon, of all people - he must have been ten or fifteen years older than her, and such a creep! But when I considered the matter rationally, I had to admit to myself that I had been the one who had invited her to the party and then disappeared for three hours without any explanation. In the circumstances, she could hardly be blamed if she amused herself in the company of another.

I got up next morning in a foul temper, and went to breakfast. All the other house officers were in buoyant mood, and inevitably the topic of conversation around the table was the party that had been held the night before. All seemed to agree that it had been an enormous success and there were demands that a date for another should be arranged at once. Somewhat tentatively, I asked whether anybody had seen what had happened to Kate, but drew a complete blank. This was not entirely unexpected, for she was a junior nurse undertaking her first attachment on our unit and, apart from Johnny, nobody else knew who she was. Simon Gresty, being a senior registrar, was better known - but nobody seemed to have noticed with whom he had been dancing, or whether he had left alone or with company.

I resolved that I must contact Kate as soon as possible, to offer profuse apologies to her, to explain why I had not been able to return to the party, but particularly to let her understand that it had been impossible to get a message through to her. Back in the privacy of my room I rang the nurses' home. I could hear the ringing tone but it rang and rang and rang. Clearly nobody was in the office to answer; it was, after all, still early on a Sunday morning. I drifted miserably to my ward round, starting on the female ward. On my very first Sunday in the job, way back in August, Sister Rutherford had explained that she liked to go round the wards on a Sunday morning accompanied by the house officer, and this had proved an extremely useful way for me to learn much about the practical management of a busy ward. In reality, it was her way of mothering the new house officers and helping them to feel comfortable and 'at home' in the job. With the passage of time we had become more equal partners, but it remained a useful exercise and was an excellent way to ensure good communication between medical and nursing teams. Before we started the round, I asked Sister Rutherford whether she knew at what time the office in the nursing home would be manned.

"I think that on a Sunday morning the Home Sister usually opens the office about eleven o'clock," she said.

Clearly this was an unusual question for me to ask and she must have known that there was a personal reason behind it, but she passed no comment, and I was grateful that she did not ask the reason for my request. Shortly after eleven am, when I had completed my round on both the male and female wards, I rang the nurses' home again from the privacy of my room. This time, fortunately, I was able to speak to the Home Sister, only to be informed that Student Nurse Meredith had already checked out. She explained that Kate had seven days leave before she started on night duty. Saying that I needed to get in touch with her rather urgently, I asked if she would be kind enough to give me Kate's address and telephone number.

"I'm afraid I'm not able to do that," Home Sister explained. "One or two of our nurses have been pestered in the past by unwanted callers, and we have to protect their privacy." I explained again that I was Dr Lambert and that we both worked on the same ward, but she was uncompromising.

"I'm sorry Dr Lambert, but the regulations have been tightened recently and I'm not allowed to give you any personal details."

Suddenly, I had a brainwave. Her friend Sally would almost certainly have her contact details. If I could contact Sally, I could probably get in touch with Kate. I realised, though, that I didn't know Sally's surname.

"Sister, Kate has a friend called Sally. I'm not sure what her surname is but she was in the same student group as Kate and has been working on the medical wards. Would it be possible for me to speak with her?"

"You probably mean Sally Bentley. I think that's the only other 'Sally' in Nurse Meredith's intake - but I'm afraid that she's left the nursing home as well. All the nurses that started in the summer have completed their first clinical attachment and they're all entitled to a week's leave before they move to their next posts."

"And, of course, you can't give me Sally's number either," I said slightly sarcastically, knowing exactly what the answer would be.

"No, Dr Lambert," came the firm and inevitable reply.

I realised that, once again, I had reached a dead end. I thanked the Home Sister, and put down the phone.

Thoroughly dejected, sitting alone in my room, I decided that the only remaining course of action was to write a letter to her addressed to the nursing home, one that would be waiting for her on her return. I sat down with paper and pencil to write it, drafting it three times before I was satisfied with what I had written. I explained in detail why I had not been able to return to the party, and particularly how I had tried but failed to get a message to her. I begged for her forgiveness. I said how much I had enjoyed dancing with her and made particular mention of the Buddy Holly number, expressing the hope that we would meet again shortly, and how I was looking forward to seeing her again. I closed with the phrase 'With my love' and hoped desperately that she would understand and accept my apology.

Chapter 14

For the rest of the day the wards were reasonably quiet. There was little to keep me occupied and I moped around, reflecting on my misfortune and wallowing in self-pity. So many questions revolved in my mind. Why did the urgent call to theatre have to coincide so precisely with the party? A few hours earlier or later would have made all the difference. Would Kate truly understand that it simply was not possible to get a message through to her? And what were her feelings for me now? Had someone else, possibly Simon, taken my place in her affections? So many questions, but I would have to be patient. They would all remain unanswered for a week.

Monday arrived and with it the routine of work on the ward, in casualty, and in the theatres. There was plenty to keep me occupied, both mentally and physically, distracting me from dwelling on my personal problems. Of the three aspects of my duty, it was the time spent in the operating theatres that was the most fascinating. Many buildings have a unique atmosphere - whether it be the awe-inspiring grandeur of an English cathedral, the close friendly warmth of a busy pub, or the gloomy oppression of a funeral parlour - and so it is with an operating theatre. Even when not in use, the marble floor and tiled walls, and the theatre table in the centre with its overhead lamp a yard across waiting expectantly to illuminate the next operation, create an aura of their own. This is a place of drama, excitement and suspense; a place where life and death decisions are made, a place where lives are won and lost. Entering the room makes the senses quicken, even for the experienced surgeon. This is where knowledge and skill are put to the test, a place where the surgeon's technical ability - or lack of it - will dramatically affect the lives of those who have entrusted themselves to his care.

For many reasons, I enjoyed my visits to theatre. There was the academic interest as the anatomy learned at medical school was brought to life, the fascination of looking at the pathology and actually seeing the disease process that had been causing the patient's symptoms, and finally the satisfaction of watching the surgeon correct the problem - possibly relieving a blockage, repairing injured tissue, or, most dramatic of all, arresting haemorrhage. Then there was the sense of teamwork. The surgeon, the anaesthetist, and the scrub nurse, supported by assistants, runners, and theatre technicians, all working together as one unit with a common purpose; for the benefit of patients who had,

quite literally, put their life in the hands of the team. There is nothing that quite compares with it.
Assisting in the theatre was a pleasant and interesting change from the more routine and sometimes repetitive work on the ward. It was very instructive to assess a surgical condition whilst admitting a patient preoperatively, then to witness the surgical intervention, and finally to follow the patient's postoperative recovery. The disadvantage was that, whilst assisting in theatre, my work on the ward did not go away; it simply remained for me to do later. Therefore, assisting in theatre always resulted in an exceptionally long working day.

There were, however, potential hazards for a young male house officer in theatre, as I was to discover on the next occasion that I was required to work there. Mr Potts was to perform a resection of a cancer of the rectum and needed two assistants. The patient was an elderly man whose tumour was situated about three inches above the anus and Mr Potts' objective was to divide the bowel above and below the cancer, remove the length of bowel containing the tumour, and then anastomose the bowel by suturing the two open ends together to restore the continuity of the intestinal tube.

Theatre clothing was unisex; both the surgeons, who were almost invariably male, and the nurses, almost invariably female, wore thin green cotton pyjama-style trousers and a green cotton smock. The only difference between the sexes was that the surgeons tended to wear rubber boots whilst the nurses, who were a little further away from the wound and anything that might spill from it, preferred slip-on wooden clogs or pumps. Mr Khan and I had already changed into our theatre clothes and were having a drink and a chat in the sister's office, when a telephone message came through from Mr Potts to state that he would be a few minutes late. He instructed that Mr Khan should start the operation and open the abdomen on his behalf. Mr Khan went to find the anaesthetist Dr Tom Lester, a consultant, who was reading a newspaper in the surgeon's room whilst awaiting the arrival of the consultant surgeon. Dr Lester was a small, slightly built man, quietly spoken, who had a rather downtrodden air and looked as if he carried the cares of the world on his shoulders. He had a reputation for being economical with words, only using the minimum number that any particular situation demanded. When Mr Khan announced that we would be starting the operation before Mr Potts arrived, Dr Lester's single response was "Right." Mr Khan and I went into theatre to scrub up, while Dr Lester went to the anaesthetic room and began to anaesthetise the patient. In due course, the patient was wheeled into theatre and transferred to the operating table. The diathermy leads were attached to the patient's thigh, the abdomen was exposed, an antiseptic iodine solution was painted on the skin from the level of the nipples to mid thigh, and sterile drapes were laid around the operation area.

During the months that I had been in post I had seen Mr Khan operate regularly, and had come to admire his careful surgical technique. Nothing was hurried, bleeding was kept to a minimum, visualisation of the anatomy was good, every step of each operation was completed with meticulous attention to detail - and yet the operations were completed in good time. He was always calm and quietly spoken. Instruments were requested, never demanded, from the scrub nurse, with a polite "Please" and "Thank you."

When everything was prepared, he made a long vertical incision in the patient's lower abdomen and dissected through the skin, subcutaneous fat and the various muscle layers, until the inner lining of the abdominal cavity - the peritoneum - was exposed. Division of the peritoneum allowed access to the abdominal cavity, and our first view of the abdominal contents. It was educational and helpful to his juniors that he had the habit of thinking aloud during the surgery.

"The first thing to do," he mused, "is to see if there is any evidence that this cancer has spread from the rectum to the glands or liver." He asked me to pull the upper end of the wound towards the patient's chest with a retractor while he first inspected the liver, and then carefully swept a hand over its entire outer surface.

"So far so good; no sign of any spread there. Now, we must look for any glands. If they are involved, we should find them along the mesenteric vessels that carry blood away from the rectum."

Fortunately, again, there was no evidence of spread to the glands, meaning that - provided the rectal tumour itself had not grown into the tissues adjacent to the rectum, and provided that no complications occurred - there was a good chance of a successful cure for this patient's cancer. Sadly, the absence of obvious spread of a cancer to glands or to the liver, as seen at the time of the operation, did not automatically mean that a cure could be guaranteed: since if a few cells (microscopic in size, and certainly too small for the surgeon to see or feel) should float away in the blood stream and lodge in a distant site, the patient would get a recurrence of the cancer.

It was at this moment that Mr Potts strode into the theatre. "Good morning all," he breezed. "I'm glad to see that you have started without me. That will save us a bit of time."

He walked over to the theatre table and looked over the top of Mr Khan's shoulder. Again, in his booming voice, he said, "That incision isn't long enough, Khan; let's have another inch at either end, right down to the pubic bone at the bottom end. This is a low tumour and we will need good exposure to get it out. There is nothing to be gained from struggling through a small incision."

Then, turning to me, "We will also need a strong assistant on the retractor at the lower end. I hope you've had a good breakfast, Lambert." Without waiting for a reply he walked to the sink unit to put on a cap and mask, scrub up, and don theatre operating gown and gloves.

It was noticeable that when Mr Potts entered, the atmosphere in the operating theatre underwent a subtle change. Prior to his arrival, the entire theatre team had been undertaking their work seriously and conscientiously, but in an atmosphere that had been calm and relaxed. With Mr Potts in the theatre the staff continued to work just as before, but there was a certain tension discernible in the air. The relaxed atmosphere had somehow melted away.

I had expected that the boss would adopt the same theatre gear as everybody else, but this was not the case. When he came to the table I saw that he had tied a length of white crepe bandage round his forehead, to form a sweatband. He was also wearing a surgical headlamp. This was a relatively new development; essentially a modification of the original miner's headlamp, which focused a strong beam of light to illuminate the area at which the surgeon's head was pointing. In operations such as this, where the dissection was to be carried out deep in the pelvis, it was much easier to illuminate the scene using the head torch than by asking the theatre technicians to manhandle the large overhead operating theatre lamp.

"Right," said Mr Potts, "all change." He replaced Mr Khan, who had been at the patient's right side, and who now went to stand directly opposite Mr Potts to act as first assistant. Mr Potts indicated that I should stand at his right elbow, in anticipation of the work that was expected of me in holding the pelvic retractor. The scrub nurse for this major procedure was the senior theatre sister who stood alongside Mr Khan, across the table from me.

"Right, let's have those theatre lights down," said Mr Potts. All the theatre lights were now dimmed, leaving just the surgical wound and the surrounding area brilliantly illuminated. This was 'theatre' in the traditional sense of the word. Mr Potts was clearly planning to be the star performer.

"Now, where are you up to, Khan?"

Mr Khan explained that he had inspected the liver and the mesentery, looking for any spread of the tumour away from the bowel.

"And has it spread anywhere?"

"No Sir, it all looks completely clean."

"Right, I'll take your word for that; let's crack on." He spoke to the theatre technician. "Tip the patient's head down, Harry."

The operating table was tipped head down to allow the coils of moist, slippery intestines to slither into the upper abdomen, allowing a better view of the pelvis and upper rectum. These coils of bowel were then held in place with swabs. He operated faster than Mr Khan, dissecting sometimes with a scalpel, sometimes with scissors, stopping the bleeding with diathermy or with artery forceps as he went. At each stage of the procedure the scrub sister seemed to know instinctively exactly what instrument was required, and usually had this to hand. Occasionally Mr Potts would say "Come, come, Sister - seven inch Spencer Wells next," and she would have them there in a flash.

Mr Potts kept up a running commentary throughout; he seemed to be in his element, and thoroughly enjoying himself. He appeared to be much more at ease in theatre than on the wards, where he was brusque and, unlike Sir William, ill at ease talking to his patients. He turned to the anaesthetist.

"We had a good game of golf yesterday, didn't we, Tom? Fine weather - a little breezy maybe, but not enough to affect decent golfers." Then, addressing the world in general, "We played at the Stretton Heath Golf Club, and a close match it was too. Anaesthetist versus Surgeon. Cut and thrust right to the end. Only settled on the eighteenth green. Now, if you would care to look down into the pelvis, you will see no trace of this rectal tumour at all. That's because it's not in the abdominal cavity - it's deep down in the pelvis, at the level of the prostate and bladder - but we'll soon dig it out. Pass me the self-retaining retractor, will you, Sister dear?"

This retractor was placed in the edges of the wound and, using its ratchet, the two blades were separated and used to keep the wound edges widely apart, to allow good vision and access. It freed up the first assistant so that he could help in other ways, such as cutting sutures close to the knot after they had been tied, or mopping away any blood so that the surgeon had a clear view at all times. I couldn't actually see how the operation was progressing because to do so, I would have had to move two feet to the left and put my head where Mr Potts' head was, but Mr Khan had a look and agreed. Mr Potts returned to his account of the previous day's golf.

"Tom had a lucky shot on the ninth. Chipped up from the semi rough thirty yards from the green and, blow me, the ball went straight into the hole! It really was a complete fluke, but it put him one up at the turn. It meant that I had to concentrate hard and attack the course on the back nine. Now, here we go - we pull the sigmoid loop of colon up, and find the space between the rectum in front and the hollow of the sacrum behind. As we develop the plane of dissection, we have to be very careful that we don't disturb the tumour, since we don't want to spread any cancer cells. Nor do we want any bleeding from those rich juicy veins on the front of the sacrum. This is where the skill of the surgeon really comes in. Surgery is 100 percent interesting, Lambert, not like anaesthetics - that is ninety-nine percent boredom."

He shot a glance at Dr Lester that the anaesthetist, busy reading The Times newspaper, studiously ignored. He was referring to the old adage that the life of an anaesthetist, like that of an airline pilot, is ninety-nine percent boredom and one percent pure panic.

"It was nip and tuck all the way to the fifteenth, but I had a glorious shot to the green on the sixteenth. A six iron from 150 yards; it went as straight as a die. The ball finished five feet from the pin, I had a single putt, got the birdie, and we were all square again."

I was hanging on to the pelvic retractor, quite unable to see what was going on in the wound, but listening to the account of the golf. I made a private bet with myself that the story would conclude with a victory for the surgeon over the anaesthetist, and I wasn't to be disappointed. I looked to see what reaction the story was having on Dr Lester, but his nose was still in his newspaper. It seemed as if the crossword was of more interest to him. He certainly wasn't going to rise to the jibe that anaesthetics was boring.

"I got a par on the seventeenth, a difficult hole with a raised green well protected by bunkers, but had to give Tom a shot. You see, his handicap is higher than mine. Surgeons have a greater sporting prowess than anaesthetists - don't they, Tom?" Again, I looked at Dr Lester, but he remained engrossed in his crossword puzzle and his face gave no outward sign that he had heard the remark. Mr Potts continued with his story.

"So, it was still anybody's game as we stood on the eighteenth tee. Lambert, you've got that retractor in the wrong place again. How can I dissect around the prostate gland if you keep hiding it from me? Let me adjust it for you. Now there it is - hang on to it and keep it still, boy."

In my own defence, I must explain that a second assistant - standing to the side of the surgeon, with a retractor held in an outstretched arm - is unable to see anything of the operation at all. The surgeon places the retractor blade where he wants it, the assistant takes hold of the handle, and then has to freeze in that position.

"Now the eighteenth is almost 400 yards long, and there is a pond just in front of the green. We both had good tee shots but Tom decided to lay up short of the water - the sort of thing an anaesthetist *would* do. It left him with a fifty yard wedge shot into the target. Surgeons are said to have hearts like lions though, aren't they? I decided to go for it. Took a three wood off the fairway and banged the ball right into the heart of the green. Two putts and the match was mine. Victory to the surgeon, hey Tom?" Tom didn't reply, but Mr Potts seemed not to notice or, indeed, to mind.

Suddenly Mr Potts was shouting. "There's a bleeder, down there, in the hollow of the sacrum. Khan, apply pressure. Sister, more swabs. Lambert, keep that retractor in place, for God's sake. Harry, get me the suction machine at once. Tom, we may need some blood for transfusion very soon."

All at once there was real tension in the air, and Mr Potts became terse and anxious. His movements were hurried and tremulous. Despite the headband, there were beads of sweat on his brow running down towards his eyes. Sister turned to one of the theatre runners. "Swab for the surgeon's brow please, nurse." Mr Potts turned away from the theatre table for a moment and one of the junior nurses mopped his brow. It took a good five minutes to control the bleeding and for calm to return, but in this time at least a pint of blood had collected in the suction bottle. Dr Lester had laid aside his newspaper and replaced the infusion of saline with blood.

The operation continued, and slowly Mr Potts regained his composure and again became more relaxed. With my inexperience and from the position that I occupied at the table, I could not see what had caused the bleeding nor how it had been controlled, but did wonder whether it would have happened had Mr Potts not been replaying the golf match in his mind. I looked across at Mr Khan, wondering if his expression might answer the question. Only his eyes were visible between his mask and his surgical cap but, so far as I could tell, he remained impassive. It seemed that surgery could be one percent blind panic as well, at least in Mr Potts' hands.

Sister had been waiting for calm to return before she asked Mr Potts a question. "Mr Potts, we have a staff nurse with us today who has come to theatre for the first time. Would you mind if she came to the table to watch the operation? It will be a good experience for her."

"No, no," said Mr Potts, "the more the merrier. Come to see the maestro at work, has she? I hope she's not the delicate sort that's likely to faint at the sight of a drop of blood."

The new nurse was already gowned and scrubbed, and she came and stood at my right hand side. She spoke to Mr Potts in a confident manner.

"No, I certainly won't faint, Sir. I've just worked for three months in the Casualty department and we see plenty of blood there. I will be fine, thank you."

I recognised the voice and although only her eyes were visible between cap and mask, I knew instantly who it was. It was Sue Weston, whom I had subsequently learned was nicknamed 'Sexy Sue' - the girl who had woken me up and brought me a cup of tea in the overnight room in the accident department. When I had spoken to colleagues in the residency about the incident during my first night of casualty duty, it had not been a surprise to discover that she had quite a reputation and was the topic of much conversation amongst the doctors. As Johnny had rather unkindly said, "She eats nice quiet lads like you for breakfast, Paul. My advice is to stay well away."

Uninvited, memories of the sight of her cleavage and the smell of her perfume stirred in my head. Her eyes smiled at me.

"Oh, hello Dr Lambert, it's you."

"Shh," said Sister at once. "Silence. Watch the operation by all means, but don't interrupt."

The operation continued. It was useful to have the running commentary to know how the procedure was progressing as, from my position, the view was limited to the entrance of the wound, the lower part of which I was pulling down with my retractor to give Mr Potts as much space as possible in which to work. My arms were beginning to cramp, so from time to time I shifted the retractor from one hand to the other. I had been standing on one spot for over an hour by this time and my legs were beginning to ache as well. Suddenly, I was aware of another sensation on my leg. Something was touching my right calf; it was warm and soft and tickled slightly. Before I could work out what it was, it had stopped, and I thought I must have imagined it. But it returned a few minutes later. There was a definite gentle stroking of the skin above the level of my surgical boot. Whatever it was had found a gap between the top of the boot and the bottom of the trouser leg. I looked down and to my horror saw that Sue had slipped her foot out of her wooden clog and was using her stockinged toes to gently stroke my calf. I frowned at her but her eyes simply laughed back at me. I turned around, hoping that there would be somebody behind us in the theatre whose presence might inhibit Sue's antics, but there was nobody there. I tried to move my leg away but was limited by the table in front of me and the solid frame of my boss to my left. Wherever I tried to go, the stockinged toes followed me, tickling me and sending my senses racing.

Mr Potts was continuing his commentary. "Pass me those cross clamps, Sister. We are going to clamp the bowel above and below the tumour, but we have to be careful not to spill any of the content of the bowel into the operating field. I know that before the operation the patient was purged well, to empty the bowel as much as possible - but if we can avoid spilling any bacteria into the wound, we shall avoid getting an infection. Tom, this would be a good time to give some antibiotics."

The soft stroking of my calf continued. Sue was now drawing circles with her toes on my skin, and she was moving up towards my knee. I cannot deny that it was a pleasant sensation but I felt acutely embarrassed and very much afraid that someone would see. Again I tried to edge to my left, and for a short time Sue kept her toes to herself. *Thank goodness*, I thought - she must have got the message that she was playing a dangerous game, and that I did not welcome her attentions. However this proved incorrect as I became aware of a new, and altogether far more distracting, stimulus. She had moved her whole body closer to me, and I felt the warmth of her thigh against mine. Then her hip met mine, and started an almost imperceptible gyratory movement.

"Hold up the colon, Khan. I need to get these clamps a safe distance from the tumour, and Sister, can you have an iodine swab to hand? I'll need to clean the open ends when we cut the bowel across."

I suddenly had a brainwave: perhaps I could get Sue moved to another position round the table.

"Mr Potts," I said, "I don't think that Nurse Weston can see the various stages of this operation from where she is standing. Perhaps she would see more if she were to move to the top end of the table."

Before Mr Potts could reply, Sister spoke. "She is here to understand the duties of the scrub nurse, so she is fine where she is."

The thigh and hip contact continued but, in addition, something warm and soft was moving gently against my right upper arm. I knew instantly what it was - Sue was gently rubbing the outer side of her breast against me. *Surely Sister must notice* I thought, but all her concentration was focused on her tray of instruments and on anticipating the requirements of the surgeon. I was quite unable to move my arms, as I was holding the retractor in the wound. Instinctively I moved to the left, but immediately came into contact with Mr Potts.

"Don't crowd me, Lambert" he said. "You're allowed to stand at the right hand of God, but God in this case is right-handed, and I can't work if you're cramping my style." Reluctantly, I resumed my previous position, ever more conscious of the warmth and softness of Sue's body against my arm.

"Right, we've clamped the bowel. If you pass me a long-handled scalpel, Sister, we will cut the bowel between the clamps, and we will have this tumour out in no time at all."

As Sister turned to reach for the scalpel, my right arm and shoulder were again caressed. I looked across at Mr Khan. It was clear that, unlike Sister, he was acutely aware of what was going on. I was certain that he was annoyed but, equally, felt unable to intervene. Afterwards, Johnny said that he would just have relaxed and enjoyed it. There was no doubt that it was a pleasant sensation, but I was terrified that Mr Potts or Sister would see what was happening and be furious. However, both were concentrating on their jobs and were completely unaware of Sue's behaviour.

With a triumphant gesture, like a magician lifting a rabbit from a hat, Mr Potts raised the rectal specimen from the wound, held it aloft, and then placed it in a metal kidney dish provided by Sister.

He turned to Harry, the theatre orderly. "Now, Harry, take that into the sluice; take the clamps off, cut it open, clean it up, and let's see what we've got. We need to be sure that we've removed the whole tumour."

Harry disappeared into the sluice with the specimen, and the surgical team, including the nursing sister, stood back from the table for a minute or two, giving me the opportunity to rest my aching arms and, with a great sense of relief, to put some distance between Nurse Weston and myself.

Harry soon returned with the specimen that he had cut along its length and opened, so that the inner lining could be seen. In the centre was a craggy ulcer perhaps an inch across, with a hard raised edge. The centre was covered in a dirty grey slough. It was a typical cancer. Mr Potts was delighted.

"That's fine. We've got a healthy margin of at least an inch above and below that tumour, so there is every prospect of a cure here. All we've got to do now is to join the two ends together and we're through. Almost time to put the kettle on."

We all resumed our places at the table and I was handed my retractor again but, as before, while Sister was concentrating on the next stage of the operation and anticipating the instruments that Mr

Potts would require, Sue Weston started her tricks. Again our thighs were in contact, and her left breast gently caressed my upper arm and shoulder. Then, she half turned to her left and strained forward, as if trying to see what was going on in the operation. On the occasion that she had woken me with a cup of tea in the casualty department, it had been impossible for me to fail to notice that she was a well-endowed young lady - and now, as her cleavage was wrapped around my right upper arm, this impression was reinforced. There was nothing I could do to escape because it was still necessary for me to hold the retractor, and I couldn't move to the left because 'God' was standing there, suturing together the two ends of bowel, completely unaware of the little drama that was going on at his side. With my eyes I appealed to Mr Khan, who clearly was aware of Sue's antics and who now looked very angry but who, like me, found it impossible to intervene.

Mr Potts continued to describe the procedure. "That's good. We have got two layers of stitches in place to join the bowel together. Now we make sure that our anastomosis is watertight and ensure there is no further bleeding. We'll put a big drain down to take any blood away, that would otherwise collect should any oozing occur after the abdomen is closed, and then I'll leave you, Mr Khan, to stitch up, if I may? You made this incision so it's only fair that you should close it."

At every opportunity Sue rubbed her soft warm breasts sensually against me and I became aware that my own body - against my will, I might add, and despite my efforts to prevent it - was responding to the stimulus on my right arm and shoulder. Theatre trousers are only thin and I needed to press forward against the operating theatre table to make sure my emotions didn't show.

"Distract yourself," I said to myself, "think of something else. Who scored the goals in the World Cup final? Too easy! In what order were they scored? Again too easy! Who passed the ball to the scorer for each of the four goals?" But I couldn't think. The sensation of her body pressed firmly against mine was too great. I glared at her to show my displeasure, but she took not the slightest bit of notice. She clearly regarded the episode as no more than a bit of fun.

I decided that the situation had become intolerable and that I had to put an end to it, so suddenly and forcibly used my right shoulder to push Sue away. The sudden movement attracted Sister's attention. She saw my arm against Sue's chest and looked at me with undisguised fury, completely misunderstanding the situation. She turned to Sue and in her sharpest voice said "Nurse Weston, leave the table at once. Go and get your lunch break immediately."

Mr Potts looked up in surprise at Sister's severe tone. "Is everything all right, Sister dear?"

"I will speak to you about it later, Mr Potts," she said, fiercely. Clearly, she was not going to let the matter rest and was planning to pursue the matter with my consultant boss. How would I be able to persuade her and Mr Potts that I was the innocent party and that her interpretation of events was completely wrong?

Sue left the theatre, closely followed by Mr Potts, leaving Mr Khan to close the abdomen. The theatre lights were raised, the atmosphere in theatre relaxed, and the operation was completed without further incident.

The whole procedure had taken over two hours and it felt good to take off hat, mask, gloves and gown, stretch my legs, and then sit down in the surgeons' room. A cup of coffee was produced whilst Mr Khan was writing up the operation notes, and I was writing out postoperative instructions, wondering how soon it would be before there were repercussions. I did not have long to wait. Sister burst in, red in the face, slamming the door behind her.

"Dr Lambert," she shouted, "I will not have arrogant young doctors molesting my nurses in theatre - indeed, right under my very eyes. In all the time that I have been in nursing I have never seen behaviour like it. I shall be reporting this matter immediately to..."

Mr Khan interrupted in a voice that was quiet yet firm. "Sister, I saw exactly what went on - indeed, I had been aware of the situation for fifteen minutes or so before you noticed. I can assure you that Dr Lambert was not responsible; he was entirely the innocent party."

Sister looked at him doubtfully. "Are you absolutely sure?"

"Absolutely positive Sister, without any shadow of a doubt. Dr Lambert was actually trying to distance himself from the girl. Do you not remember that he suggested that the nurse should be moved to another position round the table so that she could observe the surgery, but that you preferred that she should stay where she was? Remember also that Dr Lambert was actually reprimanded by Mr Potts for 'interfering with God's right arm' when he tried to move away from that nurse? She had been making a nuisance of herself whenever your back was turned. There is no doubt at all that the guilty party has gone to lunch. She is the one to whom you need to speak, not Dr Lambert."

Sister still looked uncertain. "Yes, but I saw Dr Lambert rubbing up against Nurse Weston."

"No, Sister. You saw Dr Lambert push Nurse Weston away."

Unfortunately, Sister still looked grim-faced and continued to look at me with grave suspicion but, given Mr Khan's explanation, was unable to pursue the incident further. A sixth sense, however told me that I had not heard the last of the matter; that there would be further repercussions.

Chapter 15

When I had rung Mr Khan's home, on that unforgettable day when I had been dragged so cruelly from Kate's arms, I had been answered by a female voice that I presumed to be Mrs Khan; and it had made me realise how little I knew about my senior colleague. To me, he was simply 'Mr Khan', my registrar - always helpful and supportive, a regular source of information and advice, constantly courteous and polite, exhibiting all the characteristics that you would wish to find in a perfect English gentleman - and the one who had recently rescued me from the irate theatre sister who had unjustly accused me of sexual harassment when, in reality, it had been me who had been the unwilling and innocent victim. I decided that, when a suitable chance arose, I would make some polite enquiries.

An opportunity presented itself one evening on our next urgency day, when we were relaxing together, drinking a cup of coffee after I had assisted him in theatre to perform an emergency hernia operation. I asked whether the lady that I had spoken with on the phone was indeed his wife, mentioning that although we had been working alongside each other for some three or four months, I knew nothing of his background, where he qualified or whether he had a family.

"Yes, I'm married," he replied. "You spoke to Indera, my wife - I call her Indy for short. We have been married for ten years now and have two children, an eight-year-old boy and a six-year-old girl." He seemed pleased that I had asked and went on to tell me something of his background.

Originally, he explained, the family home had been in Bombay[2] on the west coast of India, where his grandfather had started a haulage business that subsequently passed to his father. Although the business was successful and thriving, his father saw commercial opportunities in Africa and in the nineteen-thirties had moved 'lock stock and barrel' to Kenya, and started up a new haulage business there. Mohammed was his first born and proved to be his only son. Mr Khan continued the story.

"I always wanted to be a doctor, which pleased both of my parents. My father believed that England was the only place to get suitable training and I was fortunate enough to be accepted by the

---

[2] Bombay. Now known as Mumbai

medical school at St Bartholomew's in London. I arrived in this country when I was twenty years of age."

"So that is why your English is so perfect and accent-free," I interrupted.

"No," he said, "my father's business in Kenya was profitable, so I was able to study at an English school in Nairobi, and learnt my English there. English is my first language. My father has excellent English too but my mother is more comfortable speaking Marathi, which tends to be spoken in and around Bombay. Indy also prefers Marathi to English and will often speak to the children in that language when I am not around - I think she wants them to remember their Indian roots - but I insist that English is the first language in our own home. Neither of the children have any hint of an Indian accent but, of course, they were born and raised here and attend the local primary school."

"Was your wife not educated in England, then?"

He laughed. "No she wasn't, she was educated in India. When I was single, my parents decided that they had to find me a suitable wife. They obviously did not feel that I was capable of doing that for myself! Every time I went back to India for a holiday my parents would introduce me to some eligible girl from an Indian background, usually the daughter of one of their business friends. I was expected to take them out on a date - always chaperoned, you understand, by one of the girl's maiden aunts. Indy is the daughter of one of the directors of the Bombay Railway Company. It wasn't an arranged marriage, you understand. We were both free to marry whoever we wanted, but my parents put a string of eligible potential brides in front of me at every opportunity."

"And how does your wife find life in this country? It must be very different to her previous life in Bombay?"

"Yes, it is. She hasn't found it easy to settle. She doesn't go out to work. Her life revolves around the house and the children, so she doesn't have a large circle of friends, but she knows a number of the other parents from the children's school and is beginning to socialise with them."

"And do you think you'll stay in England in the future?"

"I certainly intend to. My ambition is to pursue a career in surgery in the NHS. England is my home now. Occasionally I manage a trip to India to see my more distant relatives, and I go back to Nairobi from time to time to visit my parents, but I cannot imagine returning there to live. There is a change of mood in Kenya at the moment that I fear is unsettling my father; I sense that the Africans are beginning to resent the success that Asians have made in the field of business and commerce. I'm not sure quite how long my parents will be able to stay. They hold British passports so could come to this country, but at their age they would find it more difficult to settle than I did."

I was pleased to have learned a little bit more about Mr Khan and his background. Quite apart from being such a pleasant and helpful colleague, I recognised that he was a dedicated surgeon. He worked quietly and conscientiously, being a good diagnostician on the wards, very thorough with the care of the patients both before and after surgery, and a skilled and careful technician in theatre. I would have been pleased to have him as my surgeon if the necessity arose, and particularly appreciated the time that he had taken with Johnny and me to help us in the early days when we were so inexperienced. Without his help and advice I doubt that I would have survived the challenges that we faced, and probably would not have lasted the course. Shortly, however, we were to meet a patient who was not at all appreciative of his skills.

Bert Jackson was a particularly unpleasant man who was known to his pals as 'Buster'. He presented himself to the accident and emergency department one evening, complaining of abdominal pain. It was my misfortune to be the doctor on duty at the time. He was a Bill Sikes figure; short, muscular, thick-necked, heavily tattooed and with a mean, unsmiling face, surmounted by a short crew cut. His dark eyes challenged those who chose to meet his gaze, and his chin, covered in stubble, was thrust forward aggressively. He looked as if he would be more at home walking down a dark back alley accompanied by a couple of Rottweiler dogs, each complete with a studded collar, than sitting in a cubicle in casualty. I attempted to take a clinical history but his answers to my questions were brief, blunt, evasive, and delivered in a loud voice and belligerent manner. His attitude seemed to be "Look, I've had this pain in my belly for a number of days now - you sort it out." He didn't see the relevance of the questions I was asking in my attempt to help him by diagnosing the cause of his troubles; such as whether there had been any shift in the site of the pain, whether he had any symptoms connected with the bowels or waterworks, or whether there had been any systemic upset. Eventually, I managed to ascertain that the pain had been present for four or five days, had settled in the lower right quadrant, was gradually getting worse, and that he had lost his appetite. The story was suggestive of appendicitis, though not absolutely typical.

When I came to examine his abdomen, the tenderness was compatible with appendicitis, despite not being particularly severe. Generally, it would be expected that appendicitis continuing for four days would cause excruciating pain and tenderness. Most patients with this condition are sufficiently tender within thirty-six hours of the onset of symptoms for the diagnosis to become definite, and will normally have the offending organ removed within forty-eight hours of the illness beginning. The next step was to perform a rectal examination. As Sir William had drilled into us so often, '*The examination of the abdomen starts in the groin and ends in the rectum. If you don't put you finger in, sooner or later you will put your foot in it!*' However, when I approached Mr Jackson and told him of the proposed examination, I was told in succinct fashion "Forget it Doc - there's no bloody way that you're going to stick your bloody finger up my bloody backside!"

His temperature was slightly raised, and when the blood results were reported there was a slight increase in his white cell count as well. Although not diagnostic of any specific problem, it seemed, on balance, that the correct diagnosis was likely to be appendicitis. It was clear, however, that he needed to be admitted; though probably for observation, rather than for immediate surgery.

When a diagnosis is in doubt, it is a useful exercise to admit the patient to the ward for 'observation'. In reality, it is not the observation per se but the passage of time that clarifies the situation. In many cases, perhaps surprisingly, all symptoms and clinical signs disappear and the patient returns to full health without any definite diagnosis ever being made. A diagnosis of some self-limiting condition, such as glandular enlargement, gastric flu, or viral illness, may then be attached, but can never be proven. In other cases, with the passage of time symptoms and signs become more definite, and the diagnosis becomes clear.

I had learned from Sir William that if a patient's abdominal musculature was well developed, the tenderness in a case of appendicitis might appear less marked than would otherwise be the case, thanks to the protective nature of the muscles. Therefore a thickset man such as Mr Jackson, who had experienced pains for four days, might conceivably have quite an advanced case of appendicitis without the clinical signs being particularly obvious. Having by this stage assisted at many appendicectomy operations, I had noticed that surgery was much easier in tall, slim individuals than in thickset, muscular or fat ones, who also tended to get more complications during their postoperative recovery. If this was appendicitis and surgery was required, it was not an operation that Mr Khan would allow me to perform.

Although not immediately available, over the phone Mr Khan agreed that Mr Jackson should be admitted and promised to review him as soon as he was free. I rang the male ward, made the necessary arrangements for admission and then, pleased to see the back of a rather unpleasant man, I returned to my casualty duties.

Shortly after the night staff came on duty and just as Johnny was relieving me to commence his overnight Casualty stint, I had a telephone call from the night sister.

"I'm sorry to trouble you, Dr Lambert, but there is a problem on the male ward. Mr Jackson won't allow Mr Khan to examine him. He won't even talk to him, and he is being extremely rude and aggressive."

"Why, for heaven's sake?"

"I'm afraid it's because he's coloured."

I said that I would go to the ward to try to resolve the problem, not anticipating any particular difficulty, believing that Mr Jackson's pain and a natural desire to return to good health would overcome any colour prejudice that he might have. He had an acute and as yet undiagnosed abdominal condition, probably appendicitis. He needed to be assessed by an experienced surgeon and possibly required emergency surgery. Without it, he might deteriorate very quickly. He needed Mr Khan's expertise and I had little doubt that, when the position was explained to him, he would see sense. When I arrived on the ward, Mr Khan was sitting in the office.

"I'm sorry about this, Paul," he said. "It's a long time since this last happened to me."

"I'm sorry too. I thought that this sort of attitude was a thing of the past." Mr Khan looked at me rather strangely, but said nothing.

The screens had been pulled around Mr Jackson's bed, and the patients in the neighbouring beds seemed unusually quiet and looked slightly anxious. They were obviously aware of the nature of the problem.

"Is there some sort of difficulty?" I asked benignly.

"Of course there is. I'm not having any f****** Paki examining me," Mr Jackson shouted.

"I presume you're talking about Mr Khan?"

"I don't care what his b***** name is."

"Listen," I said. "He's not from Pakistan - his parents were originally from India but he's actually a British citizen, just as you and I are. He holds a British passport."

"I don't care where he comes from. He could have come from Timbuktu for all I care. He's a wog, and he's not laying a finger on me."
I felt my blood beginning to boil but tried to keep my voice calm and quiet as I answered. "He happens to be an extremely good doctor, a fine surgeon - and for the benefit of your own health, you need his expertise right now. He needs to examine you so that we can be sure what is causing your abdominal problem. In particular, we need to know whether or not you require surgery."

"But you said I had appendicitis."

"I said I thought that was the most likely diagnosis but I am extremely junior, I've only been a doctor for a few months. I can't make a decision on whether or not you need surgery and if this is appendicitis, I certainly can't operate on you. Surely you want to be cured?"

"Who's the boss round here?"

"Mr Potts is the consultant."

"Well, he can b****** well see me instead."

"Look," I said trying to be conciliatory, "there really is no need for that. Mr Khan is a very capable doctor; you really ought to let him see you."

"I've already b****** well told you - no Paki doctor is laying a finger on me. Get Potts to see me."

"I'll see what I can do," I said, in a resigned voice.

Returning to the office, I discussed the situation with Mr Khan. Neither of us wanted to involve Mr Potts with the problem but felt that there really was no alternative. When the switchboard rang Mr Potts' home, it was Mr Potts himself who picked up the phone.

"Good evening, Sydney Potts speaking."

"Good evening Sir. I'm sorry to trouble you at home in the evening - this is Dr Lambert speaking."

He sounded surprised. "Oh, hello Lambert, is everything alright at the hospital? Is there some sort of problem?" If a case required consultant advice he would normally expect to be rung by the registrar or senior registrar, not by his lowly house officer.

"I'm afraid we have a little problem on the male ward, Sir. I've admitted a patient who refuses to be seen by Mr Khan." I went on to explain the details of the case and the patient's attitude to being examined by Mr Khan. There was a pause for a moment whilst he thought.

"It isn't right that we should be bullied, but equally I suppose we have a responsibility to stop the patient coming to any harm, even self inflicted harm. Give Simon Gresty a ring and ask him to sort it out."

"I had thought of that Sir but, if you remember, Mr Gresty is on study leave. He's at a college meeting in London."

"Ah - so he is. I had forgotten that." There was another longish pause."You say, Lambert, that you think that this is probably a case of appendicitis, but you're not completely sure."

"That's right, Sir."

"Right. Well, I suggest that you leave him on the ward overnight, and we will review him in the morning. If the diagnosis is not definite, I don't suppose he will come to any great harm. Oh, and Lambert - don't write him up for any pain relief. That way, by morning - if he really has got appendicitis - we may find that he is able to overcome his prejudices."

He rang off and I explained the gist of the conversation to Mr Khan. Since the boss had said the patient was to have no analgesia, we would obviously follow those instructions, but I wondered privately whether it was justifiable to leave him in pain. Mr Khan, however, said that it was a wholly acceptable, indeed appropriate, medical practice.

"The more analgesia that you give, the more it masks the patient's symptoms and signs and the more difficult it becomes to make a diagnosis. If you fill a patient with morphine you take away their pain, but you may be misled into thinking the patient is getting better."

I returned to Mr Jackson's bedside and explained that I had spoken with Mr Potts on the telephone, who agreed the diagnosis probably was appendicitis, but that he should be observed on the ward and reviewed in the morning. The patient looked triumphant and turned to the patients in the neighbouring beds who could not help overhearing our conversation.

"There you are. I told you so - we don't need any b***** Paki doctors. The whole lot of them should be sent back to 'Paki-land' or whatever damn country they came from."

It was infuriating to hear such arrogance and prejudice; but he was my patient, he was ill, and it wasn't my place to tackle him on his racist views.

The next day, Mr Khan and I embarked on our usual Saturday morning ward round, both keen to know how Mr Jackson had fared overnight. To our surprise, we found that he had been moved into one of the side wards. It transpired that some of the men in the neighbouring beds had been so angry at Mr Jackson's attitude towards Mr Khan, for whom they had great respect, that a number of them had taken it upon themselves to express their opinions to him on the matter. Angry words had been exchanged, the atmosphere on the ward had become difficult and, to resolve the situation, Night Sister had thought it wise to segregate Mr Jackson.

As we embarked on the ward round, Sister Ashbrook suggested to me that it might be wise to see Mr Jackson first. "He is now in quite a lot of pain and I suspect he will end up in theatre having his appendix taken out fairly soon. Oh," she added, with an apologetic glance at Mr Khan, "I think that you and I had better see him on our own; he's still being stupid and very awkward."

Mr Khan stayed in the office whilst Sister and I entered the side ward and it was immediately apparent that Sister was correct; Mr Jackson was indeed in a great deal of pain. When I examined his abdomen, the tenderness in the right lower quadrant was well localised, exquisite, and he was now running quite a fever. Despite my inexperience, I was now in no doubt that the diagnosis was acute appendicitis. Again, I tried to persuade him to allow Mr Khan to see him but, despite his severe pain, the patient remained adamant.

"No - if you can't sort it out, get Potts to sort it out."

Promising to ring the consultant, Sister and I left the room and discussed the situation with Mr Khan.

"I think that you had better ring Mr Potts at home again, Paul," Mr Khan said, "and see what he has to say about the situation. In the meantime, Sister and I will see the rest of the patients."

For a second time, I rang Mr Potts and gave him an update on the situation.

"You say that the patient still won't allow Mr Khan to see him?"

"I'm afraid that's right, Sir."

"And how definitely do you think that this is appendicitis?"

"Well, I am fairly certain now, Sir. I know I've only had limited experience but the patient is now extremely tender in exactly the right spot. He nearly jumps off the bed when you touch him there. I don't think there is a lot of doubt about the diagnosis."

"Okay - then arrange the theatre, and get on with it."

I wasn't quite sure what he meant. "Will you be coming in to do the operation Sir? If it would help, I can ring you when I have the theatre and the anaesthetist arranged?"

"No, Khan will do it. Just keep him out of sight until the patient is asleep, and let's hope the anaesthetist has a white face."

I returned to Mr Jackson, explained that I had spoken with Mr Potts, and that he had agreed that his appendix should be removed. I said that we would be arranging to do the operation within the next couple of hours and invited him to sign the standard consent form agreeing to *"removal of appendix and any other procedure that might be required"*, trusting that he would not notice the line that was printed on all the consent forms, which stated - in small print - that "*no assurance has been given that this operation will be performed by any particular surgeon*". Not that this was likely since the vast majority of patients, when presented with the consent form, signed it without reading it. It had often struck me that if the consent form was completed so that it read that the operation to be performed was '*amputation of the head and all limbs*' instead of '*removal of appendix*', the vast majority of patients would happily sign it.

Fortunately, Mr Jackson did not object to the Caucasian face of the anaesthetist - not realising, I suspect, that he was a German national! As the operation got underway, the dissection of the appendix proved to be tedious and technically very difficult. Partly this was due to the patient's muscular build, but also because it became apparent as soon as the abdomen had been opened that the appendix had burst, releasing infection and a large abscess containing pus had formed adjacent to it. Given the five-day history, this was not altogether surprising. The abscess involved loops of bowel that had to be carefully separated before the appendix could be removed. Thanks to Mr Khan's experience, patience and skill, this was safely achieved without any damage to these neighbouring structures, though the surgery took over two hours to complete.

As we worked together performing the surgery, I asked Mr Khan how often he had met such prejudice.

"Only very rarely have I met prejudice as severe as this," he said, "but I'm sorry to say that it does exist - indeed, I suppose I'm slightly conscious of it much of the time."

I expressed surprise, but he went on to explain that there were the obvious things; that many white people wouldn't wish their daughter to date or marry a black or coloured person, and they wouldn't wish to have such a family move in next door to them for fear that it would reduce the value of their own property. He went on to say that a slightly less obvious background of prejudice also existed.

"In the shops or on a bus, the shopkeepers or bus conductors will often be slightly more formal when talking to me or my wife than they would be when talking to you. And my children don't seem to get invited to birthday parties quite as often as some of the other children. In a queue for a bus or a train, spontaneous conversation may spring up between total strangers, but my family and I tend to be excluded."

"Well, at least we are free of prejudice within the hospital," I said. Mr Khan stopped what he was doing for a moment and looked at me over the top of his surgical mask.

"How I wish that were true," he said quietly, "but I have to say that you are wrong, Paul. I'm afraid there is a great deal of prejudice within the National Health Service."

Again, he surprised me. I found this statement difficult to believe.

"But surely nobody is prejudiced against you? The nurses, doctors and consultants here all value your contribution hugely. This team would fall apart if you weren't here to keep it going. I certainly would not have survived those first few difficult weeks in the job had it not been for your support, and if I should ever need an operation I should certainly come and seek you out to perform it for me. This is the only patient in four months that hasn't been grateful to you for your care and attention. All the other patients are greatly appreciative of your help, and last night expressed that view quite openly. That is why this man has ended up in a side-ward."

"Oh, I know I'm appreciated and feel that I do good work," he said, "but it's wrong for you to think that there is no prejudice. I've been a registrar on this firm for a long time now. I've passed the fellowship exam for the Royal College of Surgeons, I've written a couple of research papers and have a stronger CV than any of the other registrars in the hospital, but I regularly miss out when it comes to interviews for a senior registrar post. Most registrars get their promotion after about four years; I've been here for seven years. I've got better paper qualifications and more experience, but junior people leapfrog over me. I've actually been here longer than Mr Potts, but I suspect it suits him to have me here as his registrar. With my experience, there are virtually no emergencies which I can't manage without consultant support, so it means that he rarely has to come into the hospital to deal with out-of-hours problems." He was speaking quietly and didn't appear angry about the situation; indeed, it sounded as though he accepted it philosophically.

He continued, "Look at the wider picture. You've only got to look where most overseas doctors work. There are a few here in the teaching hospital but the vast majority work in district general hospitals, where the job prospects are less good. It is almost impossible to be appointed as a consultant unless you do the majority of your training in a teaching hospital. Those of us working in the periphery have even less chance of promotion than I do."

I hadn't considered this before but had to admit that he was correct. I knew that in some hospitals nearly all the junior hospital doctors were overseas trainees. Then he asked a question that really made me think.

"Why is it that people always refer to me as Mr Khan, and yet they refer to Mr Gresty as Simon?"

On reflection, I had to acknowledge that this was true. The sisters on the ward invariably used the prefix 'Mister' when referring to Mr Khan, and so did I. Was that because I felt it was a compliment - a mark of respect to indicate that I regarded him as a good surgeon - or was I displaying some degree of prejudice, albeit subconsciously? I had never considered that I was in the least prejudiced...but could it be that at some deeper level, I did in some way regard him as 'different'?

He continued, in a lighter mood, "Mind you, colour prejudice is not the only prejudice within the health service. What about the prejudice against women? How many female consultants do you know? Do you know of any female consultant surgeons?"

The truth was, I didn't. I knew of several female radiologists and one or two anaesthetists, specialties in which the competition for consultant posts was a little less fierce, but surgery was entirely a male preserve. Mr Khan glanced at the staff nurse who was acting as scrub nurse for this particular operation.

"Perhaps it is just as well there are no female surgeons," he said provocatively. "I'm not sure that the female personality is suited to the rigours of a career in surgery. Women aren't as tough as men and wouldn't be able to stand the long hours and the exacting work."

He had cleverly changed the focus of the conversation and it was obvious to me that he was only teasing, but the Staff Nurse didn't see it that way and was quick to respond.

"You're just as prejudiced as he is," she said crossly, indicating the patient. "Women are every bit as good as men, if not better, and would make wonderful surgeons - and I'm sure that if we did have some female surgeons, they wouldn't walk around with the fancy airs and graces that some of the consultants in this hospital have." I looked across the table at Mr Khan, and for a moment neither of us spoke. It was clear we had both decided it would be wiser not to ask her to give examples.

"You are quite right, Staff Nurse." Mr Khan had decided to pour oil on troubled waters. "I'm sure that generally women have manual dexterity equal, if not superior, to that of men and, by and large, they are much more patient - both of which traits would make them good technical operators in theatre. But they will continue to be disadvantaged so long as the postgraduate career pathway is twelve to fourteen years in duration, with much of that time spent 'on call'. That would require women to make big sacrifices. It is not a training that can be undertaken part time."

The operation continued in a more light-hearted mood thereafter but the procedure had taken more than twice as long as normal, and because of the difficulties encountered on the way, there was clearly a potential for complications in the post-operative period, despite Mr Khan's skill. There had been pus and gross infection around the ruptured appendix and a wound infection - or worse, an infection deep within the abdomen - were distinct possibilities that might lead to a stormy convalescence, and a prolonged stay in hospital.

Mr Potts was absent from the Monday morning ward round so that it was only on the fifth post-operative day that he saw 'Buster' Jackson for the first time. As it happened, his recovery had been slow but uneventful and, thankfully, complications had been avoided. When Mr Potts, accompanied by his full retinue of junior doctors and nurses, entered Mr Jackson's side room, I wondered whether he would object to the presence of Mr Khan as part of the group at his bedside; but possibly because the consultant was present, he said nothing. As usual, in my role as house officer, I presented an abstract of Mr Jackson's treatment in hospital to Mr Potts. I made no reference whatsoever to the problems we had encountered with the patient's prejudice and certainly did not mention that Mr Khan had performed the surgery but I did stress, in a voice loud enough for the patient to hear, that the surgery had been technically exacting and had been carried out with a great deal of skill - thanks to which, all complications had been avoided, and the patient had enjoyed a satisfactory recovery. Mr Potts asked to look at the patient's case record and there was a long pause as he turned to the page containing details of the operation, which he read carefully before addressing the patient, reinforcing the point that I had been making.

"This was a very advanced case of appendicitis; your appendix had ruptured and there was a great deal of pus and infection inside your abdomen. It's as well you had an operation, for without it you might not be here to tell the tale. The infection involved not only the appendix, but had also spread to the wall of the abdomen, and to loops of both the small bowel and large bowel. This was a life-threatening situation. You are extremely fortunate to have escaped without any complications and you have reason to be extremely grateful to the surgeon and his skill."

It is strange but true that patients almost always assume that it is the consultant who performs all the operations on every patient under his care. I have even met patients in the outpatient clinic, attending for their post-surgical review, who believe implicitly that the consultant performed their operation - even though they didn't see him once during the time that they were on the ward, because the consultant was on holiday throughout their stay in hospital. In this case, Mr Jackson certainly came to this conclusion, and begrudgingly offered his thanks to Mr Potts for looking after him. I suspect that this was the opening that Mr Potts had been deliberately engineering.

"You don't need to thank me - you need to thank the surgeon whose skill has saved your life."

Mr Jackson turned towards me; he seemed to be on his best behaviour. "Thank you, Doc," he said quietly. It was Mr Potts who spoke next.

"It wasn't Dr Lambert, either, who did your operation; it is Mr Khan who you need to thank. He applied his considerable skill and experience to your problem, despite your appalling rudeness to him."

Mr Jackson looked dumbfounded and shamefaced. For quite some time there was silence in the room. Finally, Mr Jackson found his voice.

"Ta, doctor," he managed to mutter, though the words were directed not to Mr Khan but to the floor.

Mr Potts turned to Sister. "Get this man out of this side ward. There is absolutely no medical reason for him to be here. Side wards are for patients who are seriously ill...not for those who are ignorant and prejudiced."

He glared at Mr Jackson, then turned and marched out of the room.

Chapter 16

I was able to find out from the nurses' off duty roster on the female ward that Kate would be coming back on duty the following Sunday, to work her first night shift. It happened to be our next 'on take' urgency weekend. Having been unable to contact her since the day of the party, and not having heard from her in the interim, I was determined to see her at the first opportunity.

The days of the week passed slowly, as did the hours of the day, until Sunday finally arrived. During the weekend, Johnny and I shared the casualty room duties. For the first time we were without the support of Mohammed Khan, who was absent on holiday. I was determined to think of him as Mohammed but it seemed strange, after calling him Mr Khan for so long. Simon Gresty took his place and lived in the hospital for the weekend. He took great delight in telling us of the research paper he had delivered at the Royal College of Surgeons; emphasising how well it had been received, and how the surgeons from the Medchurch Hospital, where he had applied for a consultant post, had congratulated him, adding to his expectation that his interview for the post would be successful. I found him much less supportive to us as house officers than Mohammed. Whereas Mohammed would see difficult cases with us, explain his findings and his thought processes, teaching us as we worked, Simon preferred to see patients on his own and simply wrote in the notes the instructions that were to be followed. He also appeared less willing to come to the casualty department to see patients as and when required, tending instead to visit the accident department every three or four hours, to review several patients - who, by this time, had 'stacked up' waiting for his second opinion. This resulted in patients grumbling at the length of time they had to wait and cubicles becoming blocked by patients waiting to be seen. All in all, I felt much more comfortable being supported by Mohammed than by Simon, despite Simon being the more senior. Possibly this was because Mohammed and I had developed a good working relationship, but possibly because I now viewed Simon through a rather jaundiced eye. Finally nine pm arrived, and Johnny came down to relieve me.

"Good luck," he said, knowing that I was going straight to the female ward to see Kate.

During the night, it was usual for the wards to be staffed by one qualified nurse, either a sister or staff nurse, supported by two junior nurses. As I arrived, I saw staff nurse and one of her assistants attending to a patient in a bed at the far end of the ward. There was no sign of Kate however and, wondering where she mght be, I spoke with the staff nurse, who was well known to me.

"I think you'll find her in the clinical office," she said, "but I think she's busy."

"Thanks," I said, and turned towards the office. The staff nurse called after me. "Paul, I think she may be occupied. She may not wish to be disturbed."

The significance of this remark escaped me. I had waited a week to see Kate, to apologise to her, to explain what had become of me on the night of the party. I was eager to see her again, to set the record straight and, I hoped, to be assured of her feelings towards me. "Don't worry," I said, and continued on my way back down the ward.

To my surprise, I found that the office door was closed and no-one was visible in the part of the office that could be seen through its glazed portion. I opened the door and walked in without knocking. The sight that greeted me stopped me in my tracks and became imprinted on my brain, to return to haunt and taunt me for many weeks to come. Behind the door, Simon was holding Kate in his arms. It was obvious that I had interrupted a romantic embrace. They both turned towards me, disturbed by my sudden intrusion, and for a moment or two, no-one spoke. Simon looked angry at the disturbance; Kate looked flustered.

All week, I had been hoping and praying that at the party Kate had merely had a dance with Simon whilst waiting for me to return, but that she had quickly realised that for some reason, I had been unavoidably detained, and had then returned, alone, to the Nurse's Home. My fear had been that, infuriated by my disappearance, she had taken up with Simon and that he had been the one to spend the evening with her, the one to walk her home at the end of the party. Here was undeniable evidence that my worse fears had been realised.

For a moment I was lost for words, as I stared first at one and then at the other. Simon continued to hold Kate firmly in his arms, the victor in possession of his trophy. My hopes and dreams crushed, I finally managed to speak.

"I'm sorry that I interrupted you," I said, the bitterness very evident in my voice. I turned and fled, slamming the door behind me.

Life on the ward was difficult for me after that. I never saw Simon and Kate together again; Kate now worked nights, and when Mohammed returned from his holidays, Simon rarely had cause to be in the hospital out of hours. On the other hand, I worked alongside both of them, coming into contact with both on a daily basis. For the benefit of the patients on the ward, it was necessary that we should maintain a good professional relationship, and by a common unspoken understanding, both Simon and Kate kept up a formal politeness when speaking with me, as indeed I did with them. The fact that my relationship with Simon was awkward did not concern me in the least. I had decided long ago that I disliked his superior manner towards nurses and junior doctors and his fawning attitude with Sir William, and that he was never a person with whom I could become friendly. I was, however, deeply upset at the gulf that had developed between Kate and myself. The trouble was that I was still very fond of her, even though I felt that she had treated me badly. I had explained in my letter why I had let her down at the party, that it was due to circumstances beyond my control, and that I had tried every possible way to get a message to her. Prior to that, I thought she returned my affection; surely it was unreasonable to fall so quickly into the arms of another? I shared my sorrows with Johnny. He was sympathetic but practical in his advice.

"I honestly thought that the two of you would get on well together, that you were well matched. At the party I was trying to give your romance a push in the right direction, but since she's proved to be so fickle, frankly, you're better off without her. Forget her, concentrate on your work, and move on."

It was probably a good, sensible, and well-intentioned recommendation, but I knew it would be difficult advice to follow. Forgetting her would prove impossible since we were bound to see each other on a daily basis, and since my feelings towards her were so strong.

A couple of days later, it was my turn to give advice to Johnny. We were in the clinical office waiting for Sir William to do his ward round, and the mood at such times was generally fairly light-hearted as we placed our bets for the regular suppository sweepstake. Johnny was normally cheerful and good-natured, but on this occasion he was clearly upset and angry.

"There's a patient in that last bed on the right called Dennis Slater, who's a pain in the backside. He's only eighteen and built like a rugby front row forward, but he's driving us all to distraction. He seems to think that he's in the Ritz, ordering this and that from the nurses; special meals, special drinks. He treats me as if I'm the ward orderly, not one of the medical staff. He got me out of bed twice last night for no good reason at all and when I remonstrated with him, he simply said, "Well, you get paid, don't you?" And he complains all the time -

about the nurses, about the doctors, about the food, about the noise. It's not even that there's much the matter with him."

"Why was he admitted?" I asked.

"He fell and bumped his head whilst leaving the pub two nights ago. He was blind drunk at the time and it was impossible to know whether he was unconscious from the drink or the head injury, so we had to admit him for observation."

"Well," I said, "it sounds as if he's fully recovered now. No doubt Sir William will send him home this morning. Just keep your cool, don't let him rile you, and with any luck he'll be gone by this afternoon."

Accompanying Sir William on his ward round was one of the more enjoyable parts of the weekly routine and today was no exception. One particular event was especially satisfying for Johnny, and restored his good humour.

When we reached Dennis Slater, the young rugby player was lounging by his bed reading a magazine, a mug of tea at his elbow. Sir William examined Dennis' head, undertook a full neurological examination, reviewed the observation charts - which were all entirely satisfactory - and then proceeded to gave the patient a long lecture on the dangers of alcohol and the necessity for moderation. Dennis listened meekly enough, though I doubted whether he would take much notice. Satisfied that Dennis could go home and that his ward round was over, Sir William turned towards the door in anticipation of the coffee and biscuits that were waiting for him in the office. I smiled to myself. When Sir William departed I would collect sixpence from each member of the team as the day's winner of the sweepstake. As I was silently congratulating myself, Johnny suddenly piped up. "I don't think Dennis has moved his bowels whilst he has been with us, Sir."

Sir William's response was entirely predictable. He turned back to the patient, raised his right index finger, and the rectal examination and suppository trays were summoned. As Sir William performed the usual pantomime, words and actions now totally familiar, I watched Johnny's face. His expression registered considerable satisfaction as he saw the young man who had so irritated him over the last two days suffer the indignity and embarrassment of a rectal examination and the insertion of two suppositories, all performed in the presence of an audience that included three young nurses.

As Sir William was occupied in inserting, first one, and then the second suppository into Dennis' back passage, Johnny casually lifted one investigation card and then a second from his right hand jacket pocket, and placed them into the left hand pocket. Not only had he wreaked his revenge on his patient, he had also scooped the jackpot. Eight suppositories had been the total that he had predicted. Nothing could be said to Johnny about the incident whilst Sir William drank his coffee with us in the office, but as soon as he left he was attacked from all sides.

"A blatant case of cheating."

"Not in the spirit of the game at all."

"Unbecoming in a member of an honourable profession."

Johnny however was unrepentant; he simply said, "A most satisfying morning's work."

As the weeks and months went by we treated hundreds of different patients, many of whom had very common surgical problems such as hernias, varicose veins and piles, with which we became very familiar. We were able to manage these cases in a routine fashion without difficulty, and without recourse to advice from our consultants. Others, however, were particularly memorable; sometimes because of the nature of their medical condition, but at other times because of their personality and character, or the manner in which they faced their disease. One or two patients in whose management I have been involved over the years remain indelibly imprinted in my brain, and one such patient was Joan Wallace.

For a number of months prior to her admission she had been vaguely unwell, and had visited her general practitioner on a number of occasions. Her symptoms had been vague: pains in the back and lower abdomen, which did not sound particularly significant on their own, but were associated with a loss of appetite and loss of energy that rather suggested something sinister was amiss. Her GP had given her painkillers and, when these did not work, offered physiotherapy. Stronger painkillers were added when the physiotherapy had no effect. All the while she had been losing weight - two stone in as many months - and her abdomen had been swelling. When she was finally referred to Mr Potts, she was clearly seriously ill.

The boss rang me from the clinic. "Lambert, I have a lady here who has a huge abdominal ascites[3]," he said. "There is an enormous amount of fluid in there. It's almost certainly malignant and it is highly unlikely that we shall be able to do anything to cure her, but we shall have to investigate her to make sure. Admit her if you will. Arrange the

---

[3] Ascites - the collection of fluid in the abdominal cavity. In the UK, usually due to an advanced malignancy.

appropriate tests as quickly as you can, but see if you can get her on tomorrow's operating list. We need to have a quick look inside the abdomen, just to make sure of the diagnosis."

When Joan arrived on the ward, I took to her at once. She had a friendly face, a ready smile and an easy manner. Now retired, she had worked all her life as a teacher at the local primary school. She obviously had loved her job and enjoyed the contact with children that this brought. Previous to her present illness, she had been favoured with excellent health, and in the school holidays had travelled widely. It crossed my mind that possibly she had a private income.

Taking her history, it was difficult to understand why her general practitioner had been so slow in referring her to the hospital. Her weight loss had been quite dramatic - it showed in her face, and in the way the flesh hung from her arms - and the swelling of her abdomen was enormous. As she said, "I look six months pregnant - and me a seventy-two year old spinster!"

Examining her I could find no abnormality with her lungs or heart, but as Joan had remarked, her abdomen looked as if she was in a state of advanced pregnancy. Tense and uncomfortable, there was little doubt that it was full of fluid, as Mr Potts had suggested.

I explained to Joan that I had been asked to arrange some investigations, including blood tests and X-rays of the chest and abdomen, and that Mr Potts planned to perform an operation on the abdomen the following day.

"He did tell me that, but didn't tell me what he thought was wrong, why I needed an operation or what he was planning to do inside my tummy. He simply said something about having a look and see."

I tried to explain. "The cause of the problem, whatever it is, seems to be in your abdomen, causing swelling. The swelling is almost certainly just fluid but we need to know what is causing the fluid to collect. We could do lots of tests over the next week or so but they might not tell us the answer. Mr Potts has suggested that he does what he would call an 'exploratory operation', to look inside the abdomen to get to the root of the trouble quickly."

She came straight to the point. "Is it cancer, Dr Lambert?"

I paused, unsure how to respond to such a direct question. "Well, yes, it could be...but it could be other things as well."

"Such as?"

"Well, it could be some sort of inflammation, or a huge cyst on the ovary."

"But is cancer the most likely diagnosis? I would like to know. I'm not afraid to be told if it is."

Again, I paused. "I suppose cancer is the most likely possibility but, as I say, it could be many other things; particularly a large cyst of the ovary, which could be removed in an operation."

"Will Mr Potts, at the operation, be able to tell what the problem is?"

"An operation will probably make the situation a lot clearer but it is usually necessary to take a biopsy - in other words, to take a sample at the time of surgery and to examine the tissue under the microscope to make a definite diagnosis. Only then would we be absolutely certain."

"And if it is cancer, will it be possible to remove it?"

"I'm afraid that also depends on what is found at the operation. Again, it is something we wouldn't know until the operation had been performed."

I had half expected some questions about the delay by the GP in referring her to the hospital but none were forthcoming. She was more interested in the future than in the past.

Whilst she interrogated me in this fashion, it was impossible not to admire her calm, controlled attitude, and bravery. She had shown little or no reaction to my answers as I had quietly admitted to her that cancer was the most likely diagnosis, and that the possibility existed that it was incurable. It struck me that she was an intelligent woman, determined to get the information that she required to understand what the future held for her. Her next comment confirmed this view. She looked straight into my face and held my gaze with her eyes.

"Dr Lambert, will you make a promise?"

"I suppose that depends what it is."

"After the operation, will you promise to answer all my questions honestly when you get the results of the samples from the laboratory?"

"Is that truly what you want?"

"Yes, it is."

"You have no doubts?"

"None. I am a single woman. I live on my own and I need to know what the future holds."

"In that case, I give you my word."

Although Mr Potts had hoped that Joan's operation would be performed the next day, this was not possible for a variety of reasons; partly because of the number of investigations to be arranged, but also because other patients had already been admitted and booked onto the next day's list. An added difficulty was that since the nature of her surgery was unknown, it was not possible to judge whether the operation would take thirty minutes (if the situation was seen to be inoperable the moment the abdomen was open), or two to three hours, if a major resection of a cancerous organ had to be undertaken.

I had occasion to speak with Joan many times whilst she was waiting for her surgery - initially to arrange her investigations, later to confirm the time of her procedure and to obtain her written consent - but whenever I went to look for her, she was rarely by her own bed and was usually to be found chatting to other patients, invariably in a cheerful mood.

"You seem very much at home on the ward," I said.

"Yes, I like to have a good chinwag - it helps me to pass the time and I think it helps other patients as well. I used to work part-time for the hospital library service - you know, bringing books round on a trolley to the patient's bedside - so I do feel at home on the ward."

I remarked that I thought her face was familiar.

"Yes, I've seen you on the ward in the last year or two. You always seemed to be quite serious and conscientious about your studies, and appeared to spend longer on the ward than some of the other students."

"There was a lot to learn," I said, "and the more I learnt, the more I found there was to learn. In fact, now that I'm qualified and working as part of the staff, I realise how little I know."

She became more serious. "There's something I've been wanting to mention to you, Paul. You don't mind if I call you Paul, do you? It's about the lady called Phyllis in the bed opposite; you know, the patient with that nasty infection in her groin. She's very worried. I don't think I'm breaking any confidences but the truth is, she's racked with guilt. A short while ago, she had a little indiscretion, and she's convinced herself that must be the cause of the infection. I feel certain that if you were to reassure her that that was not the case, you would put her mind at rest."

Several times in future years I was to discover that, although doctors are formally trained to interrogate patients about their symptoms, a patient may withhold facts that are relevant to their case from the medical staff - but may unload such information, particularly if it is of a private or personal nature, to a domestic, auxiliary, or to one of the other patients on the ward.

I looked at her with some admiration. "You're quite a star, aren't you? Thank you for that, I'll certainly drop it into the conversation when a suitable chance arises."

Joan had to wait until Mr Potts' next theatre session, a matter of three days, before she had her operation, and in that time I grew to know her better and to like her more. She never spoke of her own troubles or grumbled about the pains and nausea that I knew she suffered. She was constantly cheerful and spent a great deal of time with the other patients on the ward, having a kind word for them all. Always appreciative of the care given to her by the nursing staff, she never failed to thank them for their help. I usually stopped to have a chat with her when I did my eleven pm evening round and she would frequently chide me for working too hard.

"Don't you ever get any time off? You seem to be on the ward morning, noon and night. I am sure that there are plenty of pretty young nurses here who would be pleased to go out with you."

Despite her serious troubles, her relaxed and friendly attitude encouraged conversation. It would have been easy to share my troubles with her, but I decided to keep them to myself.

"I'm afraid there is a great deal of work to do," I said, and I left the matter at that.

Whilst Joan was waiting for her operation, the routine of the ward went on as usual. Patients were admitted from the waiting list, had their operations, and were discharged - mainly on time, but occasionally this was delayed a day or two if there were any minor complications. Urgency days were arduous but, as time passed and more experience was gained, they became less nerve-wracking. My relationship with Simon was cool but I believe it was functional, and didn't detract from patient care. Inevitably, I passed Kate from time to time when working at night on the female ward and might exchange a few formal words with her about a patient, but there was no friendship or familiarity between us and I tried to keep out of her way as much as possible; the bittersweet memories were too painful. The two consultants continued to do their regular ward rounds: Mr Potts' rounds being brisk and workmanlike and Sir William's, although ponderous, continuing to provide a mix of education and amusement, not least because of the ongoing suppository saga, especially when Sister Rutherford finally agreed to participate.

This came as a surprise because she had previously disapproved quite strongly, feeling that we were being disrespectful to her favourite consultant; but when she relented it gave the green light to the junior nurses who were to accompany us on the ward round, so that on this occasion the kitty was considerably larger than usual. Since it was

Sister's first involvement in the game, by common consent she was allowed first selection of the number of suppositories to be inserted.

"Seven," she said. This caused some jocularity since Sir William usually inserted suppositories two at a time and it was unlikely that an odd number would win the jackpot. Nevertheless, Sister was not to be moved.

In due course Sir William arrived and led his entourage onto the ward. It seemed that the theme for this particular ward round was to be the effect of drugs, since the boss had recently read a circular issued by the Department of Health that banned the use of certain proprietary medicines that had been shown, in recent scientific studies, to have no useful therapeutic effect.

"General Practitioners will have to find other treatments for patients who have nothing wrong with them," he remarked humorously.

We stopped beside the bed of a lady who had been admitted, having vomited some blood that had proved, after investigation, to be due to the considerable quantities of aspirin that she had been taking for persistent headaches. Although the aspirin had benefited her headaches, as a side effect it had eroded the lining of her stomach, causing an ulcer to form.

"You must be aware," Sir William explained, "that any drug that you prescribe may affect different people in different ways. Take alcohol, for example. That's a drug, after all, and it can have remarkably different effects in different people."

He turned to Sister Rutherford. "How does it affect you, Sister?"

"I'm afraid it makes me giggly, Sir William."

He turned to me. "And you, Lambert?"

"It seems to affect me in different ways at different times of the day," I replied. "If I take alcohol at lunch time, it makes me sleepy; if I take it in the evening, I'm afraid that it loosens my tongue and I become rather over-talkative."

"And what about you, Simon?"

"I'm teetotal, Sir," he said. *You would be*, I thought.

Sir William continued. "And we know that it makes other people aggressive, the results of which we see in Casualty every Saturday night. So you see...one drug, but many different reactions in different people. So be aware that the drugs you prescribe for patients on the ward may not always have exactly the effect that is described in the text book."

Eventually we arrived at the last bed and throughout the entire ward round only four suppositories had been inserted, a surprisingly low number. The only two possible winners of the jackpot were Mohammed, who had selected four and Johnny, on six. Could Johnny be trusted not to cheat again? We had given him quite a rough time after the last episode and I doubted that he would dare to repeat the trick again. If he did, we would have to withhold any winnings and agree on a rollover.

The patient in the final bed had undergone a piles operation, following which it is important to keep the bowels moving regularly, since the anus is inevitably painful. It is much easier in the first few days after surgery to pass a loose pliable stool than to allow the motion to solidify within the rectum, and then expect the patient to pass rock hard faeces. It was inevitable that Sir William would do a rectal examination on this patient, but would he insert any suppositories? We watched with baited breath as the examination proceeded, and sure enough the index finger was raised, indicating that suppositories were required. Johnny could not conceal his delight and took two investigation cards from his pocket in eager anticipation, a triumphant grin on his face. He was going to win again. There was more cash in the kitty than usual, and on this occasion no-one could possibly accuse him of cheating. One suppository was inserted, and Sir William looked up. Sister Rutherford gave an almost imperceptible nod of the head, and a second suppository was inserted. Sir William looked up again.

"I think one further suppository should do the trick," said Sister.

A final suppository was inserted, the seventh of the round. Without further comment, Sir William walked down the ward and washed and dried his hands before returning to the group.

"What is your favourite charity, Sister?" he asked on his return, a broad grin on his benevolent face.

Sister thought for a moment. "I think probably our own ward's amenity fund. There are a number of items that would be appreciated by the patients that the NHS is unable to afford."

"An excellent choice," said Sir William. "Now, shall we go and have a cup of coffee?"

It was clear that we had been rumbled and that the game that had been amusing us for months would have to stop. Fortunately, Sir William appeared not to have taken any offence; in fact he was in a buoyant mood during our coffee break in the office. He must have thought that Johnny was the prime mover in the escapade because, before he left, he turned to Johnny and said, "After today, I don't suppose you will ever forget that the examination of the abdomen begins in the groin and ends in the rectum. If you don't put your finger in..."

He paused, and Johnny completed his favourite catch phrase: "You'll put your foot in it."

"That's right," said Sir William. "Now, if you two boys have got five minutes to spare, there are a couple of things that I want to discuss with you in my office."

Normally such a remark might have made me a little apprehensive, but in this instance I could not recall anything that had recently gone amiss for which we might be culpable, and Sir William seemed to have taken the suppository episode in good heart. Nevertheless, it was still a slight relief to hear what was on his mind.

"I want to have a word with you about holidays. As you know, you are both entitled to take a fortnight off during the six months that you are on the unit and I don't think either of you have taken any time off so far. Is that correct?" We confirmed that this was so.

"Well, you need to get yourselves organised, remembering that you can't both be away at the same time. You also need to think about Christmas. The workload slackens during Christmas week and doesn't really pick up until the New Year. It is difficult to persuade people to come in for surgery at that time as they prefer to be at home with their loved ones, so it is not a bad idea for one of you to be off for Christmas and the other to be away for the New Year. I'll leave you to sort it out between yourselves. Just let me know what you have arranged." We agreed that we would, and Sir William continued.

"Now, the other matter relates to your next jobs. I have been impressed by the way the two of you have worked so well together and have always felt that anyone who has worked on Surgical Five with me deserves some reward. Over the years, I have made it my business to try to fix my house officers up with another job at the City General teaching hospital, if that is what they want. Johnny, I think you said that would suit you - but what about you, Lambert?"

I was taken aback at the way in which the question of a medical house officer job had been raised. The truth was that I had devoted myself to my current post and had given no thought to the next, assuming that such a decision could wait until the jobs were advertised and applications were invited. There was no doubt in my mind though; I would be delighted to get my next job at this hospital. I was already familiar with much of the routine, had a good relationship with the staff in the X-ray department and laboratories, and a second job in the teaching hospital would definitely be prestigious. I wouldn't even have to move my belongings from my room in the residency.

"I have thoroughly enjoyed working here and would love to stay on as a house physician, if that is possible, Sir." As I spoke, I suddenly realised that it was the sort of fawning remark that Simon might have made.

"Fine. Now, do you have a preference for one of the general units, or one of the specialist departments; perhaps neurology or cardiology?"

Johnny answered first. "A general unit would suit me best. As you know, I see my future in General Practice working alongside my father, so exposure to as wide a range of medical conditions as possible would be to my advantage."

"That makes sense. And what about you Lambert...where would you like to work next?"

Here was another question thrown at me out of the blue to which I had given no thought, but I had no hesitation about making an instantaneous decision.

"I confess I've been a bit too busy to give that the consideration that it deserves, Sir, but at this stage I would like to keep my options open and a general unit would suit me better than one of the specialist units."

"Right. That means Medical Two or Medical Three. I'll see what I can do but perhaps, Lambert, it's time for you to start thinking more about your long-term future. Have you given any thought to a career in surgery?"

"As I say, I've enjoyed being a house surgeon on the unit and liked working with surgical patients but whether I would make a surgeon, I really don't know."

"Well, I suspect that you might. You give it some thought and if at any stage you think seriously about surgery, I want you to come and have a chat with me about it. The next step would be to get you a job as a Demonstrator in Anatomy at the University, but I am sure we could manage that. I have known Professor Gregson for many years and I am sure that I can pull a few strings - that is, unless the hernia I repaired for him recently suddenly gives way!"

"That's very kind, Sir. Thank you, Sir," I stuttered, startled at the way the conversation had developed.

As we left, Johnny's thoughts were on the arrangements for holidays, and we quickly agreed which weeks we would take. He would work over Christmas and I would be 'on duty' over the New Year. Perhaps Johnny had already assumed, or even knew, that he would get a medical house job at the City General, but I certainly didn't. But I did know that it would be extremely helpful if Sir William were to put in a good word for me. And what about the suggestion of a career in surgery? Did he really mean it? Did he really think that I had some potential? Our conversation had only lasted five minutes but it had given me a great deal of food for thought.

Chapter 17

The next day, I went to theatre to watch whilst Mr Potts' operated on Joan Wallace. The incision that he made was small, no more than two inches in length, alongside the umbilicus. Evidently Mr Potts did not expect to be performing any major procedure. When he opened the abdomen an enormous volume of pale yellow fluid gushed out, soaking the drapes around the wound, and the nature of the problem was all too obvious; there were hard knots of malignant tissue throughout the abdomen. It was immediately apparent that surgery had nothing to offer and that this disease was completely incurable. Mr Potts took a tiny sample of tissue, simply for final confirmation of the diagnosis, and proceeded to suture the abdominal wound. The operation was all over in twenty minutes. The biopsy was sent to the laboratory and I knew that after three or four days time, the analysis would be complete, and I would have to fulfil my promise to Joan.

Unsurprisingly, after what had been a relatively minor operation, Joan was up and about on the ward the next day; indeed, without the gross abdominal swelling, she was more mobile than before. As usual, she was rarely to be found by her own bed and spent much of the time chatting with other patients, cheering them up, sharing magazines and even serving cups of tea, to help the nurses. At no stage did she complain about her own problems, though without a doubt she must have continued to experience symptoms of pain and nausea; and although she must have been anxious to learn the diagnosis from the laboratory analysis she never pestered me, or showed impatience to know the result of the tissue sample.

Eventually, inevitably, the day arrived when the tissue analysis was known. The report was delivered by the last porter's round of the day and I looked at it with sadness, although I already knew exactly what it would say. As expected, it confirmed that the tissue was malignant - but worse, that the cancer was of a particularly virulent type that would not be amenable to any form of treatment. All we had to offer was an undertaking to do our best to minimise her symptoms whilst the disease ran its inevitable course. I had made a promise to Joan that I would be honest with her and I would keep that promise, but I needed time to think about when and what to tell her. At medical school, we had received no training or guidance on how to break bad news to a patient. How I wished that my medical education had covered the practical issues of patient management and not just the management of disease. Usually I had a chat with Joan on my eleven pm evening round and decided that would be as good a time as any to speak with her, but I wondered how best to broach the subject, and spent a quiet evening considering exactly what words to use. It was with a sinking feeling in my heart that I walked slowly down the ward, pulled the screens round her bed, drew up a chair and sat by her side. Despite my preparation, I really wasn't quite sure how to start. She reached out and held my hand.

"Don't worry, Paul, I do know what you have to say. It's written all over your face; in fact, I've known for two or three days now. It is cancer, isn't it?"

I had to admit that she was right and that the biopsy, unfortunately, had confirmed this was a cancer. Typical of her, she was actually comforting me, making my job easier at a time when she was being told that her life was coming to an end.

"I thought it probably was when I began to lose weight. I tried to eat more, but couldn't. I had no appetite and felt sick when I sat down for a meal. Then Mr Potts admitted me to hospital the minute he saw me in the clinic and I knew that he wouldn't have done that unless there was something seriously wrong. I became certain when I saw that he had only made a short cut in my abdomen and, now that the fluid has gone, I can feel several hard lumps in my tummy - so I know it must be cancer, and that it hasn't been removed. I suppose that means that it can't be cured?"

Again, with sadness, I had to confirm that she was correct.

"So, where does that leave us?"

"Well, what we have to do is to try to get you and the cancer to live side by side for a little while."

"But the cancer will win in the end?"

"I am afraid that is right."

"And where has it started?"

All the while, she spoke in a calm, measured fashion, her sentences short and precise. The questions were being asked in a purely matter-of-fact way, as she sought to clarify the situation. From the tone of her voice you would not have imagined she was inquiring about her own fate; she might have been asking for information on a broken washing machine or fridge. There was no hint of self-pity. I found it quite remarkable.

"We don't know where it started. The pathologist seems to think that it probably started somewhere in the bowel."

"But I don't have any bowel problems at all, I've always been completely regular - nothing has changed recently."

I explained to her that occasionally it happens that the abnormality where the cancer starts remains quite small, giving no symptoms at all, but that cancer cells can still wash away and grow quite vigorously in other areas of the body, and the effects of these secondary deposits can produce the first symptoms and signs of the disease. There was a pause in the conversation, and she started to reflect.

"All things considered, I've had a good life, I've seen many parts of the world, and I suppose it has to come to an end for all of us sooner or later. I've so enjoyed my work in the schools. I probably spoiled the kids, but they were lovely, and I've seen lots of them grow up into fine young men and women. Believe it or not, I still get Christmas cards from one or two. And in the hospital library service I've seen patients suffer all manner of nasty conditions, but I've always been lucky and always kept well. I've really not been one to have many illnesses."

She turned back to me. "So Paul, what happens now?"

"Well, I'm afraid we can't cure the cancer, but we can help you to be free from too many aches and pains and keep you warm and comfortable - either here, in hospital, or at home." There was no hospice movement[4] at this time, and I remembered that she was unmarried.

"You live alone, don't you?"

"Yes, I have no close family. I was an only child - but I have lots of friends whom I'm sure will help me."

I knew that we would have to learn more about the support that would be available to her when she was discharged, but this did not seem to be an appropriate time to talk about such practical details. Instead, I waited to see if she had further questions, but none were forthcoming.

She obviously loved the children that she had taught at her school, and had acted as a surrogate mother to them. It seemed surprising that she had never married and had children of her own. I said so but immediately regretted it, feeling it was inappropriate to pry into her personal life. However, she didn't seem to mind.

"I was asked once - but it didn't work out."

"Was he not good enough for you?"

She smiled a slow, sad, smile. "He was not good enough for my father. My father was fiercely Protestant and Charlie was Catholic."

"And did that matter so very much?"

---

4 Dame Cicely Saunders opened the first hospice, St Christophers, in London in 1967

"It didn't matter to us but it did to Dad. He wouldn't allow it."

I must have looked surprised, for she went on to explain.

"You must remember that this was fifty years ago; such things were much more important then. They still are now, of course, in certain parts of the world. But in those days, you obeyed your father."

She paused, and then continued, somewhat wistfully. "Actually, it wouldn't have worked out anyway - you see, he joined the army. He was one of Kitchener's volunteers…all his pals were joining. They thought it was such a great big adventure and they didn't want to miss it. The trouble was, they were all so excited about serving King and Country that they didn't stop to think what 'it' was. They all went off to France in 1916 and Charlie didn't come home."

"I'm so sorry," I mumbled. I tried to lighten the mood. "You must have had other offers. I bet you were a real 'English Rose' as a young woman."

"Yes," she admitted, "there were others...but none to compare with Charlie."

"Do you have a photograph of him?"

Again, the sad smile. "Yes, I do, and I've brought it with me. It's usually in my bedroom at home. Would you like to see it?"

She reached and took her handbag out of the bedside locker, pulled out her diary and very carefully thumbed between the pages, and picked out a small photograph, slightly creased and faded with time. She passed it to me. And there he was: a clean-shaven boyish face wearing a serious expression, in the uniform of a First World War private. A young man cut down in his prime, now fifty years in the grave but still alive in this poor lady's heart. For a few moments there was silence, and I found it hard to keep the moisture from forming in my eyes.

"A handsome young man," I said, and handed the photograph back to her.

"Yes, he was, and a very kind and gentle one too," she said, as she very carefully replaced it between the pages of her diary and returned it to the safety of the locker.

"And how could you forgive your father after that?"

"It was very difficult at first. In fact, as soon as the opportunity arose, I left home and became a munitionette - you know, a female worker in an ammunition factory. Charlie had gone to serve his country and I wanted to make a contribution too. I moved up to Dornock in Scotland and lived in a large hostel with all the other girls. It was hard work…long hours, and quite dangerous too, handling all those explosives. There were a number of accidents and one or two girls died, but we had some good times as well. We lived together, worked together, and we felt that we were supporting the boys who were away fighting. And, by and large, there was a good community spirit. Some of the girls were a bit rough, but most were very pleasant. Looking back, it was one of the best things that I could have done; it changed my life completely. Before that, I was employed in domestic service as a maid at the local vicarage. I did what I was told by my father at home and did what I was told by the vicar's wife at work. Living away and working away made me much more self-reliant and independent. It taught me that I could face the world on my own and make my own decisions. It gave me self-confidence and self-esteem. The pay was good too. In service, I was receiving two pounds a month; at Dornock I earned that every week. In fact I was earning just about as much as my father!"

"And did you make peace with your father?"

"Yes, but it took a little time. I know he was doing what he believed to be right and what he thought was best for me, but if I had my time again, I would have gone against his wishes and taken the consequences. I'm sure he would have come round with time, particularly if Charlie and I had been blessed with children. My father loved children as much as I did. A grandchild would definitely have bridged any gap between us but, as it was, Charlie never came home...so it was not to be."

Whilst she had been speaking she had looked wistful, thinking of days gone by, but now she turned to me and spoke more earnestly.

"You know, Paul, in life you must take your chances while you may."

I hadn't noticed, but throughout the conversation she had held my hand. Now she tightened her grip and pulled my hand towards her, and her mood changed.

"Anyway, we must stop talking like this. You don't want to hear about the missed opportunities in an old woman's life," she said, her eyes twinkling. "What about you? Rumour has it that you're a very eligible bachelor."

"I'm too busy for romance. It's all I can do to stay awake sometimes."

"But there is a young lady that you're fond of, isn't there?" She seemed to be teasing me now.

"Oh, is there? And who would that be?"

"Do you want me to guess?"

"If you like."

"Well, my guess is that it would be a young nurse, probably from this ward, possibly by the name of Kate?"

I looked at her sharply. "And how would you know that?"

"I have a lot of time on my hands, Paul, and I keep my eyes open. Have you asked her out?"

"I'm afraid that she's going out with Mr Gresty, though for the life of me I can't understand what she sees in him. Mind you, he will be a consultant very soon and have all the trimmings that go with that."

"And do you really think that is what would influence a girl like Kate?"

I considered for a moment. "No you're right. I don't believe it would, but there's something about him that she finds attractive."

"I don't think she's keen on Mr Gresty at all."

"And what makes you think that?"

"As I say, Paul, I simply keep my eyes open. I think you should ask her out - I believe that you would get a pleasant surprise. I'm sure she would say 'yes'. I am right; you do like her, don't you?"

"Yes, I do," I admitted. "I think she's lovely. There was a time when I thought she liked me too, but I know differently now."

"I think you're probably mistaken - in fact, I'm sure you are. Would you like me to sound her out? Slip your name into a conversation and see how she responds?"

"No, definitely not."

"It couldn't do any harm, Paul. If she didn't like you it would show in her expression, and no harm would be done."

"No Joan, I don't want you to do that. I must ask you to promise not to do it."

"But Paul, what harm could it possibly do?"

"Please promise me."

Reluctantly, she agreed.

"Thank you," I said, and breathed a sigh of relief. Any association with Kate was over, a thing of the past. It would only bring more pain to rake through the embers of a failed romance. I had to forget Kate, concentrate on my work, and move on.

I stayed with Joan for another fifteen minutes or so and we talked about some of the things she had done over the years. Her life had been full and she had spread a little happiness around her throughout her journey; amongst the children at her school, amongst the patients she had seen as a hospital librarian, and even now, as her journey was coming to an end, among the other patients on the ward. Before I left I asked her if there were any more questions she had about her condition.

“No,” she said. “You have confirmed what I needed to know. Thank you for being honest with me.”

Chapter 18

When I had walked onto the ward on that first morning in August as a newly appointed houseman with no previous experience as a doctor, and had received such a frosty reception from Sister Ashbrook, I had felt like a stranger in an unforgiving and frightening foreign land. I had known none of the patients, none of the staff, was unaware of ward routine and procedures; but most of all, I was unsure of the role that was expected of me. How things had changed. Although in terms of personality Johnny and I were as different as chalk and cheese, we had formed a solid, effective working relationship; covering each other's backs, both working until all jobs were completed, and not falling out over our workload even when tired from lack of sleep, which was frequently the case. Now, as fully integrated members of the Surgical Five unit, we knew that we were important members of this close-knit group of doctors and nurses and that the unit would not function efficiently without us. We were proud to be members of the team, proud of the work that we did, and there was a great sense of satisfaction in what we achieved for our patients. Not only were we utterly familiar with the wards, the procedures, and the routine, we felt comfortable, at ease and at home there.

The male and female wards had become 'our' territory. We felt a responsibility for all the patients there. At any time, we knew as much about any one of those patients as any other member of the team, often more than the nursing sisters themselves. We attended to them by night as well as by day, and would often relate to the day sister events that had happened to individual patients through the night. In fact the time of day that I used to enjoy most, indeed to which I used to look forward, was the late evening, perhaps between ten-thirty pm and midnight, when I went to perform my late evening round. At this time, after the hustle and bustle of the day's activity, there was a stillness and quietness about the ward and a sense of peace and calm. The main lights would be switched off, most of the ward would be in darkness, and one or more of the nurses would be sitting at a small table, a third of the way down the centre of the ward, reading or writing under a single overhead light at the nurse's station. Most patients would be lying quietly or sleeping in bed, though one or two might still be reading, using the night-light on the wall above the head of the bed. After a day spent dashing to and fro, working against the clock, it was soothing to arrive at this time and survey the scene from the ward doors. There was time to walk round with the senior nurse in a leisurely fashion, checking on each patient in turn without feeling in any way rushed, and having time for a chat with anyone who happened to be awake or anxious. Invariably Joan would be awake and I would often go back to talk with her for ten minutes or so after having finished my round. She was gradually getting weaker and beginning to look gaunter as her cancer progressed, and she continued to lose weight. Mentally though she was as resilient as ever, and always cheerful. Not once did she grumble about the discomforts and the nausea from which she suffered. I noticed that she tended to take the lead in our conversations and would ask about my family, holidays and future plans, preferring not to talk about herself or her situation. From time to time I would give her openings to talk about her own future, but on only one occasion did she take up the opportunity.

"Do you think that I shall be sent home soon? I presume there are other patients waiting for this bed."

"Would you like to go home?"

"Yes, certainly I would, but I realise that I am a lot weaker now than when I first came into hospital. I'm not sure that I could cope on my own at home. I think I would need someone to help me."

"Do you have any relatives? I remember you saying that you were an only child."

"I have a cousin, but she lives abroad. I have very many friends and wonderful neighbours but looking after me with this illness would be a rather awkward and difficult job to ask them to do, wouldn't it?" It was clear that she understood perfectly well that we were talking about the terminal care that she would require shortly.

"I imagine that you have given a great deal of help to your friends and neighbours over the years...do you not feel that they would actually wish to help you? There would be support too, from your own doctor and the district nurses."

"Yes, I have helped them a good deal in the past - not just the little things like feeding the cat and watching the house when they have been on holiday, but nursing them when they have been sick and taking their children in when there has been a domestic crisis - but I do not feel that I could ask them to do this. Do some people with my problems stay in hospital?"

"Yes they do, in one of the side wards, but it's not ideal. You wouldn't see as much of your friends and neighbours as you would at home and of course, as you have already discovered, it can be quite noisy."

"But I would have you and Mr Khan to look after me, wouldn't I? And of course Nurse Meredith would pop in at night-time as well." I looked at her with some curiosity. There seemed to be no reason to mention Kate in this context. I wondered if there was some reason why her name had been included but if there was her face revealed few clues, except perhaps for some softness around the eyes and the hint of a smile. I was half inclined to press her for an explanation but my relationship with Kate remained painful to me, and I decided not to pursue the matter.

I had nothing but admiration for this formidable woman, who had accepted that her days were coming to an end, but was also considering the feelings that her friends and neighbours would have if she were to lean on them for support, should her final days be spent in her own home.

"Paul, may I have a little time to think about it? Perhaps we could have another chat in a few days time."

Two days later, my late evening round of the men went as planned, but it took longer than usual to see the ladies. Although it was nearly eleven-thirty pm, when the majority would normally be asleep, most were awake, quite chirpy and prepared to chat. When I reached Joan's bed I found it empty.

"I'm afraid she's just gone to the loo," said the patient in the next bed, "but I know that she did want to have a quiet talk with you, if you're prepared to come back later."

When I finished the round, I did indeed return to see Joan and found her sitting in a chair beside her bed, looking flushed and a little short of breath. Clearly, as the disease advanced, even walking was becoming a bit of a strain.

"Paul, thank you for coming back to see me, especially as it is so late. I did want a quiet word with you but it isn't altogether private here, the neighbours hear everything we say - would you mind if we had our little chat in the patients' lounge?"

Wondering whether she had decided to spend the last few days of her life with us in hospital, I helped her out of bed and supported her elbow as we walked slowly down the ward. Side by side, we entered the patients' lounge. To my surprise, I saw that Kate was sitting on a chair on the far side of the room.

"Now," said Joan, in as stern a voice as she could manage in her weakened state, "I am going to leave the room, close the door, and you two are not to come out until you've sorted out your differences, decided to be friends again, and arranged to go out together on a date."

And with that, she turned and walked slightly unsteadily to the door, which she closed firmly behind her.
Kate and I were left facing each other. For a moment or two neither of us spoke, each of us struck dumb by Joan's duplicity. Finally, I broke the silence.

"Look, I'm sorry Kate, this is so embarrassing. You really must forgive Joan. I'm sure that she has the best of intentions but she has obviously misjudged the situation. She seems to think that I ought to have a girlfriend; in fact she seems to think that you and I should get together. She just won't accept that you're going out with someone else. I will go and speak with her and explain, though I have already told her at least twice."

"Someone else? And who on earth would that someone else be?"

"With Simon, of course. Simon Gresty."

"Me and Simon?" She sounded amazed. "What on earth makes you think that?"

"Because when I finally escaped from theatre on the night of the party, I asked around and heard you had got together with him. When I got trapped in theatre and realised that the operation would last for hours, I tried desperately to get a message to you, and tried again to contact you to explain the situation before you went home on leave. I would have phoned you at your parent's house had Home Sister allowed me to have your contact details, but she was very protective and didn't help at all. Then on your very first day back on duty, when I came looking for you, I found you in Simon's arms in the office."

"I am not going out with Simon - I wouldn't go out with him if he was the only man in the world. He's obnoxious. When you left the party, he claimed a dance and then I couldn't get rid of him. When we were dancing he was like a limpet, the way he clung on to me. At times you'd think he had three sets of arms and hands. I was with Sally at the party, if you remember, and I explained the problem to her. She wanted to stay with John, so I told Simon that I needed the loo and slipped back to the nurses' home. I was tucked up in bed by eleven pm. Alone, I might add!"

"But I saw you together, in the office," I exclaimed. "You were in his arms. You didn't seem to be finding him too obnoxious then."

Kate answered indignantly, "Yes, and if you had been a real Mr Darcy or a gallant knight you would have rescued me. He was trying to impress me, telling me he's as good as got a consultant job and promising me trips to the theatre, a spin in his new car and so on."

"I'm so sorry Kate, I truly didn't realise. I thought I had interrupted a romantic moment. So Joan was right after all. She told me that you weren't keen on Simon, but I wouldn't believe her. How did she know that?"

"Because I told her. She's a lovely lady, but has terrible trouble sleeping. She's got far more pain that she admits but tries to avoid taking painkillers because they sedate her. I've spent hours talking with her at two and three in the morning, when everybody else is asleep. We've talked about all manner of things but we've talked about you as well."

"And what did she say about me?"

"She said we should get together - said if you didn't ask me out, then I should throw protocol to the wind and ask you - but I knew that Sue had got her claws into you." Now it was my turn to be surprised.

"Sue? Which Sue?"

"Susan Weston. When I came back from leave, I went to the theatre to look at the operation register. I knew you would not have deserted me, that something must have happened to stop you getting back to the party, and the register confirmed that. I saw that the operation didn't finish until one am and that you had been an assistant throughout, but then the girls in theatre told me the story of how you and Sue had been touching each other up while Mr Potts was operating, that the theatre sister was furious with you. Everyone was talking about it. I couldn't believe it; I was shattered. We all know that Sue is a good-time girl, but I never thought that she would take you in."

"Well, I can promise you, Kate, I would never go out with Sue Weston. She's nothing but a cheap tart. She was the one doing the touching and I was the one trying to escape. But you can't escape if you have her on one side, your boss on the other, and you are in the middle hanging on to a retractor. It was acutely embarrassing. Mr Khan saw what was really happening. He couldn't do anything about it at the time, but he put Sister straight immediately afterwards when the operation was over. Sister was certainly furious at the time but only until she accepted that none of it was my fault. I've not seen Sue since and I don't want to."

"But you've been so cold and distant with me whenever we've met on the ward, Paul."

"Only because I was bitterly disappointed that you seemed to have chosen Simon instead of me."

There was a moment's pause. Then I held out my hands towards her in a gesture of peace and reconciliation. She grasped them readily.

"So Joan was quite right then, wasn't she?" I said. "Really, it's no wonder. She'd spoken with both of us separately and realised what our true feelings were."

"We must go and thank her in a minute."

I looked into Kate's eyes, and smiled."Not before I've had a kiss."

My arms slipped around her waist, hers went around my neck, and we shared a kiss that was all the sweeter for the misunderstandings that had come between us.

"Actually, I owe you an apology for something else," admitted Kate, hesitantly.

"What's that?"

"For making you laugh and getting you into trouble when I was miming to Sir William's favourite catchphrase."

"I didn't really get into trouble; he's too much of an old sweetie to be angry with anybody."

We shared another kiss, longer and sweeter than before.

"Come on, let's go and say a big thank you to Joan."

"Haven't you forgotten something?"

"Have I?"

"You haven't asked me for a date yet."

"In that case, I'll ask you right now."

Without hesitation, she accepted, and we quickly agreed that the date should be outside the hospital where there was absolutely no possibility of it being interrupted by the bleep, the telephone, or a call from the operating theatre.

As we left the lounge to walk to Joan's bed, it was immediately obvious why so many patients had been awake when I did my round earlier. All faces were turned in our direction. It was apparent that they all knew exactly what Joan had been planning, and there was no doubt, from the expression on our faces, that her plan had been successful. We thanked Joan profusely and she was genuinely delighted that our misunderstanding had been resolved. She did, however, speak to us both rather sternly.

"Look. The truth is that you have both been rather silly. If only you'd spoken to each other, explained your feelings to each other, this whole mess could have been resolved weeks ago. So many problems in the world could be resolved if people would only talk to each other."

I knew that Kate had been away from her ward duties for some time and, realising that staff nurse had obviously turned a blind eye, I felt that I ought to leave. Thanking Joan again, I said goodnight to Kate and started towards the door, but a voice called out from one of the younger women on the far side of the ward.

"Aren't you going to give her a kiss, then?"

I hadn't reckoned on giving Kate a kiss in public but, rather coyly, I gave her a peck on the side of her cheek. But the voice was more insistent.

"Oh, come on. You can do better than that - and under the light where we can all see." I looked at Kate enquiringly.

"Why not," she said, and we walked hand in hand to the spot in the middle of the ward where the single light was shining down on the nurse's night station. Now centre stage and under the spotlight, I put my arms around Kate and kissed her full on the mouth. There were cheers, catcalls and clapping from the women in the beds all around us. The ward was alive and noisy as never before at midnight. Abruptly, however, the noise faltered, stuttered, and then ceased completely, to be replaced by an unnatural and ominous silence. I looked around. The women were no longer looking at us but were staring at the entrance of the ward. There, in the shadows of the doorway, stood a short, dark, rectangular figure, which advanced slowly towards us. Kate and I broke apart.

A deep voice boomed out, "Nurse Meredith, you will report to my office at nine o'clock sharp in the morning, is that clear?" Without waiting for a reply, she turned to me.

"And what is your name, Doctor?"

"Dr Lambert, Matron," I replied.

"Look, Matron, this is all completely my fault. I am..."

"Silence!" Matron roared. "I shall report you to the medical committee first thing in the morning."

She then focussed her attention on the staff nurse. "You will report to me at nine o'clock as well." She glared at us for a moment or two and then abruptly turned and left the ward without another word.

"Kate, I'm so sorry. There's going to be a frightful row about this."

"Don't worry Paul; whatever the punishment is, it will be well worthwhile."

Chapter 19

The next morning, gravely concerned, I waited for Kate to telephone me to let me know the result of her encounter with Matron. It was well known that Matron, who also lived in the nurse's home, was a strict disciplinarian, and it was inevitable that Kate would be punished in some way for so public a misdemeanour. Whenever I had seen her on the ward she appeared to be a formidable woman; all the nurses stood in awe of her, and she even frightened Sister Ashbrook. But what would the punishment be? Matron was all-powerful, she was answerable only to herself, and with a click of her fingers could despatch a nurse from the hospital and terminate her career in nursing. I was painfully aware that Kate had only been a student nurse for a few months; to date, the nursing school had invested little in her training, and she could easily be replaced from the hundreds of applicants that the school received each year. Kate might simply be dismissed on the spot.

On the other hand, Matron was known to hold the view that junior doctors, especially those who were resident in the hospital, were devils in disguise, demons in white coats, predators from whom her nurses needed to be protected. With luck, she would regard me as the principle culprit. Kate might then get away with a reprimand, possibly a warning as to her future behaviour, and Matron would persuade Dr Digby to throw the book at me. I had been surprised, yet impressed, that Matron had actually recognised Kate. She had addressed her by name. Perhaps she also had some knowledge of her ability as a nurse; or if she didn't know already, perhaps she would make some inquiries before deciding on her punishment. Kate was a natural on the ward. She had an easy manner, empathy with the patients, and she gave them confidence. If Matron was aware of that, perhaps she would not dismiss Kate, maybe she would show leniency.

It was difficult to concentrate on my clinical work. When clerking in a new patient, I asked the same question more than once. The first time that it happened, the patient just gave me a questioning glance. The second time, he reminded me rather sharply that he had already given me the information requested. Several times my bleep sounded and, with heart in mouth, I raced to the telephone, only to find that it was some mundane clinical matter. Finally, the call from Kate came through, and she told me what had happened. The interview with Matron had proceeded in a way that no one could have imagined.

Tired from her twelve-hour shift working through the night and apprehensive about the punishment that she knew she must expect, Kate had been in an extremely agitated state as she waited outside Matron's office with staff nurse. She too had realised that her nursing career might be at an end before it had really started. For years she had wished to train as a nurse and the prospect of her chosen profession disappearing before she had qualified appalled her. She trembled at the thought of her parents' reaction when they learned of her dismissal.

The staff nurse who had turned Nelson's eye to our behaviour the previous evening was called in to see Matron first, and Kate had been left on her own in the corridor; lonely, tired, and sick with worry. Time dragged, as Kate feared the worst. Some twenty minutes later, Matron emerged and marched off down the corridor with Staff Nurse, Kate being ordered to stay where she was as Matron walked past. For a further fifteen minutes Kate sat, sad and dejected, until Matron returned, this time on her own. Kate was then kept waiting for a further quarter of an hour before finally being called into the office. At this stage, she was in tears.

Matron proceeded to deliver a stern lecture on professional standards, the reputation of the nursing profession in general and of the City General Hospital in particular, and the behaviour expected of a student nurse. She stated that normally such appalling behaviour, particularly when a nurse was on duty and especially within sight of patients, would result in the immediate termination of a nurse's contract; but that she understood that on this occasion the patients themselves had played a part in instigating events. She acknowledged that she had been up to the Surgical Five Female ward to speak with Joan. In no way did Matron feel that this excused such behaviour, but she felt bound to take it into consideration.

"I am to be grounded for a fortnight," Kate told me over the phone, relief in her voice.

"What exactly does that mean?" I asked.

"It means that I'm confined to barracks. I'm allowed to work on the wards and I can live in the nurse's home, but that's the limit. I'm not allowed to leave the hospital campus for two weeks."

I was relieved and delighted. We both knew that the punishment could have been a lot worse and both appreciated that Joan, by acknowledging that she had orchestrated the series of events whose finale Matron had witnessed, had offered mitigation on our behalf, resulting in a lesser punishment. I would express my thanks to her later.

"That leaves us free to go out two weeks on Saturday," I said. "Will you keep it free?"

"Of course I will. Have you heard from Dr Digby yet?"

The truth was that I hadn't but was not too concerned about it, having been far more anxious about Kate's potential fate than my own. I didn't anticipate anything worse than a reprimand. It would have been far more worrying had Matron said that she was going to report me to Sir William or Mr Potts. Sir William had promised to explore the possibility of me progressing to a house physician's job on Medical Three, and might have had second thoughts if he believed that my behaviour had been inappropriate or unprofessional. It was possible, of course, that Dr Digby might discuss my conduct with Sir William, but I thought this was unlikely.

Later that morning, I went to have a chat with Joan. "I believe that you have had a visitor this morning."

"Yes, I did, and very fair she was too."

"Joan, I don't know what you said to Matron but Kate and I are extremely grateful to you. She gave Kate a lecture and she is not allowed out for a fortnight but it could have been a great deal worse. Before now, nurses have been sacked for behaviour deemed to be inappropriate."

Joan explained, "I simply admitted that it was all my doing, and so it was. It would never have happened if I had not interfered. At first she seemed disinclined to believe me - said it was an excuse concocted by the two of you - but a couple of the other ladies joined in and confirmed the story, and said how unfair it would be to punish Kate and what a wonderful nurse she was. We had her outnumbered and she knew we would find out if Kate were to be unfairly treated. No doubt she felt that she had to be seen to take some action, otherwise she would be giving the green light to every young doctor in the hospital to kiss the nurses whenever they liked. Have you heard from your boss yet?"

"No I haven't, but I'm not too worried. Senior consultants were junior doctors once upon a time, and no doubt they kissed the nurses when they had the chance," I said, with slightly more confidence than I felt, but not wanting Joan to worry on my behalf. She had more than enough worries of her own.

For over four months now, I had lived in the microenvironment that was the hospital; working, eating, sleeping and relaxing, scarcely ever leaving the complex of buildings. Everything I needed was provided for me, and I had no occasion even to go to the shops. Twice I had returned home for the weekend but only to spend the Saturday night in my old bed. On a Friday evening I always felt too exhausted to want to travel home and, since I had to start work soon after eight am on the Monday morning, it was easier to spend Sunday night at the hospital. Once or twice, I noticed that my hair was getting a little long and shaggy, but the hospital barber willingly obliged with a quick 'short back and sides'. He probably used the same instruments with which he undertook pubic shaves on our surgical patients, but I trusted him when he said that that he washed these before he cut my hair!

It was curious how my horizons had foreshortened, how my world had shrunk. The long hours, the intense pressure, and the closeted existence had combined to exclude almost all consideration of life beyond the hospital walls. Normally I would be aware of political news and sporting events, and would take an interest in happenings in my own family, but I was now out of touch on all these matters. Even the weather, that perennial topic of conversation amongst Englishmen, had ceased to have relevance for me; it was always warm and dry in the hospital.

The first week in December arrived and I was due for a week's leave, but it was not the time of year to go walking in the Yorkshire Dales or the Lake District. I had made no definite plans, having been too wrapped up in my work to give it any consideration, and had vaguely contemplated a week at home catching up on sleep, maybe seeing one or two local friends and doing some Christmas shopping. I was looking forward to the week off - not in positive anticipation of events planned, but merely as a break from duty.

When I arrived home, I got a welcoming hug from my mother. "You've lost weight, Paul, and you look pale."

She was right. When I looked in the mirror and compared my reflection with the photograph taken a year before, there was a striking change. Admittedly the photo had been taken when I was on holiday in France, but even allowing for the lack of suntan, my appearance was different. I looked gaunt, my cheeks were slightly hollowed, and my face looked weary. The house officer post was taking its toll on me, just as it had on Eleanor.

It certainly was good to be home; to be back in my old bedroom, to enjoy an undisturbed night's sleep, and to have neither a bleep nor a telephone by the bedside. In the next couple of days I read quite a lot, did some shopping, and went out with some old school-friends to the cinema and to the pub. It also gave me a chance to take stock and do some thinking, something that the pace of life in the hospital had excluded. By Wednesday, though, I had made up my mind to return to the hospital. It was not a single event that made me decide to do so; rather, a combination of things. Perhaps I was a little bored, perhaps I found the atmosphere at home a little oppressive, maybe I missed the buzz of life on the wards...but I seemed to be living in an uneasy fashion alongside my parents, rather than as a fully integrated family member. Free from the rigors and discipline of hospital life, I wanted to relax and to organise my own time, but this rather upset my father. Some of the things he said began to irritate and a little tension developed between us. He expected me to be up, dressed, and shaved, for the family breakfast at seven-thirty each morning.

"Just because you are a doctor now, doesn't mean to say that the whole routine of the house has to be changed. You can't expect your mother to cook breakfast twice." Whereas I wanted to catch up on my sleep and arrange my day's activity for myself, as head of the family he clearly expected that all household members should fall into the normal routine.

I realised that I had changed, and recalled what Joan had said about her experience in the ammunitions factory in the First World War; how she had grown up when she left home, learned how to stand on her own two feet and not to need or be beholden to others; to "throw away her corsets" as she had described it. She had learned to be independent, to stride out into the world on her own and to make her own decisions. I realised that exactly the same thing had happened to me

Leaving home and emerging from the shadow of my parents - working in the hospital, being given and accepting responsibilities, developing my own judgements and making decisions - had changed me, and given me the confidence and independence that I had previously lacked. I was still my parents' son, but I was now a man. Also, I missed Kate and wondered how she was getting on, now that she was grounded. I had spoken to her on the phone, of course, but by returning, I could see her on the ward each evening when she was on duty. Not least, I was conscious that the next day, Thursday, was our urgency day, and the workload on Johnny's shoulders would be well nigh impossible if he didn't have some assistance.

One of the patients that I admitted on my return was Rosemary Roberts, known as Rosie. It is, of course, totally inappropriate for doctors to have favourite patients, or indeed to find them attractive, but it was impossible for me not to fall for Rosie. She was absolutely gorgeous both in looks and personality. Her eyes were bright with fun, reflecting her zest for life, her full mouth was always ready to smile, and no one could fail to find the blonde curls that framed her face displeasing. Her beauty was enhanced by her complexion, her skin being smooth, strikingly pale - almost opalescent, as if moulded from the finest bone china – but, sadly, this was a result of the two congenital abnormalities from which she suffered. The first was a narrowing of the vessels that drained blood away from the liver and stomach; the second was multiple cysts in her kidneys. The narrowed veins restricted the volume of blood that could flow through them, and resulted in blood pooling in the walls and lining of the stomach. As a result, the veins there had become engorged and friable. Occasionally they would leak a little blood into the stomach, and consequently Rosie was invariably pale and anaemic. There was concern that one day she might have a more major haemorrhage.

The renal cysts affected the function of the kidneys so that the toxic products of metabolism - end products from the digestion of food, which would normally have been excreted in the urine - built up in her body, and these, in turn, slowed the production of new blood cells in her marrow, which exacerbated the situation. It was the combination of anaemia, and a tinge of yellow jaundice from her liver troubles and renal failure, that gave her the pale 'bone china' complexion.

Sadly, her whole life had been spent in and out of various hospitals undergoing a variety of treatments; multiple blood transfusions, and, more recently, renal dialysis. Despite this, nothing seemed to dampen her bubbly personality and her eternal optimism. She also had a tendency to burst into fits of giggles, which I personally found irresistible, and I was attracted to her from the first moment I saw her - which, for her doctor, would have been unforgivable, but for the fact that Rosie was just six years old!

It was most inappropriate for her to be nursed on an adult female ward, but she had been transferred to us from the children's hospital to have an operation to create a bypass of the narrow vessels. If successful, this would take the pressure out of the stomach veins and reduce the chance of bleeding, and the only surgeon in the city with the experience to perform such an operation was Mr Potts.

Rosie was given her own side ward; in fact it was a double side ward that normally held two patients, so that her parents could have the freedom to visit outside of normal visiting hours, and it allowed one of them to stay overnight occasionally, to keep Rosie company. It had its own washbasin but Rosie had to walk the full length of the ward to use the other facilities. Wise beyond her years and well used to hospitals and hospital routine, she was quite at home talking to the other ladies as she walked passed their beds. Inevitably she quickly became a firm favourite, and other patients and staff would regularly pop in to chat with her as they passed her room. Sister Rutherford, who had grandchildren of much the same age, simply treated her as one of her own in a kindly, but not overly sentimental fashion, and certainly tried not to spoil her. However, others were less aware that their visits tired Rosie and eventually, to give Rosie time to rest, it proved necessary for the door to be kept closed, with the blind down and a sign placed stating that Sister's permission had to be sought before Rosie was disturbed.

Before I went to admit her, I sat down in the office and read the notes that had accompanied her. They were about five inches thick and chronicled her care from birth to the present day. In the first months of life she had been seriously ill, but a diagnosis had proved elusive and it had taken a long time to discover where her problem lay. Thereafter, there had been numerous admissions under the care of the paediatricians to correct her anaemia and to treat the renal failure that she subsequently developed. Initially this had been managed with a special low protein diet, but she now required dialysis, and the hope had been expressed that the developments that were taking place in the field of transplantation might one day solve this problem. It was, however, the recent haemorrhages from the stomach that were now the major cause of concern and the reason for her admission for surgery.

Armed with the huge set of notes, I put my head round the door of her side ward. "Hello," I said.

"Hello, who are you?" Her parents were not with her at the time but she didn't seem in the least perturbed that yet another doctor was coming to see her. She had a quiet, open, and frank manner. I was about to say "Dr Lambert," but realised that this would sound a bit formal to a six year old.

"Paul," I said.

"Are you a doctor?"

"Yes, I am."

"Dr Paul," she said, and then repeated it again. "Yes, I like that - I shall call you Dr Paul. Are you going to look after me?"

"Well, Mr Potts is going to look after you, but I'm going to try to help him."

"Mr Potts is my new consultant, isn't he?"

"That's right. He's a very clever man."

I heard her giggle. It was the first of many times I was to do so, and a sound that I came to love.

"I call him Dr Potty."

"You mean the thing that babies sit on to have a wee?"

"No, silly. Potty, you know, potty - meaning silly." The juxtaposition of the words amused her and she giggled again. It was impossible not to laugh with her.

"Why do you call him Mr Potty?"

"Because he talks in riddles. He says things and uses words that I don't understand."

I could well believe that!

"He talks to my Mummy and Daddy and uses long words."

"Don't let him catch you calling him Mr Potty."

"Oh no, I won't. He's going to do an operation to make me better, so I'm going to be especially nice to him."

"Now," I said, "I've got to ask you lots and lots of questions, so can I sit down here by the bed?" I drew up a chair.

"You're going to 'admit' me, aren't you?" I smiled. She was obviously well and truly accustomed to hospitals.

"Yes," I confirmed. "I'm going to admit you."

"Well," she said, "I'm very special. I was born with stenosis of my hepatic veins and multiple renal cysts." She spoke the words very slowly and deliberately, but got them all absolutely right. "It means I've got portal hypertension. It's called the Budd Chiari Syndrome. Lots of doctors have never heard of it. Dr Portly says it's 'small print stuff'."

"And who might Dr Portly be?"

"Dr Portman, my doctor in the children's hospital - but he's ever so fat, so I call him Dr Portly. I have made up names for all my doctors."

"I'd better behave myself then or you might end up calling me Dr Grumpy or Dr Dopey. Am I allowed to have a name for you?"

"Yes, as long as it's nice."

"What about Miss Cheeky?"

"No, that's not nice enough."

"What about 'Sunshine'?"

She thought for a minute. "Yes, I like that. You can be Dr Paul, and I can be Sunshine."

When it came to the time to do a physical examination, she asked to feel my hands. "Why?" I asked.

"I want to check that they're warm." They met with her satisfaction, and I examined her in the usual way.

"You're better at it than Mr Potty," she said.

"How so?"

"He digs in and he's got very sharp fingernails." Again, it was impossible not to smile.

Later I was to meet Mr and Mrs Roberts, Rosie's parents, who both seemed very young; probably little older than I was, possibly twenty-six or twenty-seven years of age. They had a second daughter called Claire, who was four. They lived forty or so miles away but fortunately had a car. Both drove, and one or other of the parents visited each evening; both, if they could find a baby sitter to look after Claire. At weekends I would see all four of them together as a family and was impressed to note how well adjusted they were, coping well despite the anxiety and stress of Rosie's illness. Sometimes the family would play card games or board games together and the parents would show no favouritism to one or other of their daughters, both of whom were able to lose with good grace and without tears. At other times the parents would read or chat between themselves, leaving Rosie and Claire to play together, as might have happened had they been in their own home.

When I had returned to the hospital, Johnny had told me that Dr Digby had been looking for me earlier in the week and had been informed that I was on a week's leave, so it was not altogether a surprise to receive an invitation to see Dr Digby in his office in the X-ray department on the following Monday morning.

"Come in, Dr Lambert, come in. I've been expecting you."

I was surprised to be received so warmly and also that he had addressed me as 'doctor', my formal medical title. He was the first consultant to have done so since I started the job!

"I have set of X-rays here that might interest you. Weren't you the houseman that picked up some clinical abnormalities when you examined Harry Barlow's chest?" He was referring to a middle-aged accountant whom I had admitted electively for a routine varicose veins operation a few weeks before.

"Let me show you. This is the first X-ray taken; the one you requested which showed a shadow at the central part of the lung. Did you hear what happened to him thereafter?"

I shook my head. "No, the last I saw of him was when he left our side ward and went off to the private hospital."

"Then let me show you the more detailed X-rays that were taken subsequently." He put more X-ray plates on the screen and took out a pointer.

"There's the mass that was present on the original X-rays, but it's much clearer on these films. Radiologically, this is almost certain to be a carcinoma of the bronchus on the left hand side. In fact, I heard that

one of the chest surgeons popped a telescope down, confirmed the diagnosis with a biopsy, and he has now had his left lung removed. A smart piece of work."
It was interesting to receive information on a patient's subsequent progress and nice to be complemented, but I did not wish to appear cocky. These pleasantries were merely a prelude to the reprimand and possible punishment that was surely to follow. It was inevitable that the interview would end with a sting in the tail.

"The clinical signs in the chest were fairly obvious, Sir," I said quietly, "and he had been a lifelong smoker."

"Nonetheless," replied Dr Digby, "the signs still needed to be recognised, interpreted, and the correct investigations arranged. He came into hospital for a minor operation and you spotted a serious problem. Mr Barlow ought to be very grateful to you."

Dr Digby paused and looked pensive for a moment or two, as if uncertain how to proceed with the interview, then changed the topic of conversation; though not to the one that was uppermost in my mind.

"For my sins," he said, "I've been appointed as chairman of the consultants committee. It's a post I shall hold for three years and there are a number of things that I would like to achieve in that time. One of them is the establishment of a postgraduate tutor; a careers officer if you like, probably one of the younger consultants, tasked to show an interest in all the junior doctors that we have working here to guide them in their career choices and to support them with appropriate advice and training. Until we get a system in place, I have been trying to do the job myself and I wondered if you had thought about your own career yet. Have you thought what you want to do when your current contract comes to an end?"

I told him that Sir William had raised that very question only a week or two before, but that so far I had not thought beyond arranging a house physician post, hopefully at the City General Hospital, adding that I expected that these posts would be advertised shortly.

"Oh yes, I remember now," said Dr Digby. "Sir William's nephew is the other houseman on your unit, isn't he? And the two of you are going to do a straight swap with the two housemen on Medical Three."

I must have looked surprised, for he added "I heard it being arranged over lunch in the consultants' dining room a couple of days ago. It's not a way of making appointments in this hospital of which I approve - in fact, I disapprove strongly, and it's another matter that I intend to rectify in the next couple of years."

Again, he must have seen the expression change on my face, for he continued "Don't worry Dr Lambert. I'm not empowered to change the arrangements that have already been made, but I do intend to see that a fairer system is implemented in future."

Frankly, I was amazed. The posts hadn't been advertised, no application forms had been completed, no CVs prepared and no interviews conducted - and yet I now knew that Johnny and I were to be house physicians on Medical Three and the two Medical Three house officers were going to move to Surgical Five. Johnny probably expected to get a medical job at the City General - just as he had expected to get his uncle's surgical post at the interviews last July - but for me, this was superb news.

"For my own sake," I said, "I am pleased to hear that, but it seems an odd way for posts to be filled."

"I agree. It is entirely unsatisfactory and there will be changes. In my view, all appointments should be made in open competition. The best applicant should be the one appointed to the post. Too many jobs are being filled through the 'old boy network' at present."

I saw an opportunity to help a friend. "I have seen evidence of that, Sir, in the short time I've been at the hospital. We have an excellent registrar on Surgical Five called Mr Khan, who is overlooked regularly when it comes to promotion." I hesitated, not certain whether to go on, but Dr Digby was looking at me enquiringly, so I continued.

"He's been in his registrar post for about seven years now, he's passed the exams to become a fellow of the Royal College of Surgeons, he's published a couple of articles in the British Journal of Surgery, and he's a marvellous technician in theatre. He takes time to teach too. Dr Nolan and I have learned a great deal from him - and yet every time he applies for a senior registrar job he's overlooked, and the post is given to someone with less experience."

"You mean his face doesn't quite fit?" commented Dr Digby shrewdly.

"Yes," I said, "I suppose that's what I do mean, and it doesn't seem quite fair."

"That's exactly the sort of the case that has been worrying me and the sort of thing I am determined to change. Thank you for bringing it to my attention; I will see what I can do. Anyway, I must get on now - I've got some more X-rays to report. I hope you enjoy working on Medical Three, and should you need any career advice when that post comes to an end, please let me know."

I thanked him and turned to leave, and had reached the door when he suddenly remembered why he had asked me to come to his office in the first place.

"Oh, Dr Lambert, I nearly forgot." I turned to see him smiling broadly. "If you're going to kiss the nurses, please do it when Matron isn't looking."

"I will, Sir - thank you, Sir."

Chapter 20

The second week in December felt as if were one of the longest of my life; partly because the unit was incredibly busy as we pushed through as many patients as possible in the run up to Christmas, to compensate for the reduction in activity that inevitably occurred during the actual Christmas holiday. For obvious reasons, few patients wished to be in hospital at this time. On Monday, Tuesday and Wednesday, thanks to the over-ambitious booking of cases, the elective operating lists all overran, not finishing until the middle of each evening. This was a significant imposition on the goodwill of all the theatre staff, but the expectation was that everyone would work until the final scheduled case was safely completed. Occasionally there were grumbles, but the general attitude was that the irregular hours went with the job and that the job was worthwhile and satisfying. Then, on the Thursday, we had a particularly hectic urgency day when it was my turn to undertake the overnight Casualty duty. A succession of patients arrived during the late evening and in the early hours of the morning, none of them particularly severely injured or ill – but, unfortunately, not sufficiently straightforward for the nursing staff to treat them. The result was that I got very little sleep, the situation being exacerbated by the fact that a number of these patients required admission.

Friday also was busier than normal. Two of the emergency admissions from the previous day required surgery, and were added to the afternoon theatre list. When Mr Potts left at six pm, the operations on the elective cases having been completed, I was called to assist Mr Khan with these two extra cases, and didn't escape from theatre until ten pm. On my late evening ward visit I was literally dragging myself around, weary beyond belief; essentially working on autopilot and praying that, in my state of extreme fatigue, I would not make some horrendous mistake. It was after midnight when finally I collapsed into bed and fell at once into a deep and dreamless sleep. Fortunately, as per our agreement, Johnny took my bleep and answered all calls through Friday night and I managed to remain undisturbed until morning - when, woken by my alarm clock, I found that, apart from shoes and white coat, I was still fully dressed.

The other reason that the week dragged was that I was eagerly awaiting Saturday evening and my date with Kate. It had been particularly unfortunate that, since the terrible misunderstanding between us which had been resolved thanks to Joan's intervention, Kate had been grounded and we had been prevented from enjoying time in each other's company. We had managed to spend a few moments together on the female ward on the nights when Kate had been on duty, but conscious that Staff Nurse had also been in trouble with Matron for turning a blind eye when we performed under the spotlight at the request of the patients, it was necessary for us to ensure that our conduct did not cause further troubles, either for ourselves or for others. We were both acutely aware that Kate's punishment could have been a great deal more severe, and that Matron would not be persuaded to be so lenient should there be any further misdemeanours

As the hours slipped by on Saturday, although physically tired my mind was alive, in fact in some turmoil. It wasn't simply a matter of feeling expectant or excited. I was actually nervous and anxious. But why? The truth was, I had never felt completely at ease in female company. If in a mixed crowd of people, men and women, perhaps at a party or in the pub, I felt relaxed and would chat, laugh and joke with the rest; but when one to one with a girl, particularly an attractive girl, I felt awkward, self conscious, and was deeply envious of those who were self-confident in such situations. I had previously taken girls to dances and to the cinema but never before had I so desperately wanted an evening to be a success.

In my room in the residency I wondered what to wear for this first date, not that there was a particularly large selection from which to choose. I looked at the suit that had hung gathering dust in the wardrobe - untouched for five months, last worn on the day of the interview - but decided that this would be too formal. There was an old blazer that looked somewhat jaded which I also discarded, before eventually opting for my sports jacket. I added grey trousers, a smart-casual shirt and tie, and then looked at myself in the mirror. As my mother had remarked, I looked pale and had lost a bit of weight, especially in the face, but thought I looked reasonably respectable.

The nurse's home, like the hospital, was a detached three-story building, built by the Victorians in brick, and was considerably larger than the medical residency. It had recently been linked to the rest of the hospital with a covered corridor. Jokingly, it was said that Matron had arranged for the nurse's home to be protected by a moat, electric fences, and watchtowers manned by guards armed with machine guns. In reality, as I approached I noted that, although the ground floor windows were covered with metal grills and the front door was heavy and made of oak, it was not locked and indeed a notice actually invited me to enter and report to the reception desk. The door gave access to a small lobby overlooked on the right hand side by a glass window, where a further notice instructed me to ring the bell and to wait for attention. Presumably the nurse's home attracted plenty of visitors on a Saturday evening, for the Home Sister was already in attendance. She asked me to sign my name in the visitors' book, to state who had invited me, and then told me to pass through the inner doors of the lobby and to sit in the main hall where a row of hard-backed wooden chairs were provided. Two other young men were already waiting there, neither of whom I recognised. They were obviously known to each other and from their conversation I gathered they were planning to take two of the nurses out to a country pub for dinner and a drink. Since they seemed to be regulars, I asked at what time the girls had to be back and learned that they were required to sign in before eleven-thirty, unless specific permission from the Home Sister had been granted. The doors to the nurse's home were locked at midnight.

Shortly their girlfriends appeared, exchanged hugs and kisses with the young men, then signed out at the reception desk and went laughing and giggling on their way. I was quite happy to see them go, content to be left on my own, hoping that it would stay that way until Kate arrived. I looked around. The hall was spacious, with dark wooden panelling on the walls and a large glass chandelier hanging from a high ceiling. Clearly the building was much older than the medical residency, and had a character that our accommodation lacked. There were a number of doors on either side of the hall that appeared to give access to recreational rooms. From the noises that issued forth, I gathered that one was a dining room, another a TV lounge, and a third a games room in which table tennis was being played. A number of nurses crossed from room to room. Having been used to seeing the nurses in uniform whilst on duty on the wards, it seemed odd to see them in civilian clothes. I received a number of curious glances. No doubt, after close inspection, all visitors would be the subject of gossip, comment and speculation as to which nurse had invited each particular visitor. Already slightly ill at ease in these unfamiliar surroundings, I felt somewhat self-conscious; rather like a goldfish in a goldfish bowl.

At the far end of the hall there was a fine wooden staircase, no doubt giving access to the bedrooms on the upper floors, down which I expected Kate to descend, as indeed she did some five minutes later. When she appeared however, somewhat to my surprise, she was not on her own. She was with Sally, her friend who had joined the School of Nursing at the same time as Kate and who had accompanied her to the residency party. I rose to greet them.

"Hello Paul, I hope I haven't kept you waiting."

"Not at all - it's lovely to see you."

"You remember Sally, of course, whom you met at the party? She's got a date with John Probert. They are going to see the Christmas show that is on at the Plaza in the city centre."

Sally joined in the conversation, teasing me. "Hello Paul, I hope you're not going to leave Kate in the lurch again tonight, are you? She might not forgive you a second time!"

"Not tonight. I'm off duty, I haven't got my bleep with me, and we are going to go a long way away from the hospital - somewhere where there aren't any telephones."

Sally looked around the hall that was otherwise empty, then turned to Kate. "You're lucky that Paul has turned up...it would be nice to see my date, too. This is not the first time that he has kept me waiting. It may be time to give him the old heave-ho."

We left Sally waiting for John and Kate signed out at the reception window. The Home Sister looked me up and down as if inspecting my suitability to be escorting one of her nurses, then reminded Kate that she had to sign in again before eleven-thirty.

"Having to sign in before the clock strikes twelve makes me feel like Cinderella," she said, "but it's no different to living at home with my father. He's even stricter than our Home Sister."

As we walked down the steps and along the link corridor, we saw John Probert coming in the opposite direction. He seemed to be in no particular hurry.

"You had better speed up, John," I said. "Sally's waiting for you."

"Don't worry," he replied, "I'll spin her a yarn about a cardiac arrest or some other emergency that has detained me. She'll be so impressed that she is certain to forgive me." Then to Kate, he added, "Take care Kate, you know what they say about the quiet ones. He's been waiting to take you out for three months - he'll be like an unleashed tiger!"

He continued on his way but when he had passed, Kate remarked "I don't think she will forgive him, Paul. He rather takes her for granted, seems to think that he is the only fish in the sea. I'm afraid this will be his last date with Sally."

As we walked through the hospital and then on to the main road leading to the city centre, I knew that I should open a conversation; perhaps mention the weather, maybe enquire whether Sister Rutherford had caused any problems when Kate had asked to change the duty roster so that she could be free on the Saturday night, possibly mention the films that were showing in the city, but I was curiously tongue-tied. It was quite illogical. As a doctor, albeit newly qualified, I found myself able to talk freely with patients and get them to open up and tell me all sorts of details about their personal lives, about their illnesses, their worries and fears - but in this situation, I was shy, inhibited, and acutely conscious of my lack of confidence. If Kate noticed my silence, she was too polite to mention it, but I was grateful to her when she eased the situation by starting to chat herself. Nothing of any great consequence; how it was good to get out of the hospital and get some fresh air, particularly on a nice clear night; how the hospital and Nurse's Home had been stuffy and claustrophobic during the period she was grounded; and how the days had dragged waiting for tonight. She said she liked to have a brisk walk too. On the ward you were on your feet a lot but mainly standing around, which wasn't quite the same.

I asked if she enjoyed walking in the countryside and was delighted when she said that she loved all aspects of the outdoor life and had done a lot of walking herself, both in England and overseas. She told me of some of the high-level walks that she had completed whilst on holiday in Austria and Switzerland with her parents and brother. I spoke of my uncle, who had a small guesthouse in Grasmere in the Lake District where I had spent numerous holidays, and spoke of the walks that I had done, the peaks that I had climbed, and particularly the week I had enjoyed Youth Hostelling between the final examination and the commencement of my surgical post. She too had spent holidays in the Lakes and had climbed many of the same mountains and swum in the same tarns. As we walked and chatted, I gradually began to feel more at ease. We were talking, not as boy to girl but as friends, on subjects of mutual interest, and as we conversed ever more freely the barrier that I had felt between us melted away, and my confidence grew. Tentatively, I reached out and took hold of her hand and she squeezed mine in response; then she looked up at me and smiled. Quite suddenly my self-consciousness evaporated, my confidence returned, and I felt on top of the world as we breezed along the pavement in step, hand in hand, chatting easily.

"You're very happy all of a sudden," she said. "I've not seen you like this before."

My tongue was quite free and I simply said exactly what was in my head. "Why shouldn't I be happy? I'm off duty, it's a lovely evening, and I have a pretty girl at my side." It may sound corny but it came from the heart, and the words were spoken without hesitation.

As we walked towards the city centre, the suburban houses gave way to shops, their windows alight with Christmas decorations, then to office blocks, until we eventually reached the largest of the city squares, where the Grand Hotel stood opposite the Town Hall. Still in a buoyant mood, on impulse I said "Would you like a drink before we watch the film?"

Kate looked up the steps to the impressive façade of the Grand Hotel, four enormous pillars either side of the revolving glass door. "In there?" she said doubtfully.

"Why not?"

"All right then," she replied, but she still sounded hesitant and looked uncertain.

Together we walked up the steps where a doorman, immaculately dressed in a long grey overcoat, with buttons of gold to match the gold braid on his peaked cap, politely greeted us. As we entered the entrance hall, I knew instantly that this was a mistake. With hindsight, I realise that I should have apologised to Kate, acknowledged that this was not an appropriate place for us to have a quiet informal drink, and turned and left. But unfortunately I didn't, and we stepped into the hall. It was enormous: it would easily have accommodated a couple of tennis courts. The ceiling was high and intricately decorated with plaster moulds picked out in different colours, the whole supported by six tall marble pillars. At the foot of each pillar was a mahogany table, whose polished inlaid surface bore a large wicker basket holding a huge and obviously expensive floral arrangement. The walls were hung with tapestries and large oil paintings of highland cattle, looking bedraggled and forlorn in a misty Scottish mountain landscape. The windows were framed with curtains of the finest satin. There were twenty to thirty people in the room, the men elegantly dressed in dinner jackets, the ladies in long evening gowns; none were less than fifty years of age. Some were talking quietly in groups, others sitting on leather armchairs and sofas. One or two looked curiously in our direction. There was the sound of a piano being played in the distance.

Naïvely I had imagined that there would be a bar, but none was visible. To one side, however, there was a reception desk. I made my way there, somewhat hesitantly, and asked where it was possible to get a drink.

"Are you a resident, Sir?" asked the receptionist in an imperious voice.

I said I wasn't and was given directions to the non-residents lounge. As I turned, the receptionist spoke again. "Perhaps Sir would like to leave his coat in the cloakroom. It's on your left, at the far end of the outer lounge, Sir."

The cloakroom attendant wore a uniform just as smart and as heavily braided as that of the receptionist and doorman. When I had left the residency, I had thrown an old anorak over my sports jacket. It had served me well in my student days, but the attendant appeared to treat it as an offensive article, holding it daintily between a single finger and thumb and at some distance from his nose, as if it were malodorous. It certainly looked out of place and not a little incongruous amongst all the full-length grey overcoats, and expensive furs in the cloakroom.

Kate and I walked to the non-residents lounge which had been indicated to us, and here I was to make yet another faux-pas. I suggested to Kate that she should take a seat while I went to the bar to order drinks. The barman looked at me, somewhat inquisitively.

"Can I help you Sir?"

I started to order the drinks, but the barman interrupted.

"If you would care to take a seat, Sir, I will arrange for one of my assistants to come and serve you." They were subservient words, spoken with a superior air.

This was a far cry from the cosy pub atmosphere that I had expected. A friendly taproom, some soft music, and a warm and welcoming atmosphere would have been much more appropriate. The suggestion that we should share a drink before moving on to the cinema had been made on an impulse, but we had entered an environment to which I was not accustomed and in which I felt distinctly uncomfortable. Kate appeared ill at ease as well. We sat in huge leather armchairs about a yard apart. The togetherness that I had felt when walking hand in hand from the hospital had evaporated. The confidence I had enjoyed had disappeared. A waiter came over, a lad no more than sixteen years old, and invited us to order drinks. He brought with him a small dish of canapés that he placed on the table in front of us. He looked as if he was fresh out of school and I asked him how long he had been working at the hotel.

"Just three months." He obviously hadn't mastered the requirement to add the word 'Sir' at the end of every sentence.

"Are you enjoying it?"

His reply indicated that he had also failed to develop the need to be economical with the truth. "No, I'm not. I hate it. I have to work long unsocial hours, I'm at everyone's beck and call, and I get paid peanuts. And the chances of promotion are poor. My friend Jack has been working in the dining room for two years and he's still a commis waiter."

"I know exactly how you feel," I said knowingly. "And so do I," added Kate, with feeling. "But you must meet lots of interesting people? Customers, I mean."

"Yes, I do, but they are all so very high and mighty; full of their own importance. They wouldn't dream of talking to me. To them, I'm a nobody. Just someone who will run and fetch them a drink when they click their fingers."

Out of the corner of his eye, he saw the head barman heading in our direction, a stern expression on his face. "I'm not supposed to chat to customers. Can you give me your order?"

Kate ordered a Babycham and I asked for a beer.

"Do you have any particular choice of beer, Sir?"

"Which beers do you have?"

He ran off three or four names, none of which were familiar to me, so I picked one at random. "An excellent choice Sir, would that be a pint?" His voice was now confident and loud enough for the head barman to hear.

"No, half a pint will be fine, thank you."

When he left, I commented to Kate that his job and ours had a lot in common.

"Yes, but only at a superficial level. Our customers are the patients. They come to us when they are ill, at a time of need, and we can really help them, genuinely improve their lives; not always, of course, but more often than not. And most patients are extremely grateful for our efforts. I can't imagine that the staff here receive too many words or letters of thanks, or boxes of chocolates by way of appreciation."

"I wish we could help all our patients," I said.

"You're thinking of Joan."

"Yes, I am. She must be one of the nicest people in the world, and we can do nothing for her."

"But we can, Paul. I know we can't cure her. I know she's dying. She knows that too, but that doesn't mean we can't help her. We can ease her pain, keep her warm and comfortable, talk to her; make her realise that she is not alone, and remind her of all the help that she has given to others in her life."

On the ward, I had seen and admired the way Kate behaved; the warmth she showed to patients, the gentleness of her approach, and the calm manner in which she conducted herself. As a nurse, she was a natural. Was there perhaps a fundamental difference between those who trained to be doctors, and those who trained as nurses? Doctors wanted to cure; nurses happy to care. For a few moments neither of us spoke;

both lost in our thoughts of Joan, lying in her side room, whilst we were out on the date that she had organised for us.

However, I didn't want the evening to centre on our lives at the hospital. I wanted to learn more about Kate - her likes and dislikes, and to discover more about her as a person - so I inquired about her family and home background. She told me that she had been born and raised in Kendal on the Lancashire/Westmoreland border, which explained why she loved and was so familiar with the Lake District. She enjoyed all outdoors activities; walking, camping, sailing. She also played quite a lot of sport: tennis in the summer and hockey in the winter. Like me, she had attended a single sex grammar school.

In return she inquired about my background, but somehow our conversation had become formal, stilted and strained in this vast, impersonal room. It had lost the spontaneity that had characterised the exchange as we had walked into town. To engineer our escape, I asked if she had any preference for the film that we might see. Fortunately I had done some homework on the subject, and was able to offer her a choice.

"There seem to be three films showing in the city centre; a war film at the Ritz, a 'Carry On' film at the Odeon, and a romantic comedy at the Gaumont."

"I don't fancy a war film," Kate replied, "and when you have seen one 'Carry On' film, you have seen them all. Let's try the comedy at the Gaumont."

"In that case, let's drink up and leave. I'm afraid this isn't my kind of place."

"Nor mine - in fact, I've never been in a hotel like this before."

I confessed that I hadn't either and apologised for suggesting that we should have a drink there, but did feel pleased that we shared a mutual dislike of this hotel and the pompous staff within it.

"Don't apologise, Paul. Just put it down to experience."

"How do you think we pay for our drinks?" I asked.

"I don't think you go to the bar, I think you probably wave to the waiter or catch his eye."

Summoning the young waiter to our table to ask for the bill was another first; it seemed a most unnatural thing to do, but it seemed to work. I paid for the drinks, the cost of which seemed excessive, then asked the lad where he had a drink when he was off duty, hoping for some information that would be of future use.

"Strictly speaking, I'm underage, but my mates and I usually go to The Old Bull, two streets down on the left. It's warm and friendly and drinks are a quarter of the price that they are here."

I thanked him for the information and suggested to Kate that we might try it next time. "That would be nice," she replied, and my heart leapt at the thought that she would be happy to go out together again. We walked across to collect our coats from the cloakroom and I wondered whether it was the done thing to leave a tip for the attendant there.

"What do you think?" I asked Kate.

"I don't know, but I know how to find out," she said, eyes twinkling. "I'll accept an invitation for an evening out with your Senior Registrar and ask him to bring me here. This is probably the sort of place that he frequents. I could take the ride I've been promised in that new sports car of his, too. He says it's British racing green and soft-topped." She was teasing, of course, but she did have this happy knack of using conversation to relax a situation and to help people to feel more at ease.

Deciding that the cloakroom attendant with all his superior airs and graces had not deserved any of my hard earned cash, I studiously ignored the saucer of silver coins that had been strategically placed on the counter and, hoping that Kate would not think me stingy, we left.

It was only 100 yards to the cinema and we took two seats in the rear stalls, deliberately avoiding the double seats on the back two rows. Perhaps we might sit there on some future occasion, I thought. The secondary feature was already showing; a film about the wild life of wolves in northern Canada, which was quite interesting, with some wonderful scenery. Then came the Pathé News and the Pearl & Dean advertisements. We had ices in the interval and then settled back to watch the main feature. The film was a gentle, romantic, 'boy meets girl' story set in Cornwall, with various amusing incidents involving misunderstandings with the local farmers and fishermen. Inside the cinema it was warm, dark and comfortable. There was no need for conversation and I was simply happy to sit there, knowing that Kate was at my side. She took my hand and I felt relaxed and content, far away from the stresses and strains of life as a junior hospital doctor.

The film was undemanding and I didn't give it my full attention, my mind wandering and thinking of other things. I wouldn't be here with Kate at my side but for Joan. Poor Joan...such an unfulfilled life. Or was it? Unfulfilled in terms of marriage, children and a family life, perhaps, but full in so many other ways. She had learned to be independent, and had relished and taken advantage of the freedom she had gained when breaking away from the influence of her father. She had enjoyed her job, made the children at school her 'family', and had helped them on their way. She had travelled the world, visited places that were just names on the map to me, and at every stage of the journey had given of herself, lending others a helping hand. Even as she knew her own life was drawing to an end, she was thinking of others. What remarkable courage that was.

I thought of Kate and wondered why I liked her, and why I was so desperate that she should like me. What was it about her that attracted me, made me feel so different? She wasn't beautiful in a classical sense; hers was not the face of a film star or the figure of a model, although she was slim and good-looking. She didn't use powder, paint, or lipstick, yet her complexion was clean and fresh, and her face, with that calm expression that so bewitched me, relaxed readily into an engaging smile. But it wasn't simply her appearance that magnetised me. It was something else. There was a calmness about her; she spoke quietly, she moved quietly, and yet there was no lack of purpose in what she did, for she handled herself with assurance and self-confidence. She was very perceptive and aware of the feelings of others. Although she had only just started her nursing career, she was completely at home on the ward and with the patients. She won their trust quickly, put them at their ease, and gave them confidence. And she had the same effect on me - giving me confidence, judging my moods, and easing difficult situations.

But did she really like me? She must care for me a little, I thought. Presumably she wouldn't be here with me now unless she did, and she must have said so to Joan. Joan had engineered that meeting in the patient's lounge because she knew that the feelings we had for each other were mutual. Separately, we had both told her so. I smiled to myself. How foolish we had been. We had both opened our hearts to Joan, but not to each other. She was right. If there were differences of opinion, it was no good jealously guarding them, keeping them to yourself, nursing your grievances. Problems could only be solved if you spoke about them, brought them into the open, discussed them freely and cleared up misunderstandings. Joan had made it obvious that she felt that we were suited to each other; I certainly hoped so. It would be wonderful if our friendship could flourish.

As we sat, side-by-side, hand in hand, in the warmth and darkness of the cinema, memories of the party where I had held Kate in my arms returned. What a wonderful moment that had been as we had danced, no, *swayed*, to the music. I recalled that at first I had been too timid - afraid to hold her too close, fearful of causing offence - but she had wanted to be in my arms and she had snuggled up closer, her cheek against mine. And then had come that terrible moment when the spell had been broken and a gulf had developed between us. Thankfully, those misunderstandings had now been resolved, and she was once again at my side. My imagination began to run away with me. She obviously loved the outdoor life and enjoyed walking. That was obvious from her descriptions of her walks in Austria and Switzerland. I thought of the lovely high alpine meadows that we might wander through together, the wooden chalets and dreamy cows with their bells on leather holsters. There were all manner of possibilities...so many wonderful trips we could take, so many places that we could visit. I wondered if she'd been to the Yorkshire Dales, or Snowdonia, or Scotland. I could walk the hills with her and climb the highest mountains.

Clearly she knew the Lake District well, but there were any number of walks that we could do together. The Fairfield Horseshoe, for example. I could imagine us setting off from Ambleside on a sunny April morning, climbing up through the spring flowers, reaching the top of Heron Pike and looking down on the reflections of the hills in the still waters of Grasmere and Rydal Water far below. Then along the ridge to Great Rigg and finally the satisfaction, the sense of achievement, of reaching the summit of Fairfield - just the two of us on a mountain top with the woods, fields, and dry stone walls laid before us down in the valley, like some giant collage.

Then the descent, over Dove Cragg, catching a glimpse of Brotherswater to the east, down over High Rigg, still on the ridge with the entire length of Windermere stretched out before us, completing a classic ridge walk. In the evening, we would return to a cosy pub, have a drink and a meal, then relax in each other's arms on a sofa in front of a roaring log fire...and finally, as the day drew to an end...

All at once, I was aware of sudden movement all around and I awoke with a start. People were standing and the National Anthem was playing. In a daze I stumbled to my feet, horrified.

"Oh my God, I've been asleep. How long was I out for? Tell me it was only for a moment?"

"About an hour," she said. She wasn't smiling and looked serious, but not angry.

"I'm so sorry, Kate. Why on earth didn't you wake me?"

"You put your head on my shoulder and slept like a baby. You looked so peaceful, I didn't want to disturb you."

I tried to compose myself. The Anthem finished and we both sat down and picked up our coats. Another thought struck me.

"I hope I didn't snore."

"No, luckily you didn't, but you did grunt once or twice!"

"I am terribly sorry, Kate. Perhaps if I had not had that drink..."

Kate completed the sentence for me "...or worked 100 hours this last week," she said. "Look, you needn't apologise. I do understand how hard you've been working. Last night when I saw you, when you came out of theatre onto the ward, you looked dreadful; dead on your feet. I nearly suggested that we postpone the date to give you a chance to catch up on your sleep, but I was selfish. I didn't want to call it off. I've been looking forward to tonight for two weeks."

"I'm glad that you didn't. I might have got the wrong impression and then we should have needed Joan to sort us out again."

Kate had been right, though. As on the night of the party, my job had intruded into my social life and on our relationship. On neither occasion had I been on duty. The first time I had been in the hospital and called to assist in theatre, but this time I was not only off duty, I wasn't even in the building - yet it was the chronic fatigue, the result of my long hours at work, that had ruined this evening.

While we remained sitting, the cinema had emptied and the usherette was putting up the seats and clearing rubbish. She looked at us impatiently.

"Come on," I said, "we had better leave."

We walked back to the hospital, side by side without any physical contact, and in silence. Once again I privately cursed myself. The suggestion of a drink in the Grand Hotel had been a huge mistake and it was unforgivable of me to fall asleep in the cinema. It was understandable, of course. It was warm, dark, and comfortable in there, and as Kate had said, it had been the chronic sleep deprivation - particularly the overnight Casualty duty, and not the half pint of beer - that had caused me to nod off. At least she realised that, but I had so wanted to impress her, so badly wanted this to be the first of many meetings with her, and it had all gone so horribly wrong.

We arrived at the door of the nurses' home. I stood facing Kate and reached down to hold both her hands.

"Look, Kate, once again, all I can say how truly sorry I..."

She put her forefinger on my lips and looked at me, her face serious, but with the suggestion of a twinkle in her eye.

"Your reputation is shot," she said. "I'm going to tell everyone in the nurse's home that you slept with me tonight."

With that she kissed me lightly on the cheek, and was gone.

For a moment I stood looking at the door through which she had disappeared, and then walked slowly back to the residency. My mind was in a whirl. Had the evening been a success or a failure? At times we had talked freely, I had felt comfortable in her presence, and we obviously had some common interests; walking, mountains, and the outdoor life. Clearly it had been a mistake to go into the Grand Hotel but I felt that we had both been uncomfortable there, both out of our depth out of our natural habitat, so to speak; so again, we had some shared values. In the cinema too, Kate seemed happy enough, until...

I couldn't bear to think about it, and when we had walked back to the nurse's home it had been in complete silence - not a single word had been spoken. Yet when we had parted I suspected she had been teasing me, and she hadn't seemed angry. But then again, she was a kind, caring person. Presumably she had not wanted to upset me. Perhaps she had just been a good actress and had been hiding her true feelings, having already decided that our friendship was at an end.

Feeling miserable, I collected my white coat and did my evening round, starting on the male ward, where I tidied up a few loose ends before walking to the female ward. Again, I walked round the patients one by one with the senior nurse on duty, until I came to Joan's bed. It was sad to see how rapidly she was weakening; no longer able to get out of bed, having to be turned regularly by the nurses to prevent the development of pressure sores, and scarcely able to drink unaided. Although sedated, she brightened when I reached her bedside.

"Well, how did it go?" she wanted to know.

"I'll come back in five minutes," I answered, not wishing to discuss the evening's events in front of the staff nurse. The round over, I returned to Joan's side room.

"Well, tell me all about it," she said impatiently, and with an effort tried to lift her head and shoulders off the pillow. I helped her to sit up.

"I'm afraid it didn't go very well," I replied, and without any prompting, told her the whole story.

She listened carefully throughout, and didn't interrupt once. She was particularly interested in the manner of Kate's farewell at the end of the evening, which she asked me to describe in some detail.

"My," she said, "you have had an interesting evening, haven't you? That's the sort of story you'll tell your grandchildren one day."

"Now now, Joan, don't let your ideas run away with you," I protested.

"Well, Paul, don't you let your chances slip you by. Ask her out again, and soon, before someone else realises what a lovely girl she is."

With that, she sank back onto the bed, closed her eyes and drifted back to sleep, but there was a softness in her face; she looked content, and seemed to be at peace with the world.

Chapter 21

Any concerns that I might have had that Kate would be angry with me for falling asleep and spoiling our first evening together were quickly dispelled the next day, when I saw her on the ward. As soon as Sister's back was turned, she sought me out and thanked me for a memorable evening. I tried to apologise again for nodding off in her company, but she brushed aside my apologies.

"As long as you were simply tired and not bored with my company I will forgive you," she said, smiling.

I asked if she had taken an opportunity to thank Joan for bringing us together and organising our date.

"No, I haven't as yet, I've been too busy - but I will later in the evening, as things quieten down. When Sister Rutherford was giving us the report, however, she said that Joan was deteriorating fast."

"Yes, I came to have a few words with her last night after I left you. I'm afraid she's slipping away. She's bed-bound now, only taking sips by mouth, and since she agreed to take more powerful drugs to ease her pain, she's really rather heavily sedated."

It was true. With no effective treatment available for her advanced abdominal malignancy, Joan's general condition had deteriorated considerably during the last week. Fluid had once again accumulated in her abdomen. Her arms, legs and face had become wasted, she had no appetite whatsoever for food, and the weight had dropped off her. Initially, she had refused analgesia for her pain, and had declined medication to relieve her constant nausea. "I've never been one to take tablets if I could avoid it," she used to say. However, as her symptoms had increased, she had reluctantly accepted the need for pain relief and was now receiving morphine regularly, which was making her drowsy. She remained lucid for much of the time; usually deflecting questions about her own health and preferring to talk about others, and whenever I was with her, she never failed to ask if I had seen Kate.

When time allowed, particularly in the late evening, I would spend a few minutes in her side room; but eventually even holding a short conversation became an effort for her and she would drift back to sleep, barely having spoken a few words. So far as one could tell, she continued to feel at ease with herself, appeared not to fear death...no doubt helped by the photo of her beloved Charlie, now in a small frame on her bedside locker.

In the following days, I was able to see Kate frequently, but only as duty rosters allowed. Inevitably we met from time to time whilst working on the female ward, but on these occasions protocol demanded that we keep our meetings strictly professional. Since Staff Nurse had been severely reprimanded by Matron for turning a 'blind eye' where Kate and I were concerned, understandably she and Sister were not prepared to take the risk of getting themselves into trouble by allowing it to happen again.

As a nurse working on night duty, Kate went to bed when she came off duty at eight in the morning. I continued to work long days, my life ruled by the requirement to respond to my bleep, which only functioned within the confines of the main hospital buildings. Occasionally, when the wards were quiet, Johnny would cover for me, and Kate and I took the opportunity to walk for half an hour or so in the late afternoon in the park adjacent to the hospital. Once or twice I was able to take Kate out for an early evening meal in town, before she had to return to report for night duty. On reflection, our friendship developed in what many would regard as a very old-fashioned way. This was not due to the restrictions imposed by our respective duty rosters - after all, I had a bedroom onsite available to me - but rather to our moral standards, and the respect that we had for ourselves and for each other. We were content to be in each other's company; to talk, to share reminiscences, to gossip about hospital personalities, and gradually to get to know each other better. I would no more have thought of inviting Kate to my room than I would of asking her to travel with me to the moon. Yet our relationship blossomed and became increasingly important to me. I looked forward to our meetings. A few minutes working together with a patient brightened the day, and when she went home to see her parents one weekend I moped around the hospital with such a long face that even Johnny noticed, and teased me without mercy.

Inevitably, Joan continued to deteriorate. From a medical point of view there was nothing useful that we could do, other than to minimise the symptoms of pain and nausea that stemmed from her advanced cancer. Whenever our ward rounds reached her room, I was struck with a feeling of frustrated impotence. There were many conditions in which the surgical team could make a useful intervention, but sadly there were still many that remained beyond our reach. The nurses continued to offer every care and comfort, but Joan, at peace with the world, slipped into a coma and died a week before Christmas. I was relieved that this happened when Johnny was on duty. It would simply have been too painful for me to examine her body to confirm her death, and to attend to the formalities required of the doctor who signs the death certificate. All the staff that had nursed her and had been involved in her care felt her loss, but it came as a particular blow to Kate and I. Joan had brought us together. Kate asked if she might be allowed to attend Joan's funeral, a request that was firmly declined by Sister Rutherford, who felt that it was unwise for nurses to become too emotionally involved with their patients.

In the side ward immediately adjacent to Joan's, things were very different. The room was bright and cheerful and slowly filling with soft toys; gifts from other patients and from the staff, far more than Rosie would ever want or need. The walls were covered with paintings and drawings, some of which were Rosie's handiwork, others the artistic efforts of her younger sister, Claire. One particularly large drawing was of a man with lop-sided eyes, gaps in his teeth, and spiky hair, which she insisted was a portrait of me. I suggested to her that the likeness was more of Simon Gresty so, much to Kate's amusement, she labelled it with his name rather than mine. Kate then persuaded Rosie to add a green sports car to the picture! She had also started to make a paper chain as a Christmas decoration for her room and, never short of willing volunteers to assist, the chain lay on the floor coiled like a snake, growing rapidly with every passing day.

At Sister Rutherford's suggestion, Rosie started to create a nativity scene on a small table in the corner of her room; making the stable out of cereal boxes, of which there was no shortage of supply on the ward, and fashioning the characters and animals out of plasticine. Inevitably many of the other patients came to help - some of their models being exceptionally lifelike - but Rosie would allow only her own or Claire's creations to be added to the scene. I was at a loss to know why the lambs were green until Rosie explained, with her infectious giggle, that they had been playing 'roly-poly' in the grass. I asked what a small pink pig-like creature lying on the floor was, and was told with much indignation, "That's the baby Jesus, of course." Was it any wonder that all the staff on the unit now addressed her by the nickname of 'Sunshine'?

Due to her prolonged periods in hospital, Rosie had been absent from school a great deal so that, despite appearing self-assured and mature for her age, she was not keeping up with the rest of her school class. The hospital arranged for a tutor to teach her for an hour each weekday morning. The tutor was particularly concerned about her reading ability and asked the staff to encourage Rosie to read to them, should they have any spare time. Once or twice, if it was quiet in the evening after her parents had gone home, I would attempt to persuade her to read to me, but she wasn't at all keen. She would happily look at the pictures in her reading book but struggled with even the simplest words and found it difficult to concentrate. The only way she would agree to read a few pages was for me to promise to read a story to her afterwards.

Perhaps because I was a bit of a soft touch where Rosie was concerned, it frequently happened that she would read to me for five minutes, then I to her for twenty minutes. She was particularly keen on a book which contained 'Princess Stories' - the stories of Cinderella, Snow White and Sleeping Beauty - but she had heard these so often that she knew them almost word for word. She would ask me to tell her a new princess story and, if there were no clinical duties for me to attend to, I would oblige. Together we invented a beautiful princess who had the most marvellous adventures. She sailed to distant lands, met inhabitants of strange countries, and talked to animals, goblins and fairies. Whilst on her travels, our princess, whom Rosie decided should be called Priscilla, concocted magic potions from flowers and ferns, visited dangerous rocky mountains, dark caves and mysterious forests, and frequently found herself in frightening situations. Inevitably, there was a handsome prince who rescued her from all danger.

Sometimes Rosie would fall asleep before the story had ended, but more often Night Sister would come in and say, "Enough, Paul - time for six year olds to go to sleep."

Medically, Rosie's was a complex case with her anaemia, liver, and kidney problems. Sadly, from time to time, she suffered complications. The principle function of the kidneys is to remove toxic products, which mainly come from the ingestion of proteins, so it was necessary for Rosie to take a rather unpalatable low protein diet. Occasionally the pressure in the engorged stomach veins would lead to a small bleed. In effect, this blood within her intestines amounted to a rich meal of pure protein, and inevitably had an adverse effect on her kidney function. At such times Rosie suffered nausea and lethargy, but despite these she still managed to remain cheerful. Numerous doctors came to see her - these included Mr Khan and myself on a daily basis, and Mr Potts on his twice-weekly rounds. There were also visits from the paediatricians, who came across from the children's hospital, and the renal physicians from the medical wards of our own City General Hospital. The paediatricians were marvellous, speaking to her at her own level in language that she could understand, taking time to explain things in a relaxed and calming fashion. By contrast, the bedside manner of the adult physicians was appalling. They treated Rosie not as a child, but simply as a complex metabolic problem that needed to be resolved. Unfortunately, from Rosie's point of view, all these different visiting consultants requested additional investigations; and it fell to me to take the blood samples, and fell to Rosie to be at the sharp end of the needle. This was the one thing that she hated - indeed, the one thing that often led to tears. Certainly her renal and liver function needed monitoring but, irritatingly, one consultant might well request an investigation even when a blood sample had been taken for the same test the previous day. They would regularly ask for an investigation then at their next visit not even inquire about the result, and had to be informed if it gave rise to any concern. Had I followed all the instructions of these visiting physicians, blood samples would have been required (causing distress to Rosie) once or twice every day, so I took it upon myself to rationalise the tests, then negotiated with Rosie that we would try not to take blood more than three times a week. Mondays, Wednesdays, and Fridays became venepuncture days. Having taken blood from six or eight patients every morning for the last four months, almost invariably I would find a vein at the first attempt, with a minimum of pain for my patients. In Rosie's case, however, I started to use a tiny amount of local anaesthetic prior to inserting the venepuncture needle, which made the procedure much easier for her and reduced the frequency of her tears. The truth is that I spoilt her, just as the rest of the staff did - but as the only child on an adult ward, and such an attractive one, this was probably inevitable.

The principle objective of all the doctors from the various medical teams dealing with Rosie was to get her as fit and healthy as possible, to enable her to withstand the forthcoming major surgical procedure. The operation - designed to divert excess blood away from the stomach and thereby to reduce the chance of a catastrophic haemorrhage - was relatively new, and had rarely been undertaken in children. The chance of a successful outcome was therefore unknown, but even in adults the procedure was known to carry a mortality rate of about fifteen percent. All the medical staff involved in Rosie's care, however, accepted that the risk of spontaneous haemorrhage was much greater if the condition was left untreated, and agreed that surgery was justified. Initially the date of the sixteenth December had been pencilled in for the procedure and an entire morning's theatre session reserved, but unfortunately these arrangements had to be cancelled when Rosie had a small haemorrhage, with a resulting deterioration in her kidney function. Her condition was again improving at the beginning of Christmas week but after discussion with her parents, who were fully conversant with the risks, Mr Potts suggested that it would be kinder to let her enjoy Christmas and to undertake the surgery between Christmas and the New Year.

Hospital life has changed a great deal over the last fifty years, no more so than in the way that Christmas is celebrated. In the fifties and sixties, a unique seasonal atmosphere developed during Christmas week and for those of us who were resident, celebrating Christmas in hospital was a memorable experience. Great efforts were made by the staff to create as cheerful an atmosphere as possible for those unfortunate enough to have to spend this time away from home. Four or five days before the big day, the porters erected a Christmas tree in the centre of the ward. Each ward had its own box of decorations and the tree was decorated by the nurses when an opportunity arose, when the ward was quiet. Invariably the fairy lights - perhaps put away in a rush the previous year - declined to work, and this was a busy time for the hospital electricians.

For fifty-one weeks of the year, life on the surgical wards was significantly more hectic than it was on the medical wards due to the faster turnaround of patients, but the situation was reversed during Christmas week. Most medical admissions resulted from emergencies such as heart attacks and strokes, and this flow of patients could not be controlled. Furthermore, this was a time of year when chest infections and pneumonias were rife due to the cold weather and the city smog, and as a result the medical wards were always full with severely ill medical patients. By contrast, over the Christmas period the surgical wards were half empty because fifty percent of our admissions were patients admitted from the waiting list and it was deliberately arranged that no major surgery would be performed in the week before Christmas and no intermediate surgery in the three or four days before Christmas. When Christmas Day finally arrived, only those patients who had been admitted as emergencies remained on the ward. Despite the ward being half empty, nurse staff levels were maintained, leading to a significant easing of their workload and resulting in excellent care for the few remaining patients.

Christmas Eve arrived and, having arranged with Johnny that he should work over Christmas, I was relishing the prospect of three whole days off duty and three long nights of undisturbed sleep. I could have gone home at lunchtime - but being eager to experience Christmas in the hospital, not least because it gave an opportunity to spend some time in

Kate's company, I had told my mother (much to her disappointment), not to expect me to arrive home until the afternoon of Christmas Day. Most of my Christmas shopping had been completed during my few days leave in November, but there were still one or two small gifts that I wanted to buy, and also thought it would be nice to get a little present for Rosie…not that there was any shortage of presents already waiting for her to open on Christmas morning. It was therefore with a wonderful sense of relief that I handed my bleep to Johnny. My medical responsibilities had been laid aside for a few days and, as I walked into town with a spring in my stride, it felt as if a great weight had been lifted from my shoulders. Knowing that Rosie's side room was overflowing with teddy bears, dolls and all manner of stuffed animals, I bought her a simple silver bracelet and a single charm to go with it; a miniature silver princess.

On Christmas Eve, I joined the congregation for the traditional carol service that was held in the hospital chapel. Although christened as a child, I am not a religious person, finding that the concept of a virgin birth does not sit easily alongside my medical training; but nevertheless there is something comforting about hearing the Christmas message, and I have always enjoyed singing the carols with their familiar words and tunes. Walking through the door, I was welcomed warmly by Father Patrick Doherty, the hospital padre, and took a seat near the back as the chapel gradually filled. The congregation numbered some thirty or forty people, mainly hospital staff, although no other junior doctor was present. Half a dozen patients were there, each accompanied by a nurse; some in wheelchairs in the centre aisle, others wrapped in blankets, sitting in the pews. Bridie from the residency dining room sat with her husband, and another member of the catering staff. Rosie and Claire arrived, with their parents. They walked to the front of the chapel and admired the Christmas tree, adding a present to those already placed under the tree that would later be distributed amongst orphaned children in the city. Rosie spotted me and waved merrily before the family took seats near the front, where the children would get a better view during the nativity service.

Just before the service began, the lights were dimmed and the first verse of 'Once in Royal David's City' was heard, sung by a clear solo soprano voice floating in through the open chapel doors. As the second verse commenced, the nurses' choir entered. The nurses walked in pairs, each wearing their formal hospital cape; the nurses in navy blue, the sisters in maroon, crisp white starched caps on their heads, each carrying a candlelit lantern held high upon a long shepherd's crook. The light from the candles cast flickering shadows on the walls of the chapel. It was a moving moment. The nurses took their places at the front of the chapel and the service began.

The Christmas story was told in readings and carols as, no doubt, it was being told in thousands of other churches and chapels up and down the country; but this service had an extra warmth to it, a certain intimacy, that was a new experience for me. Sir William read one of the lessons, Sister Rutherford another, and Matron, looking relaxed and almost friendly, a third. The congregation comprised patients, some of their friends and carers, and many members of the hospital staff. This was the hospital coming together as 'family'. Dedicated, caring people who shared a common ideal; who not only worked together, but also worshipped together.

When the service was over, the nurses' choir led the congregation out of the chapel, again walking two by two as they embarked on a tour of the hospital wards. I spoke with various members of staff, had a word with Bridie, was introduced to her husband, chatted with Rosie and her parents, and even received a smile and a seasonal greeting from Matron. Later I went to the Surgical Five wards to wait for the appearance of the choir. For the patients in their beds, it was an unforgettable experience. Without being forewarned, the lights on the ward were switched off, the sound of carols reaching their ears before the choir could be seen. As in the chapel, the choir entered each ward two by two, lanterns ablaze. They walked to the centre of the ward and then formed a semicircle around the tree in the candlelight. Unfortunately there was only time for the choir to sing a couple of carols before they had to move on, but it was sufficient to bring tears to the eyes of many of the patients. How sad it is that time does not allow these wonderful traditions to continue in modern hospital life.

When I later returned to the residency there was warmth, music, and laughter in the lounge. Very few of the housemen had gone home for Christmas, and all were determined to enjoy the festivities as far as their clinical duties would allow. I stayed for about an hour having a beer and a chat, then slipped back to the ward for five minutes to see Kate, to steal a kiss and to wish her a quiet Christmas night. This was to be her last night on duty, her father having arranged to pick her up in the morning to spend the rest of the Christmas period with her family. When she returned, it would be to do a 'block' of study in the School of Nursing. Tuition would be from nine until five and I anticipated that this would allow us to spend considerably more time together than had been possible when she had been working nights. Whilst on the ward, I popped into the sideward to see Rosie, hoping that she might still be awake, but she was fast asleep, blond curls spread on the pillow and a huge red stocking tied to the foot of the bed; no doubt dreaming of Father Christmas and the presents that he would deliver during the night.

Chapter 22

Knowing that Rosie's parents would visit later in the day with younger sister Claire, I planned an early visit to the ward to give Rosie her present before breakfast on Christmas morning, and set my alarm for an early start. Christmas is a special time, particularly for children and those in contact with children, and I was at ease with the world as I walked along the hospital corridors. All the hospital staff went out of their way to be cheerful for the benefit of the patients, and I passed porters wearing Father Christmas hats pushing breakfast trolleys decorated with tinsel on my way to the ward. The office door was closed as I walked past, the routine morning nursing handover taking place. I waved cheerfully to the staff through the glass partition and Sister waved in return. I didn't call in, knowing there would be plenty of time to spend with the nursing staff later in the day.

In a buoyant mood, I hurried towards Rosie's side ward, eager to see the smile on her face and to wish her a Happy Christmas. The night before I had seen the huge red stocking at the foot of her bed and knew that her parents had left her 'Father Christmas presents' with the nursing staff, to enable them to fill the stocking during the course of the night, when Rosie was asleep. With younger brothers of my own, I understood the joy that the sight of the stocking full of presents, magically delivered in the night, would bring.

I knocked cheerfully on the door and walked in without waiting for a response, but was surprised to find the room virtually empty. A bed but no stocking at its foot, no tree, no decorations, no nativity scene and no fairy lights. Surely I must have entered the wrong side room. I looked again but no - it was the right room - and yet there was no sign of Rosie, or indeed any evidence that Rosie had ever been there. Just a big bed with freshly laundered linen, sheets neatly folded back ready to receive the next patient. For a moment I stood there confused, without understanding; then suddenly it dawned on me what it all meant, what had happened. In an instant, Sister Rutherford was at my side.

"Oh, Paul, I'm so sorry - we weren't expecting you so early. I tried to stop you as you passed the office door."

I gazed at her blankly.

"It all happened so quickly, just after midnight...a sudden haemorrhage. She slipped away in just a few minutes; there was nothing anyone could do." She ran through the usual platitudes at which doctors and nurses are so good and so practised. "It was very quick, she didn't have any pain, and she really didn't suffer."

But I wasn't listening - my mind was numb. I could not believe that such a lovely, innocent child could be so cruelly snatched away. What had she done to deserve this, such a cheerful little girl who radiated happiness to those around her? She had suffered ill-health from the day that she was born, tolerated long periods in hospital with scarcely a frown, had endured unpleasant diets and painful injections; then, just when there was the possibility that her health might be improved, she had died. Scarcely aware of what was happening, Sister Rutherford led me to the office, her arm around my shoulder. Both the day staff and the night staff were there, and the communal grief was profound. Kate and two of the other nurses were in tears. There was a shocked and sombre atmosphere in the room. Mugs of tea were dotted around the room, but nobody was drinking. Everyone sat in silence, lost in their thoughts, devastated that such a precious, beautiful and brave child should be lost.

Eventually the night staff explained what had happened. Before they had turned out the lights Kate had read her a story, then Rosie had gone to sleep as usual. She had not stirred when the nurses had filled the Christmas stocking with the presents that her parents had left for her. At one am, when routine observations were taken, the nurses had noticed that Rosie's pulse was raised and her blood pressure had fallen. Johnny had been called, but before he had time to reach the ward, Rosie had vomited a vast amount of fresh blood and collapsed. The duty registrar had been called but within a few minutes, before a blood transfusion could be commenced, there was a further huge vomit and Rosie had quietly slipped away. Her parents had been phoned and had rushed to the hospital, but unfortunately had not arrived until it was too late. The night staff were deeply traumatised by what had happened and had then been faced with the thankless job of trying to console Rosie's parents and undertaking all the dreadful tasks that are required when a patient dies and the body has to be laid out. When the story was finished, there was a prolonged silence. No one seemed to want to be the first to speak.

Slowly, hesitantly, comments were made.

"Poor little mite."

"So beautiful, so innocent."

"She suffered all her life, and for it all to come to this."

"And her poor parents, what must they be thinking?"

Sister allowed comments to be made in this desultory, morose fashion for some time as the staff, combined in grief, consoled each other. Then she cleared her throat and spoke in a firm voice, addressing her staff.

"I know how much you all came to love Rosie and how well you nursed her and cared for her. It is a tragedy that she should die, that all our efforts were in vain. Yet I'm sure you all realise as well that every patient on this ward also knew and loved Rosie, just as we did. They are bound to be just as upset as we are; perhaps more so, since we are more familiar with death. They will need our help and support. Today is going to be a difficult day for everyone but we have to remember that it is Christmas morning; it's going to be a busy day, there will be lots of visitors on the ward and plenty of work to do, so I'm sure we will all want to do our duties professionally. Staff nurse, I want you to start the drug round; the rest of the nurses and I will sort out breakfast."

Then she turned and addressed the night staff. "I'm sorry that this has been such an awful night for you but of course we all knew that a massive bleed was possible; that's why Rosie was in hospital and that is why she was to have her surgery. I know also that you did everything humanly possible to try to save her, but there is nothing to be gained by sitting here brooding. It's time for you to go off duty, go to bed, and try to get some sleep."

Slowly, almost reluctantly, the nurses stood up and went their various ways; the day staff to attend to their duties on the ward, the night staff to their beds. Sister Rutherford took me to one side and spoke quietly to me.

"Paul, Kate is the most junior nurse here by some margin; this is the first time that she's seen anything like this and she's clearly very upset. I shall have to stay here on the ward. Will you see her safely back to the nurse's home for me please?"

Sister had noticed, as I had, that although all the other nurses had left, Kate was still sitting quietly in the corner; not crying now, but stunned by the events that she had witnessed during the night. I took her by the hand and we walked slowly, heads down, along the hospital corridors, then onto the link corridor that led to the nurse's home. There I held her in my arms, her head on my shoulder, her cheeks still wet with tears. It was not the passionate embrace of two young lovers, but simply two people offering comfort to each other at a time of great sadness. Later in the morning, Kate's father would come to pick her up to take her home for a family Christmas but, reluctant to leave her on her own, I spoke with the Home Sister, who agreed to look after Kate until her father arrived.

Breakfast in the residency was a disappointment that morning. Only three or four of the residents were there, and they were mainly nursing sore heads. The usual bacon and eggs had not been provided; it was a question of cereals and toast, as all the catering staff were in the kitchens, busily preparing turkey and all the trimmings for the patients' Christmas lunch. At about ten o'clock, I joined Johnny on the ward. This was a different Johnny to the one I knew. Normally ebullient and cheerful, he looked haggard and dejected as he sat with his head in his hands. I told him that I had already heard about Rosie's death and offered my sympathy.

"It was awful, Paul. I felt so helpless. The vomit was pure blood. It just poured out of her. I have never seen anything like it. And I struggled to get a drip up. Maybe if I had managed that sooner, things might have been different."

"I was told that the blood loss was so rapid that it would have made no difference, even if there had been three drips running," I said, trying to console him.

"I suppose that's right; but to see her fade away, to slip into a coma and die and be unable to do anything about it, was terrible. She didn't cry at all. Asked for her Mummy once or twice, and then was gone."

"Was Kate there to see it?" I asked.

"All the nurses were there, Paul. They were in tears afterwards. They all knew her so well, had cared for her for weeks, had put her to bed that night and even filled her Christmas stocking. When it was over, no one wanted to go back into the room to attend to the body. And I had to speak with her parents, too."

He would have gone on brooding for some time but I remembered the tone that Sister Rutherford had adopted to motivate her nurses.

"Come on Johnny, there's work to be done before the consultants come in for lunch; we ought to walk round the patients."

We agreed that we should undertake a joint round. In truth, it was more social than medical, although the ladies on the female ward were understandably in morbid mood and disinclined to talk. To save time, I wrote in the notes whilst Johnny reviewed Sir William's patients, and he reciprocated when I saw Mr Potts' patients. Accordingly, when the round was over, all the paperwork had been completed; and, provided none of the patients developed any unexpected complications, the rest of the day promised to be quiet, though darkened by the shadow of Rosie's death.

Different patients reacted in different ways to spending the Christmas period in hospital. Feeling ill, anxious about their health, perhaps facing an uncertain future - in a strange environment and aware that in the world outside, people were on holiday enjoying the festivities - most found it difficult to stay cheerful. Generally speaking, the male patients were more accepting of the situation, deciding to make the best of it; but the women, particularly those with children, did not find Christmas in hospital easy. At a time when they would normally be at the centre of family life they became homesick, and, missing loved ones, they often got moody and depressed.

There was, however, plenty of activity to distract them. The Salvation Army brass band visited the hospital during the course of the morning. There were far too many musicians to squeeze onto a ward and too many wards for each to have an individual visit, but they played carols exuberantly at each end of the surgical corridor, which added to the festive occasion. Father Christmas arrived with an enormous sack of presents on his back. He obviously recognised me for he addressed me by name but, to my embarrassment, try as I might, I could not identify him through his heavy disguise of beard and whiskers. Nor did his voice sound familiar, though with his gruff "Ho Ho Ho's", this was not altogether surprising. Whoever it was appeared familiar with hospital routine, and spoke easily and pleasantly with each of the patients. Sister, accompanying him on his round, advised him on the most suitable present for each patient - generally bottles of beer for the men or, if they were unable to take food or drink by mouth, a gentleman's handkerchief. Most of the ladies received perfumed soap or talcum powder.

The next visitor by contrast, looking ill at ease in the clinical environment, was the City Mayor wearing his formal chain of office and accompanied by the Lady Mayoress. She looked distinctly grumpy, as if visiting the sick on Christmas Day was beyond the call of duty, and that she would have much preferred to be at home with her family. The Mayor spoke rather formally with Sister in the office and then briefly with one or two of the patients. He brought an official photographer with him, which hinted at the real reason for his visit, and a number of photographs were taken at a patient's bedside.

On both the male and female wards, the respective Sisters had converted an empty side room into a 'Hospitality Lounge' and had provided drinks and nibbles.

One table was laden with whisky, sherry, beer, cider and soft drinks; another with crisps, nuts, raisins and chocolates. Alcohol was similarly available in other departments as well, including the X-ray and casualty departments, and many staff, including medical staff, took advantage – a far cry from hospital policy today where a strict 'no alcohol' rule is rigidly enforced. Possibly these refreshments were provided courtesy of the ward amenity fund, to which Sister Rutherford's sweepstake winnings had made a small contribution!

Johnny and I retired to the male ward to await the arrival of the registrars and consultants. Mohammed Khan and his wife Indy were the first to arrive with their two children. Had I tried to imagine what the Khan family might be like in advance of seeing them, I do not feel that I would have been too far astray. Indy looked to be four or five years younger than her husband, and was slim and exceedingly pretty. She wore a most glorious sari of dazzling colours, mainly yellows, greens and gold. The two children were smartly dressed in their school uniforms: black shoes, knee length grey socks, and identical blazers. Vinay, the six-year-old boy, wore short grey trousers and his sister, Alisha, who was perhaps a year younger, a neat, grey pleated skirt. All four had a soft drink, and after Mohammed had quietly sought an assurance from me that I had reviewed Mr Potts' patients and that there were no clinical problems, he took his wife and family onto the ward to chat to some of the patients. Indy and the children, quiet and reserved, walked respectfully a pace or two behind Mohammed and only spoke when spoken to. Later I was able to chat separately with the children and found them both to be quite delightful, with perfect manners and behaviour. As Mohammed had said previously, neither had any trace of an accent.

Shortly afterwards, Mr Potts arrived with his family and joined the party in the side room. He quickly downed a stiff whisky whilst his wife partook of a generous sherry, then for the first time in the five months that I had been employed as his house officer spoke to me of matters other than his surgical patients, asking after my family and inquiring whether I was to have any time off duty over Christmas.

I looked hard at Mr Potts, wondering if he had heard about Rosie. Surely he must have done. His had been the decision to defer Rosie's operation until after Christmas. Would Rosie still be alive had her surgery been performed last week? Would he now be reviewing that decision in his mind, tormented with doubt, as I would have been had I been in his shoes? Or was his personality such that he had sufficient confidence in his own judgement that the possibility of error simply did not occur to him? Sir William had explained that when things go wrong, it does not necessarily mean that you have made a mistake; you can only take decisions based on the evidence available to you at the time. No one can act with the benefit of hindsight, but surely when something as calamitous as the death of a six year old child occurs, you must review the decision that you made, question it, and have some doubt? Or was he so hardened by the time he became a consultant that he became immune to self-doubt?

Had I imagined that Mrs Potts would be a quiet subjugated little woman, dashing about hither and thither to cater for her husband's every whim, I would have been sadly mistaken. She was the complete opposite of her husband. Tall, slim and elegant, she would have been perhaps an inch or two taller than her husband had she worn low heels, but in her stilettos she towered over him. With long platinum blonde hair, high cheekbones and a generous mouth, she had the appearance of a Nordic model. Again, in contrast to her taciturn husband, she had an effervescent personality and was extremely chatty; gushing in her praise of the Christmas tree and decorations on the ward, and enthusiastic about the drinks and nibbles that Sister had provided in the side ward. She explained how frequently 'My Sydney', as she referred to him, spoke of the high quality medical and nursing staff that supported him in his surgical work. When I was introduced to her, she said she had heard a lot about me, but knowing how economical Mr Potts was with the spoken word, I rather doubted that this was true. My first impression was that their daughter, Annabel, who was aged seven, took after her father. She seemed moody and clearly didn't want to be at the hospital on Christmas morning. She sat with a doll in her hand and a thumb in her mouth and clung to her mother's side. Mr Potts apologised for her behaviour and explained that she was shy and found it difficult to talk to total strangers.

By contrast, the son, Andrew, aged six years old, took after his mother. Short blonde hair, blue eyes and a cheeky grin, he caused chaos on the ward within five minutes of arriving. He had brought two of his Christmas presents with him; a football and a clockwork car, which apparently went disappointingly slowly on the carpet at home, but motored like a Formula One racing machine on the polished linoleum of the ward floor, usually disappearing under patients' beds or items of medical equipment. In a flash Andrew went after it, knocking over drip stands and commodes on the way. Eventually, to prevent further damage, I took him to the far end of the ward where all the beds were empty, set up two chairs as goal posts, and he took penalty kicks at me with his new football; another role not included in the houseman's job description!

At noon the Christmas turkey arrived, thanks to the efforts of the kitchen staff, who deserved great credit for producing a hot roasted turkey for every ward in the hospital, together with all the traditional trimmings. Mr Potts donned an operating theatre gown and hat and - as was traditional on the surgical wards on Christmas Day - ceremonially carved the turkey using the amputation knife from the operating theatre. Some patients were able to sit at the table in the middle of the ward, but most were served in their beds. Mrs Potts (with Annabel still clinging to her skirt), Vinay, Alisha, and I acted as waiters, whilst Andrew continued to cause chaos with his model car. With the nurses wearing tinsel around their hats and decorative trimmings on their aprons, and with carols playing on the tape recorder in the background, every effort was made to make the Christmas meal as pleasant as possible for the patients.

After the turkey had been served, Mr Potts, Mr Khan and their families went home, and the nurses and I served Christmas pudding to those that were able to eat it. Then the table in the centre of the ward was cleared, the ambulant patients retired to their beds, and the nursing staff and I sat down to eat our own Christmas lunch in the side room. When our meal was over, we chatted and drank coffee until Sir William joined us, having performed the honours with the Christmas turkey on the female ward. He held court for twenty minutes or so, regaling us with stories of Christmases past, before announcing that he wished to return home to listen to the Queen's speech at three pm. Shortly afterwards I took my own leave of the ward staff, and returned to the residency.

It was a lovely crisp winter's day, cold but sunny, and there was still frost on the ground. I had an hour or so to kill before walking to the city centre to catch the only train that was available, due to the restricted holiday service, to take me home for my second turkey dinner of the day; so I wandered out into the municipal park adjacent to the hospital, where others had gathered to walk off the excesses of their Christmas lunches. One child was riding a brand new bicycle, and another sporting new roller skates, which had arrived care of Father Christmas during the night. Others were simply strolling, enjoying the last hours of sunshine before night fell. I sat on one of the park benches and looked back at the hospital, bathed in the late afternoon sunshine against the blue sky. The buildings looked timeless. Built in solid Victorian brick they had been there for the last hundred years, and no doubt would still be there for the next hundred. From the outside the three-storey blocks with their linking corridors looked cold, inanimate, and forbidding. Inside the hospital, however, it was warm - it had its own life, its own miniature civilisation.

For me, it had been both home and workplace for many months; a place where I ate, drank, slept, but most of all a place where I had worked hour after hour, day after day, week upon week. And I was not the only one; I was just a small cog in a team of nurses, doctors and many other paramedical staff. The physiotherapists, the radiographers, the dieticians, the laboratory technicians, and all the other members of staff without whom the hospital could not function; cooks, porters, cleaners, administrative staff, all essential to the vital function of caring for the sick.

I felt sure that the buildings would still be there for many years to come. Perhaps they might not change much on the outside, but would it be the same on the inside? No doubt therapies would improve as new medicines became available, new operations were devised, and cures found for conditions that at present were untreatable. If medical practice developed in the next fifty years as quickly as it had in the last fifty, hospital routines would be very different in the future, but there was much that would not change. The hopes and fears of the staff would remain; not least the anxiety of newly qualified doctors, young men and women at the very start of their careers taking their first tentative steps in medicine, hopefully better prepared than I had been but no doubt still making some mistakes. Nurses would still be essential; maybe in time extending their skills to undertake some of the tasks currently performed by the medical staff, but hopefully still showing the care and compassion that epitomised their role. And of course, there would still be the patients; many to be cured and others, sadly, like Joan and so tragically like little Rosie, to die. Patients, each with hopes, worries and fears - some to be realised, others to be assuaged. Those solid Victorian brick walls would continue to bear witness to the hundreds of little incidents and dramas that make up hospital life.

As I sat on the park bench, I noticed two figures walking slowly down the path towards me, hand in hand, but with heads bowed. It was Rosie's parents. As soon as I saw them, I felt the tears welling up in my eyes. I stood up when they reached me. They looked gaunt and drawn, grief written large on their faces, but both seemed in control and dry eyed. Rosie's father spoke first.

"Hello, Dr Paul."

"Hello Mr Roberts... look, I'm so very sorry," I mumbled, uncertain what to say.

"Yes, it's very sad. A terrible day for us, but we were warned that one day this might happen. We've lived with that knowledge for the last six years - throughout Rosie's life, in fact." He was talking quietly, calmly, his emotions apparently under control. Perhaps talking about it dulled the pain that he must surely have been feeling.

"For the first year of Rosie's life, nobody knew what was the matter with her. She was clearly very ill, but the doctors couldn't be certain what was wrong. They were working in the dark without a definite diagnosis. All sorts of treatments were tried in an attempt to improve her health, but all to no avail. Finally, when Rosie was about two, the doctors got to the root of the problem, worked out where the problem lay, and it was explained to us exactly what was wrong with her liver and kidneys. We were also told what the implications were for Rosie. We were warned that almost all children born with this condition died before they reached the age of ten. We've lived with that knowledge hanging over us ever since, but slowly we became reconciled to it. We learned to live day by day and we've valued every moment that we've spent with her, knowing that this day might come. Of course when we heard about this new operation, we just hoped and prayed that the inevitable might be avoided - that she might have the operation and then be blessed with good health - but sadly, it was not to be."

A hundred thoughts flashed through my mind. How could he be so calm, so contained, at a moment like this? For six years, this bubbly, effervescent beautiful child had graced their family and lit up their lives with her laughter, and now she was gone, snatched so cruelly away in the middle of the night, impossible to replace. They would grieve for her every day for the rest of their lives and Christmas time for them, when everyone around would be merry and celebrating, would always be a time of the greatest sadness. And what on earth would they say to Claire? How could you possibly explain to a four year old that her sister had gone forever? Suddenly, I was aware that Rosie's mother was speaking to me.

"Paul, I would like to thank you for being a friend as well as a doctor for Rosie. She liked you a lot, spoke of you often, and we appreciate that you went out of your way to help her. We know that you spent time with her when you could have been off duty. We've heard all about Princess Priscilla and her adventures."

Suddenly, I remembered the tiny packet that I had in my pocket. "Look, I had a small gift for her...I'd like you to have it."

"That's very kind Paul, but we wouldn't know what to do with it. Please will you put it with the other presents in the chapel, for the children who are less fortunate than ours?" Then she turned to her husband, "I think we ought to go; we have to pick up Claire from my mother's, and then somehow or other we've got to explain to her what has happened."

I watched as they walked slowly back across the park to the hospital. They say the pain of bereavement eases with time but for them, life would never be the same. They would have their memories and photographs of course, but would never again hear that infectious giggle or see the smile that brought sunshine to their lives. They had to face a future without their beloved child; a future forever tinged with sadness.

And what did the future hold for me? The few days recently spent at home had made me realise that I was a different person now from the inexperienced novice who had joined the surgical unit just five months ago. Particularly satisfying was the recognition that I had matured as an individual, and developed a degree of self-confidence that was previously lacking. Last August, when commencing this job with the success of the final examination behind me, I thought that I knew a lot about medicine. In fact, I had known a certain amount of medical theory, but little about medical practice. Working on the Surgical Five unit had helped me to develop as an individual, had taught me a great deal, but equally had demonstrated how much more there was to learn. At first I hadn't coped at all well, but now felt I was on top of the job, albeit chronically tired, and realised that I was actually enjoying my work. I liked the cheerful atmosphere, the mutual respect that we each had for the other members of the team, their professionalism and expertise. All were genuinely concerned with obtaining the best outcome for the patients. If a job needed to be done, it was done, irrespective of the time. I knew that a career in surgery would be very competitive, that there would be hurdles and difficulties along the way, that success could not be assured - but I had not studied medicine in order to have an easy life. Surgery offered the ability to improve a patient's fortunes, to cure life-threatening diseases by making a practical intervention, and to help others when they needed it most. I resolved that surgery was the path that I should follow – and should I not be successful, it would not be for want of trying.